THE DEVIL YOU DON'T

By

Christine Trueman

Grosvenor House
Publishing Limited

The right of Christine Trueman to be identified as the author of this
work has been asserted in accordance with Section 78
of the Copyright, Designs and Patents Act 1988

This book is published by
Grosvenor House Publishing Ltd
Link House
140 The Broadway, Tolworth, Surrey, KT6 7HT.
www.grosvenorhousepublishing.co.uk

This book is a work of fiction. Any resemblance to
people or events, past or present, is purely coincidental.

A CIP record for this book
is available from the British Library

ISBN 978-1-78623-488-9

CHAPTER ONE
Jingly Balls

After thirty years a marriage needs 'spicing up.' I had bought lacey underwear which I hoped would be alluring, despite the tell-tale signs that I had given birth to three children. I tried to be spontaneous, although sometimes I was a little tired, distracted. Once, I scattered the last of the September rose petals over the bed and the bedroom carpet. Mostly, Lukkas laughed at my efforts.

These were my thoughts as I waited in my car, which I hoped would still be my car after our divorce. I stared at my reflection in the driver's mirror. My eyebrows were a mess and unless I held my chin up permanently, there were obvious creases in the sagging skin at my neck. I rarely liked what I saw when I glimpsed myself in a mirror. I seldom bothered to because of it.

Approaching fifty, I started behaving in a way that was frequently humiliating for me. It might not have been as humiliating had Lukkas been a different person, I reflected. In part, I blamed his old school, where it was once common for a young boy to be beaten by a prefect for being a few minutes late in accomplishing a task. Added to the degrading punishment was the prefect's insistence that the boy should thank him for the beating. Could you survive it, without becoming that prefect yourself?

I had never been to a sex shop, never deemed it necessary, but then, I felt insecure. Lukkas had been behaving oddly for some while.

I'd often enjoyed making love with him. I'd never worried about whether I was too fat or too thin, good at sex or bad. Now, along with the lack of sleep, the reduced appetite, a new shyness had begun which I had never experienced before. When we made love, he had said I should tie my hair up. He had said that my hands were cold so that now, every night, just in case, I ran my hands under the hot tap, whatever the weather.

I felt that I was being compared for the first time in my life, it was inhibiting.

My savings had depleted considerably since I had stopped teaching to care for the girls, and expenditure on sex would probably be considered a waste of money, money I didn't have to waste. But I was afraid that Lukkas found sex with me boring. If there was someone else, I would have to compete, I supposed. I didn't think it's what Charlotte meant by being the better woman, but anything was worth trying.

So, on a Saturday morning when Lukkas was away, I decided to visit the Milton Road, which has a more cosmopolitan image now, but was once the Soho of Oxford.

I parked my car in the supermarket car park, then entered the street furtively. I didn't want to be seen by friends or family, or indeed, ex-pupils who might snigger. The shop I had found appeared to be completely wrapped in brown paper but for a pink sign above the door which said, 'Strictly Sex.'

Donna, as she introduced herself to me, seemed excited to have such an ordinary person in her shop and was touchingly anxious to help me. I thought her the ideal manager for such a place; a soft, doe eyed mixture of Laurie Lee's Rosie and a touch of brothel Madame. She had honey coloured hair, a mischievous face and wore a pink, fluffy jumper and a pencil skirt.

"Hello, we're very quiet at the minute, we don't usually get busy until twelve. What can I help you with?" she breathed.

I gazed self-consciously at the many displays crammed into the small room. The plain, papered windows had done nothing to prepare me for the stupendous array of brightly coloured sex toys and videos on the shelves about us.

Dragging my startled eyes away from a picture of a young, manacled woman enjoying oral sex, I squeaked apologetically, "Actually, it's my first time in a sex shop, I'm not really sure what I want."

Donna regarded me with genuine sympathy. "How about trying on one of these outfits?" she suggested, sweeping her arm towards a cluttered rail, from which hung the kind of dressing up clothes that small children in a nursery would have loved to experiment with. Nurses outfits, police uniforms. Perhaps not the black, leather, dominatrix number. knowing if I put that on I would collapse in a flurry of embarrassed laughter immediately, I shook my head. So, she presented me with a black and white, frilly chambermaid outfit. No, the same thing would happen. I would never, ever be able to keep my facial muscles from twitching.

"I suppose," I ventured, "You don't have anything for the vagina? I've had three large babies, you see, and the muscles there are a bit slack."

"Ah. You can have an operation for that, you know..." Donna stretched her pink lips in a sympathetic smile.

I nodded. "I've done the homework," I told her, "It'll cost about four thousand pounds and I don't have that kind of money."

"You could get yourself a bigger lover," she giggled, clearly having descended that path. It was a bit cheeky though. I ignored it.

"Okay, come and have a look at these." Her eyes brightened as she hit upon a solution.

She led me across the shop to a display of elongated, spherical and oval shaped rubber things that resembled dog chews.

"These," she said in a hushed voice, "are very popular." She held up a pair of the pink rubber balls, attached to silk cord. "They're called Jingly Balls. You place them inside the vagina and squeeze your muscles. They're very good, I've walked around the supermarket, pulling them up inside me. They can bring you to an orgasm, you see, but they also tighten your vaginal muscles," she dipped her voice as a short man in a track suit entered the shop. "You can keep them inside during sex."

I wasn't sure that I wanted to have an orgasm in Asda, but it was a thought. I bought them anyway, along with a vaginal lubricant and a body cream containing glitter, thanking Donna for her help.

For the rest of that weekend, all through the routine jobs and chores, I practiced squeezing my vaginal muscles as though my life depended upon it. By the time that Lukkas returned on the Sunday evening, I had put the ash blonde hairs that I had found, out of my head. Just enough to feel strong again.

When he came to bed, I leaned against the pillows in what I hoped was a sexy, languid pose; asking him about his trip, as he undressed on the edge of the bed. He had removed his new, stripy underpants and was flexing his broad, brown back. I wanted to reach out and touch his hair, where it had grown long at the nape of his neck.

I clenched the Jingly Balls, squeezing them upward and holding them there, until in the light of the bedside lamp, so that he might appreciate the body glitter, he began to make love to me. He kissed my shoulders and then my breasts, before rolling me onto my side to enter my vagina from behind.

"Fucking hell! Ow! What the hell is that?" Lukkas shot out of me in sudden pain and confusion and my eyes widened in alarm. I hadn't thought, I hadn't considered it would hurt him.

I shrank back against the pillows, biting my lip.

"Jesus Christ, what are you trying to do to me, I'm in agony!"

He turned away from me, nursing his private parts. His naked body hopping from foot to foot before the bedroom window.

"Sh!" I implored him, hoping that our sons hadn't heard his yelping cry.

"Sh? I'm in agony!" he repeated. Then he turned and glared at me for a moment, the glass green eyes turned to narrow points of astonishment.

He reached down between my thighs to remove the offensive pink things by their string, like a butcher removing the giblets.

I watched with bated breath as he held them at the distance of the length of his arm. Then, opening the window, he hurled them into the garden for the dogs to chew.

I thought he might lecture me for hours, wondered momentarily whether he might hit me. But he did neither. He lay down beside me, staring up at the ceiling for a moment before turning off the bedside light.

"We'll try again in the morning, shall we? Don't ever do that to me again," he said.

Chapter Two
July 2014

It was a large room in a network of newly built offices. This was my third visit. I was anxious, sentiment hadn't yet turned to sediment. My heart was still passionate about Lukkas. I could tell this to no one, least of all my lawyers. I wasn't supposed to care about him any longer.

The room overlooked the motorway which lead to Oxford in one direction, Milton in another. It was painted white, furnished with a board room table and chairs. There was a water machine and a small table on which magazines were displayed, one of them a glossy advertisement for the firm. The room was large enough to swallow me up and it made me feel on edge, but then everything had scared me for such a long time that stomach churning fear had become the norm.

Each time I entered the room, waiting to be seen by Alex, I walked to the big window overlooking the continual, steady flow of traffic and I thought of that other Law firm. But Lukkas' firm was no longer my business.

I watched the magpies, hopping on the plain grass lawn that lay beyond. One for sorrow, two for joy. I paced up and down before the immense window with my hands behind my back, (in imitation of Lukkas, perhaps) but in my agitation, my heart wouldn't be still.

Go away, Mr Magpie, leave me alone. I was fretting about what I might be asked, and what I should say, or perhaps, what I should not say. All the while I worried about money and how the hell I was supposed to pay for this. How would I be able to pay Alex?

Removing my wedding ring, I dropped it into my bag, then rubbed the white skin where the ring had been for over thirty years. I had wondered so many times, since he left, how someone could rid themselves of the person who had loved them all their life, rid themselves with such ease of conscience?

"How could you, Lukkas?" I said aloud, as I had on frequent occasions, and each time with genuine surprise in my voice. His betrayal had been cold and calculating, yet long and tortuous. Almost as though he couldn't make up his own mind. As though he needed time to formulate a plan.

"You don't know what I'm like in court, Laura!" His voice cut into my thoughts.

Yes, I knew. I had heard the reports, seen social workers reduced to gibbering wrecks, I knew what he could be at home. Perhaps that threat had stopped me from taking action.

There was a slight movement at the door and Alex appeared. She smiled at me. "Hey, Laura. Sorry to keep you waiting, would you like a coffee or something?" Her voice is soothing at the same time as being business like.

I shook my head, I had drunk coffee whilst waiting for her. When I was first introduced to Alex, I thought, "He will make mincemeat of you; either that, or you will be charmed by him." She was tiny, blonde, soft voiced and with a slight, Welsh accent. Putty in Lukkas' hands, or so I expected. It didn't happen like that.

Once, she had asked me when I had first suspected that Lukkas was having an affair.

"He started cracking jokes in the morning, it wasn't like him. He used not to like getting up in the morning," I said.

"What kind of jokes?" she asked. Clearly, this was curiosity, not anything to do with the divorce.

"Well, once, when we had stayed overnight in a hotel, there were chocolate muffins on the breakfast bar, and Lukkas said, "Nothin' like a bit of muffin in the morning." He laughed afterwards, a bit like Sid James in the carry-on films."

I saw the corner of her mouth twitch irresistibly as she fought with the need to laugh.

"Yes," I said, with a smile. "Women love his wicked sense of humour."

Alex had met Lukkas on several occasions, now. During mediation, at his office, once in court on a different divorce case. As she talked about Lukkas, assessing him, so my faith in her grew. Queen Boudicca was the way I described her to Charlotte.

I had believed Lukkas was not like other men, that he was a super intelligent being. Alex told me that was what I was supposed to feel. I believed my husband was unique, that I was an inferior being. But Alex had represented other women. She knew.

"Where did we leave off?" She pulled out a chair, sitting opposite me, juggling a cup of coffee with a large, grey, ring bound file which she placed on the table. She was wearing a neatly cut grey suit which made her look even more feminine. As I watched, she leapt deftly through the paperwork with small fingers, to the end of our last interview.

"Oh, meant to ask..." She paused. "How did the wedding go?"

"It was fine," I said. "I didn't speak to Lukkas, although he confronted me twice..."

I had never believed myself capable of ignoring him, but I was proud of my own performance in doing so. And Lukkas' face was puce with anger as I by-passed him to take a different route through the hotel. After all the years we spent together, I would never have thought it possible to ignore him, but I had. The distance that now lay between us had given me the slap in the face that I needed so badly. I might still care about him, but the spell was broken, he knew it, then.

Alex smiled again and nodded her approval, leaning back in her chair with her arms folded across her chest. "Well done, it's exactly the kind of treatment he needs, now. He'll only try to get you to negotiate behind our backs, trap you into agreeing to something. Don't let him, his proposal is disgraceful, after everything you contributed to the marriage."

I had no argument with that.

"So, we got to the incident when you were pregnant with Joe. The third incident. Now Laura, no tears today, stick straight to the point. I'm your lawyer, not your councillor, okay? Speaking of which, I know money is tight, but you really must get a councillor for your own sake, nothing to do with this divorce case; but we are all agreed that you need to deal with these dreadful memories properly, with a trained councillor. We can recommend people, if you want."

I reddened. I hadn't intended to cry. I had felt like an idiot at the time. So many tears springing from nowhere and without warning. I was resolved never to do it again.

She adjusted the dark rimmed glasses, pushing them further up the bridge of her small nose. "So, it was almost Christmas and you were pregnant. What happened in the lead up to Lukkas hitting you?" The question was matter-of-fact, as calculating as Lukkas' recent behaviour towards me. It just needed an answer. I was getting used to her scientific approach.

I shook my head vehemently, "He didn't hit me, he pushed me," I said. "But I fell heavily, on my bum, then rolled onto my back, and a short while later, my water's broke; so, he had to do Christmas after all."

Alex raised her eyebrows, gazing at me for a moment with piercing grey eyes, as though amazed that I would differentiate between degrees of domestic violence.

"There was an argument before, what was that about?" she asked, at last.

"We had a difficult year, in many ways. There was an inspection at my school, leading up to Christmas, there were the Christmas performances and then, of course, I was only a few weeks away from having Joseph. It was the year that Lukkas had applied to join the Family Panel, which meant not only a lot of new cases, but nasty cases against children too. It was the first time he had really had to come to terms with that kind of abuse. I had been highly supportive, reassuring him; but I was managing a lot of things at that time…"

"What was the argument about, Laura?" Alex asked, interrupting me. Time is money. I appreciated her polite way of bringing me back to the crux of the matter. Alex has been privy to my bank statements, recently.

"Lukkas' mother and father were coming for Christmas. His parents, especially Marjorie always made me nervous. She liked things to be done, just-so, and Lukkas would be nervous too, everything had to be done well. Everything had to be perfect. I had bought and wrapped all the presents, decorated the house with the children, done all the shopping for food. It was the day before Christmas Eve. The only thing I had asked Lukkas to do was to collect the turkey from the butchers, and he forgot..."

"So, you berated him about the turkey?" Alex guessed.

"Yes, and I threw a tea towel at him. He was angry with me for that, and he pushed me backwards, he pushed against my chest."

Alex had her lap top open now, she started typing down my responses. It was stifling in the room, the air hot and heavy. Beyond the window, the tarmac seemed to shimmer in the heat. "Do you mind if I take off my jacket?" she asked.

"No, of course not..." I mumbled, thinking back to that time, long ago. I didn't understand why she wanted to go back so far. I waited whilst she peeled her jacket from her shoulders and sat down again.

"Were your children present?"

"Josh and Hannah were there. They were waiting for dinner. Yes, they saw it and they both cried when I fell. They were very upset. I pulled myself up, holding onto the kitchen unit and they both put their arms around me. I told them it was alright, everything would be alright, and they would have a good Christmas. But they were upset, yes."

She took a sip of water. "What did Lukkas do, then?"

"Nothing. He went out for about an hour, he went to get the turkey. Whilst he was gone, my waters broke, so

I was in hospital over Christmas and Joe was born on Christmas Eve."

"Have you ever reported this, or any of the incidents to the police?" Alex asked.

"No," I shook my head. "Lukkas works with the police, I didn't want to damage his reputation. I spoke to a police woman off the record, much later. She made no notes, she was a friend." I didn't tell Alex that I had told the children to be quiet about it, to forget it. I was ashamed of it.

But perhaps she guessed, because she stared at me momentarily before reviewing her own writing. Small teeth clamped upon her bottom lip in thought. She resumed her notes, typing quickly and efficiently. I had no time to wonder what the look upon her face meant.

"Tell me about the incident with Hannah."

This time I knew what she meant, but I hesitated. It was Hannah's story, her business alone. But now everything was turned upside down, now I was seeking to protect all of us. Not just her, not me; all of us. Hannah and Lukkas were very close, they always had been, she was always Daddy's little girl.

"Hannah was fourteen, Joseph only six years old. She was proving to be a difficult teenager, she'd gotten in with some older teenagers, young people you couldn't trust. Each day I had to get home earlier from work, try to stop her from meeting them... from meeting one boy, in-particular.

"It was Mothering Sunday. I went to church with Joe, who was at Sunday school then. Hannah stayed in bed. When I got back, Lukkas' parents had arrived. We ate dinner and afterwards Hannah said that she was going out but Lukkas said no, that she couldn't go because his parents were visiting."

I looked down, momentarily massaging the corners of my eyes, trying to remember the scene.

"But Hannah wouldn't give up. She said she was going, that she had stayed through dinner as he'd asked, and now she wanted to go to her friends. She got up and walked towards the hallway, but Lukkas followed her and when they got to the door, she tried to go through it. Lukkas pushed her back, and she hit her head against the door jam and cried. I went to her, but she left the house, without a coat or anything... She was gone for three days and we didn't know where she was, we had to call the police, we needed help finding her. Lukkas always wanted things to be perfect when his parents were there, he didn't want them to see him fail, not ever," I finished.

"Did you tell the police who helped you to find her, what had happened?"

I bit my lower lip, shaking my head, "Not that Lukkas pushed her against the wall, no. He was upset as I was, and he felt guilty. He loves Hannah, I know that. I gave the Police any information I could to get her back, and of course we both hunted for her. We followed all their instructions and eventually, after three days, Hannah met me in the park. She said she ran away because Lukkas had hurt her head and that she was humiliated to be talked to like that before her grandparents."

Alex nodded, saying nothing. She finished her typing and looked up at me. Her next question was asked gently, but I sometimes dreaded them. Lukkas' own lies and accusations had turned the divorce into a murder enquiry.

"There was no sexual abuse in your relationship, was there?"

"No," I shook my head in emphatic denial. "Sometimes, after we had sex, Lukkas' behaviour could be odd, but hardly abusive."

"What do you mean?" Alex asked, frowning.

"Sexism, I suppose. After Joseph was born, sometimes before that, he would be cold and distant immediately after we'd made love. I didn't understand it, but it felt like a punishment, or that he sort of disapproved, or felt guilty about the sex. I don't know...I mean, you might have expected a modicum of affection, but he would scarcely talk to me afterwards."

She pursed her lips in thought. "But you had sex throughout the marriage?"

"Yes, even when our difficulties began. Lukkas wanted to make love. I wanted to make love to him, except for some while after Hannah's birth..."

I shifted uncomfortably. It felt as though I was betraying him as he had betrayed me. But Lukkas had behaved like a man in gothic novel. He had pushed me toward madness, he had wanted that to happen and he would now, cheerfully, take everything and leave me with nothing after all that I had once meant to him.

"Hannah's birth was difficult?" Alex asked, bringing me back to her questions.

"Yes, she was a big baby, I tore quite badly during her birth, I had post-natal depression. I was in pain and couldn't face the idea of sex afterwards. I became quite insecure, but Lukkas' behaviour didn't help, he didn't understand, just seemed to see Hannah as the prize his mother had wanted. She always said that she would have loved to have had a girl, you see. But it was then I realised what a flirt he was, and we had one or two arguments about it, but nothing serious, because no matter how much he would flirt, I always felt he was faithful to me and he always seemed to love me."

As I finished speaking, the receptionists face appeared at the glass panel in the door. Alex raised a hand to her, pulling a face, as though to say, "We're still busy in here, sorry."

"What was Lukkas like when he was young, when you were first together?" Alex asked, "You told me he had a small breakdown."

"It was after he'd started working for his first Law firm, before he bought the office he has now. Lukkas was always a bit, well, highly strung, I suppose. He'd been working for them for almost two years when he started getting headaches, sometimes saying that he felt sick, physically sick. It was stress, getting used to the new roles he had to play, he suffered from vertigo, more psychological than medical." I paused, thinking back to all those years before. "He came home one day and collapsed into a chair, he was crying, saying it was all too much. So, I put my arms around him and we sat like that for a while, me kneeling in front of him. I told him to leave if that was what he wanted, or if he wasn't going to leave, at least take a few days out and give himself time to recover. That's what he did, he took three days off and when he went back he seemed much better, in fact he was stronger and more resolved if anything, and over the years he grew less fragile, until he bought the office he has now."

I watched Alex typing on her lap top, my mind drifting to the days when he had needed me, relied upon me, talked to me about everything. The thought popped into my mind, not for the first time, and I wanted to shove it away again. Had I helped to turn Lukkas into a sort of monster, by saying sorry for crimes he accused me of over the years that I had never committed? Why had I done that? To reassure small children and keep the peace, because his mother, who idolised Lukkas, believed him and would never own to him doing anything wrong? What had it accomplished in the end, a man who believed that he was above the law? I would never have said that he was mentally unstable, I tried to give him my love and support.

Alex finished typing and peered over her shoulder at the clock on the wall. I looked at it too, I had to get back soon to join Mum at the hospital.

"Okay, Laura, last thing for now, but I think we'll need another appointment soon to go over your E Form. When did Lukkas first suggest that you needed to see a Doctor, for your mental health?"

I rubbed my forehead in thought. "A few days after I first put it to him that he was having an affair. In June 2011. He told the children I was making up stories about the things I found. He told them that I was delusional."

Alex nodded. "Do you have your Doctor's report?"

I drew it from my handbag, handing it to her. It was a copy, I wouldn't let go of the original.

"I don't want anyone to see it, really," I said apologetically. "It's been hard, that side of things." I was still afraid that people would believe him. There had been times when he had been so convincing, I believed him myself. There were times when I couldn't face anyone, when I couldn't walk through Oxford, the city of my birth, in case Lukkas, the man I had always trusted, was right. In case he didn't love me anymore. My confidence gone, self -esteem broken.

Alex nodded. "The only people to see it will be the people who are trying to help you," she said. She came around the table to stand before me, and for the first time in all our meetings, she took my hand and squeezed it. "It will be well. Book that councillor before our next meeting."

I nodded. At the door as she departed, Alex hesitated. "And Laura…" she said quietly, "Don't contact him again, not about anything. You don't trust him, neither do I, so from now on you go through me. You said you still care about him, you may agree to something you will regret later."

I nodded. "I don't trust him," I agreed, "I'll trust in God."

"Never mind God. You just put your trust in me." Her eyes narrowed in a way I had not seen before, taking me by surprise. Queen Boudicca. But I got the message.

In the car park outside I leaned against the high stone wall, unseen by the Lawyers in their large, open plan office. I took several deep breaths, in through the nose, out through the mouth. Every interview I gave was like this. Dozens of thoughts clawed at my head, like irritating cats vying for attention. How could you, Lukkas? What had been the point of it all? More than half of my life, loving you. I took a cigarette from the packet in my pocket and replaced oxygen with nicotine. My grandchildren don't know that from time to time, I smoke. After a few puffs, I heard the buzz of a text in my pocket. It was Hannah.

"Please don't divorce Dad. Do as he said and see a psychiatrist. I'll find one, someone who has had nothing to do with him. He says that he'll come home then. Please, Mum. I feel as though I'm having a panic attack for the first time in my life."

I stroked the smooth surface of the mobile phone. Still, still... she would do anything to get him back. She didn't get it, she didn't understand.

CHAPTER THREE
Toya

The interior of my car is filthy. Sometimes I try to wipe the mud marks made by the children's wellies, the ground in biscuits. I retrieve the unbroken toys and wash them, I bin the broken ones. But my car is never tidy. I once discovered that sunflower seeds had rooted beneath my car seat from a spilt bag of hamster food.

As I drive, I think about Hannah. I love her so much, but she adores Lukkas in a way that she never adored me, I think. She is often critical of me, often angry with me. She blames me for a multitude of sins. She has often been secretive and won't talk to me on many subjects. Maybe it is simply that girls cut their teeth on their mothers. But I know there is more to it than that. She has not forgiven me.

I did my very best. I didn't know what else I could do, how else to tackle it. I tried to protect her. She changed when Lukkas and his mother insisted she go to a private school. It wasn't the right decision, I knew my own daughter better than anyone, knew that she was part of a small, trusted group of friends. I was friendly with their mothers. Hannah was insecure, she should have attended the secondary school with her friends.

It took her six months to feel accepted by her new school, despite the kindness of her new teacher who called me frequently in the week.

Eventually, she made new friends, but those girls lived far afield, in the countryside. Lengthy arrangements had to be made for her to meet with them outside of school.

Then Toya came along. She was the same age as Hannah, thirteen. She seemed older. Hannah said she met her at the local park. She lived a few roads away from us. When Toya came to our house she seemed friendly enough, playing with Hannah's little brother, Joe. But she was reserved with me. I remember feeling there was something secretive about her. She had dark, cropped hair and generally wore jeans. I don't remember seeing her in a school uniform, but she said that she went to one of the big secondary schools near Thame.

At first, she and Hannah spent a lot of time in Hannah's bedroom, giggling. If I knocked on the door and offered them food or drink, Hannah would be a little hostile. I put it down to her age.

After a hissed argument in the kitchen whilst Toya was upstairs, in which I told Hannah that Toya should think about getting home as it was growing dark and Hannah hadn't tackled her homework, she asked whether Toya could stay the night. I refused it, it was a school night. I remember she had a way of scowling at me, one cord of hair adrift from her pony tail. So, I decided it was time to meet Toya's Mum, that I would walk them both to Toya's home.

Neither of the girls seemed keen for me to do this. I smiled as we walked, as though I had no notion of it. They marched ahead of me in moody silence as we walked the two streets to Toya's house.

I knew the house, most of our neighbours did, although I'd not known that Toya lived there. I reprimanded myself for being a snob, for casting judgement, there was no doubt that the outside of the place was in poor shape. It had been like that for some time. For months an old mattress had leaned against the front of the building. The sparse grass was littered with dog faeces whilst empty plastic bottles littered the path.

When I went to knock upon the door, Toya hastily produced a key from her jeans pocket. At the same time a dog started to bark from within, a large dog from the depth of the bark. When the door opened, a hand restrained the Pit Bull Terrier by its collar. The young man twisted his face upward to look at me. "He won't bite," he said, but I wasn't so sure.

"Where's Mum?" Toya asked. I assumed from the familiarity with which she spoke to him that the boy was her older brother.

"Out." He pushed the dog back into the hallway and partially closed the door, casting me a half smile and extending it to Hannah.

"Okay. I called by to say hello, but I'll come back another time," I said.

As Toya went inside and the door closed on her, thirteen-year-old Hannah frowned at me. "You don't like her, do you?" She said.

I looked quickly to the door. Hannah had spoken quite loudly, I hoped they hadn't heard it.

"Whatever makes you say that?" I asked with a dismissive smile.

She stared ahead, every bit the moody teenager. "Because if she'd been a friend from school, you would have let her stay."

"I certainly wouldn't. But Hannah, the probability is that if she had been a friend from school, her own parents would have said no to it," I added. "You need sleep in the week."

"You don't like her house either, or her family…"

"I don't even know her family. Don't be silly, Hannah." I wondered then, whether Hannah had her own doubts about them.

I had no idea about the influence that Toya would have over her. But there were even worse influences to come. If Toya wanted to meet Hannah on a school night, I had a battle to get her to do her schoolwork. In the end, I would have been grateful simply to keep her at home, homework or no.

When I arrive home from the Lawyer's office there is a new text from Hannah. "Please don't divorce Dad. Do as he asks. Go and see a psychiatrist, he will come home then, he has promised me that he will. He knows people who will help. I'm having a panic attack, Mum, honestly, I've never felt like this before."

I felt terrible pity for her, for all our children and grand-children. After all this time, they didn't understand what was happening. "I bet he does," I said aloud, in response to the suggestion about his knowing a psychiatrist. A part of me had always been tempted to do anything to get Lukkas back. I stroked the surface of the phone with my thumb again, wanting to put my arms about Hannah.

"Breathe," I told her, "breathe slowly. Shut the shop and go for a little walk. I know how hard it is, Hannah, but in the end, it will be alright."

I thought about the time she had run away from us.

Once, when Ruby, her first child, was a toddler and woke several nights on the trot, I suggested that she cover her with an extra blanket at night. Tired, irritable then through lack of sleep, Hannah snapped at me, "Don't tell me what to do with my children. I will never let the things that happened to me, happen to my children!"

The words slapped my face, remained pounding in my head for ever. "It happened, you can't go back," I said to myself.

"Maybe you should talk to a councillor if you won't talk to me. I didn't 'let things happen,' Hannah, I tried to prevent them and protect you…"

At first it was Toya who pulled Hannah's strings. Before I could be aware of it, there was someone else, much older than her. Life had become a panic then. Racing home to the disapproval of the other school staff who I couldn't tell. Racing home to be there when she got off the school bus. Then Hannah started to dodge me, sneaking to Toya's and God knew where, so that I had to take Joe, aged seven, to Charlotte's house or the house of a friend whilst I went to hunt for Hannah.

For a long time, I tried to deal with it myself. Perhaps it was better that Hannah ran away, at least then the police became involved. A turning point, but by then she had grown up in a way that I didn't want her to, by then, she was under the influence of somebody else.

CHAPTER FOUR

May 2011

"You don't know me, Laura! You don't know what I'm like in court!" Lukkas had bellowed in my face, his handsome face turned puce by anger and red wine. He had never shouted at me quite like that before. The words resounded in my head through my broken sleep, losing none of their hostility the following morning. We were thirty years into our marriage, how many weeks, days, was that?

He didn't mean it, I told myself. After several months of his draconian behaviour I didn't know what to believe. Either he had started an affair or Lukkas was having a nervous breakdown.

The row began after Joe brought his new girlfriend home. There was a new sarcasm, now, to Lukkas' tone. We had been watching television, Lukkas and I, Joe and the girlfriend; an episode of the detective series which Lukkas liked. At the point where he snapped at me so rudely, we were watching a scene where the detective, deciding to part from his wife, is sitting beneath a table in his office with his pretty Italian colleague. Perhaps that had made me nervous, that innocuous scene and Lukkas' avid attention to it.

Showing kindness to Joe's girlfriend, I had asked if she would like a cup of tea, and that was all I had said.

"Will you shut up!" Lukkas yelled, embarrassing the girlfriend and infuriating me. I had known him to joke that I should get back in the kitchen where I belonged, I had known him to be extremely sexist. But this sudden, ferocious, bellowed rudeness took a new turn. Lukkas frequently talked during television programmes.

I chewed the inside of my cheek for quite some while, finally shrugged apologetically at the girl and left in silence to make tea. I had repressed too much for too long. Eventually, when Joe and the girl left the house, I bellowed back. "How could you, Lukkas? How could you be so bloody rude to me in front of guests?" A fully-fledged row began, then.

It was the first time I felt really frightened, questioning his love for me for the first time in thirty years. He had represented women I know as their divorce lawyer. Although I hadn't seen him in court since I was a young woman, I know he has a fearsome reputation. I was frightened of losing him, frightened about the prospect of doing battle with Lukkas, the lawyer, too.

Eventually, after the row subsided, I slept on my side in the small, spare room; staring at the crayon marks on the wall left by our grandchildren and yet my body ached to be next to him. It wasn't the first time I experienced that feeling of being shut out by Lukkas, but it marked the first time that I didn't apologise for a situation he had begun.

In the morning, after he had gone to work, I sat at his desk in the study, hunched over the letters that he had written to me so many years ago, trying to reclaim something I might already have lost.

Dear Laura,

I hope that you got back all right and that the journey wasn't too bad. I missed you the moment you left, I missed kissing you and holding you and all the other things too! I should be studying for my exams but all I can do is think of you and how beautiful you are. I'm glad you met my parents. Thankfully it was a mellow version of my mother. My father says you have beautiful hair. I wish you had been a virgin when we met, I can't stand the thought of you sleeping with another man.

I'm coming to Cambridge this weekend and I have a cheek to ask you, but could you pay for my train ticket if you have the money? I'm getting perilously close to the red line again after rent. I have about sixty pounds to last until the end of April.

I can't wait for the summer, Laura, for hundreds of reasons, I will have finished my degree and we will know where we will be the next year and we can start organising ourselves and we will be together! I love you much more than my dissertation, Lukkas xxx

Then, after this, I had read several other letters, protected in the cutlery box that had once been a wedding present:

Dear Laura, it's our baby, not your baby, conceived in France. Please just hang on. In a few weeks we will be together, and if your Aunts ask questions, tell them we love each other, and we are getting married soon and we are going to be the best parents in the world.

Our child will be a VIP.

I love you, you are beautiful, see you on Friday, I can't wait. All my love always, to both of you, Lukkas xxx

I let the final letter fall into the box as scenes and images from over thirty years ago flashed through my mind.

First Josh, born a couple of months after the last letter and whilst I was still teaching. Then three years later after we had moved to Oxford, Hannah was born, his little girl, and almost six years after that, Joseph arrived.

Perhaps everything got harder, less manageable, when Hannah had her first child at a young age and in an unstable relationship.

Then, I gave up my teaching job to care for Ruby and a few years later, her sister Lilly. I wanted Hannah to continue with her career, to be able to work without the expense of child care I had to pay for. Hannah worked as a buyer for a well-known fashion chain. But when the children's father left them for good, she grew lonely as young women do and she let someone else into their lives, a man who frightened both Lukkas and I.

Hannah loved this man, but on a regular basis he made life a battle ground, and all of the while I tried to protect Lukkas' reputation just as systematically, Ben caused chaos and confusion. Now I was failing to handle Ben as well as once I did, as Ruby told me, he had smashed the roof of her garden play house with a hammer.

I thought of the bruising on Hannah's arms. Hannah would deny everything. It was hard to know what to do.

Listlessly, I picked up the bullet points that Lukkas had left that morning on the study table.

"You sent me many texts last week. You said I should feel sorry for neglecting you all, Laura. What would you have me do?

So Sorry. Sorry that I am unaffectionate, often tired, working hard and often away working.

Sorry that you lie to yourself. I am not having an affair.

That you now say I am dismissive of family and friends.

I am sorry that I cannot put up with this way of living. Life is too short.

I am not having an affair but if you push me too far I just might.

Intuition, the fact that he would be away from home for ages and then bring me perfume. His defensive, then guilty, then seemingly joyful behaviour, when the joy was not about us   suggested one thing. And yet he said I was mad to think it, delusional, paranoid...

My mobile phone rang, interrupting my guilt.

I took a deep breath before answering. It was Hannah. My stomach gave an involuntary lurch, please God- not another Ben issue, not right now.

"Mum, you okay? You sound funny."

"Just the start of a cold," I said.

"Oh, sorry. I'm just calling to ask if you would have the girls on Saturday, so I can go out."

I hesitated. I felt so responsible for our grand- children that Lukkas was finding the time to fool around behind my back, and yet if I didn't care for them when Hannah asked, the alternative might be Ben as a babysitter.

"Is this really necessary Hannah?" I asked morosely. "I had them two nights ago, after all."

"Yes." It was a snappy little 'yes'. "It's Georgie's birthday and if I don't go, I'll be the only friend not there. So, will you, or won't you?" Hannah persisted, determinedly.

"Alright..." I answered, reluctant, more than a little resentful, but as my mother might say, my own worst enemy.

She thanked me, and the shop phone went dead almost immediately. I chewed my nail for a moment, then got up and wandered into the kitchen to sort a pile of drying. I wanted to nap, to shut it all out, but just lately sleep didn't come easily. The old Hall and Oates song sang through my head.

"Leave me alone, I'm a family man but if you push me too far I just might..."

I blew my nose on an old sock and stuffed it into my jeans pocket. Then I carried the pile of washing upstairs. On the bed-side table, the name of his after shave drew my attention properly, for the first time. 'L'Homme Libre,' the free man.

At night I spent a long time just staring at the broad shoulders that Lukkas had turned against me, at the thick, dark hair I loved, now flecked with grey. My sleep was broken almost every night, nowadays, where once I had slept peacefully, snuggled into his back. Now there was distance between us and my dreams were filled with jealous imaginings.

He was a handsome, charismatic, a successful man. Why had I never thought about the many women who must have been interested in him? The same, negative thoughts repeated themselves. Lukkas no longer loved me, he no longer needed me. I was fifty-three and Lukkas, fifty. I was no longer beautiful. The newspapers seemed filled with older men starting second marriages with younger women.

This insecurity was new to me, it startled. I had never questioned that Lukkas was faithful.

The night and my anxiety were made far worse by his phone. It sounded the hunting horn on several occasions until I thought I would go mad through lack of sleep. Who was texting him at this hour? Not since he was a young lawyer doing out of hours duty calls had this happened.

Lukkas himself was restless, tossing and turning in the bed, sometimes sighing like a love -struck teenager, so that when his alarm went off, we were both weary.

Tentatively I reached out with my hand to touch his smooth, broad shoulders, then recoiled as he shook me off in an instant.

I breathe to stay calm. I love him, I have always loved him, no matter what.

"I have to go and see the tenants in Croft Street, they're leaving," I reminded him, trying to regain my self-esteem after rejection. "Would you like me to make you a cup of tea first?"

"No."

He refused to turn to me, kept his back to me, then rose to the bathroom to get ready for work.

Later in the day, when I arrived at Lilly's nursery, she was sitting on her key workers lap, one finger in her small mouth, her skinny limbs wrapped about Peggy's ample body.

"Ah, Nanna, there you are. I'm afraid that Lilly has been telling me rather a sad story," Peggy said, rising with Lilly in her arms. I looked at the mischievous Lilly and groaned inwardly.

I was about to ask Peggy if we could go into her office, but she handed Lilly over to me and began speaking in front of the carpenter repairing the door and the notoriously gossipy Chairperson, Peggy's best friend.

"The thing is, Lilly says that Ben hit the window with a pair of scissors and broke the pane," Peggy began in a solemn half whisper. She drew back, awaiting my reaction. My reactions had become dulled.

"Peggy, you've done child protection training, yes? Which is presumably why you are taking this seriously, and so you should, so, you know these things are highly confidential. Do we really want the carpenter to hear, or anyone else for that matter? Could we step into your office perhaps?"

"Oh, I don't think he heard me…" she blanched, whilst the cheery carpenter beamed at us, but she walked toward the office at the end of the corridor.

"Once safely inside, I placed Lilly on the floor. "The story is true, but it happened over a year ago and Lilly is too young to recall it, so my guess is, that it's a tale her big sister has recounted. I know that's the case because I paid for the new window pane," I added.

Peggy narrowed her eyes slightly, as though she suspected me of half-truths, but she didn't challenge me.

"Well, it's not a very nice story and we have to listen to children when they are sad and sometimes record what they say now," she pointed out.

"Yes, of course," I nodded, "but honestly this happened a year ago and…" I broke off, reluctantly defending Ben, "The truth is that although Ben is capable of aggression towards inanimate objects, there is no evidence to say he has ever hurt a child, despite-the-fact that he was often hurt as a child."

Peggy digested this. My daughter's words came into my head as I watched her. "You said people could change, mum…"

"Not past thirty, and not with his back ground!" I'd retorted, as Hannah tried to persuade me to let Ben stay.

Peggy nodded slowly. "Well, we have to record it," she said obstinately, "We have to record what a child says if it's, well... dodgy."

I was trying to protect, Lukkas' reputation, trying to respect Hannah's family. Lukkas, the respected human rights lawyer. Lukkas who had said to me, "I can't get involved, I'm a family lawyer."

Lilly wriggled past me to greet a friend. I stared at Peggy. She was a kind woman and all the children loved her, that was the important thing, they loved and trusted her. Now, I felt guilty.

"I understand, Peggy. Do what you think is right but bear in mind that the incident Lilly is talking about happened in June of last year," I said.

On the way to the surgery, I thought about Lukkas' insistence I see a doctor. There was nothing different in my behaviour, other than that I found it impossible to digest his rudeness toward me without retaliating, now. I said the same things, I did the same things I had done over thirty years, why hadn't he suggested this fear for my mental health before now? For better or worse, I had agreed to iron out that possibility.

Tammy, my cousin, grinned at me from behind the reception desk. We had last met at her son's wedding, an event Lukkas had been too busy to attend. Missing that kind of family celebration would once have been unthinkable for him. Nowadays, I seemed constantly to be making excuses for his absence.

We chatted across the desk until the queue built up. Tammy handed Lilly a sticker which she promptly stuck upside down on her belly. We didn't have to wait very long to see Dr Evans.

She had been my doctor since Hannah was a baby and she was due to retire soon. At first Lukkas had said he wanted me to see a male doctor, recommended by him. But I stood my ground on that point. That had been some while ago. I had pretended to myself that he hadn't asked me, until he started to insist.

I sat down opposite her at her desk, whilst Lilly played on the floor in a puddle of toys.

Dr Evans slightly red rimmed eyes examine mine in less time than it would take an ophthalmoscope to do so, accessing stored information on me and my family situation, running data through her head as a computer would.

I feel myself go tense, as she stares into my eyes. I am wondering, in some panic, whether Lukkas is right and I am doing unusual things without recognising it.

Can you tell whether a person is mad by staring into their eyes? I am frightened. What if I am mad and they take Ruby and Lilly from my care? Ben would be overjoyed, free to do what the hell he liked, free to bully them on a regular basis.

"Why have you really come, Laura?" she asks, sounding a little exasperated.

"My husband said I must come for some tests…"

It sounds pathetic, it is pathetic, but I don't want Lukkas to leave me, to leave us.

"Oh." Dr Evans peels off a loose, grey cardigan. Neither of us have much of a regard for clothes. Perhaps this is wrong in the circumstances. "What are your symptoms, what are you suffering from?" She is smiling but her mouth is firm, a little suspicious.

"I don't sleep very well," I shrugged. "I feel tired and a little down sometimes…"

She nods at me. "When you say, 'a little down,' do you feel depressed?"

I purse my lips, frowning, thinking about it. "I'm finding it hard to eat and sleep, but I don't think I could function as well as I do if I were really depressed."

I wanted to tell her, wanted to say, "It's just that I think Lukkas is having an affair, that's what's getting me down really," but I don't say this.

She nods, reassured, and indicates that I must roll up my sleeve for the pressure monitor. Wrapping it about my forearm Dr Evans asks, "Do you still smoke?"

I look down at Lilly and say "No," very loudly, then look at the doctor whilst Lilly is busy and grimace, apologetically.

She tut-tuts unsympathetically. "You are post menopause," she warns.

The pressure-monitor stops pinching my arm.

"Are you anxious about something?"

I nod, but don't tell her what I am anxious about. "As I said, I am not sleeping very well and Lukkas says I keep him awake with my fidgeting." I didn't say that he kept me awake by heavy snoring. "It's as though I am so preoccupied sometimes, that I forget to eat…"

Dr Evans casts me a look that I might have given a class of five-year-olds, as though to say, "That's just silly behaviour." But I did not say that I thought he might be having an affair.

I had asked Lukkas whether he would see a marriage guidance councillor with me, but he had refused. I was the problem, he said.

"Well, your blood pressure is fine. I suppose it might be best to take a blood sample."

I sit in silent thought, watching Lilly play, whilst Dr Evans shoves a needle into my arm.

Lukkas could never wait for our summer holiday in Nice, but this year he had point blank refused to go. In the face of his anger, I had booked the tickets anyway. If he wasn't having an affair, what was the matter with him?

There is nothing more to be done for the time being. Lilly and I leave the surgery.

At the park, my feet are leaden, trailing after my body as I cross to the sand pit. Perhaps Lukkas didn't want to go on holiday for the first time in all these years because there was somebody he really didn't want to leave.

My concentration had gone, just a little. Where once I would have chatted with Lilly, I hadn't heard a word she said to me for several minutes. Perhaps Lukkas was right. Maybe there was something wrong with me and I couldn't see it. Maybe Lukkas was the problem.

Why did Lukkas race to work each morning? It must surely be for someone with whom he worked, a person who knew his work, a woman who had that in common with him. I felt unashamedly jealous. I had been the one Lukkas confided in over the years, listening to stories about nameless tortured children, just to help him empty his mind and sleep although, often, I wanted to cover my ears like a small child and protest, "Enough!"

Not in all the years I had known him, had he been enthusiastic about rising from his bed in the morning. Knowing that something was wrong, I had chewed my nails like an anxious child, breaking the skin around them until they were red and raw.

CHAPTER FIVE
Ben

Surely Lukkas would never carry on like that with another woman? Never in the office. For one thing, it would be too risky. For another, I told myself, it would be humiliating for me. He would never do that, not after all that we had meant to one another.

He appeared irritated with Josh, our eldest son, as well as with me. If I played music whilst I cooked the dinner, no matter whether it was Radar Love or The Lark Ascending, Lukkas would walk through the front door and turn the music off. When Josh and I went for a walk around the field beyond the garden gate, Lukkas deliberately locked us out so that we had to walk the long way around. I suppose he can have enough of Josh; after all, Josh works for his father as a lawyer, and until he has the money for a mortgage down-payment, he lives with us.

Perhaps it isn't somebody with whom he works, I muse. After all, he seems just as anxious to get to the gym. Mostly he swims, because he has a bad back. There are lots of pretty, younger women at the gym, and he likes to flirt, I know this. Nowadays he hardly bothers to disguise it. His mother said she thought he might be menopausal when I explained his marked interest in clothes and cars.

On Thursday after he has gone to work, I go to the upstairs bathroom to unblock the loo and discover the pipe leading from the tap has a slow drip. I can do lots of practical things, but I've never been a plumber. So, I go to Lukkas' desk, where various handy-man cards are stored.

As I look for the plumber's number in his desk drawer, I find a small, black, leather wallet that I don't recognise. I open it immediately and inside there are two cards. The first is an advertisement for a restaurant in Nice where we've eaten. But as I turn it over, in beautiful, sloping, French handwriting, someone has written 'Le Pot D'Etain'.

I've never been there, but perhaps Lukkas is thinking of booking a table for us.

The other card is a dress tag, I recognise the fashion brand, it's for a dress from Hannah's shop, it has a code and it says, 'Black Stella dress,' size ten.

Where is this dress? I might feasibly get into a size twelve, but never a size ten. Lukkas hasn't bought me clothes for over ten years and he certainly never makes purchases for his many, female God children. That's always been my job.

I try to imagine the dress, what it looked like, imagining the person inside it until imagining is an unbearable, toxic poison that makes my head hurt.

I call Hannah at the shop, tell her what I have found, asking her whether her father might have bought clothing there.

A little warily, she asks, "Why, Mum?"

"Oh, I just wondered…" It was a lame reply. Dejection saps creativity.

Then Hannah chortled derisively. "He's not having an affair Mum if that's what you think!"

I prayed that no one else in the shop had heard her, but then she called out to Aaliyah, her friend and assistant supervisor, "Do you remember who bought that seventy-pound black Stella dress, the last one, size ten?"

There was a longish pause. "Nope, she doesn't remember, but it certainly wasn't Dad," Hannah replied. "You probably bought it for Annie or one of the god daughters and forgot, Marge."

I detested being called 'Marge', a recent term for me on Hannah's part, a bastardisation of Madre, I think, but also the name of a rather disapproving Great aunt from my child hood.

"You've forgotten," Hannah accused.

"I don't forget things, and certainly not an expensive dress that I bought from your shop," I replied.

"Dad says you do. He says you are always forgetting things and losing things."

I frowned indignantly at the phone and said goodbye to her. This was nonsense, my memory was better than his. I felt humiliated. I should not have called her.

I would have to fetch Lilly from nursery soon, I thought, glancing at my watch and grabbing my jacket.

I meandered along the road to the school, recalling the first time I had met Hannah's difficult partner, Ben. It was one warm, summer's evening in June, not long after the girls' own father had left them.

Hannah had been lonely, I understand that. But to this day, I don't know where she met Ben Jolly, only that he clung to her like a leach from that day onward and became too strong an influence over her, capitalising upon her weakness, then.

When I arrived at her house on that evening, there were a cluster of young men, unshaven and tattooed like pirates, all gathered around her open front door. Hannah held Ruby on her hip and her face twisted into uncertainty as she noticed me before walking through the throng of pirates to meet me with the most innocent of smiles.

"They're friends," she hisses in an urgent appeal.

"What, all of them?" I ask, aghast.

"Well, Ben is, the one holding the little boy." Her eyes lock on mine, appealing for clemency. "His ex-wife asked him to look after the little boy for the weekend and they have nowhere to go, so I said he could stay here for the evening, use the settee…"

"Just him and his little boy?" I ask. "But what about your girls?"

"The girls are fine. Come on mum, I thought you were a Christian?"

That was then, and this is now, I thought. I shake my head in disbelief, knowing that I am being hoodwinked in some way.

"Just until tomorrow then? But really Hannah, how well do you know this man?"

But she had already moved away, my question was left unanswered.

It wasn't just tomorrow, in the end, it was a full-blown relationship. I knew Hannah was a good mother, how much she loved her children, but she was naïve, still.

Every weekend, Ben's little boy, a rough neck like his Dad, would return to wet the beds and introduce Ruby to nits and impetigo. Little Louis was completely lacking in discipline and left me wondering what his teachers made of him. I tried to work some magic on him after he behaved like a wild thing in the park and thumped

Ruby. I gave him toy cars which once belonged to our boys and gleefully he hurled them at Lilly, bruising her head. Ruby adored him as Hannah seemed to adore Ben, calling Louis 'my brother.'

Over the following year, Ben wrecked the house, both deliberately and accidentally.

Ruby talked about Ben smoking 'weed', although she had no idea what that was.

A tenant complained about him, and the police arrived to search for cannabis when the children were safely at school. I wish they had found some, it might have put paid to the situation; but all that they found was a large flick knife, which they confiscated.

Ben got into fights in a variety of pubs, the police came to know him well.

Hannah and Ben fought, too. I lived in terror for them all. Then one Saturday, I went to retrieve a hoover from their house.

Ben and two friends were in the garden, doing something to bits of a car again. When Ben saw me, he came to the garden gate. "Hannah isn't here, she's taken Ruby to her ballet practice," he said gruffly around his cigarette.

I hear Lilly crying in the living room.

"Oh?" I say, then walk past him and into the house through the open front door.

Hannah could have asked me to look after Lilly, but she knew that I was trying to sit on Joe, to get him through his A levels. I don't believe that Ben would hurt either child, but he won't make them his priority either.

Lilly is strapped into a high chair. Her soft, ash blonde hair is greasy with food, her face is covered in breakfast cereal and toys, bowls and spoons are strewn about the floor. She is heavy with last night's nappy and smells of wee. The television is on, switched to one of those programmes where adults who want to be famous, shout at one another.

"Come on little Froggy, Nanna is here," I croon above her sobs, lifting her out of the high chair. As soon as she is in my arms, the crying stops.

I pick up a crayon from the floor and scrawl a message to Hannah on a piece of paper.

"Taken Lilly to my house for a bath, Mum x". Placing the note inside the front door I weigh it down with an old trainer, then carry Lilly to the car.

Ben glowers at me through the gate with the expression of a dog who would like to bite me.

I nod at him with a smile that's more of a grimace.

On the short journey home, I sing nursery rhymes and silly songs to Lilly, and she is soon laughing. I run a bath with bubbles and peel the smelly baby grow from her body to sit her in the frothy bath and wash her hair and body clean. She plays with the duck Judge, in his wig. Soon Lilly is clean and happy again and I swing her in the towel singing 'Rock-a-by-baby' to make her laugh. Then I dress her in a clean, warm dress and cardigan bought at a charity shop.

As I carry her down the stairs I receive a text from Hannah.

"Ben is upset, I asked him to look after Lilly, she isn't your child, you shouldn't have taken her."

No, I don't want her to be 'my child' Hannah, that isn't the point. I will face the verbal abuse later.

"Are you home now?" I text back, "Or shall I take her shopping with me?"

I drove Lilly home to Hannah. The health visitor at my surgery had said so long as I have access to the children and a key to the house, they would not get involved, but they trust Ben Jolly no more than I do.

My greatest fear is that one day he might make Hannah pregnant with his own child, and then what would we do? Lukkas would refuse to sit at Sunday lunch with the child's father. He would have a car thief and a drug dealer as a son-in-law, more to the point, what kind of father and step father would he make? He manipulated Hannah and hated me. I had no way of solving that problem.

CHAPTER SIX

Texts and bizarre, delusional thoughts

Lukkas' phone had become a blistering bone of contention between us. It was his constant companion and of course, he needed it for his work. But recently he smiled at it as though the device were an old friend. He smiled at the texts in a way he never smiled at me. Sitting in a pub garden recently with some old friends, he had laughed out loud at a message but had shied at sharing the joke.

That night, we lay in bed in the darkened room with the window ajar. I woke to the muted hunting horn of his phone and I could not sleep again.

Outside the window, an old fox I fed with chicken carcasses barked to his young, the dogs growled softly below in the kitchen. I listened to Lukkas' breathing beside me as he lay upon his side, his back turned towards me.

He ignored the phone twice, but the third time that it sounded a text message, he rose eagerly, as though his tiredness had dissipated in an instant.

The alarm clock read five thirty.

"Who is it this time of the morning?" I asked, unable to hide my resentment.

"Nobody much," he replied, still avidly reading the text.

"It's a little intrusive when we are trying to sleep," I said. He would surely have felt this too, once upon a time. I must have lain awake for the next hour, until Lukkas rose to go to the bathroom. I noticed he carried the phone with him.

Feeling very weary, I got up to make some tea. On the way, I picked up the wash basket in which Lukkas kept his shirts, carrying it downstairs upon my hip. The smell of his after shave followed me with the basket. But there was another smell, alien, upsetting, not my perfume.

I ignored Joe's dog, Jack, who came to me in the expectation of an early morning walk. I sat on the bottom stair and lifted the top shirt to my nostrils. It was an expensive favourite, small black stripes, almost invisible against the white, making Lukkas even more gorgeous than he already was. As I opened the shirt, examining the collar, I gave a small gasp of pain and disgust.

For thirty years, I'd ironed six shirts a week and had never seen marks such as these. Brown streaks, not sweat stains, but like the golden-brown ripples of sand in the Sahara. I hadn't worn foundation for a long time, but I felt certain that these were foundation marks. As Jack pressed a cold black nose against my leg, I crushed the shirt to my chest, for there was a clear kiss imprinted in lipstick just within the stiff collar. These things happened to other people, were voiced in song, but they were not the things that happened in real life; surely to God!

"Oh God... Oh God!" I said aloud, and in an instant, Lukkas appeared before me at the top of the staircase.

"What are you doing, everything all right...?" His voice had a nervous edge to it at first, but in an instant, it turned to anger. "What on earth is it now?" he snapped testily.

The total lack of love or concern in his voice made me healthily angry.

"There are marks in your shirt, make up!" I cried. "You are always on that bloody phone; you never want to go anywhere with me, you miss weddings, weekends away...What the hell is going on, Lukkas?"

He shook his head, twisting his top lip into a snarl of disgust.

"Of-course there aren't marks! Give me the shirt, if you are going to make such a fuss about things, I'll wash them myself." He descended the staircase to snatch the shirt from my hands. "You are being perfectly unreasonable again, Laura. What is the matter with you? Did you go and see that doctor?"

I didn't reply. He knew that I had, I had told him so already.

He snorted derisively, pushing past me to the kitchen to shove the shirt into a plastic bag from the cupboard. As he did so I made a rash decision. I hurled myself to the top of the staircase and snatched his phone from the charger. I had no idea what his passcode was. As my heart thumped with the force of someone carrying out a bank robbery, my fingers fumbled to connect with my brain.

I tried 1960, his birth date and in answer the phone told me, 'wrong passcode, try again'. I tried 2006, our grand-daughter's birthdate and it denied me once more. As a teacher, computer technology had been my worst subject, but even I knew that if I kept this up the phone would block every attempt.

"What the bloody hell do you think you're doing?"

I span around, dropping the phone to the floor as I did so.

Lukkas' eyes were blazing, the green irises narrowed like a cat and dark as a forest in his rage.

"I'm sorry! I shouldn't have done that, but please let me see your phone..." I begged him, knowing with a sinking heart that he would tell Hannah and that she would be equally angry with me, but knowing too that it was imperative to silence my fear.

"Why should I do that? It's my business and it's giving into your bizarre, delusional thoughts!"

"But if there is nothing, I will feel reassured, surely? Please Lukkas..." I sank onto the edge of the bed in my desperation.

He retrieved the phone from the floor and glared at me. "There is confidential information about children on there, you shouldn't see that."

"I have my own responsibilities for children, you know that's not what I'm worried about," I mumbled disconsolately.

He drew a fresh shirt from the wardrobe, then turned to me, angrily, and snapped, "All right, if it will get you off my back..."

I felt so ridiculously grateful that I almost kissed the hand that held out the phone. For a split second his hands touched mine, soft, lawyer's hands that had once stroked my face, my back; the very feel of them conditioned my emotions. The very feel of them was like love.

Whilst Lukkas dressed, half watching me, I scrolled down the pages he had made accessible. Names and ambiguous messages from unknown people vied for my attention.

"Sorry about the migraine, see you later." That was from Holly, the new lawyer. I had met her once but didn't remember what she looked like. Why did she believe that Lukkas suffered from migraine? He didn't; only headaches after drinking too much red wine.

"Lukkas, can you drop the files to the office before you go to court?" This was from Tom, a lawyer I had met.

"Dad, could we talk about..." That from Josh, our son.

"Are you free now? Best meet outside the office." This held my attention. Charles, who is Charles, I wondered, and why did he need to meet Lukkas away from the office? But Lukkas wasn't gay, so there was probably a perfectly simple explanation.

"Can we meet...?"

"Could we talk about...?"

"Right, I need to get to work now, I'll be late," Lukkas said sternly.

I had almost forgotten that he was there. I didn't say, "Late at six am, how early do you have to start nowadays?" I should have handed the phone to him, but instead, on a crazy impulse, I rushed into the bathroom with it and slammed the door shut, locking it behind me.

"Open the door!" His voice growled like sudden thunder before a storm. He had only ever hit me once, but his muffled voice threatened to do it again.

My fingers sped to the numbers with addresses, as my back shoved against the door. Who was Ali, male or female? Seraphina... who was she?

Suddenly the door cracked on the latch as though we were cast in a horror film. The wood splintered through the white paint. Lukkas had forced the lock, he who was constantly telling our sons and grandchildren to be gentle with the house. He had forced the lock. Why, I wondered, go to that extreme if he had nothing to conceal?

When I opened the door at last, fearful of his anger, he snatched the phone from me. Grabbing the shoulder of my dressing gown, he pressed his face close to mine until I could taste the mouthwash on his breath. My heart beat was inhumanly fast now, all I could think of was that Lukkas had become the Sherriff of Nottingham.

"I told you once that if you behave like this, if you are out of control, I will leave you. Go to that doctor of yours and tell her you need something, and I don't mean lavender oil. You are the problem, not me."

He turned, and I watched him stride across the bedroom floor, slamming the door behind him. Then I collapsed back onto the bed and listened as he left the house, slamming the front door so that the sound resounded in the quiet neighbourhood.

The ache of loss inside of me was sudden and unbearable. My limbs and heart ached as though I had run a marathon. I sat, hunched and weak, staring at a toothpaste stain on the carpet with tears in my eyes, like the idiot Lukkas had suggested I was.

I couldn't keep going back to my doctor, although I believed the ultimatum from Lukkas. Go to a doctor and get pills for melancholy, or I will leave you. What pills could be prescribed for someone who suspected, with fresh evidence, that her husband was having an affair?

The door of the bedroom opened, and Josh stood there; his pyjama trousers loose on his lean body, his tawny hair standing on end; a sympathetic frown upon his face.

"What the heck was all that about, are you okay?" he asked me.

"Sorry love. It doesn't matter, it'll be alright."

"It didn't sound alright."

He sat next to me, putting his arm lightly about my shoulders, saying nothing more but trying to comfort.

"You'd better get ready for work, you'll miss the bus, then Dad will be even more cross," I said listlessly.

When Josh had gone, I stared out at the meadow, the grass a pale green from lack of rain. When we first came here, Lukkas and I often used to walk the dogs across the fields there. He never walked with me now. The last time that we walked together had been months ago. It had been his suggestion I meet him at the office on a Saturday morning. But when I arrived, he met me outside, appraising me in a way I was unused to.

"You look a bit of a mess," he said coldly.

I remember feeling so hurt. I appeared no differently than always when walking the dogs, whether on a beach or through the woods. I had always looked this way, I was just older, I suppose.

Loneliness set in. I could have talked to Charlotte, or have spoken to Mum, or to friends. But it was humiliating. Bad enough to have my own thoughts about affairs and mental illness, without sharing them with other people who believed we were a sound couple.

Every activity felt mechanical, even the girls failed to lift my spirits. I couldn't laugh or giggle, even the simple task of helping Ruby to use crayons in a colouring book failed to lift my despondency.

In his haste to get to work, Lukkas forgot about the shirt, so I took it to my local dry cleaners. Trying to be casual, I asked, "Do you have an expert on stains and removal?"

They did, she was called Pam, a large, broad shouldered girl with scraped back, two tone hair. She had a practical, straightforward manner about her, she didn't look the mischievous or catty type.

"Could you identify the marks on this shirt?" I asked, in what I hoped was a crisp tone of voice. "My son is due to be married soon and I'm very fond of the bride to be. This shirt has caused quite a row."

Pam nodded slowly, already impatient with this feckless son of mine. "We could do proper tests on it, but these streaks..." she lifted the collar to sniff the cotton, "are foundation, blusher maybe, but I think foundation. This," she pointed at the imprint of lips, "looks like lipstick to me, in fact I don't think there's any doubt in my mind. Look at the shape of it."

I suppose my immediate reaction should have been that of a heartbroken wife, but I felt a surge of relief. I wasn't mad, not mad at all; someone else recognised the stain, faint as it was.

I declined Pam's offer to have the shirt tested further. The price she asked was rather high. The brave thing would be to tackle Lukkas about it, but as soon as I reached home I received a short text from him to say he would go straight from a conference in Birmingham to stay in London, where he was going to prepare for the next week's case. There was no gentle apology, no kiss in the text.

A short while ago I had taken the girls to Cornwall, for the first time without him. I took my parents too.

Perhaps that's when I suspected Lukkas was pulling away from me. I recall playing alone on the beach with the girls, whilst Mum and Dad sat in the warm car, sheltered from the strong winds and occasional rain. I felt very lonely, with images of Lukkas before me, scenes from across the years, as he traced our son's name with the pram wheels and built a sand castle with Hannah.

I had sent a text to him which said, "I miss you xx".

"Have a good time." He messaged me back. But there was nothing about missing me.

That afternoon, knowing that his father would be absent for the weekend, Joe declared his intention to 'Have a few people around.'

My heart sank. He meant a party, which would mean my constant reminders to him to keep the noise down, reminders to his friends not to swear at full voice and to turn Hip Hop music down. He was seventeen, as were most of his friends, some of them only sixteen, so there was the worry of attempted under aged sex, also.

I had agreed to have the girls overnight. I would be hard put to manage the two things. I would have to keep the girls in one part of the house whilst Joe took over the living room.

"Can't you go to someone else's house?" I implored him. "I'm babysitting, Ru and Lilly will never get to sleep."

He grinned down at me, all muscle and testosterone, tall, like his father.

"You said if I revised for the Media exam, I could have some friends here," he reminded me.

"You didn't revise. Joseph. I had to drag you out of bed every day." But I had already lost the argument.

"Just ensure that no one is sick this time!" was my parting shot as he left the room.

Joe's parties have become notorious, even Frank, the Nigerian pastor opposite, has stopped praying for us.

After dinner, I played a game with the girls before bathing them, then read to them, sang Lilly to sleep and left Ruby reading books in her bed. Finally, I got into bed myself to the noisy accompaniment of The Grits singing "My life be like ooh-ah, ooh-ah..." I had some sympathy with the lyrics.

I tried to read some of The Big Sleep, but the plot paled into insignificance when faced with my own problems, so I stopped at chapter three. I lay, tense and anxious and staring at a crack in the ceiling, my arms held behind my head. Mostly, I wondered where Lukkas was, what he was doing, then at the sound of a shriek from a girl at about eleven o'clock, I tore back the bedspread and pulled on my dressing gown.

I marched to the living room door, yanking it open. A dozen, indolent teenage faces looked up at me, mostly girls, seated on their boyfriend's laps. No one appeared surprised or startled by my appearance there, my anger floated like a swollen, cartoon cloud, above their dull expressions.

"Okay, this party is due to end soon, so would you please keep it down or you will wake my grand-children!"

"Okay Mum," snorted Gavin, Joe's best friend.

"Don't call me Mum, Gavin, I'm not in the mood for it. You will be the first to leave if I have to come in here again!"

Joe frowned at me. Rhiannon, a recent girlfriend, lolled in his lap, unconcerned. "Why are you being such a bitch?" Joe asked, "Take a chill pill, Marge."

I ignored this. "And stop going to the toilet and slamming the living room door!" I finished.

As I strode unhappily back to the bedroom, a small voice called, "Nanna, I can't get to sleep." It was Ruby. I beckoned to her to come down the stairs then put her into my bed, tucking the duvet around her.

As she snuggled close, I decided that it wasn't unfair of me to ask for some support so, I sent Lukkas a text.

"Please will you contact Joe and give me some back up? He is having a party and has woken Ruby and I'm also concerned that George and Christina will complain again."

Then I wait, mulling over the subject of stained shirts and Lukkas' texts whilst stroking Ruby's hair to reassure her and to reassure myself, I suppose. Has Lukkas become so powerful that he can dismiss me, carry on with who he likes, doing whatever he likes? Where is he, why hasn't he answered my text? Perhaps he's asleep, or working from a hotel room, hunched over a desk. Now I feel guilty for bothering him, but after another screech from the living room and a banged door, I decide enough is enough.

I call him. After a few seconds, I hear his voice at last; his deep, manly, public school voice above the background din of a night club or bar. In the distant room, they are playing a song by George Michael.

"What?" It is an impatient, curt question.

"Sorry, did you get my text?"

"Yes, just now. I was on my way to bed. It's been a busy day. You want me to text Joseph?"

It is as if he is trying to impress someone else by being dismissive of me. His voice carries a level of authority which is unnecessary.

"Well, yes please, if you would…"

There is male laughter close to him. Then a pause. "For God's sake Laura, can't you just sort it out on your own? Can't I go away for a few days without a huge fuss?"

"Prick," I think, using Joe's favourite word.

"You don't have to do very much Lukkas. Just ask him to be quieter, or tell him the party should stop," I suggest.

"God, you are always carping on about something…" he said. Then the phone went dead.

"No…no, I'm not!" I complained to the sleeping Ruby. I do not 'carp on'. As a rule, I get on with things without Lukkas knowing, but sometimes nowadays, cheeriness eludes me. All too often, now, he says what he bloody well likes about me, and I must accept it.

So, I get up, rising from the bed. Taking the 'L'Homme Libre' after shave from the bed side table and opening the window a little further, I hurl it with all my might through the gap, deftly flinging it across the fence and into the nettles, where it would never be found again.

After a while the music and noise in the living room died down, but nothing would mute Mick Jagger singing 'Sympathy for The Devil' inside my head.

By the time he returned home, roguishly unshaven and tired, my anger had subsided. But when I lifted my lips to his cheek, he swiftly turned away, when I reached for his hand, he withdrew it. It had always been the case that Lukkas sulked if I raised any objection or disagreed with him. I suppose that's why I so rarely did. To disagree would mean silence from him, sometimes for weeks. When the children were younger, I was afraid that the silences would hurt them too.

CHAPTER SEVEN
The Hotel

Lukkas came and went during that week. He ate the meals I provided, but the atmosphere degenerated to a crippled silence, as he ignored every attempt I made at conversation.

Towards the end of that week, I decided to go away. Not for long, just for one night, but I have never done such a thing before, never walked out on my family, not even for a night. Maybe it will make Lukkas think...just maybe.

I cooked the dinner as usual, then washed up and packed a bag with clothes; my wash bag, my cigarettes and a bottle of wine; because wine bought by the glass in a hotel in July is expensive. I left Jack, the collie, to Joe; taking my old bitch, Lyra, for company. She is old and would miss me.

I didn't know where to go, so I drove up and down the country roads, within a six-mile radius of Oxford. It had been the hottest day this year by far, and the first two country hotels I arrived at were fully booked, but then I arrived at the Bayard's Hotel, close to Thame. They had room and I felt a little thrill as I parted, or to be accurate, Lukkas parted, with a hundred pounds to pay for it and an extra ten to keep Lyra with me.

The three, gorgeously made up receptionists appraised me suspiciously, or so I felt, speculating perhaps on how I came to be there. I shuffled a little on the other side of the desk, wondering whether they thought me a sad old bird whose husband was having an affair. Probably the truth. A world filled with sad old bird's and cheating, menopausal men.

"What is your name please?" the pretty Chinese girl asked.

I must have hesitated, but only for a split second. "Mrs Dalloway," I said then, in a rush, thinking of the book case and one of the novels I had meant to read, but never had. But it was a rather foolish lie, as I then had to sign for the Barclaycard in my own name. No wonder one of the beautiful receptionists glanced sideways at her friend.

I lifted my bag from the counter, pulling my cardigan across the bottle of wine which was stashed in my bag and Lyra followed me.

It was a comfortable room. Not as beautiful as the rooms that Lukkas had booked across the years, but then Lukkas wasn't here to judge. I dumped my few things onto the bed and whistled Lyra to me, leadless, for she is generally an obedient old girl. She followed me to the bar where I asked for a glass of water. Then, in the sunny gardens, I threw the water over a bed of roses and sat at a table to fill the glass with wine from the screw top, supermarket bottle.

I lit a cigarette and opening the writing pad, set down my only evidence for and against an affair.

Overwork:	Affair
Being away for longer periods	Refusing to tell me where he is going
Irritability	Being away for longer periods
Too tired for sex	Telling me not to wash his shirts
Normal guilt at being away, hence perfume gift	Guilt- perfume
	Smiling at texts
	Not being affectionate
	Wearing expensive aftershave but only when he goes out without me
	Mysterious dresses
	When he does make love, using new 'techniques'
	Saying he is not like other men,
	What??
	Lipstick on collar

It was damning. I didn't go down the route of his accusing me of madness. After thirty years of support for him, I tried to distance myself from this sinister nonsense. I didn't believe that he genuinely believed it, which suggested other, more dangerous motives… I was too cowardly to face them.

I poured a second glass of wine and staggered into the rose bushes where Lyra, emboldened by this holiday, was growling at a young Springer Spaniel.

After my second glass of wine I climbed the hotel staircase to my room, quickly becoming lost in the maze of corridors. But Lyra, with that uncanny sense of place that dogs have, lead me like a blind person's guide dog, running confidently ahead of me as playfully as a puppy on a seaside break and arriving at door number 273, as though she'd cracked hundreds, tens and units long ago.

The wine helped me to wallow in self-pity. Then, having showered myself into wakefulness once more, I dressed and followed Lyra back to the warm air of the garden.

After that, the evening became a strange business of people watching and note taking on the matter of Lukkas, and after I'd drunk half a bottle of wine, the first of many texts arrived on my phone. It was Joe, at least someone was concerned about me, I smiled, my reaction changing rapidly as I read the message.

"Where the fuck are you, Mum?"

"I'm fine, don't worry about me Joe."

"I'm not worried about you, why should I be? There are two French students on the doorstep who say they are staying here. What rooms are they staying in, do we have any spare rooms?"

From time to time to pay for various things for our grand-children, I have hosted students, but I certainly wasn't expecting these. They are not part of my plan. That's the thing about self-pity, it doesn't allow for sympathy elsewhere.

"I haven't arranged for any students," I reply, "You'll have to tell them to contact the Language school."

The following text was from Charlotte. "Where are you?" Her text said. "I called to see you, but you weren't there."

"At a nice hotel, getting quietly drunk, with Lyra; although she is sober. I'm semi flirting with old men, just to see what it feels like."

This was true. An old man had been staring at me since I sat down, but he wasn't a patch on Lukkas.

I wish Hannah had a sister. I couldn't do without Charlotte. When we were younger I had been a little envious of her, she was prettier than me by far. Lukkas had looked upon her as his own sister.

"Tell me where you are, and I'll come and have a drink with you," her next text said.

"Not today, I feel so strange, I need to think what to do. Lukkas is being really nasty, Charlie." And just admitting that bought the tears out. I sniffed them back and turned my chair away from the attentive man.

"Lukkas loves you, he always has. He's not having an affair, get it out of your head."

I gazed at the distant fields and took another glug of wine. Lyra, hungry for her supper, placed a paw upon my leg.

"I've found things. I don't understand what else they could mean but an affair. He's been horrible to me, but he's so charming to you, to others, that you won't get it."

The other guests who had finished eating in the restaurant, the families, as we once were, spilled happily into the courtyard, chattering, looking forward to tomorrow. I felt like an alien being.

"I don't know whether he loves me any more Charlotte, I think he has said some odd things to his mother about me too. The last time we visited his parents, Marjorie kept going on about what a great thing second-marriages can be, until I was sarcastic and asked her whether she was thinking of divorcing Derek."

"That was a bit naughty, they are in their late-eighty's, aren't they?" But I could hear her throaty giggle behind the text.

I was rather tired now and had drunk almost a full bottle of wine, and still no texts from Lukkas.

"Tell me where you are. I'll come there. I don't want you to be on your own."

"No. really, it's okay. I'm going to bed soon," I replied. I felt dreadfully miserable by now. I stopped answering her.

Lyra lead me to bed. I must have hit the security card against the lock at least three times before I realised that it was upside down. Swaying considerably, I fed the dog and then cleaned my teeth before falling onto the bed in a fully clothed coma. I felt sick.

At about two thirty, incredibly, considering my physical and mental state, I had an orgasm. I don't know why. I wasn't dreaming, simply in a state of comatose. Perhaps it was a simple matter of stress release. I looked guiltily at Lyra, who lifted her head inquisitively from the corner of the room, her tail thumping on the carpet. How complex and revolting human beings are, I thought.

My phone buzzed with a text and I rose immediately, willing the text to be from him. But it was from Monica, my sister-in-law; a yoga teacher and spiritual Guru.

She must have been talking to Charlotte.

"You have to love yourself," the message said, "Come and stay here if you need some time out."

I felt too tired and miserable to reply. I groaned, fell onto the bed and lay on my side, crying myself back to sleep without caring what the guests on either side of me might think. In the distance beyond my window, a hen party was in full swing. Gleeful, drunken female voices sang along to 'Heard it through the Grape Vine...'

CHAPTER EIGHT

Lies and foolish thoughts

At breakfast, I sat alone and stared at the pastries before me. I couldn't eat, all food tasted like cardboard. In the last month, I had lost half a stone, the only things keeping me alive were tea and white wine.

I decided to swim in the hotel pool. I swam ten lengths, crying silently beside a very stern looking German woman in a black swimming hat whose expression said clearly that I was raining on her parade.

After drying my hair listlessly, I decided to get my hair cut. As my hair is thick and wiry and apt to look exactly as it did before the haircut after only two washes, it always felt rather pointless. I examined my eyebrows too, wondering whether it would be a foolish waste of money to have them shaped.

I stared at my face in the changing room mirror, my skin was a good feature, but my features looked so much flatter than they had when I was younger. I was a flat fish in my early fifties. At least our forthcoming holiday might give me a tan.

I packed my few belongings, then Lyra and I started the five-mile drive home along the country lanes. I wondered where Lukkas was this morning. I imagined entering our bed room and putting my arms about him, his saying, "Laura, I've missed you, where have you been?" I still believed in it.

It was now ten o'clock. It had been his habit for some while to go to the office on a Sunday morning. For many years he had said that this was a necessity if we were going away for three or four weeks, which was what Lukkas had wanted to do in the past. We had a large apartment in Nice, family and friends would come there to stay with us during the summer months. I had accepted long ago that his work load would be greater if we did this, ends to tie up, etc.

I pulled over into the layby, Joseph took a long time to answer his phone.

"Sorry Joe, is Dad there?"

His voice is a little muffled by the bed clothes. "No, I heard his car leaving. Where are you, have you had a row?"

"No lovey, don't worry, I went out with some old friends and stopped the night. Okay, see you a bit later."

He grunted and went back to sleep.

I wanted to talk to Lukkas. We needed to have some-kind of a conversation, rather than his permanent avoidance of me. I bypassed the turning to our home and drove on to his office. As I turned into Oxford, I caught a glimpse of sunshine on a charcoal coloured car ahead of me, it was Lukkas' car.

I followed it as it swung through the open barrier. He saw me and gave me a look close to pure hatred, which gave out a heat of radiation so intense that it temporarily zapped my internal organs.

I saw us together, in a picture in my mind, sixteen years ago, entering these offices hand in hand as he moved in. So different, now.

He hesitated, reaching for his work bag, glaring at me. "What are you doing here?" He barked, so loudly that I prayed there was no one around to hear it.

"I wanted to talk to you," I said lamely, looking from his wet hair, black as a seal to his chic, striped shirt. That was what my Russian friend Anya called him, chic, the chicest man she had ever seen, she said.

I knew I was not welcome there, but still he held the reception door open for me, letting the latch close as I entered. I followed him up the staircase like Lyra, like a bitch in disgrace who would do anything to be stroked.

On either side of us the little offices I had not seen for so long drew my attention. These were the rooms where lawyers and trainee lawyers, including Josh, had arranged their desks and filled spaces with files and photographs of their families. The desk tops were neat or untidy depending upon the personality, in the case of Josh and Tom, there were several rolled up ties on each desk.

We reached Lukkas' office on the top floor, his desk facing his secretaries, above it hung the large black and white photograph I had bought for him long ago, of the two attractive young lovers kissing in front of the Eiffel Tower as they crossed the street.

This was the most frenetic office of all, as a rule. Here, the complex child care cases were dealt with. Lukkas had told me once he was worried about the time when Josh would come here because the things people did to their children could be truly horrible, and he believed Josh to be too kind, too sensitive. There were large, dog eared files piled everywhere, gruelling to the eye, let alone to read.

"What? What do you want? As you can see, I have rather a lot to deal with," he spat impatiently.

Then he sat at his desk, studiedly ignoring my presence, opening a file with one hand and starting up his computer with another.

I bit my lip, shuffled uncomfortably for a moment. His face was set in a snarl of contempt. Every movement that he made was intimidating. The old me might have snapped back at him, but the woman I was now had lost her confidence, the woman I had become was no longer sure of her place in the world.

"I'm sorry..." I began but didn't get any further.

"Sorry? Last week you sent me seventeen texts..."

"But you wouldn't speak to me Lukkas, and they were mild texts, I don't understand what's happening to us," I pleaded with him. I looked around for a chair but for the first time in my life, in Lukkas' own office, I felt afraid to sit down.

"What kind of support is that? You know we are trying to launch the advice booths, which could help thousands of neglected people, and you appear to be trying to pull me down. What the fuck do you think you're doing?"

He had started shouting again, and twisting words around, so that I was to blame, as if I were the one returning with lipstick marks on my clothes.

"I've always supported your work, Lukkas..."

I sat down opposite him, feeling weak, vulnerable and stupid, intimidated by the files as well as the lawyer before me, who now scrolled down his phone to text someone far more important than I was to him.

A slight, dull bump, like the closing of a door came from behind us and I turned my shoulders to look behind me.

"Hardly supportive now!" He barked. Then he smiled nastily, nodding slowly, his eyes widening as though in dramatic realisation. "Oh, I see… You think I might be having an affair with one of my Lawyers, do you?" His voice suddenly rose to shouting pitch, "What about my reputation Laura, have you considered that?"

No, I hadn't thought that he was having an affair with a colleague. I didn't believe his humiliation of me would ever take that turn. I shook my head, speechless, senseless and opened my mouth to speak but couldn't find any words there.

Had it been my imagination, or had he glanced towards the far door behind me as he spoke? Was he raising his voice to impress someone else? For he was using his actors voice now, and I'd not seen him in court for ages, but I knew Lukkas well, knew that he loved nothing better than an audience.

"What are you looking at?" He sneered. "There's no one there, Laura. This is what I'm worried about, you see. You are starting to become paranoid. I think you should go back to that Doctor."

"No, Lukkas, I…" But as with many times during our marriage, I was not going to be allowed a voice.

"What about your aggression, Laura? You are physically abusive." His voice was smooth now. I wanted to call him a liar, it was such an abominable lie. I tried to breathe slowly, to control my angry resentment at this rubbish.

"I am physically abusive? Lukkas, when I was pregnant with Joe and you were trying to find the money to buy this office, you pushed me over in the kitchen and made Josh and Hannah cry. You have held me so tightly by the arms, so that I couldn't leave the room on the many occasions you have berated me for something silly, that you left bruising!" I cried, finding my voice at last.

His face twisted into a sneer of contempt, his voice rising to a shout as though to silence me. "Do you really believe that anyone will ever listen to such rubbish!"

I could feel my own voice shake as I projected it to be heard across his own, loud voice. I knew the pattern well. I knew some of his behaviour now was my fault. I had said sorry so often in the past to keep the peace that Lukkas believed in my guilt alone, believed in his own perfection.

"You goad me Lukkas, often. You have said that I dressed like a Nun when we went to your last office do, on an evening where I had been nursing Lilly and comforting Hannah; I didn't want to go with you after that. I must never disagree with anything in case you sulk, so I didn't disagree because the children would be afraid of the silence. You hurled your case at me recently, saying you didn't want to go to France this year, you threw it! There is nothing wrong with me, you are the one who is behaving differently!"

His eyes were sheer green pin points now, hard as emerald stone, radiating anger.

"Liar!" He breathed.

"No. I am not a liar. These things happened."

"You, Laura, hit me with a frying pan."

As he said it, I collapsed into a chair, stunned into silence once more. Did he have no more imagination than to invent a punch and Judy scene? Did Lukkas believe what he was saying, did he expect me to believe this too?

"Hit you with a frying pan?" I repeated. It would have been darkly funny, but it wasn't.

"I have never hit anyone with a frying pan, let alone you," I said in a whisper, shaking my head at him.

He got up. He turned away from me, staring out of the window behind his desk, towards the university buildings, his arms folded across his chest.

"You don't even remember, do you?" He said, shaking his head.

"Of course, I would remember that. My memory is better than yours and always has been. I'm the one who reminds you about things and I always have done, remember?"

And the voice admonished me once again. This is your fault. For years you have apologised for crimes you didn't commit to keep the peace, in order that he wouldn't refuse to talk to you, because when you said sorry for these non-existent crimes, Lukkas would buy me flowers; and it was an unreal life which you played your part in, offering sex to placate.

Lukkas turned back to me. He stared into my eyes intently, waiting, maybe waiting for this response, for me to say, "Why, yes Lukkas, I remember it now, I did hit you with a frying pan after all, silly me!"

But, "I don't remember 'cos it's not bloody true," I said.

He skipped over the denial and his voice took on a lighter tone, as though he was denouncing his own lies as unworthy of pursuit.

"Well, anyway, this has all gone too far, Laura. Trying to get into my phone messages? You need cognitive therapy at the very least, perhaps a psychiatric assessment would help. Oh yes, Hannah told me all about the dress by the way... I know nothing about it, I assure you."

I might have known, Hannah told Lukkas everything, as once upon a time would I, I supposed.

"This can't go on, Laura. Go to the doctor," he said, deliberately looking down at the file before him, dismissing me now.

But I hardly heard him. Another thought had entered my head.

"The lights were all on when we came in…" I said.

He frowned now, as though his belief that I was mad was justified.

"I mean," I explained, "that there is someone else here, isn't there? Otherwise the lights would have been off. You don't leave them on overnight."

He shook his head slowly, indicating that I was a tragic imbecile and that little could be done for me.

"Get out, Laura. Go away, please. I have work to do."

His voice was so cold that I could feel frost on my skin. He had used this voice on Josh, but for the first time I could feel how hateful it was, knife sharp, reducing a person to nothing.

I rose from the chair then and turned away from him, no longer knowing what to say, my eyes rooted on the floor. Slowly I walked towards the winding staircase, away from him, feeling like a woman in a Gothic novel, mad with grief. Not knowing what my next action might be, only knowing that I had lost in some way.

It was as I descended that I heard the heavy file thump to the floor. But it hadn't come from the room I had just left; the sound came from the room behind it.

I hardly cared at the time, only later did I wonder about it. Perhaps one of his colleagues had been there all along. What did it matter? Lukkas appeared to despise me.

CHAPTER NINE

Passion, by Gheorghe

There had been someone listening to us from the adjoining room and that person had turned the lights on, entering before Lukkas. Perhaps it was Heather, I told myself. But Heather was a friend, my age, married for ever like me and definitely not Lukkas' type. Lukkas would never have spoken to me like that in Heather's hearing. It was as though he was showing off, as though he wanted the other person to hear the strong, macho tones of his deep voice, lecturing me, putting me down.

I sat very still in the car for a long time, feeling numb, unable to function. Random thoughts clamoured for attention as I gazed ahead of me, feeling unable to move. I wanted to talk to Hannah but discussing anything with Hannah had become so difficult.

Marjorie, Lukkas' mother, always wanted a little girl, she has told me this frequently. If she had a little girl, she would have called her Susannah, apparently. But she had Lukkas.

When Hannah was born, after the hardest, the longest birth imaginable, during which I tore and after which I felt as though my life had been sucked out of me, Lukkas did something he didn't do with the boys. He took her from my arms, so that I could sleep, he said, which could be construed as helpful. The young nurses, deeming him such a handsome and attentive father, allowed him to do that and it's true, I fell asleep in an instant after a pang of doubt and insecurity when I watched him walk away from me with Hannah in his arms. When I awoke, he still had Hannah in his arms and I felt robbed of her. The first thing that happened after the boys' births was that they were put to my breast.

I felt robbed and after all that work, a little resentful too. It was a long time ago, and call it silly if you will, but the feeling continued afterwards. Hannah's was the only birth that caused me post-natal depression. It didn't last for too long, but it was the first time that I thought about Lukkas' relationships with other women. During the first year of her birth, it almost appeared that he was going out of his way to flirt whilst my sore vagina took some while to heal.

And in the years after her birth it became clear that, though Lukkas loved all his children, she would be treated differently. He seemed fascinated by her, buying her little dresses so frequently. I thought, you are glad of her because it is what your mother wanted, a little girl. And as though to prove me right, as soon as Hannah was old enough for school, Marjorie suggested to Lukkas that Hannah should board at a public school close to her home and live with her.

I said no. No. But I felt almost threatened by the idea.

Now, I drew in a deep breath, tried to smooth my puffy eyes in the driver's mirror as I turned on the engine at last. I didn't want Joe to think I had been crying.

Lukkas didn't mean any of it, he didn't mean to be hurtful. I had to give him time to realise that I wasn't mad, time to feel bad about things, I told myself.

It wasn't like Lukkas to feel bad about anything.

The wall calendar said that Sarah and Tom had invited us to dinner and to stay the night with them in Pinner.

"I'm not going, can't, I've too much to do…" Lukkas declared flatly on the Monday morning.

He sipped his tea, staring through the kitchen window at the place where he had fought with Josh over a year ago. Mercifully, touch wood, their last big fight. The two physical battles they had were both in the garden. I never, really understood what they were about, but the last had been the more menacing; perhaps that was why they were so much more careful, nowadays.

On both occasions, I had run between them shouting for them to stop. Lukkas was larger than Josh, who had always been a skinnier version of his father, but it hadn't stopped Josh from antagonising him.

"But we must go," I protested to Lukkas. "They are our oldest friends and you've never missed Tom's birthday before! We accepted the invitation ages ago, they'll think it's really odd."

Lukkas grunted softly. "Maybe that's the problem, it's your behaviour that's odd."

I said nothing in response to this. I didn't want to rock the boat.

"Anyway, I've got two new adoption cases starting this week…"

"Please, Lukkas…" I pleaded.

He set down the mug which said, ironically, 'Keep calm and carry on.'

"I'll see what I can do. I'll let you know mid-week," he agreed at last. It was better than a refusal. I left off the subject then.

After I had taken the girls to school and nursery, I returned to the house to do a bit of Miss Marple sleuthing. I went to our bedroom and stood before Lukkas' large wardrobe. Before me were hung the ten or so suits he wore to work. Old favourites and new, ranging from black to grey.

Alone in the house apart from Joe, who said he had a 'free period' and was still in bed, I started placing my fingers into the little pockets of the more recent purchases. Lukkas had suddenly begun to buy himself new suits and shirts, and a colourful collection of new pants and socks. I was bemused by this, until recently, he had grumbled if any of the family spent too much on clothes of any kind, suddenly he'd become a peacock. But, I supposed that the new purchases came with more work and career advancement; although it didn't account for the pants and socks, unless he had grown ashamed in the swimming pool changing rooms of the old ones.

It was as my fingers explored that the smell of perfume reached my nostrils. Not after-shave but perfume, sweet and romantic, making my nose twitch like an angry cat. Rarely did Lukkas buy me perfume, rarely did I buy it for myself, but I knew an expensive perfume when I smelled it.

It wasn't my imagination, although I wanted it to be that and I could understand why a jealous woman might trash a man's clothing. But I didn't trash them. The feeling of hurt and betrayal swells inside, until you must do something about it, or be poisoned.

My fingers fumbled inside the breast pockets, finding only small advertisement cards for his firm. Susan Mace, Family lawyer, who was she?

I found crumpled tissues in his pocket, until I realised that the third crumpled tissue was a serviette from a restaurant, a small, white napkin. I stared at it in my palm, wondering where it had come from, then noticed the two, tiny punctures as though someone had wiped their mouth upon it. Something else. Burgundy coloured lipstick, the same shade as the lipstick on his collar. This serviette hadn't been used by Lukkas, but by a woman wiping food from the corners of her mouth.

It had been kept by him as a treasure, a lady's favour, why else would it be in his pocket?

I moaned aloud, a mixture between a sigh and a cry, wavering like a broken song.

Quickly I rifled through the other pockets. There were more, each with the same puncture marks, each of them smeared with lipstick. This was about something more than sex. It was about infatuation, love, maybe? I couldn't bear it any more. I held them in my balled fist as though they were small, repulsive insects, with the intention of flushing them into the toilet, then stopped; noticing something else.

There were tiny, powder blue pin-pricks of shining glitter on the lapels and shoulders of a new, black suit. Miniscule shards, but when I brushed my fingers there, they met with the whorls of my finger-tips. Not the kind of children's glitter that he might have inadvertently collected on a visit to children, this was eye shadow, eye powder.

"I hate you," I said aloud; but it was meant for her, not him.

I went to the bathroom toilet to destroy the tissues, then stopped in my tracks. I should show them to Lukkas, ask him about them, but I was afraid. A voice in my head asked me whether I wanted to lose him completely; that Lukkas, who had lied to my face, saying that I had hit him with a frying pan, would tell the children that I had made these marks and placed the tissues inside his pockets.

They would believe him, the father I had taught them to trust, I knew this. "Never get caught out, never admit to anything." Who had said this? Lukkas' father for one, Lukkas himself.

But I wasn't going to destroy this evidence, not yet.

I went into the corridor, searching for a safe place to hide them. My eyes fell upon my grandmother's old Singer sewing machine, dusty from lack of a needle. I placed the tissues inside the metal box that held bobbins, covering them with the lid. No one would ever go in there, not even the girls would be interested in anything but turning the machine handle.

I walked away from it, wondering about this woman without a face. Did they talk about me, mock me? I hated the thought that someone, a stranger to me, unknown to me, might know things about me, about my children...

Later in the day, having collected the girls from school, I took them to the park. Then I read with them and cooked their tea. I waited for Hannah to collect them whilst they watched the television.

Hannah was a little tired and told me off for giving them crisps because it wasn't a good habit to get into. I shrugged, saying nothing, but ran after the car as they drove away to make them both giggle.

The dinner was ready for when the men came home. So, I did something that I had wanted to do all day. I drove to a large, local, chemists.

This time, I could no longer be bothered to worry myself about what the middle-aged lady with the honey blonde bun and pink false nails thought of my visit to the shop.

"Could I sample some of your perfumes?" I held the crumpled tissue with the strongest fragrance before her. "I'm trying to identify this," I explained.

The slightly bored expression left her face instantly. "Oh, yes!" She beamed at me enthusiastically, as though we were about to play a game of cards. "I'm good at that sort of thing." She ploughed her small nose into my tissue without a moment's hesitation, then, between us, we travelled along the tall glass cabinets, clutching our perfume sticks.

After about twenty-five minutes of playing Sherlock Holmes and Watson, we had narrowed our choices down to four perfumes. "It's this one," my new friend stated decisively, and I nodded in agreement.

"'Passion,' by Gheorghe," I murmured. I wanted to hurl the bottle at the shop window, as I had thrown Lukkas' after shave into the bushes, the impulse was very strong… but although I had imagined myself doing a number of things which would have given me an exclusive invitation to the mad house, at the very least brought about my arrest, I smiled calmly and thanked her profusely for her help. After that I bought a bottle of expensive perfume of my choice on Lukkas' Barclaycard, a thing I would never have done before.

I didn't want Lukkas to cancel the weekend with Sarah and Tom, which was why I said nothing about the perfumed tissues. So, I pulled the Scold's bridle over my own head.

Lukkas rewarded me by agreeing that we should go to Pinner after all, and we drove there on the Saturday afternoon. I was so excited. I said very little, because recently, when we drove anywhere at all, but particularly to visit Lukkas' parents, he seemed to pick arguments about silly, inconsequential things, as though he wanted to provoke an argument.

Today, Lukkas was smiling.

"I've had to part company with Gwen," he said, as we drove along the motorway.

My mouth fell open, I stared at him in disbelief. "But why, you mean you fired her? She's been your office manager for years. You said you couldn't do without her, not so long ago."

He tapped his fingers on the steering wheel along to the radio, seemingly unconcerned.

"It's unfortunate, but it's her own fault. I didn't fire her, we simply agreed to part company. She had an issue with one of my lawyers, someone on who the firm depends. Then she did something rather silly. She believed a member of staff was stealing stock from the filing cabinet in her office, so she placed a small spy camera on her desk to catch the person out."

"That's it, you fired her for that?" There was a squeaky indignance in my voice.

He grunted. "You don't seem to comprehend the seriousness of the matter. I won't have my staff spied upon. Apart from anything else, it's illegal and we are a law firm."

No, I hadn't realised it and felt sure that Gwen wouldn't have, either. We all make mistakes, and this was Gwen's first mistake over many years. Surely a warning would have sufficed. After all, she had been loyal to Lukkas for so many years, not to mention her care for her elderly mother and now, her husband.

"I gave her a good reference," Lukkas said, reading my thoughts, "Which was rather better than she deserved in the circumstances…"

I puffed out my cheeks and stared at the distant fields and farm buildings. I wondered whether Gwen had caught the thief but didn't ask it. I would have to contact her, I wanted to do that. She had been very kind to me across the years.

Knowing my feelings, Lukkas said, suddenly, "I don't want you to see her again, at least not for some while. You would be undermining me if you did."

I nodded but said nothing.

Sarah ran along the front path of their house to meet me. She threw her arms about me and I felt so pleased to be there. It was always her greeting and her skill, too. She was good at making everyone feel welcome. "Good God Hinny, you're so thin!" She laughed. "Are you dieting?"

Tom leaned against the front door, grinning broadly. He led us to the living room, which was flanked by a modern, glass conservatory. It had been a sanctuary for us over the years, a way to escape from our grandchildren. We had known Tom and Sarah all our married life and being with them had always been an entirely comfortable thing. Soon we were buried beneath cushions and newspapers on the settees, listening to Led Zeppelin and The Pet Shop Boys whilst the smell of the Moroccan Lamb on the stove made us hungry.

As Sarah said, "Let's go away on holiday together this year," I almost forgot that Lukkas and I had troubles. We discussed where we might go to, and everyone appeared to be enthusiastic, including Lukkas.

Then Tom said, "Know what I found the other day?" He went to lift some photograph albums from a box, handing the first album to Lukkas. "I found this in the attic," he said.

I lodged on the edge of Lukkas' chair to peer over his shoulder and smiled. They were photographs from thirty years ago, many of them showing a very young Lukkas and I. In one of them, Lukkas sat cross legged on the grass. He had longer hair, wore spectacles and a Superman tee shirt and he was looking down at me as I lay with my head in his lap, laughing about something. I remembered the day, at a friend's house in Birmingham. In the photograph, Lukkas was gazing at me with such love, such rapt attention.

"Oh, Tom, they're fantastic!" I said. I smiled at Lukkas, expecting a similar reaction, I suppose. But all that he said was, "Such a long time ago." He gave a half smile and it felt as though he wanted to dismiss them as unimportant. For some while after it I said little. Neither Tom or Sarah seemed to have registered the comment as I had, and during dinner, Lukkas was his usually funny, charming self; at least in company; making us all laugh, even putting his hand on my knee.

Their two teenage children came home, and we sat with them, picking at the cheeses on the table and drinking wine until late into the evening. After half-past midnight, Sarah and I said goodnight and gave in to bed, leaving Lukkas and Tom still drinking.

I didn't sleep, thinking about Lukkas and the photographs as I stared at the stars through the window and listened to the distant rumble of trains. I heard loud laughter in the hallway at the foot of the stairs as he came to bed, calling goodnight to Tom.

I smiled as he came in the room, smelling the red wine on him as he sat upon the edge of the bed and pulled off his clothes. Then he turned to look at me, his face in shadow. He took my hand and lifted it to his lips.

He collapsed upon the spare bed beside me. Suddenly, his hand reached across my chest as he gripped my arm tightly.

"I'm sorry... so, so sorry..." he sobbed drunkenly, and he started to cry into my shoulder. I drew in a breath, shocked, but filled with compassion for his distress. Lukkas had never apologised to me in his life.

"But why, what for?" I asked softly, placing my arms tightly about him, kissing his shoulder.

"I was talking to Tom," he mumbled, then, "Only you, Laura...only you..."

What he was talking to Tom about, I would never know. Seconds later, the long, dark lashes closed on his cheeks and he fell asleep in my arms.

I thought our troubles were over... but each time I believed this. I always believed it, that we would start again.

CHAPTER TEN

What Lukkas said

The weekend after visiting Tom and Sarah, we drove to see Lukkas' parents, Marjorie and Derek. They lived some seventy miles away. In thirty years, we had scarcely missed a Sunday without seeing them. Now that they were elderly, it was even more important to do so.

We drove past the low, tumbling stone walls beyond the Blenheim Estate, through the gentle, Cotswold countryside and fields of dun coloured sheep, sweeping down the dangers of Pony Hill to stop in Evesham for a cup of coffee and to buy Marjorie flowers. Lukkas' mood seemed mellow. On recent journeys, he had found so many reasons to be tense and angry.

Often, as he drove, I would gaze out at the window with my own thoughts. The journey often triggered thoughts about the past. Today, memory leapt to another journey, when Hannah was not yet fifteen and Josh at University.

I remembered driving with Joe in the car. I remembered wishing that Hannah was safe, with us; remembered thinking I should have made her board at her school, she would be safe then. That particular day was terrible. Hannah had shouted at Lukkas that she wasn't coming to see her grand-parents. Lukkas ordered her to get in the car when we were already late, having told Marjorie that we would take them out to lunch. Hannah shoved past me and ran through the front door and along the road.

"Leave her!" Lukkas growled, "I'm not going to be late again. She can sort herself out."

What I knew by then, had told Lukkas too, was that it wasn't Toya that Hannah was interested in, now. It was the nineteen-year-old brother who I had met on the doorstep. When I spoke to her about it, she scoffed at me, so, I went to see Toya's mother. She wasn't in the slightest bit interested. "What could she do about it?" she wanted to know.

After that encounter, I would stand in the shadow of the alleyway which ran beside their house, staring up at the bedroom windows, wondering and fearful, willing Hannah to come home. Lukkas said he couldn't get involved, he was a family lawyer. I knew that public knowledge of this would destroy him. That's what he had intimated to me. But I had to do something to stop it.

It became my daily mission to stop her from self-destruction. Searching for her in local parks, in shopping centres, sometimes, at weekends, discovering that she had gone to parties attended by young people who were older than she was. On one occasion, Charlotte came with me to a local house where we burst into the kitchen like Starsky and Hutch, threatening to call the police unless she left. She did, hating me afterwards. On another I arrived, breathless, parking my car on the pavement outside an Oxford night club which she was far too young to enter. I pushed past the door man in my cardigan and middle-aged mummy clothes to find her, a whim only, but she wasn't there, unless she hid from me.

My mother knew, my sister, too and they did what they could to help me. But I could tell nothing to Marjorie and Derek, Lukkas said that Marjorie wasn't strong, that she would faint. Lukkas always contrived stories about where Hannah was, that she couldn't visit because she was staying with a friend from school, that kind of thing. I knew now that his mother wasn't the fainting kind, she threatened it whenever she wanted a change of plan. She was certainly strong enough to be cruel about those she saw as weaker than her.

When I was younger, I almost believed Marjorie was better in some way, than my own mother. It went further than being loyal to Lukkas and his family, I believed in some way that I had to be like Marjorie. I was in awe of her too, as were my own parents. I took her coldness for the self-control that my own large, noisy family lacked, especially at meal times when we would all talk at once. I saw her aloofness to others as a kind of superiority. But then, years later, I realised that Marjorie lacked the confidence to talk with strangers and had unconsciously turned this into regal snobbishness. In my forties, I realised that Marjorie wasn't better than my mother, so often my strength and resolve. Mum isn't perfect, but she would never threaten to faint, there are too many difficulties to resolve.

I think, had Marjorie's life been a matter of easy comfort, in which she had been kind and forgiving, I might have forgiven her, then. But she belittled so many people from the comfort of her carefully arranged home. She belittled the small people, people with lives far more difficult than her own. She belittled the women that she called friends. Sometimes there was jealousy in this.

On this Sunday, I sat beside Derek on the sofa. I listened to him talking to Lukkas about cricket. I knew little on the subject beyond what Josh had explained to me and the avid fans in my class over the years. Rounders was enough for me. I sat on the hard edge of the sofa, sipping my sherry, sometimes gazing out at the distant Malvern Hills, blue as a sharp-edged cloud.

Then, Lukkas said, "Anyway, what kind of a week have you had?"

Marjorie stood behind Derek's chair. She hummed a small sigh of regret. "Not bad. We've been to two, very nice funerals. Those are the only parties we're invited to, nowadays. All of our friends are dying!"

I didn't hesitate. Both Lukkas and I had suggested it before. "Then why don't you move closer to Oxford? We could see you far more frequently and care for you. You would be closer to the grand children."

Derek smiled. In contrast, Lukkas glowered as though I had suggested that his parents move to Africa, whilst Marjorie's swift glance in my direction held distain.

"I don't think so. We are very happy here," she said. Having just stated that there were few friends left. She picked up the flowers we'd bought for her and retreated to the kitchen. I got up slowly to follow her, wishing I hadn't said anything. Suspecting, not for the first time, that I had taken her little boy away from her. But this wasn't true. She had sent her little boy away to board at public school from the age of eight. There, Lukkas' emotions weren't dealt with. There, he had been abused.

In the kitchen, Marjorie snipped at the stems of the daffodils and tulips to arrange them into a vase. She moved stiffly. Tall, erect like her son. She deigned to acknowledge me. I was reminded of the Queen of Hearts and allowed myself the briefest of smiles.

"The funerals, were they close friends?" I asked. I couldn't think what else to say in that moment.

"Bob was, yes. It was a lovely funeral. At a church in Evesham. The church was filled with flowers. Derek and Bob were members of the cricket club and the British Legion for years." She gazed out across the front lawn where cherry blossom drifted across the grass. "We used to have such fun," she sighed. "I think Bob's wife is going to move to Wales, now. To be closer to their daughter."

I softened in my own feelings. Perhaps that was why she was a little snappy when I re-suggested that she should move closer to us. Maybe she wanted to, perhaps it was Derek who refused, after all.

As I was about to ask her about the other friend, she turned her face towards me. Her lips popped together in a sound I had heard her make often, like a fish at the surface of a bowl. It was a sound she made unconsciously when she was thinking something through.

"And you, Laura. How have you been recently?" she asked. It sounded like an accusation.

"Oh, fine, thanks." As I was never able to tell her anything in case she fainted, it was my standard reply. Another world into which you didn't bring your problems, no matter how great they were.

She set the scissors down and sniffed, the kind of sniff when you have a cold coming. "Lukkas says you haven't been yourself recently, that you are anxious."

I couldn't resist the short laugh. We had been through so much, with Hannah, with Josh too and now with Joseph. Marjorie had no idea but now, when it suited

Lukkas to tell her, I was anxious. I was so tempted to say, "Well, Marjorie... as a matter of fact I've been upset about Lukkas. He's been unkind of late, then there are the text messages at night, the marks upon his shirts..." Instead I said, "Really? No, I don't think so. I've been fine."

I had drained the glass of sherry. "Would you mind if I made a cup of tea?" I asked.

She nodded towards the tea pot. "Good. I'm glad about that." But she didn't sound convinced. What she said next came in a rush. "You know, if you are anxious, you should get some support for his sake. Lukkas does a very hard job, he needs your support, Laura." She hesitated briefly, as though gathering her thoughts. "I had a hysterectomy," she smiled, "Remember? I felt so much better afterwards..."

I remembered. Derek had insisted she have one.

I nodded. "I don't want a hysterectomy, Marjorie, I don't need one. It would make no difference at all. Lukkas gets my support every day. He has had my support for thirty years, I hope I don't have to convince you of that."

I stated it calmly, then took my tea into the living room, leaving her. In all these years, I couldn't remember receiving the tiniest morsel of praise from her. Lukkas was everything, Lukkas was all. I wondered who it was she believed comforted him when he was troubled? Perhaps he gave her the impression that he was never troubled in case she might faint. But he had been. Frequently he had needed to talk problems through with me. Did Marjorie think that Lukkas helped children with school work, taught them to read, monitored their coming and going? Did she think

Lukkas cooked the meals, that he did the washing and the shopping? I had never seen him empty the trash or wash a grill pan! I bridled with righteous indignation, tried to calm myself.

I caught Lukkas staring at me. He had noticed the rosy redness in my cheeks. Perhaps he would think it was the sherry, that would be best. But I knew Marjorie would tell him about our conversation, just as I knew now that he had talked to her about me.

Chapter Eleven

The Opportunity to Cheat

At the start of the summer holiday, I remembered that I was supposed to be taking Ruby for her tennis lesson at the sports club.

Ruby's school report said she tended to duck when a ball came towards her, so Hannah and I went halves in paying for her to have lessons in her summer holidays. I drove to collect our granddaughters, scouting around for their swimming costumes, sun creams and hats. I arranged to meet Charlotte and her thirteen-year-old daughter Ellie there too, for a swim afterwards.

I waved goodbye to Ru as she disappeared with her group and settled down to watch Lilly in the play area whilst I sipped a cup of coffee and idled through the pages of the newspaper. Occasionally I glanced up and realised, for the first time in years, that although Lukkas came here to swim because of a bad back, it would be a bonus for him to be surrounded by so many gorgeous, tanned females of all ages, perhaps especially the younger ones in their skimpy sports gear. I had many young and attractive acquaintances and friends. I hadn't thought about their own or my appearance since I was in my thirties, but now I looked at them afresh, with a new, nervous suspicion. No wonder Lukkas seemed in such a hurry to get here before work.

As I sat back, pulling in the stomach made slack by three babies and three hernias', the most gorgeous and feline predator of them all appeared before me.

"Hello, Laura, I didn't know you were a member here!" her voice trilled. The greeting was pretty-false, Sarah Child's had done everything she could as Headteacher to oppose any kind of Educational reform that I attempted at the school I had taught at for almost twenty years. My suspicion of her went far beyond her physical looks, they had more to do with her nature. She was shallow and lazy, the type of person who would rise through the ranks by accepting credit for another colleague's ideas.

Let sleeping dogs lie, I thought, the last thing I need now is an enemy.

She was several years younger than me. Headteachers resemble business managers now. No more the flat footed headteacher of my youth, with basin haircut, who spent their summer holidays climbing the Himalayas. Toned physique, long, black hair, bright, hazel eyes and sharp red nails. This was how Sarah now appeared before me.

"Oh, we've been members here since the place opened, but I expect we come at different times, I'm usually here with my grandchildren," I smiled.

"Mind if I sit here to drink my coffee?"

My heart sank, but I nodded at the chair opposite me, "Please do."

"So, do you miss teaching now?" She asked.

I nodded towards Lilly, "I'm teaching every day!" I replied. "Where are you working now?"

"Oh, I'm working as an advisor for the local authority. I miss teaching sometimes, but I have to say that it's not such hard work!" She winked. I smiled.

"And Hannah's shop?" Sarah asked.

I nodded brightly, "It's had its ups and downs, but things have settled down a bit now."

"Oh good, I bought a top from there a couple of weeks ago, as a matter of fact. One of your old pupil's is working there, isn't she?"

"Aaliyah..." I replied.

The red claws tapped gently on the table top. "I've seen Lukkas on a few occasions recently, as a matter of fact. He's buying a new house for me..."

I doubted Lukkas was involved, he didn't do conveyancing, but I nodded interestedly.

"We've bumped into one another here of course, and since I started working at the local authority, we sometimes use the same pubs."

He hadn't told me that, but I said nothing. Lukkas rarely told me anything nowadays.

She took her dark hair in her hands and drew a band around the long tresses. "And, of course, he's been on television recently, talking about these legal aid shop booths, he's quite a dynamo, isn't he?"

Whether it was that Lilly fell off a colourful stack of cushions with a small squeal of surprise just then, or whether, for all kinds of reasons, the subject matter had turned to Lukkas, I don't know; but I had begun to squirm uncomfortably and wanted my distance from her now.

I picked Lilly up from the floor and retrieved the bags with towels. "Well, Sarah, it's been really nice to catch up. I think Ruby's tennis lesson has come to an end, so we'll have to make a move. It's been lovely seeing you again." A lie. Couched in socially acceptable good manners. "Good luck with the new house," I added.

The deepest thoughts in the most mundane surroundings, as I walked away from her, I thought of how much love and trust there had once been between Lukkas and I. People see Lukkas as a charming, funny and friendly man, they don't understand that he can be totally ruthless, manipulative in the pursuit of something he wants. I know this. He would never own to it. Lukkas believes he is a balanced person. Once or twice in the past, when Josh was younger, he had fought with Josh, not just verbally, but a physical fight between a younger and an older stag. I remembered running into the garden to separate them before one or the other was hurt, and the hurt and scars would always be emotional ones, and Josh the one who really suffered.

As I turned the corner to the tennis courts, my thoughts went back to Sarah Childs. I licked my lips in discomfort. Why had she focussed on Lukkas? Because he was an interesting man, I supposed. But what if they had formed a friendship? After all, she was very beautiful, the size ten black dress would certainly fit her. She had appeared very interested in him. I didn't believe for a moment that she would have any qualms about dating a married man.

The girls ate their sandwiches by the pool and I rubbed sun cream into their skin before their swim. Ruby is a good swimmer, whilst Lilly is fearless and has started to swim short distances with her face below water. Their favourite game is called 'Dolphins and Mermaids', which entails riding on my back and chasing imaginary sharks. It is exhausting, so I was very grateful for Charlotte's arrival with her younger daughter, Ellie. The girls love Ellie and half child, half woman, she instantly got into the pool with them.

Charlotte sunbathed beside me, saying nothing for a while whilst I chewed my nails.

In a week or so we would be travelling to Italy with Lukkas, then to Nice. It was a hot day and in previous years, I would be excited about the prospect of a holiday. Just now, I felt as though I were in danger, as though something terrible was looming above me, clouds to burst, axes to fall, bitten nails, thumping heart.

She raised her sunglasses to look at me. "Did you talk to Lukkas? How did things go?"

"Not so good. There's not much point in kidding myself, I'm sure that he's carrying on with another woman."

She drew a breath but shook her head. "I can't believe that."

I ignored her instincts, she hadn't discovered the things that I had.

"Something just happened," I said, "Here, at the pool. Do you recall Sarah Childs from the school?" And I began to tell her about the conversation, whilst she smeared fake sun tan into her legs in preparation for the holiday. As she listened her expression changed, her lips parting slightly until her mouth widened in horror.

"But Laura, really, she was just talking about Lukkas. You can't assume that every woman connected with him in any small way is having an affair with him! Apart from the gross unfairness of it, you'll go mad! Lukkas is a very attractive and powerful man, lots of women are interested in him, but it doesn't mean that he's having an affair!"

"I don't assume that," I said, although I half wondered now, whether it was his true intention to drive me mad. "It's just that she has taught Joseph, and Ellie too; she might have asked about them, surely? If anyone bears a resemblance to that woman in 'The lives and Loves of a She Devil', it's Sarah Childs. She wouldn't think twice about tearing a family apart if she wanted a man enough."

Charlotte laughed, then stopped, regarding me differently. She placed her hand over mine.

"Please stop worrying about it. I know Lukkas loves you," she said.

I didn't challenge her. Wasn't that one of the strengths of it, that everyone believed Lukkas loved me, from our children, to our friends?

I didn't tell her about the things he said. "I want my life back," and "You don't know what I'm like in court." I didn't tell her about the scrappiness of the Valentine card, sent to me in February or "Shut up woman," when I had talked to Joe's girlfriend during a romantic kiss in a film. I didn't tell her these things. It was as though he had found some-kind of nasty strength to be rude to me and dismissive as often as he liked.

"Well, the point is that I don't know, and I don't like not knowing. So, I'm going to do my own private detective work and find out."

"And Sarah is all you've got?" she smiled.

"Yes. But there's something else I remember now. She has a house that she rents out, just as we do, and her house is four doors down from ours." I shook my head slowly. "I know there's something going on, Charlie. Apart from anything else, I can feel it," I touched my breastbone with a finger. "I know that can't be called rational, but for so many little reasons that are hard to explain, I can feel it..."

In the kitchen, the evening after meeting Sarah Childs, I watched as Josh, hot and tired, pulled off his tie and shirt and dropped them onto the floor.

"How did you get on today?" I asked. He started tearing at the bread, ravenously hungry as always.

"Fine. David's a pain. He's a bully, no matter how hard I push myself, he wants more... desperate to go on holiday, don't think I can afford Iceland so have to be France."

Hannah liked a mixture on holiday, water parks with the kids, eating good food and the occasional clubbing spree. Joe liked clubbing, full stop, whilst Josh slept on the edge of volcanoes in Iceland in a sleeping bag and listened to Drum and Base.

"Can't be easy working for Dad or David," I sympathised, but as Grandma says, at least you've got a job."

He grinned. Then, because he's my son but a trusted friend too, I said, "Dad wants me to see a doctor. He says I need cognitive therapy or hormone treatment or something." I didn't say that he wanted me to have a full on mental health assessment and had recently called me psychotic.

Josh puffed his cheeks out in a long sigh. "Do you feel ill at all?"

I shook my head. "No, definitely not but," I dipped my voice, "I want you to keep this to yourself please Josh, but I think it's possible he is seeing someone else."

His reaction was normal, comforting me; but neither did he dismiss the possibility beyond a mild "I'm sure that's not the case."

"I thought you two hadn't been getting along recently. But no, there's a whole world of difference between being a bit sad and a bit mental and; not that I want to see you divorced; but if it happens, I think it might, you know, weaken your case if you've had assessments like that, especially as you will have to request them yourself."

I know our children love me no more than Lukkas. I put my arms about his neck in a hug and felt such gratitude for his advice.

"That kind of thing could end up with Ben having more access to the girls than you," he added as I drew away, "I don't believe that's a good thing, do you? No, don't do it," he said emphatically, "you've been a strong person all your life. I'm a bit surprised at Dad."

He drew back, staring at me intently for a moment or two.

"The thing is, I'm confused. I've always trusted that Dad would do the right thing by us all but now," I left off, rubbing my forehead in confusion. "So...actually... I saw the doctor, who did some physical tests, but she hasn't found anything and whether I'm right or wrong, there must be many people who suspect infidelity, but it doesn't make them mad, does it?"

He shook his head, then kissed me lightly on the forehead as his father might have, once upon a time. "Just don't bother with doctors again," he said.

After cooking the dinner, I rang Jennie, an old teaching friend.

"What on earth do you want Sarah's number for?" Jennie asked suspiciously in an accent still flavoured with Manchester, although she'd lived in Oxford for most of her life.

"I thought I might start teaching again, do a bit of supply," I explained.

"You'll be lucky to get any help from Sarah after the stick you gave her! I don't have it, but I know someone who does. I think she's just bought a house in the Fernley Road in Foxlea."

After the call, I went to google the whereabouts of the Fernley Road. Then, with a guilty look at the two dogs beyond the glass doors, wagging their tales optimistically, I grabbed my phone and my bag. I tell myself to calm down, but a sort of panic has started in me, an unstoppable feeling that it must all be accomplished now. Lukkas' secretary recently told me that he usually left the office by seven, so why, quite frequently now, didn't he come home until eight-thirty?

I drive as though the end of the world is nigh, just about resisting the urge to beep at the other cars melting in the heat at the end of the day. I can't explain it, other than what I was doing felt better, somehow, better than accepting everything, but doing nothing.

Lukkas' car is a sleek, silver grey Ferrari. My car is a tatty old Chrysler, used for family holidays, for packing surf boards and tents, for golf clubs and dogs. It isn't easy to hide, so I didn't try. I would stop by the office firstly, find out whether he was still there.

I parked the car on the pavement close to the police station and walked to the office car park, passing hordes of tourists. His car was still there. I chewed my nail like a child, wondering what to do next. It felt silly because it was silly, silly that I, so sensible; whose every moment was filled with practical endeavour; should be trying to track down my husband's lover, or potential lover. But however desperate it seemed, I was doing something, at last.

If his intention was to meet Sarah after work, he would take the route that skirts Oxford. This meant that if he went straight home after all of this, I would miss him. So, I got back into the car and drove to a little slip road leading to some private houses and pulled into it, parking the car so that I had a clear view of the road and would spot Lukkas if he passed me.

I waited and watched like a hawk about to pounce on its prey.

I thought of the many things I should be doing, washing up, ironing shirts, offering to read to Lilly, testing Ruby on her times tables. I waited for twenty minutes in mounting frustration, then picked up a pad and pen and wrote an indecipherable shopping list, so I didn't have to take my eyes off the passing cars.

A woman glowered at me as she struggled to get her pushchair around my car. A gaggle of European students, heading towards the ice rink, stared in my direction.

I did something I'd not done in twenty years and smoked a cigarette out of the car window. As I flicked the butt onto the grass, I froze. Lukkas' young, heavily pregnant secretary walked straight towards me.

She half smiled, uncertainly. No doubt she thought this an odd state-of-affairs and would tell people in the office tomorrow. I had to acknowledge her.

"Oh, Hi!" I trilled, a tad eagerly. Then, "Are you still at work, it must soon be time for your maternity leave, surely?"

She smiled, he cheeks pink in the heat. "Almost, thank goodness, it's getting a bit much now."

"I'm just picking someone up from the ice rink," I lied, thinking on my feet.

After she had gone I pouted. This was getting me nowhere. Restlessly, I decided to go in search of Sarah Childs new house.

The Fernley Road wasn't difficult to find, the only thing I didn't have was her house number.

The continuous thumping in my chest now slowed, becoming still, under control at last. I scanned the street, a wide street, curving gently. There was no sign of Lukkas' car here. But then, of course, such a thing would probably take place in a hotel and why assume they would use his car, why not hers?

As I wandered rather furtively along the road, examining the houses, the sky had changed colour, now a plummy blue. With it, the intense heat gave way to heavy drops of warm rain.

I thought guiltily of my vegetable patch. The old me would have celebrated the rain, but my vegetable patch had been sorely neglected, for the first time in years. The old me would have listened to radio four, worrying about the shortage of water and the state of the planet. If I felt I didn't know Lukkas now, I scarcely knew myself. I was a fifty-something year old woman whose once stable emotions had distorted, out of all recognition.

I begged God as I walked, begged the angels of a dead grandmother and sister too, "Please let him be faithful to me, please let this not be true…"

My lips parted at the rain, my clothes were now soaked as I explored the road. I had arrived at a yellow skip placed outside the door of an ordinary looking house. I glanced up and down the street. Thankfully the rain fall meant there was none to see me. Hastily I dodged towards the wide front windows and then, resting my hands upon the chipped wood of the sill, I peered inside the front room. It was filled with unopened boxes and packing cases. Someone had been living here for a while, according to the debris of unwashed cups and open bags that littered the room, but then Sarah had never been one for clearing up in the staffroom, I thought.

There was a small estate car, parked in the driveway of the house next door. I knocked and waited, until at length a young man holding a baby against his shoulder, answered it.

"Hey," I started. "So sorry to bother you, I'm looking for the house of an old teaching friend who has just moved in." He stared rather blankly at me, but without any interest, his priority was to get the baby to sleep.

"Sarah Childs," I explained.

He nodded, recognising the name at last. "Next door, we haven't seen much of her, I don't even think she lives there on a permanent basis." He smiled wearily, still rhythmically rubbing his baby's back, and I thanked him.

I retreated towards Sarah's house once more, hoping that I wouldn't be watched, smearing the window with my breath. Had I been able to observe myself, I would have conceded that I had become a desperate fool as I hunted for clues, looking for pictures of Lukkas in her house. I saw no pictures, but as I moved towards an expanse of kitchen window through a broken, wooden gate, I spotted two leaflets on the inner sill, the one for an Italian Restaurant, the other for Lukkas' firm. His face smiled from the leaflet: reassuring... cheesy.

I leaned my forehead against the pane for a moment as a kind of madness took over, the kind of madness Lukkas seemed to want from me. I wanted to see Lukkas, to hold him and speak to him. I wanted reassurance, wanted it now.

So, I drove home then, at the speed of light, with all kinds of questions and anxieties in my head. When

I reached home, ignoring the questions from Joe, who wanted to borrow a tenner and asked, "Where have you been, are you checking up on Dad?" I paused for a moment on the stairs.

"No, don't be silly, why would you think that?" I asked.

"Because you never go out this time of day and 'cos Dad says you are behaving strangely, checking up on him."

But he grinned at me, as though my life was a joke, and went to ask his brother to 'borrow' a tenner instead.

Lukkas wasn't home yet, my feet pounded the stairs to the bedroom where I stripped, squirting myself liberally with perfume and changed into a fresh, clean summer dress.

"I must look nice, I must look nice…" I muttered to myself, in a frenzy of insecurity.

On heightened alert, I listened for his car whilst reheating his dinner. I was now the replica of a perfect, fifties, wholesome housewife. My grandmother would have been proud, but my mother would have raised her eyebrows.

When he came through the door I gave him the usual peck on the cheek, resisting a full-on snog as when I had attempted one recently, he glared at me as though I had stripped off my clothes in a busy street. I left him alone to do the usual things; putting his bag away, changing from his work clothes, hanging up his suit, and then as he sat before the television, I took his dinner to him on a tray.

"Would you like a glass of wine?" I trilled.

Lukkas continued to stare at the television over the top of the glasses he generally put on when he settled into home life.

"Not just now, thanks."

He ate his dinner in silence, as though I were invisible. We sat like that for a long, long time, until I broke the silence.

"Do you remember Sarah?" I asked, picking up a pile of sewing, mostly children's clothes, but a button had come away from one of Lukkas' court shirts.

"Which Sarah?"

"Childs, the Headteacher?" I tried.

"I've met her a few times, I think, but I can't remember what she looks like."

He yawned, staring at the television as Libyan rebels attacked a city. Once upon a time, I mused, concepts such as democracy, freedom and events in the world news had mattered to me, enough to argue with other people about them. But recently I had stopped being aware of what was happening in the world, even in my own country, of the crying infants and the wailing women, the elderly with dementia and the suicides. It was though there was only Lukkas in the world.

I rose from the chair and went to my sewing box to search for a needle and cotton.

"Isn't Sarah using your firm to do her conveyancing?" I asked lightly.

Lukkas grunted. "She may be, for all I know," he replied. "What is this, the third degree? For your information, I have twenty-four members of staff. I wouldn't know whether one of them is doing her conveyancing or not. Do you mind if I watch this now?" His voice was gruff, his tone accusing me of speaking to him whilst he watched television.

I nodded and turned my attention to the sewing, biting the inside of my cheek to quell my hurt. In my aggravation, I stabbed my finger on the needle and a bubble of blood spilled on the cuff. I rose to find the soap.

The rain fell relentlessly against the window pane now, making my body ache with loneliness.

CHAPTER TWELVE

Young people

On Saturday morning, Lukkas came home early to pick me up. We were going to Gloucestershire to visit old friends. Every year since they moved away from Oxford, we had holidayed with them. Every summer they held a garden party, afterwards we could stay if we wished, but this year Lukkas proclaimed he had too much work to do on the following day, so we would drive back in the evening.

He was a little irritable on his arrival home, but I put this down to work overload rather than anything else. We weren't taking children or grandchildren this time, which once would have meant Lukkas' eagerness to stay in a hotel, but I didn't mind, he had refused so many invitations of late, leaving me to attend things alone. I just wanted to be somewhere with him, enjoying the freedom from family.

From the car window, we said goodbye to Joe, who was not visiting his would-be cousins with us on this occasion but giving a hip-hop performance at an Oxford club. He had raced across to the car to ask for money once again.

"Can I borrow twenty?"

"Borrow twenty? You mean I'm going to get it back?" I asked sceptically, through the car window. "What happened to your allowance from Dad?"

"It's gone," he said flatly.

"Look, it's only Saturday Joe, and Dad keeps asking me to spend less money…" I looked over at Lukkas then, at the steering wheel, but he stared into the distance, he didn't want to be involved.

I sighed, fishing around in my purse for a twenty-pound note.

As we drove away, Lukkas said, "Must you keep complaining about money, anyone would think you were poor."

"But…" I began, but I didn't finish. Lately it was as though he wanted to argue with me constantly. "I just want to get him to cut his cloth," I said, borrowing a phrase of my mothers.

We drove out towards Witney, Lukkas driving quite fast. The sky was heavy with rain once again. I wondered how many people Simone had invited and whether she would have room in her house for everyone if the heavens opened. I gazed down at my old sandals doubtfully. They were open toed.

There was a mark on the floor close to my foot, a thick blob of flesh coloured something. Mud, maybe, but in Lukkas' pristine car? I put on my glasses, leaning down to examine it. Even before I had dabbled my fingers in the silky-smooth stuff, I knew what it was.

Foundation, the same colour, the same texture as the stuff on Lukkas' shirt collar. Slowly, indignantly, incredulously, I drew in a breath then withdrew my fingers as though they'd been stung, rubbing the tips of my fingers together to brush the stuff away.

The intensity of feeling was too great to manage, too high a price to pay for silence, for self lies.

"There is foundation on the floor, quite a big blob," I blurted.

At first, he appeared defensive, frightened, even. His lips twitched with restrained anger, then he let out a false, bitter laugh.

"It's mud," he said, casually glancing from my fingers to the stain.

"No Lukkas, I may not wear it anymore, but I know what it is," I said quietly. "It isn't mud."

I bent down to scoop up some more of the stuff. Anyone within our family would receive a severe telling off for messing up Lukkas' car, so who was this person, so important, so respected that they could squirt make up on the floor?

"Absolute rubbish," Lukkas argued. "It's sandy mud, it probably came off Josh's shoe when we called in at Swinbrooke College the other day."

This was my warning signal. The angry expression, the way his fingers clamped tightly on the wheel, the way he worked his jaw in that distinctly masculine way. I fought with the wife inside of me, but she won.

"No, Lukkas. It is, definitely foundation." My heart had started to palpitate as though I had a small animal trapped behind my rib cage.

When he shouted, so suddenly, so violently, I had the very real desire to leap from the car.

"Right, that's it, I'm going back. I didn't want to go to this bloody thing anyway, I'm certainly not going with you, not in this mood!"

The glint in his green eyes as he turned to narrow them at me was a devilish light, whilst his face had turned the colour of the thunderous sky beyond the window.

"In what mood? I have been in a great mood," I fought to keep my voice steady. "Really, Lukkas, I'm not in a mood and I'm not making any observation other than that is foundation. Maybe you gave someone a lift and they dropped it, I don't know." Then, "What are you doing now? Please Lukkas, don't…" I spluttered as he started to turn the wheel.

His face was filled with spiteful anger as he indicated, before turning the car back in the direction from which we had come. I leaned back in the seat, my body rigid, as though we were about to crash. I had meant what I said, what was the point in lying about it? I was so sick of his rule, that if I was a good girl, saying nothing, all would be well, but if I objected, stated the truth, we were done. I was torn between these choices all the time now.

But like Cinderella, I wanted to go to the ball. I stared down at the folds of my skirt and swallowed my bile. I rested my hand lightly upon his shoulder.

"Please Lukkas, don't do this. Maybe it was Hannah, perhaps you've given her a lift recently."

He never gave Hannah lifts, she had her own car, and anyway, Hannah never left the house without make up.

Savagely, he pulled his shoulder back from my wheedling caress. "I never wanted to go anyway."

Why had he felt like that? He used to love their company, all of them, love drinking beer and cracking jokes to make them all laugh, love teasing his godchildren. I thought of Joe's hurt if we arrived home unexpectedly, of the mistrust and doubt in his eyes. He would blame me and then text Hannah as he always did, and she would question me. I thought of our friends, my friends, and what they would think and say if we didn't show up.

Without too much thought, I placed my hand upon the steering wheel beside his, I didn't tug or yank at it, I just rested my hand there.

"Please turn around again..." I begged.

"You fucking mad woman, what are you trying to do, land us in a ditch?" He took my hand in his fist, shoving me away.

I recoiled into the passenger seat, thinking of all the times he had derided my driving whilst I had driven him to-and-fro so that he could drink over the years, it wasn't fair, he wasn't fair.

"Lukkas, please take me back again. I won't mention the make-up."

Begging, begging again. I knew him, over the years I'd begged when he refused to speak to me over minor things, apologising for things I hadn't done or said because young children would be so unhappy I couldn't bear it any more.

I fought back tears, clamping the soft inner cheek between my teeth as he stared stonily at the road ahead of us. Love and hate fought for supreme place, choking my emotions.

Then Lukkas checked the driver's mirror, his strong chin jutting forward. He sniffed.

"I want you to go to the doctor again, a doctor of my choice this time, not one of Monica's happy, clappy, hippie friends who prescribe yoga and lavender oil. You are becoming delusional and it's time to face up to the fact that there is a problem." His voice was calm once again, quiet, the voice he used with other people, a gentle, reassuring voice that acted like hypnosis upon me, at times-but it carried real determination, now.

He put a hand on my knee, a gentle hand that used to hold mine to cross a road or when I felt unhappy. "Stop crying," he told me.

"Alright," I said, "I'll go back to the doctor." I stopped caring then, but like a child I thought, "Anything you say Lukkas."

Lukkas found a lay by then and turned the car around. Perhaps he really did believe that I was deranged, I told myself. But it was convenient, then, to say that. I felt as though I hated him, hated the feeling that he was perpetually bullying me.

I could have done with feeling a little brighter, a little more confident. I felt drained by the journey although we had only gone a short way, as though I had undergone a kind of emotional torture. I sat very still, with my hands in my lap. The vanity mirror showed my face chalk white.

I was grateful that our friends were pleased to see us. They greeted us warmly, and they seemed not to notice that Lukkas had immediately distanced himself from me, even if I felt that we were frauds.

Simone and Piers had decorated the garden with bunting, and when the sun came out at last, it all looked very pretty. They had set up a large marquis in the long garden and there were drinks in the conservatory and food laid out on a trestle table.

Simone and Piers have three children. Gemma was seventeen and about to go to University whilst the younger two, George and Jonathan, are adopted. They had invited their Oxford friends to arrive a little earlier than everyone else, then, later, came the local friends from the town and the work colleagues.

I watched Lukkas laughing and joking with his godchildren as he used to. I am godmother to one or two of them, but Lawyers carry more weight than teachers, I guess.

His head was thrown back in loud laughter. I wanted that reaction from him so badly that it was an almost physical pain.

Young people admired and adored him.

Gemma wore a short skirt and flowery top, her fair hair reaching the middle of her back. Molly was there, and Sam too, and Tania's daughter who wore a tight-fitting leopard skin dress with her chestnut hair in a pony-tail. Apart from Ellie and the twins, most of the girls were sweet sixteen. Then there were Lisa and Jack's two daughters, Mya, twenty and Betty, also sixteen.

Betty looked stunning, like a model. She had cut her dark hair in a bob and wore a red shift dress with a silver belt around her waist, her long pale legs ended in the highest pair of black high heels that I have ever seen.

We watched them now, Charlotte, Simone and I, as we sipped wine.

"I can't believe how they've all changed since I last saw them!" Charlotte exclaimed. "How old is Betty now, sixteen? She looks so much older than that, it seems only yesterday that she was Lilly's age, with little blonde curls…"

I winced, "Don't remind me, they make me feel so old. I suppose at fifty-four, I am old."

Simone laughed. "Rubbish, Laura. You're very attractive for your age."

"Thanks," I said, "But I don't feel it, not nowadays."

Charlotte shook her head reprovingly. "You know what? You look a whole lot younger since you went to the hairdresser and got a proper cut, and you're so thin now. Why don't you go to Hannah's shop and get a few things before we go to Italy…and buy make up," she added. "It's years since you wore make up!"

"Ha! So, you feel I need a make-over, then?"

Simone grinned. "If you can't take advice from your sister, then you're in trouble. You told me yourself that your lovely skirt came from Oxfam, but is there anything wrong with buying yourself a new outfit from time to time?"

Charlotte nodded, "You have spent every penny you have on family, you know you have, start splashing out on yourself a bit before people see you as a martyr."

The accusation hit a raw nerve. "I'm not a martyr!" I snapped at Charlotte. I hated that label, but maybe there was some truth in it. I had revelled in the role of wonderful granny, maybe at the expense of losing Lukkas to someone else.

Lisa appeared at my side, a voluptuous Madonna, someone who would never be seen without make up and who knew exactly what to wear to compliment her figure. Her Salsa dancing was so sexy, she had once provoked a row between a married couple we knew.

She was a nurse, and Jack, her husband, the Head of a local school, an amazing artist in his own right. When Lisa greeted me with a hug, her breasts felt like safe, warm cushions against me.

"Are you okay?" She asked quietly, tactfully, placing a hand lightly upon my shoulder. Maybe the years of examining women in all conditions had given her the kind of intuition the others lacked. There was kindness in her voice, but was there something else also? Momentarily, I wondered whether Lukkas might have said something to her, suggested something, but perhaps that was paranoia.

"I'm fine!" I smiled. "I've not been sleeping too well, but I feel great apart from that."

I wanted to turn the conversation to everyone else now, anyone else but me, so I was relieved when Lisa started talking about Betty and her future. She asked me about Hannah's shop, how things were going there and whether Mya might get a temporary job there before returning to University.

But I wasn't giving Lisa the attention she deserved. I found myself half listening to her as I watched Betty, her younger daughter, clinging to Lukkas' arm. Betty was giggling animatedly. Every now and then her dress would fall from her pale shoulders and she would tuck her straight black hair behind her small ear. It was flirtatious. Betty was flirting but she was not even aware of this because she was sixteen, and Lukkas was like an uncle to her.

Still, she appeared to dance and prance before him, laughing at each joke, devouring every word and gesture whilst Lukkas revelled in her movements. The effect was like a stab to my belly. There was never a time, now, when Lukkas responded to me in this way.

Charlotte returned to me then, squeezing my arm. "Hey, don't be offended by what I said. You are still beautiful," she smiled. She must have been watching me, watching me as I watched Betty with Lukkas.

"She's a bloody little flirt, isn't she?"

I turned to her sharply, taken aback by her tone and the way that she said it.

"In Polzeath, last Easter? She was all over Neil in much the same way."

My eyes widened, "Really?" I asked.

"Yup. Look, since the beginning of time, marriages have been made between old men and young girls, from Juliette to Helen of Troy. It only recently became illegal. You think the male libido has really changed though? I don't."

"Obviously not," I remarked, a little bitterly.

CHAPTER THIRTEEN

A Bitter Pill to Swallow

"You promised to go to the doctor again, a real doctor…" Lukkas promptly reminded me when we arrived home after the party.

"But, Lukkas, please rethink this, there isn't anything wrong with me," I pleaded.

"Nonsense, Laura. Your behaviour is entirely irrational," his lips twisted as he stared at me with grim, impatient determination. "This is serious, you promised me, and if you don't go, I'm going to leave you."

He would never have said that or thought it, once. I had been his right-hand woman all our married lives. How he had changed towards me, what on earth was happening to us? It hurt so much. My face puckered, ugly in sorrow and self-doubt. I took a step towards him. "Please, no, I don't want you to do that. It's mostly the things…"

"The things," he scoffed, knowing what I'd been going to say. "What things? You make them up."

There was no point in arguing with him. But I was afraid of his leaving. He would go to someone else, to her, whoever she was. In panic, I rang the surgery. They had an appointment that day, a cancellation. I could see elderly Dr Griffiths, who had known me since I was a young woman. He was my mother's doctor.

Across his surgery desk he stared at me with pale green eyes set in a high forehead. His long, thin fingers were folded together in front of him and he rested his sharp chin over them. His gaze was that of a psychiatrist, his smile kindly but slight.

"How nice to see you," he said as I walked into the room. I think I had distanced myself some years ago when, without checking for her age on his computer screen, he had proposed to a thirteen-year-old Hannah that she should take the pill for stomach cramps.

"Dr Griffiths, could you prescribe me with an anti-depressant?"

I asked it quickly, it must have sounded almost comical, because he smiled, but I had been terrified of asking it.

"Are you depressed?" He asked, reasonably enough.

I should have said yes, a firm yes, if I wanted Lukkas to stay, but it was all so silly that I hesitated then.

"I'm... anxious," I said. "I've been finding it hard to concentrate, sometimes."

He nodded slowly, "But that isn't necessarily depression. What makes you think you need anti-depressants?"

I hesitated again, swallowed, then couldn't lie. "Lukkas, my husband, says I must ask for them because he thinks I'm changed in some way. But the truth is, Dr Griffiths, I believe he's having an affair and I'm afraid. He says he will leave me if I don't ask you for something."

"Ah," he nodded a second time. "You came to see Dr Evans quite recently; did you talk about this with her?"

"No."

He sighed. "I can't give you anti-depressants on the basis that your husband is threatening to leave you."

"No, I suppose not." I panicked then. I had come all of this way for nothing, and Lukkas would go..." I made up my mind in a rush. "But I can't get over this feeling of sadness," I said, "That's genuine enough."

He clicked his tongue against the roof of his mouth in an irritated admonishment. For a few seconds he tapped his fingers upon the desk, watching me. Then, to my surprise, he said, "I suppose that I could prescribe Temazepams, a mild dose, but I must say you seem calm enough to me."

I nodded, gratefully. "Thank you," I said.

"It may make you feel a little drowsy at first. It might even make you feel sick," he warned me.

I didn't want to be drowsy or sick, I had far too many things to do each day. I didn't want to be some pliable, meekly obedient little woman who couldn't feel her emotions at all and did everything her husband and a possible mistress told her to. But still, I was afraid of Lukkas leaving, for all kinds of reasons. I would have to do it, I told myself.

I waited silently for my prescription, then walked briskly from his surgery to the exit, crossing the road to the chemists.

The tablets lay inside my bag for the remainder of the day. Once, when alone, I took the packet out and fingered it tentatively, then popped the foil at the back to remove the first one, but I couldn't make myself do it. I suppose it was a small step to the mouth, but it felt like a dangerous, detrimental action, that I was about to change my life for ever. I didn't want to have different thoughts, or to be slow, unable to care for the multitude of people I loved and cared for. I didn't want to be a different me, I had always been as I was and Lukkas had been happy with it for over thirty years, that was what I didn't trust.

What was really making him so unhappy with me now?

When he came home, he came straight to our bedroom to find me. I watched him hanging up his jacket as I paired his socks, going about his usual routine. He said nothing at first. Then he cleared his throat and turned to me suddenly, with a stern look upon his face.

"Well, did you go?" He asked.

"Yes."

"Did you get something?"

"Yes, temazepam," I said.

"Have you started taking them?" He asked.

I hesitated, considered saying yes, but then I would have to act like a person who takes temazepam, I would have to pretend to feel sick, I would have to be sleepy, switched off from life. I couldn't carry on like that, I would drop the act sooner or later.

"No," I admitted.

He scowled at me. "So, what's stopping you? Get them now and take the first."

Why, why did he want me to do this so badly? Then, I think for the first time, I asked myself whether this was about money. Was he intending to leave me anyway? In which case there would be a divorce and Lukkas might be shielding finances for himself. I didn't want to believe this of him. It was like some cruel, stupid game.

I got up and fetched my handbag from the living room, to prove that I had them. As I looked up, I caught my reflection in the mirror. I looked tired, dishevelled. Lukkas thought me stupid, he had said so before. I wasn't a trophy wife, he wanted a trophy wife. He wanted to be free of me, to be free of family problems. I couldn't move for a few seconds, my body was suddenly very heavy, my feet rooted to the spot.

When I returned to him, he shrugged his shoulders. "A doctor with some common sense at last. Just take it," he said, looking out of the window towards the fields, as though it didn't matter to him, but I knew that it mattered very much.

When he turned around, I shivered at the new intensity in his face. His words had been gentle but insistent, where once he would have encouraged me lovingly to do something to make me better, this was another matter, this was not to help me in any way and I felt it as he studied me.

"Do you want me to put it on your tongue for you?" He asked. He said it so lightly, as though it was an insignificant thing, as though it were a sexual act, offering me a strawberry.

As I held the pill between finger and thumb, in an instant, I loathed this new Lukkas.

"You would like that, wouldn't you?" I said quietly, knowing that if he left, my heart would be broken but knowing that if I swallowed it, it would be completely against my will, against my right to choose.

"I'll be a good girl," I said sarcastically. "I'll try to be the person you want. But no, I'm not taking it, no. I don't want to be changed, I want to be who I am. Whatever you decide, I'm not taking pills."

Rage illuminated his eyes, now he held so much anger inside him that he couldn't speak. He turned away, stomping from the room, banging the door, going to the kitchen to find the dinner that his stupid, mad wife had cooked for him.

I put the pill back inside the broken packet. Tomorrow, I would return them to the surgery, none taken, with a brief note to Dr Griffiths, apologising for having wasted his time. Lukkas was wasting their time; the Family man, the Family lawyer, the Human Rights Advocate. Lukkas didn't believe that I was mad. He was a liar.

He didn't leave after all. Perhaps he hadn't yet achieved the right result.

I thought I had escaped punishment. For almost two hours, we managed the house by avoiding one another, moving cautiously about our home, a nervous employee rather than a wife, wiping sticky finger marks from the walls with a cloth and generally cleaning up.

Josh was at the gym and Joe had gone out, I was glad neither of them had been present. I was upstairs when the front door opened and banged shut. I peered across the bannister to see Hannah. The children weren't with her. I searched her face for the kind of misery Ben caused, but her expression was angry, rather than upset.

"We need to talk," she said. "Is Dad in the living room?"

I nodded. "Talk about what?" I asked anxiously. "Where are the girls?"

"With Ben." She mounted the stairs. With Ben? I felt anxious each time she chose to leave them with Ben.

She peered into the living room, smiling sympathetically at her father.

Her anger was with me.

"Come in here, Mum." It was an order, not a request, instantly making me feel as though I were under house arrest.

"Why, what's the matter?" I gazed at her nervously. Closing the living room door behind us, she sat on the settee. I sat beside her, at the edge, keeping my distance. Lukkas placed his tray upon the coffee table and waited, hardly giving me a glance. I tried to steady my breathing whilst my stomach was tight with nervous knots.

"You promised Dad you would see a doctor and he has given you medication. Why haven't you taken it?" Hannah demanded.

When I opened my mouth to speak, the air seemed to leave my lungs. "It wasn't like that Hannah. He didn't want to give me anything at all, I persuaded him to, on-the-grounds that Dad had threatened to leave and that I was sad about it, but I can't take them, it was stupid of me, I don't need them. How will I function, how will I look after you guys if I take pills?"

"I don't believe you!" she snapped, "I'm going to call the surgery tomorrow and ask them." I should have said something sarcastic, like 'Good luck with that one,' but I hated Hannah's snappiness, her distress that he father might leave, her willingness to believe him and to stop him from leaving at all costs. I was upset, too, that she would try to alert other doctors to the prospect that her mother was mentally ill in some way.

Lukkas said nothing in all this time. He stared down at his slippers, as though he was a spare part in the conversation.

"He's going to leave you: don't you get it? Going to leave us, is that what you want?" Hannah's voice rose to a squeal, a woman, a mother, still young.

"I don't want to take medication on-the-grounds that Dad his having an affair with someone else and he and she want me out of the picture," I pleaded, entreating her to see my point of view.

"He isn't having an affair, you're deluded! Dad wouldn't do that to you. You're going crazy Mum and you can't see it. You hid his passport for God's sake, why?" Hannah shouted in despair.

My mouth had fallen open. I stared towards Lukkas. "Hid his passport? Why would I do such a stupid thing? I didn't even know his passport was missing!" I stood up and stared at him, willing him to say something, watching his calm appearance with so much anger inside me I could hardly breathe. "You know that's a lie. How could you manipulate us like this?"

But Lukkas turned his face to Hannah alone, shaking his head sadly to gain her support.

"Have you found it now?" I cried.

Hannah rose from the sofa then. "You have to have a proper assessment, Mum. Please stop delaying things."

I stared across the room at the black and white photograph of my grandfather. He had been a strong man, a good man. "Help me," I begged him silently, in need of a friend.

"Do you know what medication does to you? Do you understand that I might be tired and sick? When Catherine took pills during post-natal depression, her mother had to stay to look after her children, she could barely rise from the bed. What about your girls?"

"Dad feels you should not be looking after them right now, anyway. Not in your present state." She said it reluctantly. I knew she relied upon me, and she knew the girls trusted me and loved me. Even so, it was the final shitty blow to bring tears to my eyes. I had cared for them and protected them for so long, taught them to swim, paid for their ballet and now they were going to be removed from my care?

"Perhaps you ought not have them until you've seen someone," Hannah said quietly.

"Is that what he said Hannah? The final blackmail after he persuaded me to give up my career to care for them, for your sake. What did he say all those years ago? Oh yes, that after all I didn't need to work with his salary." I turned away, hugging my elbows. "So, where would they go to?"

"To a childminder, I suppose." Her voice was clipped. I knew she didn't want this, didn't have the money for it.

Clever Lukkas, sitting quietly all the while as though this was nothing to him. Who was the woman who was trying to hurt me like this? In an instant I wanted to tear her to pieces. My choices were to take pills or to lose my grandchildren, to lose Lukkas. I watched him go to Hannah now, kissing her on the forehead. That kiss was a betrayal. His love was betrayal.

CHAPTER FOURTEEN

Blood at Nice airport

This year, we were travelling to Nice with my parents and with Charlotte and Ellie. Lukkas' passport had mysteriously re-emerged in the interim.

Charlotte's partner and his two girls would join us a couple of days later. We would all be staying in our apartment on the Promenade des Anglais and then we were to drive to Tuscany in a hired car to join our friends. It was the first holiday without the girls, who would arrive with Hannah in a couple of weeks-time. Leaving them made me nervous. I felt great trepidation too, at taking my family whilst Lukkas behaved as he was, he had hardly seen them in a long time, and I felt almost apologetic about their coming with us; a little concerned about the atmosphere Lukkas might engender.

A few weeks before the event, I had started packing a suit case whilst speaking to Lukkas about various arrangements. When I said that I thought we wouldn't need a new push chair for Lilly, he flew into a rage out of all proportion to the comment, throwing his suitcase across the room. After that, I said nothing and packed in secrecy, like a smuggler.

Hannah had a great deal to do in the run up to the holiday. I wanted to support her with the shop as well as the children, so I went into Oxford on a couple of occasions to hand out leaflets to female tourists. Some of the young women Hannah had employed to do this job were obviously either lazy or less than confident about it, as we had recovered thick wads of advertising material from the city bins. I wasn't concerned about what others thought of me, but I was a little worried about what Lukkas would think, so I kept away from the main roads.

I collected a box of designer dresses from Oxford Station for the shop, too. Hannah had sold an incredible one hundred and forty-two outfits during one of the sunniest days in the city. As I staggered beneath the weight of the box, having parked illegally in the space of an absentee street trader, closely watched by the college porter opposite, I saw Lukkas.

He was walking towards the city centre, talking animatedly to the woman beside him who fought to meet his stride. She must have been in her forties, perhaps. She was small, a little shorter than me, but more elegant and with dark hair, cut almost in the same style as Betty's. She wore, not the standard black skirt and white blouse donned for court appearances, but a light green dress.

Staggering beneath the weight of the heavy box, I set it down upon a low wall and gazed after them as they strode towards the City Centre. They made a handsome couple. I was glad they hadn't seen me, hot, sweaty and almost invisible behind a box.

I thought I knew the woman, but couldn't be sure where from, wasn't sure where I might have met her.

I quizzed Josh again after work, trying so hard to ask the question lightly, as though it was nothing to me.

"A woman?" his tawny hair was dishevelled, standing on end because he had a habit of running his fingers through it and it needed cutting. His expression was distant, dreamy as he stared through the kitchen window into the garden, where the girls were chasing an escaped chicken.

"Oh, I know who you mean, you mean Holly. She works with Dad in the Family team…"

He came back to earth, staring at me with a bemused expression upon his face, then dipping the ladle into the spaghetti Bolognese, dripping a blob onto the tiled floor.

"Holly," he said, around the mouthful of food, "is probably the most expert lawyer on child care cases after Dad, she's a bit bossy; but on the whole, she's alright Mum and I think, I'm pretty sure in fact, that she's married."

"He's married too," I mumbled childishly.

Josh put his arm around me. "Stop worrying. Dad isn't having an affair. You're not mad," he said quietly.

When people asked me if I missed teaching, I would say, "I'm always teaching…" which was true. But I missed my relationship with other children and with colleagues too. Sometimes Lukkas and I would represent the same children, I as the school Special Needs teacher, and he as their lawyer. I had been very proud to represent the same child as Lukkas. I missed my colleagues, missed the strength they gave me.

It is humiliating to be reduced to imagining women of various shapes, sizes and colours making love to your husband and often, so that you can't sleep. There is nothing kinky about it, your confidence begins to slip away little by little…

On the Saturday morning, I drove the dogs to kennels and then returned to Lukkas and followed by Charlotte, bringing our parents and Ellie; we joined the queues to Luton airport.

"Can we not fall out with any of the air hostesses this time?" Lukkas asked me on the way there.

I remember turning slightly, arching an eye brow. "I asked for assistance Lukkas, I had a baby squirming on my lap if you recall and had asked three times for help, she chose to help three single men, having asked me to wait a minute. If you need to remonstrate with someone, you do it, why do you expect me to be different?"

I waited with baited breath. I had answered him back, he was unlikely to forgive me. But to my surprise, he left the subject and after a little while, I relaxed into the journey.

I thought about the name of the lady lawyer in Oxford with Lukkas. It had been on his phone. What had she said? That she hoped his migraine had gone. Josh had said that she was an important colleague now, but she couldn't have been at the office for very long, as I knew all the other lawyers. I felt sure that Lukkas would never start a relationship with someone with whom he worked, he would never do that to me, I was the Boss' wife, it would be too humiliating.

As we approached the air terminal car park, Lukkas handed me his phone. "Can you find out which area we are meant to take the cars to?" He asked.

I listened to the answering instruction and told him.

"But is it Gate A or gate B?" he snapped testily, "Here, give me the bloody phone."

I heard the man on the other end of the phone try to explain, in his faltering, Polish accent.

"Wanker," Lukkas exclaimed dismissively at the end of the call.

I glimpsed Charlotte at the driver's seat of the car behind us. My elderly father waved at us and I waved back. Lukkas stared sideways at me, elongating his face as though I had done a very odd thing and I knew I was right to feel ominous about this holiday. We are all nuisances to him, slowing down his new, James Bond existence.

As we pull the wheelie luggage through the airport, Lukkas strides ahead in his cream, Brian Ferry suit topped with a white panama.

As the man who Lukkas called a wanker calls out to us that he is having a problem starting Dad's old hatchback, Lukkas raises his eyes to the sky and walks away to buy himself a cup of coffee, leaving us, including poor little Ellie, who just wants a nice holiday, to sort it out.

This lack of respect is so out of character for him that I stare after him open mouthed, but I am indignant for my family, who would never, once, have been treated in this way.

Charlotte opened her mouth to call out to him, to tell him what is happening.

I put my arm on her hand. "Leave it, selfish git. We'll sort it out ourselves."

The Polish guy is great. He tells us not to worry, he will tow it to the garage and have someone look at it and then call us when they know what the problem is.

Charlotte and I help our parents with their luggage and we go off to find Lukkas then, who we find sitting with his coffee and a newspaper. He glanced up at us with more of a smirk than a smile and that look tightened the hard, angry knot in my stomach.

I bought everyone coffee and a drink for Ellie, in the meanwhile Lukkas had taken up his phone once more and made himself busy with that. Once again, he dismissed us, if he wanted to be rude to me, it was something I frequently tolerated, but to be rude to my family made me feel doubly vulnerable.

As we joined the queue for the plane, he carried on texting, smiling at his phone and the person at the other end until my blood boiled with resentment, and I did exactly what Lukkas wanted. I reached for his phone and snatched it from his hand.

He threw me a look of pure, unadulterated loathing. Reaching to snatch it back again, it clattered to the floor.

My dear family, the holidaymakers in the queue, all stared at us in gape mouthed horror. Never had anything like this occurred at Luton Airport.

The phone was intact, more's the pity, I thought bitterly.

"Laura, I really don't think that was necessary," my poor mother, unaware of the deteriorating atmosphere between Lukkas and I, hissed reproachfully.

Charlotte shook her head and grimaced at me for my lack of self-control but said nothing.

"Look," I accuse him, before my father and mother and little thirteen-year-old Ellie in her fake pearl earrings and new holiday bag, who had been so excited; before the American woman and her two teenage sons, embarrassing everyone further. "Look, can't you just be nice for two minutes, you've hardly spoken a word to anyone. You didn't lift a finger to help with Dad's car!"

And his eyes flash at me in the handsome face like small, hard emeralds. "That's it, Laura, I've had enough and I'm going home." His tone is clipped, like a machine. It is the last thing I want, and I know I shall regret saying it, but the hurt inside me won't stop.

"Good," I say, trembling inside, "Go home then."

My mother puts a trembling hand over her one kidney, and I feel dreadful for her and close to stupid tears myself. My father takes the crook of her arm nervously and looks away into the distance. Lukkas and I were the backbone of our family, supportive and dependable. They don't understand what has happened and no more do I.

"Don't say any more, Laura. No more. This isn't very nice for any of us and especially not for Ellie," Charlotte warns me.

I nod, trying not to watch Lukkas as he walks briskly to the rear of the queue with his mobile and his travelling bag.

Charlotte followed him then, persuading him not to leave. In the back of my mind a song, popular with Joseph, resounds loudly, "You need me, but I don't need you... you need me, but I don't need you..."

On that occasion, Charlotte persuaded him to stay.

I've known happier plane journeys. This one certainly wasn't to the strain of 'Fly me to the Moon' or 'We're all going on a Summer Holiday.' We settled my parents close to the front of the plane with a gin and tonic, attempting to erase unhappy thoughts, then Charlotte and Ellie tuned into their headphones.

Lukkas seated himself as far away from me as he possibly could. I glimpsed him once, stony faced at the back of the plane.

I was less angry now but consumed with fear. I couldn't envisage being single after more than thirty years with him.

Then my panic multiplied. Over the years, Lukkas had punished me on occasion by withholding things. Now I imagine him withholding my passport, even the keys to the apartment. What would I do if he raced off, leaving us to book a hotel we didn't have enough money for? I don't have enough cash on me. I have Lukkas' Barclaycard, but I'm unable to use it in France. I speak a little French, but not half as well as Lukkas.

I sit and stare at the clouds, ignoring the cherubic baby beside me where normally I would have tried to make it smile. His Jewish parents regard me suspiciously, the baby is very cute, and I know instinctively that they've been told so by countless people, but I am so miserable that I can't manage more than a wan smile.

As we alight from the plane, I find myself scurrying after Lukkas, leaving the rest of my family behind. When I reach him, he is still stiff and angry. I touch the sleeve of his jacket gently, an apology forming on my lips, but he brushes my hand away.

So, "I want the keys to the apartment," I say, with more force, but he hurtles on to the baggage carousel, still ignoring me. Others stare, watching unreservedly, some amused, others incredulous. I am embarrassed, but Lukkas seems not to care about any of it now.

"I need the keys, if you are going elsewhere..." I say, nodding at his holiday bag where the keys are stored and when he turns away from me, I yank at the shoulder strap.

"Give me the keys, Lukkas," I insist. Then we start to fight over the bag like children before the astounded holidaymakers and staff, and in front of all these people, Lukkas brings his fist crashing down on my forearm, making me wince in pain and I forget where and who I am completely. I reach up to his handsome nose and squeeze it between thumb and forefinger.

Lukkas' yelp is like a dog. Turning away, he strides away from me to the far side of the airport and I am so ashamed that we have sunk so low.

My family appear from the passport desk, blissfully unaware of our fight until they see Lukkas, clutching a tissue at his bloody nose, and go to him.

Suddenly, Charlotte is there as I stand, a helpless zombie, staring after my husband. She organises our luggage, shepherds our parents, takes my hand as though I need shock treatment and wheels us all through Nice airport into a wall of heat and sunshine.

I hear my own staccato as I tell a taxi driver where we want to go. The taxi isn't large enough, so we arrange ourselves into two taxis. Finally, in the rear of the taxi I share with my parents, I have a fully-fledged breakdown in Mum's arms; crying, sobbing, repeating Lukkas' name whilst the taxi driver watches us from the mirror, his eyes soft with sympathy at whatever bereavement I am suffering.

The strip of bright blue sea flashing past us along the Promenade des Anglais does nothing, this year, to excite me, neither the sunlight dappling the water, or the swimmers and sunbathers and coloured parasols on the beach, or the families walking, or the roller skaters or the bikes. They are visions to lift the heart, but not today.

On the sunny pavement outside the apartment where we had spent every summer for fifteen years, we stepped out of the taxis and Lukkas kissed my mother and then Charlotte on the cheek and wheeled his case along the pavement towards the old town without looking back. They all believe it is my fault, it is my fault.

I wanted to die, I was dying inside. My intestine had untwisted, but this was worse, I felt nothing. I loved him and wanted to love him, and the ache of rejection was impossible to bear.

For a long time, I stood on the balcony whilst my family unpacked their bags, each with their own thoughts. It was the start of a period where, without my grandchildren I smoked one cigarette after another. Sometimes that day, I cried silently, sometimes loudly.

"If things have gotten this bad then maybe it's all for the best," said my mother, hugging me. The sadness on my father's face was obvious and I begged their forgiveness for ruining their holiday.

Some while later, because we had to eat and because I had to revive their spirits, we went to the 'Jardin', the restaurant next door to us, and our mood is no longer solemn and to my amazement I am hungry enough to eat the whole chicken salad.

After dinner, I try to make it up to Ellie by swimming in the sea with her, as though there is nothing wrong. Once I was nervous about swimming in the dark, now I no longer care, such things don't frighten me anymore, real life frightens me far more.

When we go to bed, Charlotte offers to sleep with me as though I'm a child. "I'll be okay," I assure her with a hug. But I don't sleep at all. I cry out his name, get up, smoke again, drink water, pace the balcony, miss him so much. At last I find myself in the kitchen.

Charlotte comes to join me at this late hour.

"Do you think he's gone back, to the UK?" I ask her.

She shrugs, "I don't know. I think it more likely he's here, at the other apartment or in a hotel perhaps."

We sit in the darkened kitchen, at the breakfast bar, speaking in hushed whispers.

"Don't contact him," she pleads with me, "If things have gone this sour, you need to think about it first…"

At two thirty in the morning I disregard her advice and send Lukkas a text.

"Please Lukkas, come back. I love you so much, I'm sorry about your nose." It sounds almost comical in a situation that isn't comical at all, but I send it. I know there will be no reply, but I send it.

I lie in his shirt, one that he keeps at the apartment and listen to the sounds of Nice winding down.

There is a pattern to night life everywhere, most particularly on the Promenade des Anglais. In the earlier evening, there is the chattering of voices, the families with push chairs, the girls, dressed to kill; the wealthy coming from hotels to greet the evening, the clubbers and those sitting on the night time beach listening to bongo drums that add their voice to the warm evening.

Then, much later, the prostitutes emerge to ply their trade, leaning languidly against the cars, watched by a hidden pimp. They are mostly Russian girls, very pretty, with white skin and dark hair.

Once I had felt jealous when one of them turned a secret smile upon Lukkas as he held my hand in the street and he smiled back at her. When I let go of his hand, aggravated by it, he said, "It's their job, to look at men."

Gradually, past three in the morning, the traffic slows; the cars returning to Cannes, the cars to Monaco in the opposite direction, all traffic stops. The drunks cease their song, the Casino goers lose their money, the late-night revellers give in to sleep and even the smoking, gum chewing prostitutes leave.

Then it becomes so quiet that at last you can hear the gentle lapping of the sea on the pebble hard shore.

I lay in his shirt, listening to the waves. I cannot bear to be here without him, haunted by memory. I clutch his pillow to my stomach, curled like an embryo. Half-awake and half asleep I think of the easiness of death for the second time that day. I think of taking pills, then walking unnoticed and effortlessly into the dark waves until the pain stops.

I do the most thoughtless and selfish thing I have ever done in my life, I send a text to Hannah.

"I don't want to be here, I don't want to live anymore." I am drunk on emotion.

As though she hasn't had enough to deal with. Hannah replies quickly.

"Where's Dad?"

"Gone. I don't know. Maybe Massena, but he won't reply to my texts."

Her message comes quickly. "Don't be stupid, we will work it out, everything will be okay. I'm going to text Dad."

I slump back onto the bed and cover my eyes with my arm, waiting for a call that never comes.

CHAPTER FIFTEEN

Sunshine and persuasion

I must have slept for an hour or two.

In the pastel, early morning light, I rise before the others. Lukkas is all I can think about, and I write to him.

"I have loved you all my life, that's how it feels. But I was brought up to think for myself and I suppose my respect for you was so great that in some ways you became my parent. I came to accept your way but often; your way is domineering. Too frequently I have used sex to soften your moods. It isn't only me, in one way or another our children have felt frustrated also.

Latterly, because I want to avoid your shouting or banging tables in front of the grandchildren, I have said what I wanted to in a text.

I chose to give up my job to help bring Ruby up, but it was difficult for many reasons. I have worked all my life, including when our children were growing up. Hannah was depressed when the girls' Dad left, and resigning my job meant I had to rely on you for income. You said that you wanted that too, you said, "After all, you don't need to work." At a time when I had lost my sense of worth, you started to be very rude and sarcastic and sometimes, Lukkas, your parents would behave in the same way. Your mother has said pointedly on many occasions that other women support their husbands, as if I don't support you!

I have brought in an income, done the housework, cooked every night, raised three children, sorted the trash, been the laundress, acted as a plumber and gardener as well as teaching our own children and undertaken many jobs that were either below you or you failed to notice, but whereas I respected your work, you failed to respect mine.

The student from Brazil left because she said that you shouted a lot. When I asked you to remonstrate with Joe for using the term 'cunt' in front of his nieces you did nothing of the sort but told me off for demonstrating his language to you, whilst you continued with his allowance.

What doctor could help with these problems? Then, more recently you have started to goad me, or I have felt goaded by the things that I've found, what doctor will help with this?

I love you Lukkas, truly I do, and you know it, but much as I enjoy making love with you, only prostitutes and slaves have sex when their pride is so destroyed by their lover. You will like me no less for this, but when I asked your father not to use the term Paki in front of our children, he told me that I needed a Scold's bridle and asked me if I knew what that was. He labelled most of your aunts and his own sister as mad, and he meant it. I am no relation to them and for the previous thirty years, there was no suggestion of there being anything wrong with me, so what's going on?

Please see a marriage councillor with me to try to work things through."

It was only half past six and the family were still all abed. I showered and put on a bright, strappy dress, which Lukkas had once loved, and set out, closing the apartment door softly behind me.

At that time, there were only a few people about, the old ladies and mothers heading for the supermarket, the early workers and the dustcart. On previous holidays I had taken the girls for an early swim, for at this time, the sea was still and smooth as a swimming pool.

As I turned into the Westminster Hotel I passed several early morning joggers. The hotel was one we knew well, the girls loved to climb aboard the stone lions at its front.

I asked the young concierge whether my husband was there, it was just a thought, and he smiled at me in a friendly way but said that it was information he wasn't allowed to give me. I nodded, without further explanation and he wished me luck in my search.

I descended the steps of the Westminster, walking towards the park with the carousel and crossing the road to the very expensive boutiques and to our other apartment, Massena.

This was our first buy in Nice, or to be exact, Lukkas' first buy. Nice was where we had our first holiday abroad, I hadn't even known he was thinking of buying the apartment. He came to Cornwall at the end of a sunny week, having told me that he had to go to Belgium for a client, when he sat on the picnic rug, he told me, "I've bought a present for you."

Lukkas is like that, he likes to choose what money should be spent on, but he likes to spoil with grand gestures. At the time I had mixed feelings, it was churlish in the extreme not to be pleased, but perhaps we ought to have made the decision together.

I had no key for the apartment in Massena. I wasn't sure how I would get inside the building and our apartment is four storeys high. So, I walked to the rear of it, staring up at the yellow façade. Through the railings surrounding our courtyard, I could see that the shutters were open. Someone was there.

I was tempted for a moment to bellow his name at the blue sky, startling the pigeons and sleeping holidaymakers in a country where people seldom shout, but I imagined the angry faces staring down at me.

Then, our song, for every couple has a song, came into my mind in a rush and falteringly at first, but confident in my voice, I started to sing.

"There's a place for us, somewhere, a place for us... Hold my hand and I'll take you there..."

I sang for quite a while, knowing all along that Lukkas prefers the rusty, broken Tom Waites version, but that would have sounded comical and right then, I had little to smile about.

There is no answer from him, although I think the little old man on a bench in the sunshine enjoys my song.

Dejectedly, still clutching my letter to Lukkas, I start the journey through the back streets of Nice and to the supermarket, to purchase breakfast things.

And then a text from him arrives on my phone, my heart leaps with joy, even though it says, "Go home Laura."

"Please come back. I'm sorry. I love you so much, we can work things out," my fingers work like pistons, desperately. But he doesn't reply.

If Lukkas was here, we would go to Zeus Plage, one of the private beaches. It is our favourite and we have been on very friendly terms with Thomas and Veronique and their family, who own it. In the past, Lukkas and I have played host to up to thirty adults and children there. Lukkas and Thomas smoke Cuban cigars and talk rugby.

But sunbathing and swimming at Zeus Plage takes a degree of self-confidence, of Savoir Faire, and currently I lack both. Sensing this, after breakfast on the balcony, my family say they would be happy to go onto the public beach. We take the parasols out of the outside lock up, shaking the pigeon shit off them and rescuing two eggs to show the girls when they come. We retrieve the beach chairs, bought last year and make a picnic.

We walk to the beach, helping my father down the steep steps, and set up camp amidst the other parasols, leaving our parents in the shade with English newspapers, whilst Charlotte, Ellie and I have a swim.

The water is warm, soothing, like swimming in blue jelly. I try not to think of Lukkas and immediately remember a time when Lukkas and I were young and made love in the sea.

I stifle the urge to cry once more by submerging myself beneath the waves. I don't want Ellie to suffer any more from her damp squid of an aunt. I smile at her lovely little figure in the bikini with affection and vow to buy her a new one. Last year, an Italian man who was twice her age or more, patted her bottom as she passed him in the street. I shouted at him that she was twelve years old, and he beat a hasty retreat.

Now, I stare along at the private beaches, Lukkas wasn't generally given to allowing other people's sadness to spoil a good time, I thought bitterly, as

I imagined him lounging on a Matalan with the first beer of the day.

After a while I left Charlotte and Ellie splashing each other in the surf to swim along the shore line in search of him, swimming in a crowded sea to peer up at the beaches that I might catch a glimpse of him. Once I would have been too proud to do any such thing, but now, my salty hair plastered to my cheeks as I looked for a needle in a hay stack, I scarcely cared what anyone else might think.

When I returned to Charlotte, she was waiting at the place where I had left my shoes. I clamber from the waves in an undignified waddle, having forgotten my beach shoes, a necessity for the hard pebbles.

"Don't look now," she warned. "Lukkas is sitting on our balcony, smoking cigarettes!"

"Lukkas hasn't smoked for ten years!" I exclaimed, "Are you sure that it's him?"

I look upwards, cautiously, toward our apartment. It is him, sitting below the awning. I feel such relief that I hug her.

"Don't be desperate," she cautions, "Let me go, let me talk with him first."

So, despite my urge to go to him immediately, I wait, my heartbeat growing ever more rapid. My mother knows, Charlotte told her, she holds my hand very tightly, her nails digging into my skin as though to keep me there.

When Charlotte returns, she nods at me. "Be cool," she tells me.

Lukkas finds it easy to be cool with me, I don't find it as easy to be cool with him.

When I reach the balcony, he is sitting at the table and an ash tray is full to brimming with stubs. He hasn't smoked for ten years, or, at least that's what I believed. I felt a stab of protectiveness, as though he is my child.

"Lukkas, you don't smoke! What are you doing?" I cry out.

He stared ahead at the beach, but it felt a little that he was acting a part, like Noel Coward. "You did it," he said. I didn't argue with him.

"I want to know what Charlotte means by 'your side of the story,' what exactly is your side of the story?"

I sat beside him, resting a hand on his knee, this time, he didn't pull away.

"I guess she meant that she was trying to be fair to us both."

He kept his profile turned towards the beach. "But what is your side of the story, Laura?"

I was nervous, it was a little like feeling trapped now, this life with him; but it was also impossible to escape, love is a trap of your own making.

"I guess I told her that whilst you are working so hard, I've undermined you with my own insecurities," I said truthfully.

"And that you believe I'm having an affair?" He asked in a monotone.

"Well, yes, I've wondered," I said truthfully. Then, against all instinct, "There have been things to suggest that you are," I said.

He continued to stare over the balcony towards the crowded beach but shook his head.

I wanted to say that sometimes it was as though he were goading me, deliberately provoking me. I was too afraid. I reached out to him, gently touching his cheek. "I'm sorry I hurt your nose... I was afraid that you wouldn't let us into the apartment."

"Huh!"

I looked at him intently, conscious that I was about to say anything to keep him there. "Maybe I could do with cognitive therapy or something," I volunteered.

He blew a ring of smoke into the air. "Tell me about the time your mother took you to a child psychiatrist," he said.

I frowned at him, not only had it been forty-four years ago, Lukkas had never shown any interest in it before. "Why do you want to know that, now?" I asked, suspicious, never-the-less, I kept the fixed smile upon my face.

"It was such a long time ago. I only had one session. I think the psychiatrist told Mum that I needed a little space, that I felt too responsible for three younger siblings, so I kept picking arguments with Paula because she was my next sister down. He said I would grow out of it and I did...What has that got to do with now?"

But he didn't answer me, he shook his head and then reached out to stroke my cheek and the feeling was so wonderful, I melted like Italian ice cream in the sunshine.

"No more of this then," he said. "I'll come down to the beach with you."

He did that, it was as though he had become a changed person. He told me that he had loved me since the first day he saw me and that he would never love anyone else and I believed him. I believed him. He was kind and attentive to my family once more and he smiled and seemed happy.

At night we made love, Lukkas made love to me with the soft touch of his hands, deftly undoing my bra as he used to and caressing me until I groaned, and he shushed me. I relaxed at last, feeling that all would be well again, feeling that everything in life was wonderful.

On the following day, Lukkas suggested that we should all eat at a well-known restaurant in the old port, 'La Reserve'. He booked a table for twelve thirty as the lunch time menu was a little less expensive. Normally we would have walked the distance, but we took a taxi for the sake of my parents.

Lukkas seemed nothing like the man at the airport. He was charming and attentive, and I felt ecstatic at our reunion, like a teenager in love.

We drove through the lengthy underground tunnel used by the notorious Robin Hood of Nice, Spaggiari, in his robbery of a bank. Lukkas admired the man for the risks he took and told me as such.

'La Reserve' is built high up in the white rocks that overlook the little coves and caves where local children leap into the azure sea. Three sides of the restaurant overlook the ocean, so you can see the millionaire's yachts bobbing in company with fishing boats and sailing boats and the giant yellow ferry coming to and from Corsica.

I sat opposite Lukkas and next to my parents at a spacious, white clothed table; our backs to a giant, silver framed mirror that ran the length of the wall. Lukkas and I argued politely about who should sit facing the restaurant, until he insisted that I should.

Seated opposite me, he was handsome as always, on this occasion he resembled a slightly unshaven Errol Flynn. He wore a sky-blue shirt and cream shorts and was the picture of a well-to-do-man on holiday. He joked with Charlotte and helped Ellie translate the French menu, he talked to my father about the fish caught in the region and was charming to Mum.

It wasn't until midway through a conversation about the prospect of the journey to Italy that I smiled at Lukkas, opposite me. I was about to ask him who would do the driving and to all intents and purpose, he was part of the conversation, but the words dried in my mouth. His eyes were firmly fixed upon the reflected smile of a young woman and through the mirror her eyes were locked upon his.

They had been gazing at each other for some while, as in a game, utilising the mirror to good effect. When Lukkas realised I had noticed it, it broke the spell. The girl's eyes darted back to her friend, a young blonde seated opposite her, whilst Lukkas smiled at me as though I had just this minute walked into the room; a false, hasty smile.

The girl had dark, straight brown hair cut stylishly to the nape of her neck, a small, rather spoilt expression and ruby red lips. She wore a little black dress with a white belt at the waist, almost as soon as she had looked away, her eyes darted back to Lukkas' compulsively, but seeing that I had taken this all in, her eyes fell to the napkin on her lap in an expression of annoyance rather than guilt.

I wanted that look that had passed from Lukkas to the girl far more than the delicious but expensive food on my plate. It was as though they were making love with their eyes.

My face must have registered my hurt and discomfort. "Is everything okay?" he asked.

For a reply, I stood up to address Charlotte.

"Could we change places, please?" I asked her quietly.

She frowned in confusion. "Yes, of course, if you want, but why? The main dish is about to arrive."

I resisted the temptation to tell her that the main dish was already here. I did not want to be patronised, to be some extra party in a silly game, some silly woman who could be treated without regard whilst my husband flirted with younger women!

"I just want to sit overlooking the sea for a while, and to talk to Dad," I said, fumbling with my napkin.

"Okay," she replied uncertainly.

But as Lukkas' eyes followed me, he knew without my having to say a word. We didn't speak for the rest of the meal. Before leaving the restaurant, in the ladies' toilet, my mother regarded me anxiously whilst Charlotte hissed, "Whatever happened, why is Lukkas so quiet?"

I told them what I felt, or at least I tried to. I told them what I had seen.

"Oh, dear God no," poor Mum said, shaking her head, "Not another argument!"

"Are you sure, Laura, or do you think you imagined it?" Charlotte raised her eyebrows, having heard 'Lukkas' side of the story, which I am sure, wasn't anything like mine.

"No, I didn't imagine it, how dare he, how would he feel if I carried on like that? He is doing it deliberately and it's getting worse, as though he carries on elsewhere like it and it's infectious! Unless he knows how upsetting, how sexist it is to behave like it and he's deliberately goading me."

Charlotte shook her head despairingly.

We returned to the restaurant to pay the bill. Lukkas' body was stiff with anger, his back turned against me.

The girl stood on the pavement outside, studiedly ignoring us, speaking to her friend. Before everyone, Lukkas turned to me, his eyes were blazing with fury.

"That's it Laura, I've had enough of your imaginings. I've had enough of your spoiling everything!" He shouted it, so that everyone from the waiters to the passers-by on the street and the pretty girl with whom he had been flirting heard it. My poor parents had gripped each other by the arm and were trying hard to stare in the opposite direction.

It was humiliating for everyone but came from his humiliation of me in the first place.

"I'm going, this time I mean it, and I won't be coming back!" Lukkas barked.

He turned away from us and marched briskly towards the port. My heart pounding inside of me like an overwound machine, I ignored Charlotte's entreaties to come back, following him.

"No Laura!" She called after me. "You will only make him angrier, leave him…"

But I couldn't, I wouldn't be able to function in a world without him, I would fall to pieces, I told myself yet again, a demented female swan.

I hurtled after him. He had reached the sea wall now, all I could think of was catching up with him, of begging him to stay.

"We're going down to the beach," I heard Charlotte call, "to take Ellie for a swim!"

I heard a passer-by snigger as though we were actors in a terrible play and she the audience. Actors in a dreadful tragic comedy.

At last I caught up with him, tried to keep pace with him and reached for his elbow but he tore away from me. "Go away," he snarled, "I don't want to be with you, it's over!"

The dreadful finality of his words made me feel sick in my stomach.

"No, Lukkas, please!"

But he was walking so fast that it was almost impossible to keep pace with him. His feet slap-slapped upon the pavement in his sandals. I had begged over the years when he wouldn't talk to me, but never so hard. I knew then, and I felt now, that he didn't mean it; it was Lukkas, what Lukkas was like.

"No!" he shouted back, "You told me there would be no more fuss. I will not be told what to do or how to behave. Clearly, I am not good enough for you, clearly, I am not what you need. I am too old for this rubbish…"

I bit my tongue, resisting the temptation to say, "Not too old to flirt with younger girls than Hannah though, not too old to sulk like a child if I don't agree with you…" Instead I dodged this way and that, like a player in a football match until, raising his eyes to the brim of his panama hat so that for one split second it occurred to me that he was enjoying the situation. He skirted me and began walking back along the pathway we had followed, descending the steps to the beach, even before I realised that he was turning back once more.

My parents were seated upon a rock by the sea, as we approached, they hurriedly turned away from us and stared out at the ocean, frozen statues of English people on holiday, they were so still, only the ribbon on Mum's hat fluttered in the breeze.

But at last he allowed me to take his hand.

"I love you Lukkas. I promise it will be alright. You make me feel vulnerable and I'm not handling it very well, I won't behave like that again…"

Two young women lying upon their stomachs in the sand peered up at us, the younger one laughing, her shoulders lifting up-and-down in silent mirth.

Lukkas gave a long sigh and took a cigarette from the packet in his jacket pocket. He lit it and the flame spluttered on the sea breeze. He drew on it heavily.

"Look, Laura," he started, "I came back yesterday for Hannah, not for you. You have to stop harassing me," he said.

Harassing him? He was my husband of over thirty years, had I harassed him during all those years of love and support? I dug my nails into the palm of my hand, it hurt and humiliated me even more that he had returned for Hannah's sake and not mine, but I couldn't say it, not now. I kept silent.

Then he started to take his shorts off for a swim, and my parents seemed to collapse like a butter sculpture on the beach in the sunshine; whilst Charlotte and Ellie, appearing before us in their bathing costumes, stifled yelps of amazement at the sight of him.

Later, walking back past the boats and cafés of the harbour, my mother took my arm as Charlotte talked to Lukkas some way back.

"What's really going on here?" She asked. "Are you alright? Lukkas says that he wants you to see a doctor…"

I bit my lip. "I don't need to see a doctor, Mum. Lately Lukkas has been, well different, towards me. He's never seen women as equals and I think his childhood was far more complex than I understood when we were both young, he was sent to a public school when he was very young and there's some emotional understanding lacking in him. Also, well, he had some pretty appalling experiences at school." I said no more, that was private, he had told me in confidence, something his parents had never known, one of the worst things that could happen to a child, to a human being.

She frowned, as though my own explanation lacked clarity. "But he's been like that for thirty years and you two were such friends. What's changed?"

I shrugged miserably. "Perhaps it's me, I'm just older, I don't feel as though I want to be treated in certain ways," I said.

But I didn't say "I think Lukkas is having an affair, I think Lukkas is emotionally weak and it's possible that loving someone else means that he can simply drop me in the 'of no further use' basket," just as he got rid of long time partners at work, or staff, or anyone who stood in his way. I didn't tell her because it hurt me too much to admit it and by deed of the relationship, it would have hurt her too.

Chapter Sixteen

Provocation

That evening, Neil arrived with Becky and Isabelle, his children. The mood changed considerably, memories of Summers before, as we yelled to them over the balcony when they alighted from the bus.

We had prepared the dinner in advance. We ate, talking animatedly, and whatever Charlotte may have explained to Neil, he kept to himself and I was grateful for his tact.

After dinner, we sat on the balcony, talking, whilst watching the three girls cavort in the warm sea. Isabelle, at twenty, was in charge.

Maybe Lukkas was tired, but he is seldom morose when in the company of others and as his tone changed to joyless sarcasm, I was confused. Perhaps, I thought, he is acting now, trying to impress upon Neil what a pain I am, glad of another bloke to confide in.

I left it. The last thing I wanted was another scene. I stood at the sink, washing up with Charlotte whilst the two men drank beer on the balcony. When we had finished, drying my hands upon a tea towel, I wandered out to them, "Charlotte and I read that there are going to be music bands on the Promenade later this evening, shall we go for a stroll?"

In previous years, Lukkas would have leapt up enthusiastically. He loved Nice, he loved Mojitos and no matter how exhausted, he would have agreed. Now, he said, "No thanks, I'm tired."

I was disappointed, but I didn't show it. I wanted to go for a walk, smell the evening smells, tap my feet to the music; but there was something more, there was the memory of all the times Lukkas had returned from places he wouldn't talk about, breath reeking from various cocktails. Why shouldn't I dress up and do the same?

I went into our bedroom and opened the wardrobe. Peering at me from the rather non-descript outfits was an emerald green, boob tube dress that Hannah had given to her daughters to dress up in, which I had optimistically shoved into my case.

Undressing in front of the long mirror, I examined my figure. I had lost a lot of weight, this had been unintentional, but the result wasn't bad at all. My skin had a light tan, my legs were sturdy but without cellulite. Perhaps I could get away with the boob tube dress after all. If I didn't wear knickers, there would be no line, but I mustn't forget and bend over. I pulled it over my head. The bottom part was fine, but the top made me look cheap and nasty. I drew out a semi-transparent black shirt, put it on over the dress and tied it in the front. It all looked quite good.

I wasn't disappointed, as I walked into the living room, the girls were back from the beach, dripping water all over the slippery marble floor.

"Oh my God, Laura, you look fantastic, where did you get that dress from, I want it!" Isabelle shrieked.

I grinned at her, "You can have it, it will suit you better," I said.

Lukkas was seated at the breakfast bar, examining a message on his phone, but he had looked up at me when Izzie shrieked her approval. He stared at me over the top of his glasses and I felt ridiculously pleased.

"What are you doing, Laura?" His voice was stern.

"I smiled, clip clopping across the floor in a pair of strappy sandals. "I'm just going for a stroll, as I said, if anyone would like to join me. I thought I might have a drink at the Westminster or the Negresco."

"Thank you, God, at last I have his attention," I thought, in a cheap prayer.

"What game are you playing now?" He asked.

Beside me, now, I heard Charlotte's sharp, anxious, intake of breath.

"I am not playing games at all," I said in gentle surprise, "If you get dressed up in your best suit to go out and wear aftershave for the occasion, I don't suppose that you're playing games."

I knew then that Lukkas didn't want me to go out looking this good, but I didn't know enough to decide whether his were feelings of love or ownership. I decided to go with the former.

"I'll come with you, hang on a minute," Charlotte said then, whilst our mother supressed a smile, a gin and tonic rattling in her hand, "Gosh, you look nice Laura, have fun," she said with an element of pride and provocation, "Better take a key in case we've gone to bed."

Charlotte and I went down in the ornate lift and wound our way into the street with the other late-night revellers. It felt good, it was such a rare thing for us to do that I wound my arm through hers as though we were young again and on our way to some disco or other. We found an empty table at the Westminster Hotel, opposite a temporary stage set up across the street where a Reggae band were in full swing.

"You know," she said, the survivor of two marriages, "Things will be alright if you leave Lukkas."

"If I leave Lukkas," I said, "I might lose my right to my home, and anyway, I love him Charlotte, I really do."

"I don't know the law, but will leaving him really mean that?"

I shrugged. "I don't know, but anyway, is it a good idea to leave my family at this moment? Leave Hannah and our granddaughters?"

"No, I suppose you're unlikely to do that at any time." She beckoned to a young waitress to order our drinks.

"I've loved Lukkas all this time. I really don't believe I can survive without him, so what do I do, throw in the towel to another woman?" I asked.

"You genuinely believe that there's someone else, don't you?"

"Yes, yes I do. There have been too many things and he's too..." I searched for the right word, "defensive," I finished. "He skirts the issue. He has said that he wouldn't do anything that I didn't like, that fundamentally, he isn't doing anything that would hurt me. It's all legal jargon, why not be straightforward? Why not just say, "I'm not having an affair and I don't intend to either, you know how clever he is." I stopped speaking briefly to sip at my glass of Kier. "There are the things I keep finding and this feeling I can't explain, as though there's someone else, egging him on to be dismissive and rude to their own advantage."

She nodded slowly, watching me.

"Then, he said that I'd hit him with a frying pan…"

She started laughing then.

"It's not funny, it's hurtful, lying crap," I said.

"It's funny because it's so lacking in imagination!"

Charlotte wiped her eyes and straightened her face, putting her hand over mine. "Laura, it's quite dangerous where you are concerned, if he is going about saying that kind of thing to people, well… I've been really fond of Lukkas and you know that, but perhaps it's time to see a lawyer now, one that you're not married to."

"I can't. He's controlling and domineering but I have all these feelings of love and loyalty towards him."

She nodded. "Well, thanks for bringing me on such an unusual holiday," she joked. "Seriously though, Laura. If there is another woman, I would think she's being far cooler than you are…"

"I've been me all of our life, it's harder to change now," I pointed out.

But I felt better for the conversation, I felt as though I had some stronger support.

Several men of varying ages had stared in our direction. I'd always been conscious that Charlotte attracted male attention, but rarely that I was. I suppose I should have been flattered at the middle-aged man staring at my legs beneath the short skirt, but I wasn't. Instead, I was experiencing a kind of revulsion. He was seated at a table close by, with a wife who I assumed was a little bit younger than me and his own daughter. "Yuk," is what I thought, "Yuk, doesn't he even realise what a put down that is for his wife? What a creep."

Was that Lukkas now, did being good looking make him less of a creep?

We drank two Kiers each and wandered back to the apartment. The girls were watching a film, Neil was sitting on the balcony with several empty cans, Charlotte muttered, "Oh no, he'll snore all night now."

Our parents had gone to bed, Lukkas too.

His long body was outlined by a single sheet. He breathed softly, facing away from me and towards the door. When I climbed into the bed, he didn't stir. I got in beside him and curled about his back.

I awoke the next morning after a long sleep to the sound of a cup being placed upon the bedside table.

I smiled at him. "Thank you, I love you," I said. When he smiled back I believed in new beginnings, it was as though the poison had gone.

"Are you coming with me to collect the hire car?" he asked.

I wanted to do anything that meant being with him. I dressed, and we walked hand in hand through the shadier back streets to fetch the people carrier.

When we returned, everyone was ready and had eaten breakfast but for Becky, who was still applying her make up.

Whilst we drank coffee with our parents, Charlotte and I lectured them as though they were small children about safety whilst we were in Italy. We were both concerned about leaving them there, but our mother was fiercely independent and loved being in Nice to choose to do as she wished.

"Don't trip down the stairs, be very careful…"

"If anything goes wrong, just call us…"

"Oh, for God's sake, stop treating us like children and go!" she said at last.

Charlotte and I had stocked the fridge with enough food for a month and had told each other that if we had to drive back from Italy for any reason, that's what we would do.

We clambered into the hire car, which Lukkas would drive for the first part of the journey, waving our goodbyes at the balcony. I settled into the back with needle and cotton and a pile of skirts, determined to have shortened them by several centimetres before we reached our destination. No more retro Laura Ashley for me. The sewing was interrupted by conversation and several hundred miles of interconnecting dark tunnels following the coast from France to Italy, always emerging next to the sea which glistened like a shimmering blue shawl beside the road.

Within a few hours and after a couple of stops to change driver and visit motor side restaurants to fight in queues with babbling, excited Italian families, we reached the verdant evergreen of the Italian mountains Blue pine and cypress beneath an Azure sky, surrounding mountain top villages. The colours of clay, white and sienna.

I felt so happy, so reassured, as Lukkas squeezed my hand and kissed me frequently during the day and if I hadn't stopped believing in the elusive 'her', at least I thought, "He is mine now, you are not here."

When we arrived in Arezzo at about four in the afternoon to stock up at the local supermarket first, he looked down at me as we stood by the car, alone, saying, "You know, when it's good, it's really-good with you, Laura." And I wanted to push the supermarket trolley singing Italian opera but contented myself by floating around the place like Sophia Loren on a film set.

I had only visited Italy once before, in the year after our sister died aged only thirty-three. Josh was eleven then, and Hannah, nine, whilst Joe was just a baby. We stayed in a house high in the mountains in a village called Bastia. We swam with tiny frogs in river pools of green water at the foot of the mountain.

Oh, Lukkas, so gentle and considerate after my sister's death. Such a contrast with the man who booked us into a country hotel in Ludlow and made love to me with such ferocity and impatience last Spring. It was almost, I thought then, as though he had done something that I wouldn't like and was trying to remember me once more. It had been fucking, not love making, and his eyes were as cold and intense as a shark's, almost as though his lust was aimed at someone else, as though he couldn't overcome his frustration. It bruised me in every way. After it, he lay on his side in a damp dressing gown as though he was alone, sleeping long into the evening.

The next day he dragged me impatiently around Ludlow Castle, knowing nothing of its history. But I thought of Katherine of Aragon, who visited the place with the young Arthur, Henry VIII older brother who died, so that Henry became Katherine's new husband who she loved and revered and eventually lost to Anne Boleyn. I remember that shiver of fear I had experienced in the shadow of the castle, a premonition of something bad that would sever us as surely as the axe.

But now, in this place, I smelled roses and warm, scented air and those thoughts were forgotten as Lukkas reached for my hand, steering the car deftly with the other to drive along the dusty white track to the Villa Romano, whilst in the distance there were the bluish mountains and, in the foreground, the tall, evergreen cypress trees which flanked dense woodland.

As the car jerked along the bumpy road, Charlotte, the three girls and I sang along to the radio, our voices joining with 'Supertramp', "Give a little bit, give a little bit of your life to me…"

CHAPTER SEVENTEEN

Unreasonable jealousy

The villa was white, beautiful; with curving stone steps reminiscent of an illustration from Cinderella. The large, stone urns at the front of the house were filled with Bougainville and the shutters were thrown back before elegant gardens that surrounded the house. It had all the opulence of Italian nobility.

The black, wrought iron gates opened without being told to the moment we arrived. Lukkas parked close to the house, whilst the girls fell out of the car to explore the gardens, suddenly much younger versions of themselves.

Izzie and Ellie peered over the wall which housed the swimming pool, whilst Becky leaned over the slimy, lurid green of a walled pond that had once been a well, yelling to the others, "Massive frogs in here!"

As the lizards scuttled away from their sunny spots on the stone walls at our noisy arrival, we took our luggage and the groceries from the car. Lilyanna, our hostess, later dubbed 'Lilly Allen' by the girls, came from beneath her family's coat of arms to greet us. She was slight, brown haired and with an intelligent face. We were the first of the families to arrive and were rewarded with a grand tour of the villa. Lilly Allen's family could trace itself back to the thirteenth century, her family had lived here since the sixteenth century when the villa was built over the site of a monastery, she told us.

After an hour, Simone and Piers and their children arrived, having taken a plane to Florence and rented a hired car. Between us, we set up the cold meats, olives and bread with wine on the table beside the pool. It was five o'clock in the afternoon and the heat was intense. From the woods came the distant, rasping sounds of sawing, from the grass the softer sound of the crickets.

Lukkas sat beside me and stroked my arm gently as we talked and laughed; it was a moment of utter joy for me and for the first time in a long time, loving our grandchildren as I do, I was glad they weren't there. Watching Lukkas' genuine laughter as he chatted with Piers, I ventured, "I love you…"

"I love you," he returned, kissing my cheek, and I saw Charlotte smile in unabashed relief.

Lukkas' phone broke the spell, but this time it was Lisa. She had sent several texts as they made their way to the villa, saying that they had missed their flight and that Jack, and the girls, were thoroughly fed up.

"Oh, they are in Arezzo and lost, apparently," Lukkas said. "They're driving around the baseball stadium without a Sat Nav, trying to find us." He jumped from his seat, "Better go and find them, are you coming?" He held out his hand to me.

We found them in the car park of the sports stadium, looking squashed beneath large suitcases, but they grinned when they saw us, and Lisa called, "Laura, you look like Katie Perry, you're so thin!"

I didn't know who Katie Perry was, but took it as a compliment.

We lead them back to the Villa and left them to make themselves comfortable until they joined us by the pool. The two girls, Betty and Mya came to join the other teenagers, first testing the water with their brightly coloured toe nails before jumping in with excited shrieks and peals of laughter. Jack, their father, wandered about the villa for a while, examining the landscape for the right scene to paint. Lukkas and I had several of his paintings hanging on our walls.

Gradually, the weariness disappeared from Lisa's face, but I couldn't help but notice the look of curiosity she gave me from time to time.

"Oh my God, it's so good to be here," she told us as she sat beside one of Simone's boys, curled in a chair in a white towel with a Harry Potter novel before him. "Mya and Betty quarrelled the whole time because we missed the plane, then they felt squashed in the car, and Jack was as moody as hell!"

She held her wine glass with immaculately painted red nails.

"You look great, Laura," she said, for the second time that day.

"You too, and I like the way you've done your hair." I didn't understand why the compliments made me feel uneasy, somehow. Perhaps, looking back later, knowing that Lisa and Lukkas were close friends, closer perhaps than I was to Lisa; I had half wondered whether Lukkas had said something to her about my 'madness'. She was a nurse, after all.

"Be wary of those mosquitos," she added. "Remember what happened to you on holiday last summer?"

I didn't want to be reminded of it, not in front of Lukkas. On the same night that Hannah had called us, crying about Ben's behaviour whilst we had the children in France, a horse fly, rather than a mosquito had drifted through the open bedroom window and bitten me on the eye lid. I spent the next three days looking as though I had been punched in the face.

"It was a horsefly, I think. I'm taking precautions with a super repellent this year," I assured her, and she smiled and leaned back in her chair, wrapping her arms about her legs.

Jack sat beside the other men at last, and Mya finished in the water and came to sit beside him.

"How is university, Mya?" Lukkas asked.

"Great, we've been busy opposing the raise in student fees, the government are such liars!" She said it as though she were the first person in the world to make that point, with a kind of naivety. I remembered being the same, once, quoting boyfriends as if their research was my own.

Then Isabelle, Gemma and Betty came to sit with us too, all wrapped in towels, dripping water on the patio and chairs.

I watched Betty as she smiled innocently at Lukkas. Or was it innocent? She was on the cusp of womanhood, leaving childhood behind and beginning something else. Her towel slid down her shoulder revealing a plump, Venus like shoulder and white breasts in a bikini top.

"Mum said you were planning a trip to Arezzo tomorrow, according to Simone, the shops are quite good for clothes... could we come with you when you go?" Betty asked him.

I couldn't mask the dip in my smile. Lukkas hadn't said anything to me about a trip, perhaps he hadn't had time yet, but the past, he had made plans with Lisa and the girls without talking to me. I just didn't want to do the tourist thing on our first day, much as I loved visiting old places. I had thought that he and I might lie by the pool or go for a walk on our own somewhere.

I said nothing. So long as he was away from her, the woman, whoever she was, what did I have to complain about? I told myself.

That evening, Lillianna brought in a chef to cook for us all. The dining room was separate from the house, in a large conservatory.

Below us, beyond the conservatory, the lights of the town sparkled like the jewels on a velvet, black dress.

By now, Sam and Tania had arrived with Molly and Ted and their younger daughter, Kate. We sat at a long trestle table, Lukkas sat opposite me whilst Charlotte sat to my left. I wore a little black satin dress which was old, now, and I had lost weight, so I had to pin the back of it; but Lukkas always said that it was his favourite of my clothes.

My steak was delicious, but too large for me, so I cut it and Ted gratefully accepted half. I looked up at Lukkas and leaned back in my chair with a small sigh. He was staring at Betty with that same, rapt attentiveness reserved for the girl in the restaurant, whilst she was looking back at him beneath her long fringe. We had known her since her babyhood. As with the girl in the restaurant, Betty had her black hair cut in that same bob with a swept fringe. Lukkas stopped looking at her suddenly as he caught my eye, his cheeks reddening visibly.

"Everything okay?" He asked again, just as he had in the restaurant in Nice. I hadn't wondered it before, but now I thought, is he trying to provoke me in some way, trying to make me mad so that he can prove to everyone what a freak I am?

"Yes," I lied, "but I don't want to go tomorrow, with Lisa and the girls. Can't we stay here, or go off on our own somewhere?"

His thin lips thrust forward in a look of disappointment and annoyance. "But I've already said that we'd go, and Jack is staying here to paint, so he can't accompany them."

Charlotte seemed to be listening, waiting nervously beside me. I wanted to say, do you have to be the chivalrous hero, always Lukkas? But I didn't.

"Okay, never mind. We'll spend some time together the next day," I smiled, to be rewarded by the fall of my sister's shoulders as she relaxed again.

After dinner, we all trooped into the evening air to sit by the pool. Most of the young people changed into their costumes to swim again, their laughter drowning out the sound of the crickets and the hooting of owls in the woods behind us.

I noticed that Betty had changed into a black and white swim suit, but she didn't join her sister and friends. Going straight to the chair beside Lukkas, which Neil had just vacated, she sat with a towel about her, hugging her knees.

She watched Lukkas avidly, all the time, whether he was holding the conversation or no. I tried to concentrate on the subjects that the women around me were having, but the anxiety I had felt for so long made me uncomfortable and nervous. As I watched, Lukkas drew Betty into conversation, making her giggle once more.

I got up in the end, wandering away from the group to the low stone parapet overlooking the lights of the town to light a cigarette, unseen. Jealousy was getting the better of me for sure, but there was something more than this, something Lukkas hardly seemed to understand himself, he was attracted to a certain female. The females he had shown interest in were similar in looks, as though he missed one person particularly, and would replace her, temporarily at least.

A loud giggle from Betty brought my attention back to her. She was dancing at the side of the pool to the stereo system, but the only person watching her, the only one paying her attention, was Lukkas.

I drew a sharp intake of breath. "Oh, bloody hell…" I muttered to myself as I wandered back to the party, unhappy once more and disconsolate.

I hadn't planned it, but as I walked past Betty, smiling, my sandaled foot caught her bare toe and she yelped and fell backwards, her arms flailing as she landed on the surface with a smacking sound. She disappeared beneath the lights of the water, to remerge a second later, her eyes glistening with shock, a very angry expression upon her face; the expression of an angry child; which she was.

In a split second, I was ashamed of myself. Piers and I offered her a hand at the same moment, but she accepted his alone.

"I'm so sorry, Betty. That was clumsy of me," I said. But her eyes narrowed dangerously. Catherine De Medici confronts Lucrecia Borgia.

As I turned away, there were two people staring at me whilst all others took care of Betty. Jack was one, and the muscles of his face were clenched in suspicion, the other was Mya, Betty's big sister.

Chapter Eighteen

Our Own, Private, Riot

I went to bed before everyone else, feeling heavy of heart. I had wanted to stay up with Lukkas, who liked to be the centre of attention, but suddenly a dreadful weariness took over, coupled with guilt about Betty. She was sixteen and would have no idea about anything. I remembered the hurt in Jack's eyes. Lovely, kind Jack. My life was spinning out of control.

Lukkas had always been a flirt, there were times when it hurt me and times when I brushed it off, but he had, mostly, considered my feelings. Not only did he not appear to be considering them now, but he seemed to be deliberately provoking and goading me, often.

On the day that he had thrown the case across the bed recently and bellowed at me at full voice, then left the house, slamming the door; a friend called for coffee. "I've just seen Lukkas in his car," she told me, "Singing at full voice to the radio."

So how upset had he really been, when he threw the cases across the bed, and to what extent was he acting a part to punish me?

But nothing could be the fault of a sixteen-year-old girl I had held in my arms as a baby. I had become the wicked witch to Snow white.

My dreams were fitful. I dreamt that we, our family, with the children and grandchildren, were on a boat, but Lukkas was on his own boat, his back was to us and his hands were shoved into his pockets as he sailed away from us, whilst overhead the storm clouds gathered.

I didn't hear Lukkas come to bed. When I awoke, he was lying on his side facing the wall, snoring and smelling of beer and sweat.

I pulled on some shorts and a tee shirt to wander through to the hub of the villa where Charlotte and the three girls were having breakfast. Neil was also still in bed.

Charlotte glanced up from the cooker where she was frying bacon. She started to say something when the sound of shouting drifted from Jack and Lisa's apartment.

"That's been going on for about twenty minutes," Charlotte said. "Want some bacon?"

"No thanks," I shook my head. "Can you turn that cooker off a minute, so I can have a quick word?"

She frowned at me, puzzled, but followed me through to a little side room. I told her what had happened.

"And did you? I mean, I saw her tumble into the pool. But did you do it, deliberately, I mean?" Her face was lined with suspicion.

"Possibly..." I said, ashamed. "I was annoyed, yes, and I'd had three glasses of wine."

"Laura! Really! What an idiotic thing to do," she tutted. "You are now, officially, your own worst enemy!"

Neil got up then and she went back to the bacon. I followed her, sitting limply on an arm chair. "What's all that about?" Neil asked, pointing at the ceiling then stumbling around the kitchen in search of vitamin c tablets, which Izzie found for him.

Then Lukkas stood in the doorway, all dressed, in shirt and shorts. He began to set up his lap top on the kitchen table, trying to run a business in England from Italy. "Yes, it woke me up, what is that all about?" he said, adding his voice to Neil's.

I grimaced at Charlotte and got up to wash the stack of plates in the sink and make coffee whilst Lukkas accepted a bacon sandwich. Perhaps, I thought; if I hid behind a newspaper beside the pool in a pair of dark glasses, it might all go away.

They left at about ten thirty. Lukkas asked me whether I felt sure that I didn't want to come, and I kissed his cheek and told him that I would see him later. I really didn't want to spend the first of three days in the shops admiring outfits for the girls, even before last night's incident, but I certainly didn't want to go now.

Betty, with an admirable look of unbeaten defiance, marched past me with her nose in the air, whilst Mya shook her head in my direction and Lisa threw an icy 'Goodbye, Laura," at me.

When they had gone, I went to put on my bathing costume and borrowed a sun hat from Simone, intending to keep my low profile and write a letter to Hannah in our absence. I took out my pad and pen and wrote:

"Hannah, I love you so much, I love you and your girls, even if we don't always see eye to eye about Ben.

He isn't the right partner for you and I am very much afraid that he will spoil the girls' lives, as well as yours.

I know you are angry about the information I gleaned about him, but Lisa wasn't being malicious when she gave me that information, she was concerned for us all.

Why, for example, would he need to keep weaponry in your house? Why this fear that he will be attacked at any moment? What is he mixed up with, drugs?

Your relationship with Ben has caused significant problems for the family. The fact that Dad, that we can't merely invite him to dinner is not the way this family operates. Everyone is invited to dinner as a rule, but Ben has a significant criminal past and Dad is a well-known and respected family lawyer, he can't have anything to do with Ben.

Ruby told me that Ben shouts at you and she is afraid for you and her little sister. You say he is lovely with children, but in what way is that lovely for the children?

After two years and the involvement of various societies, Ben still doesn't have any money to help you pay the bills of buy food. You say that he gives you money, but I ask you, where does that money come from?

You are beautiful and intelligent and motivated, why in God's name are you still with him…"

I paused, sighing and pulling the pen from between my teeth. You are with him because you think you love him, I thought, just as I love Lukkas. You are with him because my relationship with your father lacked balance and you need to control things, but you choose less intelligent men with difficult backgrounds, and you can't 'control them'. There again, Lukkas has always controlled things and I let him, so it's my fault. I should have left him when he pushed me over, I should have left him when he pushed you and you ran away. I should have left him long ago, but I couldn't bring myself to, and I still can't.

I carried on:

"He isn't doing your reputation any good and he is making it hard for Dad to work. The relationship is embarrassing for Dad, who you also love. I implore you to tell Ben to go.

Mum X

I folded the letter into my hand bag, meaning to post it in the town tomorrow. I glanced around at the hum of voices from those friends who had come to join me by the pool.

Tania brought me a cup of coffee and we chatted for a while about the children.

I shaded my eyes to scan the landscape for Jack and spotted him at last. He was seated on a chair on the brow of the hill, his pad attached to an easel, painting. I wanted to go and talk to him, to explain as best I could, to apologise.

I made up my mind that when Lisa returned I would try to say sorry. I shut my eyes beneath the cowboy hat and tried to concentrate upon the sound of crickets in the grass.

It was Charlotte who woke me, to ask me whether I wanted to have lunch with them. I wiped a smear of drool from the corner of my mouth, feeling sure that I didn't drool when I was a younger woman. When I followed her through to the shady kitchen, Isabelle and Becky were hunched over their lap top, engrossed in a news item from England.

"What's all that about?" I asked.

"Riots," Becky said.

"What, about the student cuts?"

Izzie shook her head, her long silver earrings flashing in the light. "No. According to the news reader, a teenage gang member was shot by the police in London last night and the gang turned on the police, it's sparked riots everywhere."

"What, in Oxford?" I asked, incredulously.

"Actually…yes, a group of youths came down from London and were joined by other teenagers quite close to home, they smashed the windows in Macdonald's."

"Oxford Macdonald's?" I asked, incredulously.

"No, the one on the roundabout near you," Becky said.

I grimaced, peering over their shoulders at the images of young people lobbing stones at shop windows in Birmingham. The last time we had riots in Oxford, they'd been in Blackbird Leys. Since then a lot of money had been put into the place, but I suspect those riots had been about more than poverty and overcrowding. They'd been about racism.

When Lukkas appeared at the door, I smiled at him. His expression was grim enough to erase the thoughts of riots in the UK. I swallowed hard, all drool drying in my mouth in an instant.

"Did you have a nice time?" I asked.

"Oh yes. We had a great time. But Lisa wants to talk to me away from the girls, something about you and Betty. Would you have any idea what that's about?"

My stomach squeezed in on itself once more, as though it would collapse.

"I'm very sorry, Lukkas. Yes, I think I might know. Do you want me to come?"

He shook his head. "No thanks," he said, coldly polite in front of Charlotte.

After he had gone, Charlotte put her arms about me.

"I won't have lunch," I said. "Not very hungry right now. I'm going back to our room to wait for him there."

She nodded. "Stay cool," she said.

I stood, stock still for a long time beneath the vaulted roof of the apartment in which we slept. Once it had been a wine cellar, it was cool and comfortable. I stood as if in a dream, musing on the people who lived here hundreds of years ago, other people's lives.

I crossed the room to the open casement and breathed in the warm air, trying to be still, trying to decelerate the beating of my heart. Then I stood on tip toe to peer out of the windows at the olive grove and the town at the foot of the hill. I tried not to think of Lukkas, not to think about what Lisa might say, not to think of any of it.

I heard Simone's voice and Piers' car, pulling onto the gravel outside. Normal sounds, freeze framed in a time capsule, the calm before the storm.

I went for a shower, washed myself, then heard Lukkas' sandals slap, slapping on the tiled floor and doubled up with the knot inside my stomach, feeling sick, a child's reaction to anger. The sound that his sandals made was pure fury.

Just before he reached the bathroom door, I lifted the brush and began to brush my hair, trying to 'be normal', to compose myself anew. Tying a towel around me, I walked to the bedroom to meet him.

His face was puce with rage, like thunder before a storm.

"What the hell have you done?" he hissed. As I faced him I was afraid, he looked as though he would choke the life out of me.

I drew in a long breath, pulling my shoulders back, preparing for fight, not flight.

"It's partly your fault Lukkas. You were encouraging her and she's sixteen!" I hissed.

He flinched at that and his face twisted into something malicious and evil, something I scarcely knew of him. "You twisted, mad woman; she's my goddaughter!"

"And the woman in the restaurant, was she your goddaughter, and the other women you have humiliated me with? Humiliated me whilst you say that you love me? Start respecting me, Lukkas, start respecting the woman you said you needed and couldn't get on with your job without!" My voice had risen to a shout of accusation and disgust. "There are barriers, you might have shown Betty a more responsible barrier, you might have made something clear to those other women, other than 'let's play silly games whilst my wife isn't looking.' Who do you think you are, what have you become?"

I pushed past him to the wardrobe, searching for something to wear, anything.

"That's it Laura, you are talking rubbish again…"

But this time, I didn't wait to listen, my words tumbled one over the other like irresponsible bullets. "You are becoming a fucking bastard, Lukkas, how could you? After thirty years of marriage, how could you keep hurting me like it, how could you tell people I need mental health treatment just because you've grown so big for your boots, because your male menopause is out of control! Someone has been telling you that you are so God damned wonderful you can do what you like!"

"Ah," his expression was smooth for a moment. "There we have it, don't we? This non -existent woman I'm supposed to be having an affair with…"

"I'm sick of it, sick of being taunted by you. You are a fucking bastard, fuck off then. I've stuck with it all these years and if I'm not good enough now you can just fuck off!"

I pulled on a pair of trousers and a top. I had to get away, get out of this room, into air, into space, get away from this person who abused my love. "I've done everything I can, for everyone, day in, day out and you treat me as you do?"

But he stood, solid in the doorway to bar my exit.

"Move!" I yelled, no longer caring who heard me, feeling claustrophobic.

"You are quite; quite mad, aren't you?" he taunted now; a wide, sadistic smile across his face.

I pushed myself beneath his arm and he held me fast to stop me.

"Do you know what you've done? We've had these friends for years!" he growled.

"These friends? These friends that recently, you never want to see, these friends you are cheating on, as well as me? Move, Lukkas, get out of my way, I want to leave…" I pushed with all my might against his chest, desperate to go through the door.

In an instant, he raised a shaking fist as he had never done before, he thrust it right in front of my face, his own face twisted into malice. I felt afraid, but in a second that fear dissipated, replaced by my own sense of humour, he became a caricature of Bella Lugosi.

"Move!" I yelled, forcefully, and when he did not I turned and grabbed his bag filled with work. I ran to the open window in my fury, tipping the contents onto the gravel outside in one, senseless but purifying act of vandalism.

"Fuck off Lukkas, I'm sick of your male menopause! You're the one who needs the doctor, not me!"

Furious now, he leapt towards me, grabbing my arm in a tight grip. I shook myself, tried to wrench away, but he wouldn't let go until at last our wrestling match ended beside the bedside table. I grabbed the mosquito repellent and squirted it straight into his eye until he leapt backwards in pain.

I fell backwards onto the bed then, trembling and panting like an animal, unable to feel anything, silently watching him drag his clothes from the closet to push them into a bag.

He stomped from the room and I listened as he retrieved the things I had thrown out of the window.

He wouldn't take the car, I felt sure; he would travel back to Nice by train.

I lay there for ten minutes, doing nothing, wondering what to tell our friends, but for the first time I was resolved that he would go. And then there was a knock at the door.

It was Charlotte, thank God. I couldn't have borne seeing anyone else right then. She put her arms about me and I sobbed into her tee shirt, until it was soaked with my tears.

"I told him to fuck off!" I wailed, pulling away to blow my nose. "He's gone, Charlotte."

She smiled at me. "I think that would have been a better idea. But no, he's talking to Neil. The riots have grown worse and he's deciding what to do."

She took my arm in her hands. "You've got large, purple bruises spreading on your arm, look…"

I shrugged. They didn't seem to matter. "I'll wear long sleeves to hide it," I said.

He hadn't gone. Weariness and relief spread through me in equal measure. I got up and went into the bathroom to splash my face.

"Why don't you sleep for a bit?" Charlotte suggested.

I gazed at my red eyes in the bathroom mirror and slid drops into them. "I'm okay, really," I said.

Charlotte shook her head at me as she examined the bruises. "Far better if he did go..." she said.

In the kitchen, Lukkas was hunched over his mobile phone. His bag of clothes had been thrown onto the settee. His face was impassive, betraying nothing. No one would have known what had just happened.

"No, don't take the girls with you," he was saying. "Get someone to look after them, in case things turn really nasty... okay, you'll need a team of people, ask Josh and Joe for a start and anyone else you can get. I'll call you back when I've found out what the police are advising."

He was speaking to Hannah. He averted his eyes from mine and spoke to Charlotte.

"The riots have spread to Oxford, there are groups and gangs threatening to smash shop windows, they've broken a window along the road from Hannah's shop and she sounds understandably nervous. I think she will have to move the stock somewhere else." He rubbed his forehead in thought.

"Tell her it'll have to be taken to our house," I suggested. As I heard myself speaking, I thought, this is surreal. What just happened to us?

"Not a bad idea," Lukkas agreed. "None of the retail outlets will be insured against riots."

He wandered outside into the garden, holding the phone to his ear. I made coffee, for him, for me.

Charlotte smiled, "Coming for a swim with me?" she asked.

I nodded, "In a while, I'll just see what happens," I said.

"You need a break from him…" she mouthed.

As Lukkas paced about beneath the trees, speaking to the policeman, I placed the coffee in his hand.

He looked up as I walked away.

"Laura," he called, "You are wrong about a lot of things."

It felt reassuring again, just to hear his voice, but I knew our own riot would take longer to resolve.

It was as though nothing had happened. No fight with Lukkas, no jealousy, no Betty. It was as if we had started a courtship all over again.

During the day Lukkas took my hand frequently. We were quiet, we were together. We visited Arezzo alone and the surrounding towns also. Jack and Lisa were generous in their forgiveness, at first Betty was less so and I understood it, I deserved her silences. Mya also took a little time to forgive me, until one day we found ourselves alone in the kitchen and a conversation started between us. "Betty isn't as confident as people think," she told me, and I felt sorry for all of it.

Looking back, it might have changed everything if Lukkas had left on the train, but he didn't, and now I am glad of it, because I have the memory of peace, of just being together and loving him, like the feeling of September. I didn't want to leave him and then, I don't think he was sure that he wanted to leave me, or perhaps Lukkas was a coward underneath, but then, I may be called that too. Whatever happened to us at that time, even if he was biding his time, it felt like improvement.

At the end of our stay in Italy, we drove back to Nice to join my parents and Joe and his girlfriend and Hannah and the girls. We had the best time there, at the beach, at the castle ruins, picnicking on the hilltop which overlooked the vast harbour and taking the girls on the little white tourist train. Ruby now leapt fearlessly from the white, iron jetty into the sea and Lilly grew in confidence, doggy paddling without her arm bands.

I tried to change my outlook, when Lukkas stared at other women, mostly blondes now that I had accused him of preferring brunettes, I thought, "But he sleeps with me."

When the time came for Charlotte and Neil, the three girls and our parents to go home, I felt the usual sadness at the end of a holiday but far more relaxed than I had been for a long while. Lukkas and I were left to care for the girls in Hannah's absence, as she had no one else to run the shop, (now with its stock safely returned).

I admit to feeling a little embarrassed before Lukkas in the role of Nanna as I had never done before. It was hard to act out that role with the one I now believed, to keep him with me, I should adopt. All the while too, I imagined that he yearned for another life, a life of casinos and bars, the Havana club and the Moscow bar, watching him as he strode out into the sunshine, tall, handsome, eye catching in a way that I could never be, now.

Somewhere, perhaps, I wondered, now that he paid attention to tall, blonde, Russian girls, is a girl who accompanies Lukkas to London Hotels, to Law dinners. A girl half my age and without dependent grandchildren.

I tried and succeeded in pushing away these thoughts by throwing myself into play with the girls, covering myself and the marble floor in paint and glue, reading with them, wrestling them down to smear them with sun cream, or being Nanny dolphin in the sea.

When Lukkas played in the sea with them, I noticed that he drew a lot more attention from females than I did.

His relationship with the children often amused me. He wasn't so keen on the paint and glue bit, he enjoyed telling them stories, but his favourite activity was to walk the two little girls through the streets of Nice in their pretty floral sun dresses, except when they refused to walk another step, of course. He was irritated when Ruby declared she wanted margarita pizza in a restaurant and then wouldn't eat any of it; in fact, he didn't believe in negotiation with under sixes at all and was so embarrassed when Ruby called him an idiot in front of a German woman and had to be lifted off the beach one day, that he locked her in the far bedroom. I suppose it was mostly interesting because dealing with our grandchildren was a thing I did every day, sometimes in the face of Lukkas' criticism, but I couldn't see how he did them any differently.

We made love every day. Sadly, it could hardly have been called spontaneous as we had to push a wardrobe against the door whilst the girls watched cartoons. It made me a little fearful, that Lukkas might be having spontaneous sex elsewhere, that this simply wasn't good enough. But it felt too as though we had found each other once again and Lukkas became playful, smacking my bottom and tweaking my breasts as he used to.

I was calm and happy until the evening before our return.

I could not bear to lose him again, to the long Autumn evenings, to London and Milton Keynes and perhaps to another woman. I couldn't bear to go back, I thought, as we did the last-minute tidying jobs and drew the white curtains against the sea, following the excited chatter of the girls into the lift.

CHAPTER NINETEEN

Mr Toad

We had been home for about a week when Lukkas announced that he wanted to change his car. He said he thought his car reflected a staid and boring personality, although it was only a year old.

He asked me to go with him, to test drive a new car. It would be 'our car', Lukkas said, although we both knew this was nonsense.

Lilly had to come with me. As we waited at the garage, Lilly jumping up and down beside me at the prospect of a ride in a car without a roof, I looked at my reflection in the garage window and was pleased. I was skinny now, and the new jeans suited me.

Lilly and I pulled faces at one another as she jigged about on the forecourt and as Lukkas drew up outside, I felt excited too.

Lilly ran forward to clasp Lukkas' hand and we were met by Geoffrey, the large, jovial sales rep who would accompany us. We were taken to a green, BMW convertible. Even I, a person who doesn't know one make of car from another could see that so far as cars went, it was beautiful.

Lilly sat in the back beside me, safely bound in the child seat, although she weighs no more than a feather and I was a little afraid the wind would pick her up and carry her away over the hedges. Lukkas drove us to Islip village whilst Lilly shouted and giggled over the engine as though she were on a fairground ride.

For the next few days I watched Lukkas leave the house for the pool in his new toy and thought of a handsome Mr Toad whizzing through the countryside, blowing his horn at the other drivers.

"It's the male menopause," his mother warned me. "No doubt he wants to reassure himself that he's still sexy."

The evenings were not too dark yet, not too cold; and the girls and I went blackberrying in Shotover Forest. Lukkas, in the meanwhile, went to work every day, smelling deliciously of aftershave. I also noticed how regularly be bought new underpants and shirts now, where once he wouldn't have bothered, even new socks on a weekly basis. I put this down to the male menopause too.

One evening, when he arrived home much later than usual having been on a conference in Birmingham, I was in our bedroom putting the washing away when I heard the sweep of his car on the road and looked out of the window. I watched as he alighted from the car, taking his work bag and resting it upon the boot. He put a hand in his pocket, I thought for a key, but instead he drew out a tissue. He didn't blow his nose; but lifted the thing delicately to his nostrils as though it were a kind of heavenly scent and he smelled it.

He smelled it with a look of intense happiness, as though it were a trophy to be treasured for ever.

I bit my lip, drawing back from the curtain. But when he came upstairs as he always did, I could not kiss him, could not look at him. He put a hand on my shoulder and I pulled away a little from his touch.

"What's the matter with you?" he asked. I shook my head.

Lukkas shrugged then, grunted softly. He hung his coat on the trouser press and went into the bathroom.

Silently, I slid my hand into his coat pocket and pulled out the tissue. I left the bedroom for the landing and leaning against the wall, opened the tissue onto my hand.

The mark of her lips was as clear as the mark on the shirt. Pink lipstick, fuchsia pink, and there too, running across the tissue, was a long, ash blonde hair. I held it to the light, not Ruby's, or Lilly's or Hannah's, my hair was dark, our daughters too.

Perhaps if we did more together… It was a long shot perhaps, but either I would keep trying, or give up completely. I shoved the tissue into my pocket. When he emerged from the bathroom, I said, "Tom and Sarah do Salsa. Could we do that? They have classes in Oxford, would you come with me?"

His lips twitched as though he wanted to laugh. "Salsa?" he mocked. "I don't see why not…"

I smiled, pleased; suddenly almost forgetting the tissue with a pink lipstick smear. "But I was forgetting your back, will it be too much, d'you think?"

Lukkas shrugged. "It'll probably be alright, if not, I'll have to stop. 'Tisn't so much my back, but the time factor." He grunted like the elephant Colonel in Jungle Book, an, 'I'm a busy man,' noise that he sometimes used to dismiss me. "Get the dates and times and maybe we could do a couple of sessions."

The classes were held in a hall in North Oxford. Lukkas was late for the first session, but I didn't really mind that, or that our progress was rather slow. It was just nice to have Lukkas to myself, to do something that was fun and that I could share with him. In fact, I found that I was much better at it than I believed I would be. I had never been confident about formal dancing as Lukkas was, but this was different, a dance that you could feel as you moved, and I didn't mind that we had to change partners either; although it was very noticeable how much other women of all ages loved being his partner.

How gallant he was, how they fiddled with their hair and giggled and blushed.

On the third Tuesday, an hour before the Salsa lesson, Lukkas sent a text.

"Sorry. Can't make it. Power cut, all the power has gone in the office. I'll have to wait here until it comes back on."

I frowned at the text. A power-cut? I'd never heard of such a thing in Oxford, sometimes in winter in the villages around, but this was early Autumn. This was Oxford, not Havana. I tried to call him, but his phone went to voice mail.

When Josh returned, I said, "That must have made life difficult."

He stared blankly at me. "What must?"

"The power cut," I said. "Dad said you had a power cut in the office."

He frowned, shook his head. The thing about Josh is that he is disarmingly honest, he finds it impossible to lie, even when it might be the kinder thing to do.

"I've been in the office since mid-day, in the empty board room," he said. "My course in High Wycombe was cancelled, so I had a chance to catch up on all of the work I needed to finish before Dad gives me a whole load more. I was there till after the people on reception had gone and I think Heather saw me before she left. I was using my lap top the whole time, so I know there wasn't a power cut."

I bit my lip, angry then. Lukkas was mocking me. "Who was in the office, Josh?"

"Just Josh'n Holly, I think, I heard Tom go, anyway." He lost interest then, lifting the lid of the chicken casserole to dunk a piece of bread in the sauce.

I wandered to our bedroom, opening the wardrobe door to run a hand thoughtfully down the arm of one of the jackets. Then I took my own perfume from the bedside table. Aiming the bottle at the suits, I sprayed each of them with the scent, dousing them until I had used half of the remaining liquid in the bottle. I smiled with satisfaction and closed the wardrobe door.

CHAPTER TWENTY

The Witch Doll

Two weeks after buying the car, Lukkas packed his bag to go to Lille with some old male friends for a birthday celebration. True, he had not long returned from Nice, but again, he seemed almost reluctant to go, this time. In previous years he would have jumped at the chance.

He left the house at five in the morning, kissing me goodbye.

I had wondered, aching inside with the thought so that I scarcely slept at night, about the tissue; eventually flushing it in the toilet where it belonged. I wondered too, why after all this time, Lukkas insisted that I must not swim with him in the morning. He said it was a time when he could think, and yet I didn't speak to him, doing twenty or thirty lengths before going to the children to get them ready for school.

I wondered whether his eagerness to leave me was because he would meet someone else.

On the morning Lukkas left, I went to the health club again, taking my costume.

There were only five or six swimmers beside myself, most of them in their sixties, grey haired lawyers and bankers, rather plump, certainly none I could see that Lukkas would get excited about.

I relaxed and entered the rather chilly water to do my lengths.

I had done five or six when she walked through the swinging doors from the ladies' changing room.

She was stunningly beautiful in a youthful, pixie like way. Ash blonde hair tied up in a ponytail. What had Lukkas said to me recently after we made love? "Why don't you tie your hair up." He had never suggested that before in all these years.

The girl was in her twenties, I think. Skinny, white limbed, her gold and black bikini clinging to the meatless bones of her body. She couldn't have been much older than Hannah.

In an instant, I knew why Lukkas came so early, why he didn't want me with him. To give credence to this, the girls behaviour was puzzling.

As I swam, watching her, she glanced up and down the pool as though searching for someone. After this she went to the sauna, pulling open the door. It was empty. She went to the jacuzzi, nodding her hello to an elderly gentleman; but then she turned about, with a look of petulance on her small face, heading straight back to the changing room.

Clearly, she had expected to see someone there. How odd, to take all that time to change into such a lovely costume but not to swim.

I decided to finish my lengths, climbing out of the pool, and followed her into the changing room. As I walked behind the slight body I saw a bruise on her calf and wondered. Lukkas had given me a bruise such as that, long, long ago.

I have never had the leisure time that the young woman had to get dressed. Most of my life, getting dressed after a swim has been a matter of dealing with noisy children who drop their dry clothes onto wet floors.

She took over an hour to prepare herself for the day; drying her hair, making her face up as though she were creating a masterpiece. I pretended to text someone as I half watched in fascination.

Then, suddenly, she was dressed and ready to leave. She sent a text herself, on a small white phone, picked up her bag and walked out of the room. I followed her. I don't know what I was thinking, what I thought I was going to do. She had ash blonde hair, she was pretty; that's all I had, other than that I felt anger at Lukkas for wanting to be here with her, without me.

I watched from my car as she unlocked the new bicycle with the wicker basket.

And then she turned. That same, slightly petulant expression. She knew what I was doing and very possibly, as Lukkas had borrowed my car from time to time, she knew who I was.

I saw a small smile on her face, half self-satisfaction, half grimace. She threw her leg over the bicycle and started through the lane which lead to the Woodstock road whilst I drove the car parallel with it, in the bus lane, she paused, looking for me.

I hesitated. I wanted to see where she went to, but I would have to manoeuvre along a one-way road. Not a very clever idea.

In the end, I drove around the school near bye and pulled into the road I assumed she had entered and there she was, at the end of the street, cycling at speed towards the smaller houses at the end of the terrace. I followed her progress then parked at the corner opposite the wine bar, just in time to see her locking her bicycle up. From the gritty expression on her face, she believed she'd shaken me off. When I emerged from the overhanging rose bushes, her eyes widened with surprise.

"Hello!" I greeted her, with cheery normality. "Sorry, I didn't mean to freak you out, I've a feeling that I know you from somewhere."

I smiled. She smiled too, but it was very forced.

"Um, have we? I'm sorry, I really don't remember you…" She had a slight, Canadian accent. At least she hadn't screamed, I thought.

"Perhaps I've met you in company with my husband?" I ventured. "Lukkas, he's a lawyer."

Her eyelashes lifted, just slightly, as she put her head on one side. Her cheeks were rosy with cycling, but they had flushed even more as I said his name.

"Ah, yes; I know who you mean, yes, I've chatted with him."

I nodded with an encouraging smile which didn't explain why I had made such effort to track her down. "And your name is?"

"Morgan, Morgan Windward," she said.

"Laura," I volunteered, offering my hand. She was almost hopping from one foot to another, desperate to lose me.

"Well, nice to meet you. I'm sure I'll see you again at the pool." I smiled my most convincing smile and threw her a little wave of the hand.

I tried to resist it but couldn't.

I sent Lukkas a text. "Hope you're having a good time. I met Morgan this morning, when I went for a swim."

The text came back promptly. "Yes thanks. Never heard of her."

To this day, I regret the primeval superstition that took hold of me. Perhaps it was the influence of my grandma, whose beliefs hovered between the Christian and the Pagan. A woman who believed you should never turn a visiting gypsy away without crossing her palm and who threw lavish amounts of salt over her shoulder to cancel out bad luck. I know I will never do such a thing again, it's like wishing death upon someone, I didn't even understand who I was attempting to murder.

At first, I found myself wandering about the dining room, my mind upon Lukkas' denial as I retrieved various pens, crayons and toys scattered about by Ruby and Lilly. I rarely throw toys out unless they are in a damaged state, preferring to wash them. I have a doll with a squashed face who is several years older than I am, several action men who now wear dresses, ancient cars, quite a lot of building bricks. This morning, the Barbie dolls caught my attention. One by one, I picked them up, dropping them into the toy box. I suppose I was still thinking about Morgan.

Sindy is now in her forties. One hand has been chewed by a dog, her hair is a frizzy mess, but I always liked her because her body is less improbably sexy than the Barbie sisters. Then, my eyes light upon one of the oldest Barbies, old, but curvaceous still. She is wearing a Hawaiian skirt and a bikini-top, her hair is still long and glossy. She only has one leg, but I have no compassion. This Barbie doesn't represent anyone, in my currently warped imagination, she might be any woman.

In an act of sheer, sadistic, childish vandalism, I snap off her remaining leg and throw it into the kitchen bin.

Whistling to the dogs, I grab my coat from the hallway, shoving the legless, loveless Barbie into my pocket. I stride out along the garden path with purpose. Through the gate and beneath the branches of trees that are wet with newly fallen rain. I head for the well-trodden pathway leading to the muddy stream, where I have played poo sticks with two generations of children. Today, my journey has a far more sinister purpose, I am getting rid of a body.

I trample through the undergrowth of the pheasant copse, followed by the two excited dogs who know this isn't a place they are permitted to enter off lead. My coat snags on the broken barbed wire fence and I snatch it away impatiently. Then I scramble down the bank to the ancient stream, gurgling at the bottom.

Here, there would be no one to bother me, none to witness my ritual. I take despised Barbie from my pocket, flinging her in a well-practiced, over arm bowl with all my angry energy behind it so that she is propelled through the air to land in the undergrowth on the other side of the stream. A kind of madness, I suppose, but I feel the same release as a boxer might, hitting a punch bag.

Jack, who will chase anything from sticks to motorbikes, hurtles after the toy with his tongue hanging out. I yell at him to come back in my deepest dog trainer voice. I hadn't considered Jack's reaction in all of this.

It was then that I saw him, camouflaged by a long green coat as he stood against an ivy clad tree. I didn't know the man, had never been close enough to acknowledge him, but I'd seen him about the fields. Once, fixing the broken fence to the woodland copse. On other occasions he had lopped down some of the lower branches after a heavy wind. I had supposed he was a game keeper. I froze in some surprise.

He was shorter than Lukkas, with grey stubble on his chin and an outback style, broad brimmed hat on his head which dripped rain.

"Hello," he smiled. "Not very safe for walkers down here, you know."

I hoped, beyond hope, that he hadn't noticed what I had hurled into the bushes. If he had, he was polite enough to skip over it. Lyra was sniffing his coat and wagging her tail, a good sign, at least he wasn't a rapist.

I sniffed and returned the smile. "Oh? It isn't shooting season is it? I come down here quite often."

He rubbed the stubble on his chin with a rough hand and regarded me. "You've not seen the signs that say 'no trespassers' then? I'm letting you know for your own good. The farmer who rents this land from the University often comes here and carries a gun, too. He's been known to set wire snares before. If your dog got caught in one of them, the wire would tighten and strangle him."

I reached for Lyra's collar, attaching her lead. "Surely that's illegal?" I said, a little indignantly.

"It depends upon the kind of snare, either way they're pretty nasty." He shrugged his shoulders. I had been warned. "I don't have any say in what the farmer does. I work for Stanton College who own most of the land in this part of Oxfordshire."

He had green eyes, like Lukkas, but more of a hazel-green in colour, I noticed.

Jack appeared then, his tail wagging gleefully, his hair smeared with mud as he bounded through the undergrowth and dropped his trophy at my feet.

I felt my cheeks burn cherry red as I tried not to look at the distorted torso of the doll at my feet. The gamekeeper or forestry man, or whatever he was put his head upon one side to scrutinise the thing. He grinned. His face lit up with a smile which I might have thought attractive if I hadn't been riddled with embarrassment.

"Never seen anything like that down here before," he mused. "Sticks, balls, dog chews... but never dolls."

All the while, Jack lay before it, panting; desperately anticipating my every movement, waiting for the second throw.

"Jack has some unusual toys," I smiled. I picked up the muddy doll, turning my back on the dog as he leapt at me. "Thanks for the advice."

I tried to smile as I left him there, aware of the broad smile on his own face as I scrambled to the top of the woodland bank. When I reached it, I looked back; briefly. He was still there, watching my progress.

When I reached the bottom of the field I held Jack tightly by the collar whilst throwing Barbie to the depths of the muddy stream, where she belonged.

CHAPTER TWENTY-ONE

Manacles

I imagined myself as the second or third wife. Or in a Bourka. Turning a blind eye and being 'the better woman' was harder than anything I had ever attempted.

During September, he seemed happy, sometimes jovial. But whilst I troubled myself with the family and tried to match his moods, I did not feel peaceful beneath it all. What I felt, when he cancelled dates at the last minute, or changed them, and when I found other, lipstick smeared trophies, was that our life was being dictated by another woman; a woman with less than I had to lose. A lonely person, perhaps, or an ambitious one.

The smell of a heady, unfamiliar perfume was the most haunting thing of all. Sometimes it was so strong it felt as though his clothes had been sprayed with the stuff at close range in retaliation for my 'perfume attack.' So, I found myself desperately examining his clothes before I washed them, in the manner of a forensic scientist.

Accordingly, one evening I lifted a pair of pants from the wash basket. Since the incident of the Jingly balls, Lukkas had not made love to me. Now, in the confines of the room, I could smell sex on them and I hated her afresh, whoever she was; more than I had ever hated anyone. I stared down at the underwear. it wasn't my imagination, I could see faint white stains splashed upon them. This feeling damaged me, not just emotionally but zapping my internal organs with radioactive intensity that burned.

No one would believe this, not our friends, not his colleagues. Surely, he would never be as careless as this. To treat me in this way was to view me as a housekeeper, not a wife.

As my face twisted into bitterness, I dropped the pants into the basket. Several small bits of twig and pine needle went after them.

"In a wood, for God's sake?"

"What are you doing now?" He had opened the door softly, had been watching me. I jumped, guiltily, turning to him. No, I wouldn't apologise, I wouldn't be treated like this anymore.

"For longer than four weeks, since we returned from our holiday, I've been finding things that don't belong in this house. Blue and gold glitter on your coat, long hairs, broken cuff buttons, twigs in your underpants, sequins in your new car..."

His face reddened, but he didn't explode with anger, shout as the tension inside me told me that he would. After a moment where he stared at me, he laughed. A low, dangerous, humourless laugh.

"The old affair thing again?" He closed the bedroom door behind him and crossed the room, coming softly towards me in a way that made me flinch.

"Do you know how lucky you are, Laura? Other women have to work, pay the mortgage, you stay at home and look after your grandchildren..."

I felt anger surpassing every other emotion. "I know what it is to work, Lukkas, to work and look after a family. I did it for over twenty-years whilst you built a career, remember? You were the one who suggested I stop work if I recall. What exactly are you saying now? That I should turn a blind eye to your cheating on me because I'm a very lucky woman?"

For better or worse, the argument that was brewing had to stop, because Hannah's car arrived outside.

"I'm really worried about you. You are delusional, obsessive, now you appear to be sniffing my underpants. From now on, I'll do my own washing and you need to see a doctor."

I don't know what Hannah heard, but I think she heard this. She opened the door and glared at me, her face as stony as her fathers. She had enough problems with Ben, and if her father was bonking other women, she would never want to face up to that truth.

"Not again? Drop it Mum, he's right, you're behaving like a mad woman, Dad isn't having an affair. He's told me all about your behaviour and I think he is right, there's something wrong with you, you should see a doctor, I'll come with you, if you like."

I blew out a long sigh, I wanted to argue, to ask why he had woodland in his pants if that was the case, but Ruby was standing behind her.

Lukkas shook his head dramatically, dismissing me, and left the room. I stood with the door closed and listened as they talked about me on the landing.

After that I became more afraid. Afraid of the doctor, afraid that Hannah would stop me from seeing the children, afraid of losing Lukkas for good.

Lukkas came home from work late on many occasions and when he was at home, I was torn between pleading with him and snapping back. He asked for an old blanket to cover his car when he stayed away from home on court cases and I laughed without humour.

"It's for the soft top when it gets frosty!" he barked.

"Why can't you just stick it in the hotel garage?" I asked, turning my back on him.

He asked whether the old fan heater was in the garage because the office was chilly in the mornings and I shook my head derisively. I had never been asked for these things before.

"What's the matter with you?" He snapped, one day.

"Nothing…" I muttered, with the latest tissue in my pocket, smeared with burgundy lipstick this time.

But towards the end of September, finding a cuff button broken clean in half for the third time that month, smashed and broken, not misplaced, when Lukkas never did practical jobs and having no idea why, I sent him a text at work.

"Why are your cuff buttons broken again?" It was better to send a text, I never knew what our children would hear if he was at home, better by far to avoid the shouting.

A minute later, he sent the reply. "They break in the washing machine."

My thumb worked angrily on the phone keys. "Then why don't Josh's cuff button's break? They are all washed in the same machine."

My life was being reduced to this, I thought; by some, selfish, greedy woman.

On that, morning, when I took the girls to school, I felt as though my heart would break. In the school playground, I could find no conversation and walked away from the chattering groups, smiling, but never joining in.

Valeria, my Russian friend, elegant mother of two, walked towards me.

"What's the matter with you today?" she asked. "You look so sad and tired."

Just those words of sympathy were enough to make my chin wobble uncontrollably. I looked down, clamping my teeth on my lower lip. I was the class representative for heaven's sake, I couldn't have people witness my breakdown.

Valeria put her hand on my shoulder. "Come to my house," she said, "I do some Reiki on you, I not charge you, or just talk if you like…"

And I followed her, mindlessly. I had no idea what Reiki was, I just needed a friend to talk to.

Valeria's hall way was sweetly scented and scrupulously clean, decorated with Russian Icons in bright colours and gilt, mostly of the Madonna and child. I took off my shoes and went inside, through to the living room.

"Want a coffee before we start?" she asked. I smiled and shook my head, I was coping, just about managing to keep my emotions in check.

"Come on then." She led me upstairs, past the bedrooms and to the very top room in the house to her own bedroom, a large room, feminine in every way. It had a large double bed and smelled pleasantly of Jasmine. Valeria took a box of matches from the dresser and lit some candles.

At the foot of her own bed was a high, single bed, the kind that you find in a hospital or physiotherapists. It had a bolster pillow and a single blanket over it.

"Just climb up and lie down," she said. The simple invitation was enough to provoke hot tears of grief, they coursed down my cheeks.

"Oh, Valeria... I don't know what to do anymore, Lukkas loves someone else, I'm sure of it, at least he is seeing somebody else."

All the pent-up anger and fear burst to the surface like pus, lanced from a boil. She had asked me nothing and before her, the only person I had spoken to was Charlotte. But even with Charlotte, there had been barriers. Lukkas was her family too, and I wanted her to love him still. In between sobs and blowing my nose on the tissues Valeria offered me, I began to tell her the chronology of it all until I couldn't speak any more and when my ranting had ceased I begged her. "You can't tell anyone Valeria, you mustn't. I've worked so hard to build his reputation, I don't want anyone to know these things!"

"Listen to me. Everything you say to me is confidential, I promise you, Laura. Nothing will leave my head. Now, you will be surprised at something..."

I sniffed and waited.

"Do you not know that Alexie and I divorced two weeks ago?"

I stared blankly at her. What was she talking about? They had dinner with us only last year, she had the cleverest children in the school, her house, her life was perfect. They were the happiest and most sociable couple in the street.

"He lied to me, Laura, over a long period of time. He had a mistress in Russia and I had no idea about it, his business was there, and I trusted him. But then, he became... what is your English word? Sloppy, that's it, sloppy about it. I too found things on his shirts, and in his suitcase when he came home. It made me feel ill. Then, the guilt first, buying me things, taking me to dinner, spoiling me. Only she grew too strong for him, too strong for me. One moment he would snuggle up to me in bed at night, the next he would be rude, sarcastic. He behaved as a cockerel with two hens. I hated it, hated being treated like this. I found out her name, she was a worker in his firm and within a few months, he had made her a managing director."

My mouth hung open in total surprise. I could not fathom it. I told her how sorry I was.

"It doesn't matter. You think you won't survive, and it's hard, I can't lie to you. Now the children blame me. I lose my house I love so much, but it gets better with time. You know what I did in the end, to get proof?"

I shook my head.

"I got my mother and my sister to follow him for me, in Russia. I could not go, I had to stay here with the children, I had no one to stay with them and they had to go to school. It took a long time, but they caught up with him. He stays with her in a hotel and then my sister got her number." She pursed her lips, remembering. "Then I rang her and put this affair to her and you know what she said? She said, 'Alexie loves me, not you.'"

"Oh God, Valeria, I am so, so sorry, to burden you now when you've been through so much." I put my hand to her cheek.

"No matter, I am well, I am strong again. I put the affair to Alexie and he confessed to me, he broke down in tears like a little boy with his hand caught in a cookie jar and like you, although we weren't married as long, I thought I would die if I lost him but no, you don't die and all you need is a little strength and family love. Like me, you have love. Leave him, Laura. Don't let him treat you like this. He is a fool."

"He says I'm mad, Valeria. I think he's trying to persuade the children of it." My voice was weak with weariness.

She tutted. "Don't let him do that to you. However difficult it is, you can't stay with him if he's doing that. You aren't mad, there will be enough people to defend you."

"But, I don't have any real evidence that he is, yet…"

"It sounds as though he is," she shrugged. "All of your experiences were mine. Do you know what I would do if I had the money?"

"What?"

"If you really want evidence, to prove to your children that you aren't mad, for one thing, pay a Private Detective."

I stared at her long and hard, thinking about this. As much as I knew what I had found was real, I dreaded being wrong about him, "His shirt and jacket cuff buttons keep breaking, snapping in two!" I said.

She placed her arms above her head in a star shape and wriggled. "I don't know the English word for it," she said solemnly.

"Manacles," I groaned, in a voice of dread.

CHAPTER TWENTY-TWO

An Abuse of Civil Liberty

The Reiki was calming. I felt relaxed, but strangely energised by it. When she explained that the point of Reiki was to release bad energy, I admit to being sceptical, but that's what it did. She passed her hands over my fully clothed body, never actually touching me, but the sensation of intense heat from her hands was very real.

I felt sleepy with emotional tiredness and my confession to Valeria, on her advice, I went home for a nap before collecting Lilly.

Later, much later, I waited for Lukkas to come home with the unwanted image of him in manacles in my head, like a scene from Dracula, with Lukkas as Jonathan Harker. Would there have been one voluptuous vampire or two, I wondered?

I wasn't strong, like Charlotte, like Valeria; I was afraid. I had started catastrophising everything. I loved Lukkas, although I resented his behaviour.

On the following day, I took Joe to Oxford with me, with Valeria's advice in my head. I had applied for Lukkas' business and Hannah's shop, as well as other interested retail outlets to advertise, using a redundant bill board in the centre of the City. Now, after a meeting at the Town Hall, we had permission, but Joe was the strongest person I know, the only one with the strength to lift the board from its glass case.

I couldn't afford a Private Detective and anyway, I felt sure that Lukkas might have used some of them through his firm.

Joe trundled ten paces behind me, afraid of being seen with his mother by one of his friends.

"I'm hungry," he called to me.

"Okay, let's get this done and you can get something to eat."

"This isn't going to take for ever, is it? I'm recording some stuff this afternoon."

Tired of calling back over my shoulder, I dropped my pace, forcing him to walk with me.

"No. It won't take too long."

We were passing the Randolph Hotel, where Lukkas stayed the night before our wedding so many years ago.

"Why do you and Dad keep arguing?" Joe asked suddenly.

"Arguing, are we?" I asked lightly.

"Yes, you are," he scoffed. "You didn't use to argue, not like you do now. Hannah says you think he's having an affair. It's crazy, Mum. He'd never do that to you."

It sounded so simple. "Really, what else does Hannah say?" I asked.

"That she agrees with Dad, you've got something wrong with your mind." Joe chuckled, but it was a slightly nervous laugh. I wondered how scary it was to be young like Joseph and imagine that your mother was suddenly mental.

I stopped, standing in-the-midst of a group of Japanese tourists to stare at him.

"I'm not mad, not crazy, Joe, whatever they say. There's nothing wrong with my mind, honestly. Please stop worrying…"

He frowned at me, his head on one side in a mannerism of Lukkas'. "Then why are you going through his underpants?" He asked.

"I'm not," I lied.

"You are, Mum." He smiled at me fondly, shaking his head.

"It's complex, Joe." I could think of nothing better to say. Seething anger and resentment swept over me. It was enough to have my nose rubbed in the things I was finding, without Lukkas encouraging the children to question my sanity.

We started walking again, past the Martyrs Memorial and the chattering foreign students feeding pigeons with Macdonald's chips.

"I promise you, Joe. There is nothing wrong with my brain or mind, it's been fully effective so far. Please stop worrying," I said.

He took a fifty-pence from his pocket and flipped it into a hat lying beside a homeless man and his two dogs.

"Well, for your information, Dad texts Hannah and talks about you, then she texts me."

"Poor Hannah," I said bitterly, but with real sympathy. He heard the note in my voice, tutted and rested a hand on my shoulder. How like Lukkas he was at that minute.

"I don't believe you are mad, no more than you ever were," he joked, "but maybe don't look for things, if you see what I mean…"

I thought, you mean I should turn a blind eye? But I didn't say it. I thanked him and kissed him on the cheek, although he leapt back instantly, presumably in case there might be a rapper friend in the vicinity.

Carfax, at the very centre of Oxford, was jam packed with afternoon shoppers.

"Right-o Joseph, if you could just get that bill board out for me, I need to go and get some pins to attach the posters."

"Mum, can we get a move on with this? Some people are waiting for me," he asked in exasperation.

"I know, you said, so I promise not to be long."

It made me feel shaky and nauseous simply to purchase the thing. I hadn't used a Dictaphone since I was a young teacher. But there was no way of affording a private detective. I didn't trust Lukkas, I loved him, but I didn't trust him, I told myself. Furthermore, I could feel my potential visit to 'the Doctor' getting ominously close.

So, that evening, whilst Lukkas was in the shower, I took his keys from the bedside table and stole out of the front door with the Dictaphone pushed to record. I held it in the palm of my hand, hidden in one of Lukkas' old black gloves. A new car, recently valeted and Lukkas' pride and joy might be a good place to start, I thought. Quickly, I unlocked the door and shoved the machine beneath his car seat, then, my heart hammering wildly, I sped back inside the house to replace the keys.

I prayed that he wouldn't find it, but it wasn't until two days later that I found my opportunity to retrieve it again.

I took the dogs for a walk across the fields beyond the gate. It was dark then and windy, but I seldom feared muggers whilst the dogs were with me and I had so much more to fear now.

I squelched across the muddy fields in my wellingtons with the dogs running at my heels, threatening to knock me over at the bark of a fox, whilst pressing the device close to my ear so the wind wouldn't detract from the sounds of the day in Lukkas' car.

It took a long while to realise that the nothingness I was listening to, was in fact a whole thirteen hours of recording through the night whilst the Dictaphone had lain beneath the seat, interrupted by a fight between two cats.

I fumbled with my cold fingers, swearing to myself and running the thing forward to the next morning when at last came the sound of his clicking the door unlocked and then music from Lukkas' favourite radio station. 'Gonna run to you..." How appropriate. Then Michael Jackson and Guns and Roses. I heard the cars rushing past on the motorway. He must have changed his mind about the early morning visit to our dentist, the sound of speeding traffic didn't indicate that route at all. He was on the motorway to Thame or North Oxford.

The car slowed down and pulled off the motorway. Lukkas turned off the engine and the radio. I heard him get out and the crunch of his feet on gravel. I heard the lowing of a cow in a near bye field. The countryside. Then feet, his feet on a metal staircase and finally his knuckles banging on a door.

The car must have been parked for almost an hour before whatever door it was, opened, and his feet descended the metal stairs.

He travelled on alone and it would have been a boring journey if not for the music and for a brief but shockingly funny moment when he spat out the words,

"Come on then, you fucking cunt!" at a motorist who proved too slow for him.

It told me little and the battery petered out a little while later. It was only much later in the day, puzzled by the metal stairs, that I realised where metal stair cases often belonged.

In motels and Travel lodges.

CHAPTER TWENTY-THREE

The Cockerel

I could not work Lukkas out, I couldn't fathom his moods. I knew how difficult his job was. Once, I would return from teaching and he would be desperate to talk things over with me, the children he had responsibility for, neglected children, abused children, young prostitutes. He would talk, and I would listen. Sometimes I wanted to put my fingers in my ears as though I were a child myself. I was a teacher, I had tried to protect young people, but these stories were harrowing.

We had dinner with some of the many Guardians Lukkas worked with, kind women, rational, sensible women. But now, he hardly talked to me at all, upon any subject, we rarely went out with his staff.

Mostly, Lukkas was cold towards me but sometimes he would be an old friend once more, laughing even, cracking jokes. It was as though his emotions were playing havoc with him, as though he didn't know and wouldn't say what he wanted. Up, one minute, down the next.

On the morning of my birthday in October, he was the cockerel, all confidence, all generosity.

Although he had to work in the morning, he had booked a restaurant for us over lunch.

When we woke, he handed me various beautifully wrapped presents. He had bought a dressing gown for me, some 'Paris' perfume and, well, a couple of things I thought odd. Namely shower cream and body lotion with a naked blonde girl on the packaging, they were for a much younger woman. I didn't say anything of course, other than to give him a kiss and to thank him.

But then there was the birthday card with Marilyn Munroe on the front, blowing a kiss.

Every birthday that we had been married, he had given me a lovely scene of a Cornish beach or a landscape, waterfalls, woodlands, that kind of thing.

I smiled and read the inscription inside. 'To Laura, have a happy day, be happy in life, lose the suspicion, it is ill founded.'

'I love you,' perhaps, or 'with love from Lukkas.' Ill founded? It had a legal ring to it, like 'You'll never prove anything.'

I didn't point out to him that Marilyn Munroe was a manic depressive who may have committed suicide. I didn't want to spoil anything. But it rather felt as though someone else had chosen both my presents and my card.

I dressed, reading my happy birthday texts and got ready for the big day, a day with Lukkas and without children.

He drove to the courts in Banbury and whilst he worked, I did some early Christmas shopping. At twelve thirty, I met him for lunch at a little restaurant in the centre of town.

Lukkas was quiet, but he smiled and listened to me talking and I was happy that morning.

It was as we got into the car I saw it, it wasn't difficult to see, I wasn't looking for it but there it was. The end of a long, slim, cylindrical container, pink, pushed into the runner beneath the driver's seat. The tip was sticking out, just as though someone had intended it to be found there, just enough to ruin the whole, lovely day.

I pulled it out and as he saw me do that, Lukkas' cheeks turned ruddily red.

"What have you found," he snarled, turning in an instant, as though the finding of it was my fault.

"A lip gloss," I replied blankly.

He gave a little shrug of the shoulders. "One of the girls put it there, Ruby or Lilly."

"No," I said, indignantly. "Neither girl has been in your car yet and it was cleaned by the garage, just after we went for that ride, remember? Ruby complained that you hadn't taken her in it yet."

I wanted there to be an innocent answer. Did Lukkas really believe I wanted to find such things, had he no idea of how much it hurt? And yet I was starting to believe that they were being left in his car to hurt me, directly, by someone who was jealous.

Then he turned to me before starting the engine, his jaw thrust forward so that he looked like a monster as he said it. "You put it there yourself, didn't you Laura?"

"I? I put it there myself?" I might have laughed but the insinuation frightened me. Did he really believe that? And I said, "Are you trying to protect someone, Lukkas?"

He stared forward then, starting the engine, spluttering in fury. "That's it, Laura. How could you be so unreasonable? I'm not going to Cornwall with you at half term, go on your own. Got it now?"

I stared out at the trees, at the Autumn fields, looking away from him; clutching the lip gloss with tears scalding my eyes.

We didn't talk for several days. Lukkas told Hannah about the lip gloss and when I collected her children and returned them, she too, treated me to silence or snapped at me that it was my fault that Dad wouldn't go to Cornwall.

"Why are you crazy, Nanna?" Ruby asked me one day.

Anger made me bold and foolish both. I had nothing to go on still, no idea who would have left such a thing in his car. So, on the morning he searched for his trunks in the washing machine, I decided to go for a swim, to disregard the rule he had set me, that I mustn't swim with him.

I said hello to Sandra, the girl at reception, and wandered nonchalantly through to the changing rooms.

As usual, there were few swimmers this time of the morning. I got into the pool, shivering a little, but more intent upon looking for Lukkas and as I relaxed into easy breast strokes I caught his eye, or rather he caught mine and the look he threw me was filled with poison.

He was alone, reclining in the Jacuzzi with the air of a James Bond minus the martini, tanned still after Nice, his black hair sleek from the swim.

Just before I reached the end of the pool, Morgan appeared. She walked with care, on a direct path towards him. Small, as I remembered her, but somehow changed, older. The black and gold bikini had been replaced by a new swimming costume, in black and white, with large scoops carved out of the sides. She looked sultry and sexy in it.

When she reached the Jacuzzi, her toes upon the very edge, she smiled and opened her mouth to speak to Lukkas, but he shook his head, twice; so that a startled look appeared on her face as he shook her off. Then she frowned a little and turned to the pool and seeing me, scuttled away to the sauna.

Lukkas rose from the water then. Ignoring me completely, he walked towards the male changing rooms and left me there.

That day, I kept my anger from everyone except Charlotte.

"Guess what?" She told me over the phone, having researched Morgan on the internet. She's a cognitive therapist."

"Oh Charlotte…" I sighed heavily, my brain working overtime, "What if she's the one giving Lukkas these ideas about my mind?"

"She could be bloody useful if he tries to slam you away," Charlotte said, helpfully.

Hannah persuaded Lukkas to go to Cornwall in the end, although he had been scarcely talking to me. I think Lukkas wanted her to get away for a while. She wouldn't talk about it, but things with Ben had grown worse in a way we didn't understand.

We had rented a house in Polzeath since Hannah was five or six, with the same friends with whom we went to Italy. If I had been hesitant about seeing them, I should not have been, they were true friends, as understanding as true friends can be.

The beach at Polzeath is wide and lovely, sheltered by high cliffs. Across the years, we have built a million sand castles, eaten a million ice creams, played rowdy games of cricket and football and taught the young how to belly board in the cold Atlantic.

Josh appeared for three days but we hardly saw him. He spent all his time surfing, fishing and chatting up a very pretty barmaid in the local pub.

On the second day of the holiday, trailing happily down to the beach with Hannah and the girls, their spades scraping on the high path above the sea, Hannah called out to me, "Slow down Mum, I want to talk to you."

I stopped then, retrieving a hairy, brown caterpillar from a crop of green Samphire for the girls to see and they instantly squabbled about who should hold it, threatening to pull the poor thing in half.

Hannah smiled, but pursed her lips before speaking to me. "Mum, I don't want to spoil your holiday, but I have to speak to you."

I knew it before she explained. I knew Lukkas had set her up to this. "I'll come to Cornwall, Hannah, but I want you to talk to Mum." I thought I had escaped. At least she hadn't talked again about removing my grandchildren from me, letting me see them under supervision.

I looked at her face, the large and expressive brown eyes, the long, brown hair blowing about her cheeks.

"What lovey?" I asked.

"Dad is right. You need to see a doctor. When you are calm, like this, everything is great. But sometimes you've been behaving irrationally, you know, going through his clothes and things and he's told me…" she paused, "He's told me that you plant things in his car."

She was right, I didn't want anything spoiled and she seemed not to believe me, anyway. I knew her, her relationship with her father. If Lukkas maintained that shitty lie, she would believe him no matter what.

"I don't want to talk about this with you, no. Except for one thing, hard as it is to accept. It makes me feel ill when I find things in the house or in Dad's car. No,

Hannah, I don't think any doctor could resolve that." I picked Lilly up to carry her down the steep steps to the beach, feeling more than a little irritated, then spoke without looking at her. "I want you to remember this time, Hannah, and one day, if some man tells you that you are mad because you find things that suggest an affair, just tell him to get stuffed, will you?"

She shrugged her shoulders. "Alright Mum, but don't say I didn't warn you. He will leave you if you carry on this way. He says that last November, you heard voices in the kitchen pipes."

"I have never heard voices in the kitchen pipes or told Dad that! He is telling you lies, Hannah, as he tells me lies. I said he was away a lot last November and that I was lonely. November is a dark month and sometimes the pipes hum in the winter, which got me down. Loneliness, the dark and the bloody moaning pipes. I certainly didn't say or believe they were communicating with me. Think you'll find that feeling is quite common. If he used the term 'voices' then he's lying to you."

I turned away from her then. I didn't want to row, to spoil it all with an argument. Not this week, away from whoever it was who made my life, our lives; a misery. Perhaps it was all pretence, I could easily believe that it was a charade for the benefit of other people, but Lukkas appeared to be happy and jovial.

There was a morning, grey with mist, I will never forget to my dying day. For some reason he woke early, as he used to when we were in Cornwall and our own children were babies. He put cold feet on me and we giggled, like children; spontaneously. Then he made love to me. Afterwards, we went for such a long, lovely walk together, to Rock, where we stopped for a coffee.

But there were times too when we circled each other as dancers in the Tango.

I noticed that sometimes in the evening he would withdraw into the dark shadows of the Canadian pines behind the house, unnoticed.

Whilst we cooked and drank wine and played games with the children, all of us together in the brightly lit kitchen, Lukkas would slip out like a ghost.

The first time, aware of his wandering away from the kitchen by the back door, I thought he had gone for a cigarette. None of the children knew that he smoked, but he had lifted his mobile phone from the charger on the mantelpiece.

I said nothing until the third night, when I followed his progress again and he took his phone with him. This time I went up after him, into the little copse, and saw his quick movement as he put the phone into his pocket. "Hello," he said. There was sadness in his voice.

He took me into his arms and hugged me. "You can't go everywhere with me," he said.

"I never used to want to," I reminded him.

In the middle of the week, when Lukkas went surfing with Neil in the rain, I watched them retreat along the winding garden path in their wet suits and when they had disappeared, I picked Lukkas' phone up from the bedside table, prepared to fumble for the code as I had once before. I didn't need to, he must have been in a hurry because he had left it unlocked.

Hurriedly, my heart beating fast, I found the numbers there and ran my fingers along them. The numbers of friends, of colleagues, of the lawyer who had joined the Family team and, Irina?

In some ways, unsurprising. Irina was a tenant now at the house we owned in Croft Street, Russian, pretty, blonde, in her late thirties, but I dealt with the tenants there. Lukkas didn't have Brad's number, or Daisy's or Katie's numbers, I checked to see. Why Irina's?

She worked as a receptionist in a hotel, although I didn't remember which hotel, she was doing a course in hotel management too. She was always less respectful than the others, somehow, and having been at the house for a while, she had argued with me about the rent. I remembered how cross I had felt at the way she spoke to me about it. When I told Lukkas, he had leapt out of his chair in the living room and told me, "I'll go and deal with it."

His 'dealing with it' had simply meant agreeing with her and I was annoyed and surprised, it was something I'd never known him to do before. As a rule, he would flummox people with legal jargon.

Not Irina?

There was a knock at the door and I dropped the phone heavily and rather guiltily upon the table.

"Aunty Laura, Mum says do you want a pasty?" Ellie smiled at me, her smooth cheeks glowing with youthful innocence.

"Yes Ellie, thanks, I'm just coming down," I replied.

No. Not Irina. I shoved the thought into the cobwebbed corners of my mind.

CHAPTER TWENTY-FOUR

Dr Lamb

I did not mention Irina until we arrived back in Oxford.

"What...who?" He asked as he ironed his own shirts for the first time in thirty-three years, making a bit of a hash of it.

"Irina from Croft Street, you still have her number and she's not a tenant any more. I saw it on your phone." This last statement didn't ring true, because it wasn't true, but I'm not much of an actress. His lip curled. He stopped ironing and stared at me. I tried to look normal, tried to breathe slowly.

"I refuse to answer any more of your silly questions. You've been spying on my phone again, haven't you?"

I didn't answer, looking down at my thumb nails, trying to defuse the time bomb that I had ignited.

"Listen Laura, because I'm deadly serious. For the last time of telling you, I'm seriously contemplating leaving you. You interfere too much in my life."

"I'm your wife, Lukkas," I reminded him.

He turned the iron off and rested his hands on the back of the sofa, bearing over me. "I'm going now. I'm leaving. I am sick of your lack of trust, of your misguided beliefs. I'll give you a few days and if you haven't booked an appointment to see Dr Lamb in that time, I'm not coming back."

"But where are you going?" I pleaded with him.

"None of your business," he barked from the door.

I didn't cry when he had gone, but chewed my fingernails, staring out into the dark, feeling lonely as hell. Josh had advised me not to go under any circumstances. When Josh and Joe returned, they would both be upset, but only Joe was likely to rant at me.

Then I thought of someone I could ring. David.

I'd not seen him in ages, he was Charlotte's ex-husband and Lukkas' friend, a skilled Carpenter, fluent in Spanish and German, a philosopher (which reminded me that I still hadn't read the copy of Zen and the Art of Motorcycle Maintenance that he'd lent to me some while ago) and occasionally but by no means regularly, a bit of an alcoholic.

I went down to the kitchen and outside into the garden, where I hoped no one would hear me.

He seemed pleased that I'd called him, although very shocked at the state of our marriage as outlined.

"Laura, I had no idea. I love you both very much, but I don't understand what you think I can do to help."

So, I told him about the doctor.

There was a long pause after I had finished. Maybe, I wondered, he's trying to diagnose me himself.

"Okay. Tell them this. You've always been an intense person, passionate about things. Lukkas was married to you for thirty-three years and these are things he loved about you. The next thing you need to remember is that unless you've physically attacked someone, you can't be made to agree to any treatment. I thought of Lukkas' bloody nose at the airport, then thought of his physical attacks upon me."

"So, you are saying they can't make me do anything against my will?"

"No," he said emphatically, "But don't be persuaded and always remember…" he chuckled then, "They can't do anything if you're drunk."

"Is that from personal experience?" I asked.

"Maybe."

I went to bed after my call, fuelled by dreadful thoughts of incarceration in a mental institution and wondering where Lukkas was staying and who he might be staying with.

At nine o'clock the following morning I received a text from Lukkas.

"I have an appointment for you with Dr Lamb at eleven am. I'll pick you up at ten thirty," it said.

I bridled with anger. But I would have to go, it was the only way to get him back. "No thanks, I'll drive myself," I replied. He would have loved that, I suppose, driving me there as if I couldn't handle driving myself.

There was never a time, in all the years of our relationship, I could have envisaged this, my journey in a tumbril to my execution. I sat beside him in the waiting room, in silence.

Dr Lamb was nothing like Dr Evans. She oozed psychiatry. Small, in an above the knee tweed skirt and soft pink jumper, she must have been about my own age, I supposed. But her blonde bob, slightly greying at the roots and high heels gave the impression of a younger woman.

When she greeted Lukkas it was with an expression of sympathy and admiration, to me she said, with slight coldness, "Take a chair."

I took the chair. She opened her mouth to speak to him first and I knew that I was going to be treated very much as a third party in this, so I said, "I'm afraid that this is a waste of time. I'm only here because Lukkas threatened to leave me if I don't come."

She lifted her eyebrows, that one movement told me that I was an animal, a specimen, as though she had analysed me already and anything I might choose to say was wasted breath.

"Your husband is very concerned about you, he feels that your behaviour is interfering with his ability to work…"

"Ah," I nodded. "I see. But for thirty-three years, my support was the very reason that he could work," I said.

She skipped over that, it wasn't anything that she wanted to hear.

"He has shown me the messages you sent him."

So, Lukkas had indeed prepared the ground for this appointment. How stupid am I? I thought.

I nodded, feeling a little shaky, trying now to keep the tremor from my voice.

"Those messages were in response to what he said before he left the house. Lukkas shouts, I didn't want to upset our family and often he has refused to discuss important issues, sometimes also, I've asked him to support me with a family matter. He's sent some pretty blunt messages to me."

Dr Lamb resented my arguments, she hadn't expected me to do that.

"When your husband came to me, he was very depressed."

I could imagine, the little boy thing; but Lukkas was far too robust to be depressed, he was a fine actor, however. If he hadn't been a lawyer, I think he could have chosen that as a career.

"Dr Lamb, Lukkas is capable of shouting very loudly, believe me..." I contemplated telling her about some of the ways that Lukkas had behaved over the years, but he would hardly stay with us if I did.

"He also told me that you have followed him in your car and that on one occasion, you tried to ram his car..."

My mouth half opened in disbelief. This was preposterous! Ram his car, me, the person who has been terrified over the years of what Lukkas will say if I get one tiny scratch to the paintwork of my car?

"Doctor Lamb, that is an...untruth!" I burst forth, aware that Lukkas was a God and therefore I must not say 'a lie.'

I took a few, calming breaths. "I have followed him, yes, but if you are married, Dr Lamb, and you thought your husband was having an affair, you might do the same thing."

I felt, rather than saw, Lukkas shrug his shoulders beside me. He was still playing a part, the maligned but supportive husband of a mad woman.

"I have asked Lukkas to attend a councillor with me, but he won't do that," I added, quietly.

"This isn't a relationship problem," Lukkas said.

"What are the things that I've been finding, in your house and car, Lukkas, if this isn't a relationship problem?" I asked, turning to him.

Dr Lamb cleared her voice, ending that line of conversation abruptly.

"You have also hit him with a frying pan..."

It was a statement, not a question. She had made up her mind. I was both shocked and incredulous at it.

"I've never hit him with anything!" I cried. These were lies, Lukkas was a liar, suddenly he had become the greatest liar on earth.

Dr Lamb shook her head slightly. This lovely, caring man, this Human Rights lawyer, tell lies?

"Look, doctor Lamb, I believe that Lukkas is having an affair!"

There, I had tried not to say it, really tried not to humiliate him and suddenly, I felt sluiced in cold water. Why was I here, why? Because this was Lukkas' super injunction to keep me quiet or because it he left me he stood to lose money? I shuddered.

Doctor Lamb cast a small, smug smile in my direction. "I don't believe that is the case," she said.

"How could you know that; how could you possibly know that?" I blurted.

"Your daughter has also spoken to me and expressed her concern," doctor Lamb said, skipping over my question.

"Hannah?" That hurt a lot and I didn't conceal it very well.

My Hannah, my little girl, the person for whom I worked tirelessly.

"Hannah doesn't have the experiences that I have, she is only twenty-six." I groped in my bag for my phone, flashing it before her whether she wanted to see the messages or not. "However, if she wasn't merely scared by all of this instead of believing that I had a serious mental illness, I doubt she would ask me quite as often as she does to care for her children. I tried to show her, reading out the first message I came to, "Mum, I have a really bad headache, please would you have the girls…"

222

But doctor Lamb looked away. "I believe that your behaviour is obsessive and that you are becoming a danger to your husband," she said.

There were unwanted tears in my eyes now. "For all these years I have kept Lukkas' reputation and career safe and now I care for our grandchildren and next is to care for elderly parents; mine, Lukkas' too." Words came out in an unstoppable flood. "What hope is there for all of them if you do this thing to me, based upon lies?"

Lukkas leaned forward to the doctor. "How long will it take for her to calm down if we give her something now?" He asked calmly, as though I were one of the dogs visiting the vet.

"Oh, in an hour or two she would be as right as rain, after a good sleep," doctor Lamb assured him, as though I weren't there.

"What, are you serious?" I gasped. "Why, because I'm crying, you would medicate me?" I looked from one to the other of them and leapt from my chair.

"Laura, sit down!" Lukkas ordered. Then, as I shook my head, pushing past him to the door, he asked in a gentler voice. "Please, sit down."

But I turned my back on them both not even bothering to shut the door behind me, scooting along the corridor, only to slow down at the reception desk, because I wanted to cry, to howl; in my panic, I even envisaged them holding me down to inject me.

Nothing could be the same between us again. Lukkas was trying to control me, not the other way around. I didn't fully understand why, but I felt sure he would never come home now.

CHAPTER TWENTY-FIVE

A Rational Woman

He did come home, that same evening. We said nothing to one another. What could be said?

The silence continued for several days until Saturday morning, when he saw me preparing to visit his parents with him.

He shook his head, "I'm not taking you with me, you can't be trusted," he said. So that was my punishment.

I stared after him. "What do you mean, we visit your parents every weekend. I've cared for them every bit as much as I have for my own parents. What do you mean, that I can't be trusted, what do you think I'm going to do, Lukkas?"

"You might upset them," he said, making for the door. I wondered what he thought I would do, what mad action he thought I would take, what strange wild dance he believed I would perform in front of them. So, this was to be my punishment.

And just as we were arguing, Hannah arrived in her car. She looked from one to the other of us and waited.

"She's going on about affairs again," Lukkas said, with a sigh, coolly examining the back of his hand.

"No! This began because you said that I couldn't visit your parents with you," I reminded him.

But Hannah's disapproval was directed at me.

"Please, Mum, do as he said, he told me that you ran away. Stop running away from this, go back to her and tell her the truth, get a proper assessment. If Dad goes, I won't let you see the girls, Joe will leave too, you'll be very lonely then."

Did she mean that… she wouldn't allow me to see Ruby and Lilly? There was such a dull pain in my heart, a real, physical ache which restricted my brething.

Joe descended the stairs, drawn by the commotion. "She's right," he said, "I will leave if this stuff doesn't stop."

He placed himself between Lukkas and I, standing in the doorway.

"We are all in agreement, Mum," Hannah said. "Please see a psychiatrist who will diagnose you properly."

Joe put a hand on my shoulder then. It wasn't meant to be threatening, but with the three of them actively blocking my exit now, I had started to feel claustrophobic.

Where was Josh? Oh, how much I wanted him there with me.

"Please Joseph, this is all wrong. You can't expect me to go to a doctor again based upon a relationship difficulty."

"Relationship difficulty…" I heard Lukkas scoff.

"No, Mum. Dad is right." Joe's voice was weary, and I felt sorrier for him than for myself. But then he blocked my exit as I tried to walk through the door, in a tactic that his father had used before.

"Joe, let me pass, I can't breathe," I pleaded with him.

"No," he said, solid in the doorway.

I looked to Hannah in an appeal, but she said nothing.

"We thought it would be good to have a meeting with you," Joe said.

"Okay, but I would rather a meeting with a councillor present, not like this. I can't think, I feel as though you are imprisoning me like this. Please let me pass..." I wondered what they were going to do. In the back of my mind, I knew that Lukkas might goad me and then we would argue and then, what? I had a vision of Joe picking me up in a fireman's lift in preparation for the straight jacket.

Then I realised the back door was standing open for the dogs and that I had left my car keys on the kitchen unit. Without hesitating, I shot beneath Joe's arm, past Lukkas and through the kitchen whilst the dogs leapt up at me, thinking this was a game. I grabbed my keys from the side and escaped through the garden gate and to my car before Joe could catch up with me. When he reached me, he banged angrily on the passenger window, but I locked the doors with a click of the key and reversed, escaping.

It took me a long time to stop shaking. I drove to a nearby village and bought a packet of ten cigarettes and getting out of the car, stood by a field to smoke one of them. I tried to think where I could go to for advice and could think of only one person.

Heather. I supposed that it might compromise her, as she was one of Lukkas' senior lawyers. But if Lukkas was aware I had talked to her, he might stop persecuting me and I had known her before she came to work at his office. I was running out of defensive ammunition now.

I drove to the house behind the high, neatly trimmed green hedge. Her car was there. I parked mine and trod the stone steps to her front door.

Much to my shame I collapsed in tears as soon as she answered the door, whilst Heather stared in amazement at the bosses wife having a nervous breakdown.

"Laura, come in love, what on earth has happened?" She said after a moment. She brought me into the hallway, her arm about my shoulder until I was safely inside and surrounded by her paintings and tapestries hanging on the walls there. I tried to compose myself, scraping at my puffy eyes.

"Oh, Heather, I don't know where to begin," I said whilst her son, a boy of Joe's age passed us on his way to the staircase, nodded uncertainly and beat a hasty retreat to his room.

She led me through into the kitchen and I collapsed in a heap on a wooden chair and rested my elbows on the table amidst the colourful crockery. Heather handed me a large piece of kitchen towel and I blew my nose loudly. Whilst she made tea, I started to tell her as much as I could, as much as was relevant. She handed the cup of tea to me and pushed a sugar bowl in front of me, sitting down herself. As I came to the end of the story I looked at her, half expecting her to say, "Yes, I think it's probable that you are mad." Then almost collapsed with relief when she said, "But this is so common. Most of the women who come to us talk of these things. It sounds highly probable that Lukkas is having an affair. If you don't mind, I'd rather you didn't repeat that."

She stared at me for a moment. "Does he talk to you slowly and reasonably in public and lead you by the arm, sometimes?" She asked solemnly.

My eyes widened in acknowledgement. "Yes, he has done that two or three times, notably when we went to the staff wedding in February," I said.

"Is he stopping you from seeing friends or family?" she asked.

"Yes, both," I nodded.

Heather nodded. "You aren't mad. These are old male tricks to control a situation. Affairs are common, they have nothing to do with age or class, in fact they often cross class."

I sipped the tea, feeling a good deal calmer. I told her about some of the things I had found in his car.

"That too, is very common. Young women especially like to leave parcels like that, it's to do with envy and ownership."

I told her about the times that Lukkas, always so gregarious, had shied away from events; twice claiming that he felt ill, once lying in a darkened room as though he felt depressed.

"So, what are you going to do now?"

I shrugged, having no idea. "I don't want a divorce," I said, "Despite all of this, I love him."

I pursed my lips in thought. "I want to find out who she is," I said at last.

"Why? What will that achieve, anyway?" She asked me. "You don't need to know to get a divorce, you just claim unreasonable behaviour and chop everything down the middle. After all these years, you might get half of his business profits."

But I didn't want half of his business profits, I wanted him to love me, to stop treating me like this.

"If I find out who she is, I can at least prove that I'm not mad as he says, as the children now believe and the doctors he has talked to." I told her about doctor Lamb and my visit to her.

She widened her eyes in shock. "Good grief, that's appalling, like something from a Gothic novel. Why though? Why did you see her and not your own doctor? He would have prepared her, he would have seen her first. It's never a good idea to follow up a meeting like that."

I drew in a long breath. "Lukkas has been threatening to leave me, he said he wouldn't come back until I had seen someone of his choosing, a psychiatrist, I mean." I could see how pathetic this must sound. "But recently he cried about something when he'd had too much to drink, he didn't tell me what he was crying about, only that 'I was the only one."

"When people are sexually charged up, obsessed, they do some dreadful things," she sighed. She patted the back of my hand. "You must be very confused. So, if you stay with him, how do you cope with all of this without actually going mad?"

I shook my head. I had no answer to that, other than that I wasn't really the kind of person who does go mad, and this I knew.

When I left, it was with a feeling of calm. She hugged me and told me to come back if ever I needed to. "Go to Relate," she advised me, "The marriage guidance people. If Lukkas won't go, see them on your own."

It wasn't until we reached the door that I remembered. "Heather... why did Gwen have to go, what was the reason?" I asked, without mentioning the paper clips or the spy camera.

She shrugged, if she knew the answer, she didn't betray it. "I was away at the time, on holiday. I'm not entirely sure," she said.

Nothing was said on my return. Lukkas had gone to see his parents alone. Joseph treated me to silence until he wanted to 'borrow' a tenner, Hannah had gone out for the day, with the girls and Ben.

When Lukkas arrived back, he said nothing to me but for the next week treated me to some of his special rules. The house was too tidy one minute, it was untidy, and I should clean it, the next. I was controlling, I should respect his individuality, he was 'not like other men', I was lucky compared with other women. The list seemed endless, as though he wanted to provoke a fight. No matter how hard I tried to jump through his hoops, I never, ever succeeded.

Lukkas' emotional absence from me continued until November 5th and bonfire night. He returned late or stayed away often, never telling me where he was going, like a house guest. I was distraught about it, but both Hannah and Charlotte told me not to follow him or try to discover his whereabouts. One evening, though, feeling desperate, I did try to call him and to my surprise, he answered. It was pitch black outside, all trace of summer gone. Perhaps that added to the ominous nagging inside of me.

He coughed once, as he always did if he was nervous or not telling me the truth and I heard the woman's voice, close by to him. He shushed her too, I heard that. When he spoke to me his voice was clipped, but not actually unfriendly and he told me that he was staying in a hotel in Milton Keynes.

When he came back the next evening I found the nose plasters in the bathroom and the hurt, the ache of knowing he was lying to me was so painful. Lukkas had always snored, but he had never used the plasters that are placed over the nose to prevent it, not in all the time we had been married. The box was in his wash bag, empty. Why would he want these things in a hotel, whose sleep was he so eager not to disturb? There was a small sachet of KY jelly there as well, we had never used this either. I said nothing to avoid another row.

Chapter Twenty-Six

Irina

We continued doing the things we always had, the children and I and because of what was happening, these events meant even more to them. Joe and Hannah made a bonfire for the girls and some neighbours who were joining us that day, as well as a handsome but physically weak Guy Fawkes to go on top of the fire.

We gathered in the damp garden when it was dark, huddled together, now in winter coats. My brother and his wife, Monica were there, as well as Charlotte and Neil and the teenage cousins. My parents came too. We munched on hot dogs and tinned soup.

We didn't wait for Lukkas as he hadn't told anyone whether he would come. My father, muffled against the cold by Mum, in a peaked cap and with a scarf wound about his neck, lit the bonfire. My brother and Neil lit the fireworks.

AS the coloured lights lit up the garden and the sky, against the "Ooh's" and "Ahh's" of our voices, the mobile phone in my pocket signalled a message, 901, a voice mail.

I held the phone to my ear, wondering whether it might be Lukkas. The message was muffled and indistinct amidst the laughter and voices around me. I walked to the kitchen where my mother was stirring a pan of tomato soup and kicked off my wellington boots, then went into the hallway for some quiet.

Pressing the phone tightly against my ear, I listened once more. I was sure that, somewhere there, I could hear Lukkas' voice, but it was a little like listening to a conversation under water. Lukkas' voice and a girl, or rather a woman.

"Please..." Yes, I could hear that, again, "Please..."

Then Lukkas, it was his voice, rising in tone, in anger or alarm as he might have spoken to me or to the children over the years. The call wasn't being made to me, it was as if the recording had been made somewhere and then sent to me.

I stared at the phone, I was disturbed by it. Was Lukkas in trouble, I wondered? Then I heard the noise of his key, slipping into our own front door and I placed the phone into my pocket just as he arrived in the house.

He smiled at me. A warm smile. I was so confused by it that I went shyly towards him and kissed his cold cheek. He didn't turn away; but allowed me to plant it there.

Much later, after Lukkas had gone to bed, I stood at the living room window, staring down at the dying embers of the bonfire and listened once more to the voice message. I repeated it again and again, although it was indistinct, so that I was sure. It was Lukkas, after all this time I knew his voice. I recognised the female voice too; but couldn't be sure who it was. Sometimes what they were saying seemed to be on speed dial. Why had it been sent to me?

"Ten, twenty, fifty...okay?" His voice.

"Please...? The girl.

"Tuesday, okay? Goodbye."

"Please?"

"Just a minute... what are you doing, what the fuck are you doing?"

A muffled noise and some movement followed and then a third party again, a girl, calling something as though she was outside the room. What was she saying?

There was a muffled noise and some more movement and the third party again, calling the name I couldn't make out. There was the sound of footsteps retreating and a long pause before a door slammed sharply. The recording device made a loud, screeching, scraping noise that hurt my ear and ended abruptly.

I gave up at last, feeling irritable and exhausted. I got into the bed beside Lukkas who snored softly like an angel fallen from hell.

But I couldn't sleep. The words I had heard played themselves again and again in my head. The woman had an accent, like Valeria's. Counting? Then it had to be money. The woman had sent the recording to my phone number quite deliberately, she must have known my number and the only person she could have taken it from was Lukkas.

Then just as I was drifting off to sleep, my eyes opened suddenly in realisation.

The third voice, from somewhere outside the room called once at the start of the recording and once at the end, they were called at a high pitch in small, broken syllables.

"Rina...Rina..."

Carefully I drew back the cover whilst Lukkas tutted in his sleep. I picked up my mobile phone and went back to the living room. I listened through to the end, because after Lukkas said "What the fuck are you doing?" it was so much clearer.

"Irina!"

I listened a few more times, until, along with the weariness there was excitement now.

I had an answer of sorts.

CHAPTER TWENTY-SEVEN

Dog Fox

I said nothing to Lukkas before work. As soon as he had gone, I grew nervous about confronting him with the call to my phone, ridiculous to spend an entire morning in that state, I thought, and so I tried to put it out of my mind until the evening.

As things turned out, I didn't get around to confronting him at all. An hour after Lukkas returned from work, or wherever he had been in the evening, I had a call from Hannah's friend and next-door neighbour, Amira. When she speaks there is a cautious dip in her voice.

"Laura, I'm sorry to call you so late, but I think there's a problem at Hannah's and I'm worried."

My heart sinks. It goes down like a tug in a storm. Amira called us once before, I've been waiting for this.

"What is it Amira?" I ask the question knowing the answer.

"For the last two days there has been shouting on and off, from Hannah's; but tonight, it's especially bad and I heard a scream. One of the children is crying, Laura…"

That is why, I think, Ruby was tired this morning, tired after the bonfire party but because something else might have happened.

"I'm just coming, Amira, and thank you," I say.

"What's the problem?" Lukkas asks and because of his work, because of his reputation, I tell him, "I'll deal with it, I think it's Ben."

He nods. "Call me if you need me," he says.

My tyres grate upon the gravel as I arrive. I look up at the bedroom windows but hear nothing and let myself in with the key Ben would prefer I didn't have. In the hallway, I listen, hearing Hannah's sobs. Ben is saying something to her, but he hasn't realised that I'm here.

I mount the stairs, two at time until I reach her bedroom and when I peer around the open door, see Ben kneeling upon the floor by her bed as though he is begging forgiveness, and so he might, the room looks as though it has been ransacked. The dressing table stool is broken, there are papers and clothes strewn everywhere, the door itself has been attacked with a blade of some kind.

When Hannah and Ben and Ruby, who is sitting up in bed beside her mother and snuffling softly; big, stifled sobs from such a little girl; when they turn to see me, they have all been crying, but I no longer give a damn about Ben's tears. I've witnessed them before, once I almost felt sorry for him, but not now. They are the tears of a little boy who knows that he's been caught out in the act of bullying.

"It's not my fault, Laura…" Ben starts, wiping his nose on the sleeve of his leather jacket and Ruby begins crying again and buries her small face in her mother's armpit.

"Get up, Ben, and get out before I call the police!" I warn him. I don't want to call them, for Hannah's sake, but we can't live like this anymore.

"Where's Lilly?" I ask Hannah urgently.

"Asleep, in her cot in the bedroom," Hannah sniffs.

"Get up and get out!" I tell Ben, noticing damage to the bathroom door as well. He is still kneeling on the floor in a repentant posture which fails to move me.

He clambers from his knees, drawing himself up by leaning on the bed. He reeks of beer and he is swaying. "It's not as bad as you think, Laura. There's some blokes after me, I needed money, that's all."

I stare at him in disgust, is he expecting me to give it to him? I know it without being told, this is the way Ben has exonerated himself from blame since his childhood. I don't care about him now, I just want to protect Hannah and the children. I forget myself in front of Ruby. "Fuck off, get out now. I will call them Ben, I'm not joking!"

Hannah once said to me, "You said that people can change." But it's me who has changed, not people like Ben who play on softer hearts.

Weakly, from the bed, Hannah sobs, "But he hasn't got anywhere to go…"

I shake my head in despair, "He'll find somewhere, Hannah. He's not going to terrorise my grandchildren anymore."

I turn away from her, directing my attention to Ben. I feel my arms shaking now.

"Please, Laura…" he pleads with me.

"Get out," I say, pointing to the door.

But he won't move. All my protective instincts and fury take over then as I throw myself at him, full force, pushing against the black, leather jacket; throwing myself to make him move, inch by inch as though I could push him off his feet. He is heavier even that Joe and could easily hit me, hurt me, but instinct tells me that he won't dare. At last I succeed in shoving him back through the doorway and out of Hannah and ruby's sight.

There, he stands obstinately at the top of the staircase and his expression changes to one of ugly hatred, he would like to kill me, I am certain of it in that instant.

"Go, go away you idiot!" I bellow at him.

He sways before me, says nothing, looks at me through the drunken eyes, but he won't budge.

"Get out, go!" I cry. Behind me, in the bedroom I can hear Hannah crying. I must bring an end to this, I must, my voice tells me, and with gritted teeth I lunge at his chest, pushing him backwards until at last he stumbles drunkenly against the wall and tumbles down the staircase to land in a heap at the bottom.

There is no movement for a second or two. My heart beats are out of control. I am scared in an instant, thinking that I've killed him, until Ben clambers to his feet, rubbing his head. His face is alert once more as he stares up at me and mounts the bottom step as though threatening to seek revenge for what I have done. But he stops, instead he turns his savagery on the book case, kicking the wood with all his strength. Then he leaves the house.

I lean against the wall, trying to steady myself, to slow down, adrenalin pumps through every vessel in my body. Then I hear his motorbike start up and thank God for now that, he's left and that perhaps Hannah and Ruby will be able to sleep.

"Nanna," Ruby is standing at the bedroom door. I pick her up and kiss her. "It's all okay now Ru', you need to go to sleep, Mummy must go to sleep too." I settle her back in the bed beside Hannah and go to make a baby bottle for her, she's far too big for a baby bottle but I hope it might soothe her.

"He doesn't have anybody, he doesn't have anywhere to go to Mum, please don't call the police," Hannah begs me.

"I have to," I tell her. "This time I must, and you can't have him back again."

The two, armed policemen come quickly. They ask to check on the girls, who are asleep when they come.

They interview Hannah and I in the kitchen, Hannah tries to be truthful whilst defending Ben in the same breath. The police officers look at one another sometimes, knowing the likelihood that when a few days have passed, Hannah will have him back. But they warn her that if anything like this happens again, the social services will be called, and she is frightened of that at least.

After giving our statements, Hannah returns to bed with a cup of tea whilst I put on my jacket and return to my car, because I feel sure that Ben will return. So, I sit in the driver's seat and wait, watching.

At half past one in the morning, when I am starting to doze off, I hear his motorbike turn into the close and shake myself awake.

I get out of the car and wait. Hannah is dangling from the bedroom window above.

"Mum," she whispers through the dark. "He's been watching the house for about half an hour, texting me."

"Then turn off your phone or give it to me," I hiss back. "I'm exhausted Hannah, go to sleep."

He comes back one more time that night, a ragged dog fox on the prowl. He stops before my car, astride the motorbike, his black leather jacket hanging open to reveal a hairy chest. He has abandoned his tee shirt. His eyes glare daggers at me from within the helmet.

Chapter Twenty-Eight

"I Have a Man"

Hannah didn't take Ben back. But she was lonely and a little depressed. When she asked if she could come home to live with us I was overjoyed, albeit a little concerned about space in the house and how it might affect things between Lukkas and I. At least if she lived with us I could try to make her happy again.

Lukkas was clearly relieved about it, that she had chosen to rid herself of Ben.

The girls thought it fun to be with us, like a holiday. I became even more involved in their lives. The trick was to help Hannah but stick to her rules where the girls were concerned.

Ben didn't leave it at that, oh no. One night, my car was broken into. It might have been anyone, but in all the years we had lived in the quiet neighbourhood, nothing like it had happened before. After that, my half dozen hens were stolen from the chicken coup. Not a fox, foxes don't use pliers to cut holes in a fence. I reported the incidents to the police, of course, but I didn't talk to Hannah or Lukkas about my suspicions. I didn't want Hannah to have anything to do with Ben, now, and I didn't want her to feel badly about it either.

A few days after Hannah and the girls moved in, I remembered the message sent to my phone and Irina.

When the house was empty and the girls at school, I rang half a dozen hotels in the Oxford area, explaining that I was Irina's old landlady and that I wanted to pass on some post to her, until I came to the Hotel in the country, where I had spent an eventful night with Lyra. What an irony, it was the hotel where Irina worked. The receptionist knew of her immediately.

"Oh, yes, Madam. She is working in our accounts department; would you like me to put you through to her?" The receptionist asked.

"No, thanks," I said. "I'll call in with the post later today."

Outside the hotel, in the busy car park, I tried to think about what I was going to say until I gave up. It wasn't likely to be the sort of conversation that I could predict after all. As I crossed to the hotel, I found myself searching for Lukkas' car.

I was met by the same, tall, thin Manager I'd seen upon my previous visit. I asked whether I could have a brief word with her and having explained my visit with the lie I'd invented, he sent a young woman to fetch Irina for me.

As soon as I saw her, I wished I'd worn something a bit smarter, wished that I didn't look so much like the housewife I was.

She was cool as ever, although her cheeks were slightly flushed as she smoothed down the tight fitting blue uniform. It appeared that she'd recently changed her clothes, but then, she had only just arrived to work at the reception desk, I supposed.

Her hair, pulled into a chignon, was no longer the ash blonde I remembered, it was a darker, golden colour now.

I looked at her eye lids, they were painted with blue glitter. Not the kind of glitter used by children, which is hard and gritty, but the finer stuff I had found on Lukkas' coats and jackets.

She smiled at me with a suspicion she couldn't hide, her grey eyes widening slightly beneath the plucked and painted eye brows.

"Hello, Irina," I greeted her, with as much amiability as I could muster.

"Laura." She smiled back. "What can I do for you?"

"Might we have a word in private?" I asked, "Perhaps over there..." I indicated a deserted part of the lobby.

She nodded, but her red, lipstick smile had become rather fixed upon her face. She walked away, stopping to turn to me. "Will this do?" She asked.

I nodded, and we stared at one another for a moment. She was about my height, which is not tall, but with a willowy, reed like body and the features of a model. A very attractive woman.

I drew a short breath, letting it escape from my nose. There was only one thing that I could honestly think to ask her, only one thing I wanted to resolve.

"Irina, are you having an affair with Lukkas?"

I suppose I must give her credit for her cool. She didn't redden, this time, her cheeks remained ivory white. "Would it really matter if I was?" she asked me.

It threw me, and I spluttered a little. "Yes, yes of course it would," I said indignantly.

She examined the long, shining almond nails of her right hand for a moment, before looking at me again. "Besides, I have a man," she smiled. "and I have only met Lukkas on a few occasions."

I didn't believe this. I took the phone from my handbag. Did she flush, then? Just the merest hint of pink?

"I had a rather odd message sent to my phone a few nights ago. A friend of my sons is going to enhance it for me, it's a little obscure, but the woman in the message sounds like you and someone in it calls your name. There can't be so many Irina's in Oxford."

Instinctively, or perhaps nervously, her long, slim fingers reached for my phone, then withdrew as my own hand curled protectively around it. As I regarded the highly polished finger nails, I thought of the false nails I had found in Lukkas' car.

She shrugged her small shoulders. "I know nothing about this message," she said.

I nodded. "One last time, Irina, are you and Lukkas having an affair?"

"No," she denied, a little more forcefully now, adding, "But it wouldn't be the end of the world if I was."

"Maybe not in Russia," I said, "But if you are, it's the end of my world and perhaps yours too..."

I had not seen the man until this point. He was leaning against the reception desk, watching us. A large, blonde, red faced man who oozed bouncer or henchman from every pore.

He stepped towards us. "Is everything alright, Irina?" He asked. He had a Swedish accent, I think.

I remembered the middle aged American lady in Paris, thrown out of her hotel with her cases, literally thrown out by a Parisian doorman. How shocked I had been, how much Lukkas had laughed. I felt sure that he would laugh at me now.

"Is this lady bothering you?" The Swedish man asked Irina in a low growl.

Instantly there were soft tears in Irina's eyes, worthy of Chekov. The kind of tears from an attractive woman that Lukkas would respond to instantly.

"Yes, Gregory, please ask her to leave now," she whispered, in the manner of a dying woman.

I looked up at Gregory's florid face. "It's okay, I'm leaving," I said, adding for good measure because, quite honestly, I didn't want to be thrown out on the pavement like the poor American lady who couldn't pay her bill, "She's quite an actress, isn't she?"

I drove home, disquieted but resolved not to talk to Lukkas about it because the girls were living with us now. This had added to the strain of finding semen stained underpants and other things when he returned from hotels. I could not talk to him or accuse him for fear of his wrath or his leaving and the girls had endured enough, because of Ben.

There was nothing funny about it at all. Finding such things filled my heart with murder, clawed at me as though parasites were draining my energy, tearing my heart out.

CHAPTER TWENTY-NINE

Gaslighting

Lukkas started to make love to me once more. Having children in the house again made this harder, but we had a lock on the door and we had always had children in the house one way or another. It wasn't only this that made me jumpy and sometimes reluctant. I had started to feel inadequate, that somewhere, a woman had his heart and was doing it better than me.

I never used to feel frozen, shy even; about sex with my husband as I did now. Even whilst we made love, I fretted about whether Lukkas was enjoying it, or whether he merely thought that he ought to make love to me.

I visited doctor Evans and she prescribed a pessary called Vagifem to thicken the muscles of my vagina. I was told how regularly I should take it, desperate to please Lukkas, I took too much, more than was good for me.

Then came the Sunday morning when we were to visit Lukkas' parents again. I don't know what he had told them when I didn't visit on the last occasion, I didn't ask.

We had made love the night before, and I had fallen asleep against his back. That morning, I awoke with the sunlight streaming though the bedroom window and quiet in the house- but for the cheerful chatter of the magpies in the chimney. We were the first to wake and Lukkas was already showering in the bathroom when I went downstairs to make two cups of tea.

It was his mother's birthday and as Lukkas suggested, I had bought a silver necklace as a present from his father, too old now to visit the shops, to give to his mother. It was a lovely idea and I had chosen the locket carefully.

As Lukkas emerged from the bathroom, towelling his hair, he said, "I can't find the necklace you bought for Mum. You put it in the bedside drawer, didn't you?"

I reached across the bed to find it for him, but after rummaging around for some while I had to give up. I had put it there, he was right, I knew that I had. As I was the one who bought most of the Christmas and birthday gifts, I had various hiding places, and could always lay my hands upon things.

He stopped towelling his hair, saying nothing for a moment, but I was worried by his expression, midway between being critical and something else I wasn't sure of.

"Hold on a minute, maybe I moved it." I stood on the edge of the bed, gripping the duvet with my toes to reach up into the next hiding place, the shelf at the top of the wardrobe. For several minutes, I hunted for the necklace, in shoe boxes, amidst the bath salts, batteries and socks. "It's here somewhere," I assured him, but when I turned to look at him, his lips were pursed in anger.

"You've hidden it, haven't you?" He said.

"Hidden it? But Lukkas, I took ages to choose it, I want to see her reaction today when she opens it. What do you mean, why would I have hidden it?" As I stare at him, I wonder if he's joking, or whether he really believes it. My heart starts to palpitate, warning me softly of the danger. The allegation is dreadful.

My fingers clamber across the dusty shelf. I must find it, I hate losing things.

"I've had enough of your silly games. You stay here, I'll buy her something else," he growls at me.

"No, no! I'm coming with you, I've been a part of their lives for over thirty years. You know I wouldn't do such a stupid thing, why would I do that?"

Then Hannah appeared at our door, Lilly in her arms. She looked weary, her eyes were puffy as though she had been crying. "What's happened?" she asked quietly.

Lukkas sat on the edge of the bed, lacing up his best shoes. "She's hidden Grandma's present," he said. "It's the last straw. I'm going to see them without her. I'll be back this evening."

I started crying then, stuffing my tongue inside my cheek to stop tears. "Just give me a few minutes Lukkas, I'll find it," I said.

"I don't have time, I promised Mum we'd be there early…"

He crossed the room, kissed Hannah and then Lilly on the cheek and dropped the door with a bang.

Hannah said nothing. She held on to Lilly for a while, watching as I carried on searching for the necklace. She was not sure who to believe, but I know she was willing me to find the present before Lukkas left the house.

I wasn't even dressed yet. Over my shoulder I said, "I will find it, Hannah. It's not true, it's a stupid thing to say. I haven't hidden it. I have no reason to hide it."

She didn't make any comment.

Minutes later, we heard his car start and he drove away from the house, winding his way at speed to the top of the hill which joined the motorway. Now I was hurling things onto our bed in anger and frustration, the things that had lain at the foot of the wardrobe for months. As I did so, my fingers closed upon the soft coating of a small box. I drew it out from the corner where it lay and looked at it. It was the black box with the silver locket inside.

I turned to show Hannah, but the sound of running water was the bath she was preparing for Lilly. My face puckered into a frown. I knew that I'd put the box in the bedside drawer, remembered doing so. Even if I changed my mind and placed it on the wardrobe shelf, had it fallen, it would not have been shoved into the corner of the cupboard like that.

It had been placed there.

It haunted me all day, that I knew I hadn't put the necklace there, but that, perhaps I had and had forgotten. I was upset too that Lukkas had marched out, leaving me there. I sent him a text, telling him I had found it, but he didn't reply. It was all upsetting and as I walked with the dogs I realised that I was talking to myself and wondered whether I was going mad after all. I needed to speak to someone about it, someone I could trust.

He came home later that evening. I asked him how my parents-in-law were, but he had little to say about them.

The next day I made an appointment with Relate.

I saw a Chinese lady called May. She must have been a little older than me, she was wise and calm and asked many surprising questions, but firstly how and why I came to be there. In the end, I told her everything. When I elaborated too much, she stopped me. She scribbled notes as I answered and seemed to believe in the relevance of some things I told her, that I was the eldest child from a large family seemed to be important, somehow.

Towards the end of our interview she said, "I believe what you say, I think there is enough to say that you may be right. It's a huge risk for him to have taken, but he won't be the first. I don't feel there is anything wrong with your mind, it sounds as though your husband is trying to control a situation which has become too much for him."

Then, just as Heather had, she asked, "The question is, what are you going to do next?" She sat back in her chair and waited for my reply.

"I don't want us to part, if that's what you mean," I said.

Her lips disappeared in thought for a moment as she regarded me. "In my extensive experience, it's highly unusual for a woman to have the staying power to cope with this kind of situation. Sooner or later, your patience will become exhausted, you may become angry, bitter and frustrated."

"I've been all of those things," I said. "But my children blame me, at least two of them do, and he wants them to believe it."

She nodded, "They are adult children and one day they will understand if you part. You are hoping he will stop this affair?"

I nodded.

"And if he doesn't?"

I couldn't answer.

She hesitated. "Some of the things you have told me make me very concerned for you. For example, on two or three occasions he has accused you of taking something, or of planting an item in his car. He is also saying that you have a madness. There is a term for this, Gaslighting someone."

"I don't know what that means," I said, feeling stupid.

"There is an old film, in black and white called Gaslight," she explained. "In the film, a man perpetually tries to persuade his wife that she is mad by lying to her and trying to convince her of the lies…"

"Alfred Hitchcock!" I said at once, "with Bergman. I've seen it."

She nodded. "Yes. Gaslighting can make a person quite ill. You may be putting yourself in a vulnerable position."

As I ascended the stairs from the basement offices, I thought about what May had said. Lukkas might be having an affair, he might love someone else more than me, but he would never try to Gaslight me. Never. He was a Human Right's Lawyer.

CHAPTER THIRTY

Better to reign in hell

I told no one about my visit to 'Relate'.

I wasn't ready to believe that things would improve between us, but I wasn't ready for the end, either.

It was a little like being in the middle of a nightmare, on the edge of a sheer cliff, and I was constantly alert to the signals from Lukkas. There was nothing wrong with my mind, once again, anger swelled inside of me that Lukkas should have suggested to our children and to our family and friends that there was.

So now, when I found tiny twists of dusky, pink wool on his jackets and tissue smeared with lipstick in his pockets, I shut up about it. If I spoke of these things, his campaign against my mental health became more ferocious.

On the one hand, I think I must tempt him with love, food and sex; on the other, that I must leave him. I no longer know who I am, or what to think.

Rational, sensible behaviour was the only way to prove him wrong, I told myself. I was so sensible that Joe remarked at Sunday lunch, one afternoon, "What's the matter with you, you never act the fool as you used to..."

I shrugged and shook my head in unexplained disbelief. They couldn't see that if I 'acted the fool,'

Lukkas might say that I was mad or immature, as he had before. I couldn't win. Life followed an uncomfortable path, paved with egg shells.

I tell Charlotte that I have been all of Henry V111 six wives in turn.

"Yes," she says sagely, "but Lukkas has remained Henry V111 during all of it."

Lilly asks me why Mummy cries sometimes. She misses Ben, I know this, and I admire her resolve to be rid of him whilst I can't be rid of Lukkas. "We all cry sometimes, Mummy will be alright," I reassure Lilly. "Give her lots of cuddles."

Josh begins a relationship with a frail, skinny girl from a book shop whilst Joe's ex-girlfriend phones me frequently, crying over the phone because she misses Joe. Considering all the fights they had, which left many items broken, she has a cheek, but I feel sorry for her, as I do for anyone suffering from unrequited love at present.

Lukkas had agreed to leave work earlier to attend an art exhibition of my brother's paintings, which would be held in Oxford Town Hall.

As we walked along the High street, Lukkas held my hand, rubbing the side of my left hand distractedly, in an old familiar way that I loved. I couldn't bear the thought of his doing that to anyone else. He seemed to have forgiven me for hiding the necklace, or perhaps he felt sorry that he had accused me in the first place.

"You look nice," he said with a half-smile.

"Do I, Lukkas?" I venture.

"Of course, I do," he says, giving my hand a squeeze. But I check my thoughts. I am conditioned by him, by his moods and his beliefs, waiting each time for forgiveness so that we can start again.

The broadness of Steve's grin as we entered, and the number of people present told me that the exhibition was doing well. Monica and their sons had been handing leaflets to tourists all week so they all deserved the success.

Lukkas shook Steve's hand whilst I greeted Monica with a kiss on the cheek. She reached to the table to grab a glass of white wine and handed it to me. "Your Mum and Dad have only just left. Your Dad wasn't very impressed because there's no beer," she laughed.

"Mum spoke to me this afternoon, she's so proud of Steve, she's told everyone she knows, I think."

"Have you sold very many paintings?" Lukkas asked.

Steve nodded. "Four, so far, each at a good price. Three of them scenes of Oxford City life and one of a nude to a lady from Summertown. She's interested in the whole collection, so I'm keeping my fingers crossed. She appears to know you, Lukkas, one of your clients, perhaps?"

He nodded towards a large but elegant blonde lady, draped in a blue pashmina.

"Oh yes, that's Helen," Lukkas nodded. "She's very wealthy," he added in a whisper. "Mind if I say hello?" He asked, turning to me.

I watched Lukkas cross the floor, a commanding figure, towering above the woman from Summertown who had to stand on tip toe to kiss his cheek.

I hugged Monica's arm as I stared at the long, naked spine of the seated woman in the canvas before me. "We all know that it's you, Monica," I giggled conspiratorially.

To my surprise, she gave me a rather tight-lipped pout.

"Some of them are, but not all of them," she said, a little irritably. I had always assumed that Monica didn't care about Steve's passion for painting nudes. I suppose that was naïve of me. I wouldn't want Lukkas to paint nude women, after all.

"If you look at that woman, for example, the figure is very like mine, she's someone of roughly the same age, but look at her back, her hips, doesn't look as though she has had any children yet, does it?"

Monica's grey eyes stared into mine for a moment as though in thought, then she swigged her wine quickly and looked away again, a woman trying to hide her feelings.

Perhaps, fortuitously, a sharp voice greeted us from across the room, a familiar voice, bringing back fond memories.

"Hello, you lovely people, long time, no see..." The voice was very distinctive, a gentle voice with an Australian twang to it.

This was Simon, a friend from childhood. More startling was the strip of white, bloodied bandage strapped across his nose.

"Forgot to say, Simon is staying with us for a few days," Monica explained.

"Oh, Simon, what on earth happened to you?" I cried, putting my arms gently around his neck so that I didn't hurt him.

His fine features broke into a friendly smile. "No, darling, not a homophobic attack! A very handsome surgeon in London broke it for me to set it straight."

"But Simon, your nose always was straight," I frowned.

"Not nearly straight enough. But look at you, gorgeous as ever," he complimented, holding my hands at arms-length to admire my dress.

"Older than ever," I reminded him. We chatted about the past two years of his life in Sidney and I thought how happy he was, now that he could be as gay as he wished, not having to hide his sexuality as he once did in England. Perhaps his mother's death had helped him to move on in every way.

As he talked to me, his brown eyes roved around the room. I knew who he was searching for, Lukkas of course. Strange that this failed to upset me. I wondered for the first time whether I would care if Lukkas were in a relationship with a gay man.

As I followed Simon's gaze, I saw Holly for the first time that evening. Lukkas had advertised the Art exhibition in his office, but I suppose I had not thought that she would come. I watched them in conversation. There was something so intimate about their behaviour that I felt a sudden pang of jealousy. As Lukkas towered above her, he inclined his head low, very close to hers to catch her words, whilst self-consciously, Holly hooked a strand of chestnut brown hair behind her ear. Watching them, I knew in that split second, they were aware of each other only, and it hurt.

"Come and speak with Lukkas," I suggested to Simon. Happily, he crossed the room with me. But when we reached them, Holly flushed pink, whilst Lukkas looked annoyed at the intrusion, and it wasn't Simon he was upset with. No, I could tell that he was irritated with me. He may as well have snapped at me, "What do you want?"

Holly smiled and said, "What a lovely jacket."

Why do women mask the things they might wish to say by complimenting people's clothes?

Several unwanted thoughts ran through my head as I gazed at her, predominantly their discomfort as

I approached them with Simon, who had now become animated in conversation by Lukkas' presence. Why that, why had she been uncomfortable? She was a lawyer, even if she resembled a librarian, she was younger and prettier than me, though not that much younger... she must be used to conversation with all kinds of people, surely?

She resembles a hen, I thought. A small, pretty, little hen who might suddenly snatch at a mouse and tear it to shreds.

As we both made a game of listening to Lukkas and Simon in conversation, her dark eyes watched me frequently, I noticed, just as though she would like to know more about me. But I did not feel flattered, only wary.

Then, only ten minutes after we had interrupted their conversation, when Simon offered to fetch her a glass of wine, Holly said, "Thanks, but I really ought to be going."

She had a soft, pleasant but faintly Warwickshire accent, I noted.

"Really? But you've only been here a short while," Lukkas said. There was disappointment in his voice.

She didn't just say goodbye, but reached up to kiss Lukkas on the cheek, leaving a smear of burgundy lipstick on his skin, then went to a coat stand in her sharp heels to retrieve a pink shawl.

Pink wool. Pink on his jackets, pink on the carpets in the house and on the soles of his shoes, blonde hairs on his suits. Holly, Irina...? Pink wool and blonde hairs told me nothing. Perhaps I would go mad in the end, mad with loss, mad with grief.

I shoved those feelings aside, once we were home, and smiled as Lukkas trod the stairway in his comfy slippers, wondering what Holly and Irina and Megan would make of this seemingly tired, older man as he clutched his back.

"Would you open a bottle of wine in the cupboard?" Lukkas calls to me. And in an instant, we could be the couple we once were.

In the cabinet there are two bottles of white wine... and a bottle of Vodka. I stare blankly at it. Two days ago, it hadn't been there. It was not a label I was familiar with, not that I ever bought Vodka. I held it at arms-length, wondering. Irina was too obvious a suspect. It was too silly for words.

But after I have taken his wine to him, risking all, wanting everything to be well, for us to be the family we were, I ask him with as much innocence as I can muster, "Where did the Vodka come from, was it a present?"

The speed at which that question separates us is frightening. Fury floods colour into his face.

"Vodka, what are you going on about now? It's probably been there for ages. I don't know anything about it! If this is one of your tricks to disrupt and upset the household, think again. I will leave, Laura, I mean it!"

The children had gone to bed and Hannah was resting.

"Please don't shout, Lukkas," I implored him, "It doesn't matter." I took two deep breaths to steady myself. He got up then, his slippers slapping impatiently on the stairs as he descended to the kitchen. I listened as he slammed the cabinet door shut. I stood, frozen by the changed atmosphere, staring out through semi-drawn curtains at the dark and the white flakes of snow that had begun to fall again.

When Lukkas returned, I asked, "Okay?"

"Don't talk to me," he said. He said nothing else to me for the remainder of the evening, but left the living room before me, without saying "Goodnight."

I was fast asleep beside him, somewhere in the middle of the night. In the snow lit bedroom, the needle stab of a sharp fingernail stabbing my eyelid made me screech in pain. I saw Lukkas' fingers, the fingers of his left hand, retracting like poisonous tentacles. Long, white fingers, attacking me. He smiled, apologetically at me as I covered my eye with my hand, but his eyes told a different story. They were alight with angry glee.

"You poked me in the eye," I said, sounding stupid in my surprise.

"Did I? Sorry." But there was no sorrow in his voice. He nestled down in the blankets, returning to sleep.

I had the most horrible dream that night, and woke suddenly, at the very point where I was about to be locked in a room and attacked. I had been at a party of some kind, in a big, dark house. Lukkas was there, somewhere in the room, and some of our friends, too. But I was alone, I felt isolated from everyone. They didn't appear to know that I was there at all as I drifted from room to room like a ghost. I entered a room and that was when it happened. The door slammed behind me and this large, ugly man threw himself at me, holding me by the neck.

I woke, then, breathing heavily, panting, but relieved that it was a dream, relieved that I had woken. I almost laughed when the name entered my head. Aleister Crowley.

Aleister Crowley had been a pupil at Lukkas' old school many, many years before Lukkas was sent there.

Lukkas had talked about him often, though. The subject held some fascination for him. But I had never taken any of it seriously. Neither did I see the man as 'The wickedest man in the world,' as he was named. More wicked than Hitler?

If what Lukkas had told me was true, he was an occultist, a magician, had started some secret sect or religion called 'Thelema,' took Heroin and became addicted because a doctor had prescribed it for asthma and eventually descended into total debauchery. He also worked as a double agent for military intelligence. These were things I had gained from Lukkas. Oh yes, Crowley killed cats, too. Perhaps Public school, as it was then, had done this to Crowley.

Why had I awoken to think about Aleister Crowley? Perhaps that was who had been strangling me in my dream. What a nasty thought. I shivered, lying down in the bed again. Perhaps public school had done this to Lukkas, too. I couldn't recover from the thought that Lukkas had deliberately stabbed me in the eye.

I had never taken Lukkas' fascination for Crowley seriously because he thought it fun to talk about him, would laugh at the stories.

I closed my eyes, tried to fix my thoughts upon the tide rolling onto the beach in Polzeath. There were too many thoughts in my head. Holly, pink wool, mysterious bottles of vodka, then the row and Lukkas hurting me like that. Maybe, at long last, I had really started to go crazy.

Lukkas loved his old school but had told me things that must have left scars, things that little boys shouldn't have to put up with. Where had his vertigo come from? The headaches? Symptoms of feeling out of control.

He said that he saw the school as a second family, yet he had been rebellious against it in his youth, and that rebellion against the school carried on even after Josh was born. A love hate relationship.

Lying in the bed, rubbing my sore eye, I remembered a party we had been to, close to Lukkas' old school. Lukkas, our friend, Tom. I, in the back of his old banger. He drove past his old school on the way back to his parent's home, where we had stayed for the weekend. There was no need to go that way, but Lukkas said, as he often did, "I just want to have a look at it."

I stared from the car window at the red turrets rising above a low mist that poured like liquid Nitrogen from the hills beyond, almost covering the school grounds.

"That's the cricket pitch," Lukkas said. He drove to the end of the road, then. I thought he would park for us to get out. He didn't. He turned off the headlights with a chuckle, revved the engine and drove straight onto the carefully managed, green expanse of the school's pride and joy, the cricket pitch. He drove at full throttle, the tyres spraying out clods of earth as though we were in a tractor. As he did this, he laughed with abandonment. The laughter of revenge.

I remember looking up at the windows of one of the oldest, Victorian buildings. I saw a sight I will never forget. Dozens of little boys were leaping up and down at the lattice windows having jumped out of bed to see what the noise was about. They stared, pointed. Some seemed shocked, their mouths open, whilst others grinned in delight.

They looked so angelic, like doves. They wore white nightshirts. Little men in long, flannelette nightshirts.

CHAPTER THIRTY-ONE

DC Jane

Christmas was drawing closer. I forced myself to think about cards and presents and covered my bare, brown legs in tights. I made an angel costume for Ruby and I fretted about Lukkas' whereabouts over so many of the long, dark nights. Mostly I was distracted, less organised this year, troubled by Lukkas and his actions, but I did my best to maintain a semblance of normality for the children and grandchildren.

And then one morning, Lukkas went into work a little later than usual, sitting at his study desk downstairs to write his own cards to the lawyers and guardians and businesses with whom he worked.

It had always been a nice feeling, to have him there, before he seemed so anxious to leave me. But I had found it hard to accept that a bottle of Vodka should arrive from nowhere, that strange, unrequested recordings had arrived on my phone, carrying the name Irina.

I passed the open door and he looked up and smiled at me in the absent-minded way he always used to, thoughtfully twiddling a pen between his fingers.

He packed away the cards and his papers then and put down the green pen he'd been using to write.

When he had gone I stood in the study for a moment, wondering. I looked down at the pen he'd left behind.

I'd never seen it before. On the soft, rubber gripper there were the miniscule shards of blue glitter I had seen on his black coat and on the side of the pen, a logo written in Russian and some numbers printed in white.

"Prostituta!" I muttered venomously, using a choice, Russian term of abuse learned from Valeria in one of her less spiritual moments. Where else would Lukkas acquire the pen from?

It snowed that evening, just the merest few inches of snow but the girls awoke with excited giggles at the prospect of my dragging them on sledges to the school, mercifully not very far away.

I had one of the most eccentric ideas I have ever had and whilst Lukkas was shaving in the bathroom, I stuffed green peppercorns and frozen peas into his exhaust pipe, packed in with ice and snow, deciding that, like a demented Gretel, I would follow Hansel to discover which direction he was taking. To the office, or to the hotel where Irina worked.

But by the time I had reached the top of the road, the trail of vegetables had been emptied into the slush covered road.

It had been a stupid idea. Or had it? The peas were splattered across the road on the left, just beyond the traffic lights, I noticed. He had turned towards the hotel after all. I sped after him, examining the road ahead for peas in the snow, but on the motor way there was no snow and the peas were invisible, so I kept going, heading for the hotel. Perhaps I would find him there, perhaps I would know at last.

I parked outside the hotel car park, behind a tall hedge, then edged to the entrance and walked swiftly towards a delivery lorry, stacked with crates of milk.

From the open rear of the truck I scanned the hotel car park for Lukkas' car. I must have waited, hovering there, for about five minutes. I couldn't see the car; but gasped as I saw him and hurriedly pulled back behind the trailer.

He was in conversation with a younger man, a tall, slim fellow in a light brown, leather jacket, but his back was to me and I couldn't see his features. It was Lukkas, they were quite some way from me and my eyes are not good, but it was Lukkas.

I breathed rapidly, terrified that Lukkas would spot me and as I watched, Lukkas held out his hand. I thought to shake the proffered hand of the younger man, but no, Lukkas handed him something. It looked like an envelope. Lukkas handed him an envelope and in that split second, all I could think of was the recording that came to my phone, and Irina's name with it.

He turned then, going into the reception area of the hotel.

"Are you okay?"

I jumped, stifling a cry. The delivery man stood before me, an empty crate in his arms, a half amused, half puzzled look upon his face.

"Yes thanks, fine... sorry..." I mumbled, as though I had caused him a problem. I walked briskly away then, without looking back.

That evening, when we were alone, having mulled events over during the day and arrived at a conclusion, I ventured, "Have you ever been blackmailed, Lukkas?"

He stared long and hard at me, one eyebrow raised, then grunted softly. "Nobody blackmails me, Laura," he growled.

But the thought haunted me. I didn't know what to do. In the recording sent to my phone, it had sounded as though Lukkas was counting, what was more, Irina's name was on the recording. The envelope he had handed to the man in the hotel car park, the hotel where Irina worked, might have contained money. Perhaps he was frightened, had done something very wrong. I knew him better than anyone, he would often cry and stress about things when he was young, just as he had when we stayed with Tom and Sarah and he said, "Only you…"

Perhaps. I didn't know what I could do. But an evening came, late in the month, when he called me from Milton Keynes. He told me that he would have to spend the night at a hotel there, that his car had broken down, and for once he sounded genuinely sorry and upset rather than indignant that I should want to know where he was.

I drove to Milton Police station because Lukkas didn't go there often. I went on impulse, what Lukkas would call a 'knee jerk reaction,' I drove in the dark and parked in the grey slush of a side street. I hoped that she still worked there, because I'd heard that she was going to be promoted. No longer DC Jane, but CID Jane.

I didn't know exactly what I would say to her, only that at that moment, nothing in my life seemed concrete any more. I carried on as I always had, caring for my family, including Lukkas; whilst he behaved oddly, badly and called me mad. There was just this last possibility and just then, I clung to it; that he was frightened, being blackmailed, perhaps forced against his will.

Treading the ramp towards the doors of the sixties building, my cold hands shoved into my pockets, my nose starting to run with a new cold, I pushed against the swing door with my shoulder. There was only one young man waiting to be seen, he was Chinese. I sat down in the waiting area and heard the conversation between him and the Duty Sargent. The young man had been robbed of his wallet. He took a form and started to fill it in whilst I came forward to the desk.

The Duty Sergeant was about the same age as Lukkas, but his features were earthy, worldly. He glanced up at me and smiled. "Can I help you?" he asked.

"Is DC Jane about?" I don't know you, I thought, I hope you don't know Lukkas.

He was a little more interested then. "Do you have an appointment with her?"

I shook my head, "No, I don't, I do know her though…"

He nodded. "Could you give me an idea what this is about, is it urgent, I mean, a domestic incident?"

"No," I said hastily. Just as I struggled to explain, the swing doors behind the desk opened and there she was, just as I remembered her; tall, self-confident; handsome, rather than pretty.

One of the Rugby Mums. We served coffee and hot dogs on a Sunday morning.

"Laura, how are you? It's so nice to see you, Maggie and I were just talking about you the other day. She was going to call around and see you…" We chatted for a while about Joseph and her son, Andrew, who used to play for the same rugby team. "All those muddy sessions on the rugby pitch, eh? It seems like yesterday!"

I grinned as she reminded me, my toes as cold now as they had been on those Sunday mornings, until she paused and frowned, remembering her job. "But, is everything okay?" she asked me.

"Sort of," I said. "Are you very busy, or about to go off duty or something?"

She shrugged. "No, actually, it's been pretty quiet, I expect things'll hot up over Christmas and after New Year, that's when tempers flare." She closed one eye and regarded me with her head on one side. "Do you want to come through for a chat?"

I nodded, with a sudden tightness in my throat which could easily turn to tears.

I followed her through a corridor painted the colour of nicotine, it also smelled of cannabis, presumably not a police person, I thought. She jerked her thumb towards an open door. Outside the room a lopsided Christmas tree valiantly attempted to lighten the grim surroundings.

Jane nodded towards a chair, sitting herself opposite me. She poured a glass of water for me from a half-filled jug. I understood that she was trying to put me at my ease, she talked about her son, Joe's old friend, Andrew, who was now at Hendon Police College. She waited patiently, whilst her pink nails tapped gently upon the surface of the desk.

"The thing is, Jane, I need this to be strictly confidential. I'm here because, a little while ago, I had a voice mail sent to my phone. It appears to be Lukkas' voice, with... a woman." I paused. "It's odd. I don't recognise the other voice and don't understand how the other person got hold of my number, but there's a women's name called on the recording, Irina, and I only know one Irina. She would know my number. But..."

Jane's expression hadn't faltered, her training had been excellent, but even so, even though there wasn't a hint of criticism there, I felt such a fool.

"But Lukkas is counting, that's what it sounds like, and the thing is…" I paused yet again, then it came out, when I had wanted to restrain my speech. I told Jane about his behaviour towards me, not the really ugly stuff, but the suggestion that I was mad when I wasn't, the sanctions, the influence over the children.

Still her expression didn't change, until she said at last, "Has he used any physical violence against you?"

"No," I said. "No."

"Do you feel that he is in a relationship with someone else?"

"Yes, well, possibly. I've wondered that for some time, but when I ask him, he denies it."

Again, I felt humiliated. However nice, however reasonable a person, worldly wise; Jane, with her successful children, her lovely cottage in Stanton, her successful marriage, made me feel small, made me feel a failure. Yet I wasn't in a position to be proud, I had brought myself here.

"I don't understand what you want me to do, Laura. Having an affair isn't a criminal offence, much as we might like it to be." She smiled sympathetically. "Have you got the recording?"

"Yes, here, but the thing is, I wondered, could he be being blackmailed?" I said in a rush, groping in my bag for the phone.

She didn't answer me but held out her hand.

I went to the voicemails, listening for a moment before handing it to her, then she took it and placed it by her ear. I watched as she listened once, then ran the recording back to the start, listening again. After the third time, she said, "It sounds like him, you would know your own husband. I think I can hear the name,

Irina and I can hear him counting. The voice saying please sounds more like a young male than a female."

I frowned, but thought then; yes, it does.

Jane shook her head. "I don't know what this is, Laura. There's no evidence to go with it, nothing you can pin point. Have you played it to Lukkas?"

"No," I admitted.

"It might be the Irina you know, but this is someone calling the name. There are probably a few Irina's in the Oxfordshire area, Russian, isn't it?"

I nodded.

She sighed then. "Presumably this Irina is who you suspect as the other woman? If you knew what this was about, and could persuade Lukkas to admit it, do you really think it will make him give her up?"

I shrugged. "I suppose not," I said slowly, biting my lip all the while like a school girl before the Head teacher.

"But you want to stay with him, or are you looking for revenge?"

For the first time I wondered whether I did want that. I had been angry inside for a long time, perhaps I did.

"The Police can't find revenge for you, Laura. Only divorce might do that. Do you know that Ken and I divorced?"

I brought my chin up swiftly, staring at her in surprise. "Really? No, I didn't, I'm sorry."

She gave a chuckle. "Don't be, I was down for a long time, but I'm over it all now. He left me for another woman. Truly, I'm happy, the children are happy too. It all worked out in the end and I've moved on. I don't have any regrets and though I can't promise you that it's easy, it gets easier." She handed my phone back to me. "Or, if you are determined to prove what you feel and face him with it, get a private detective."

I laughed then. "After stopping my job to look after Hannah's children, I've less than a thousand pounds in my bank account," I said.

It was the second time I had been surprised at a marriage break up and the second time someone had suggested a private detective, first Valeria, now DC Jane. She had said that she thought the pleading voice belonged to a man. I had that thought, too. But what did that mean? At least she had heard Lukkas' voice, I supposed.

On the pavement outside the police station, feathery flakes of snow fell to the ground and I lifted my face to them, breathing in the clean air brought by the snow.

Suddenly I wanted to go back to my parents, to my childhood, to safety and security. I thought I had that with Lukkas, I was wrong.

Chapter Thirty-Two

A Private detective

I had several hundred presents to buy and some very small savings left from my teaching, but I felt tortured enough to follow Jane's advice. The Private Detective seemed as necessary an investment now, as a new boiler.

I searched through the yellow pages, wondering whether you could find hit men in the yellow pages too.

In the end, I settled on a London agency, believing that they wouldn't have heard of Lukkas. But they had many offices and a receptionist put me through to one of their people in Oxford. I was so anxious that my voice rattled in the receiver.

Mr Macpherson did not have a Scott's accent as his name implied. He had a deep, rough edged, cockney voice.

The question repeated itself inside me, "How could you do this to Lukkas?"

Mr Macpherson was very business-like, barking short, sharp questions at me, which I answered as best I could.

"What kind of car does he drive... is he a fast driver?"

"Very fast," I told him. "He's been followed by private investigators before, through his own court cases, so he might be wary."

"In that case, Madam, we will need two investigators on the case, one to follow him on foot and one to drive. We'll also need a tracker placed on his car just in case we lose him."

A Tracker, what was that? I wondered. It sounded terrible, as though he were a fugitive on the run.

"All right, how much will that cost?" I asked.

"About two thousand pounds, plus VAT," Mr Macpherson said.

I swallowed hard. "Mr Macpherson, I don't have that kind of money," I pleaded.

"Then I can't organise it for you, Madam. That's the price," he said, politely but very firmly.

I mulled it over on the way to the nursery and then, with Lilly, went to the supermarket. It was full of ordinary, Oxfordshire people, not the kind of people who call private detectives at all. I didn't even have two thousand pounds. At the vegetable counter, Lilly counted twenty red apples whilst I felt so distracted I could hardly count the fingers on my hand.

"Are you going to pay for those?"

I looked straight into the steely eyes of the lady on the checkout, realising that in my frenzy I'd eaten half a bunch of green grapes.

In bed that night, in the early hours of the morning, whilst Lukkas snored beside me and muttered bits of conversation in his sleep, I had an idea.

I called Mr Macpherson the next day.

"Is it a bit cheaper, and is there any reason why you can't just place the tracker on my husband's car, so that I can get the postcodes and things from that?" I asked.

There was a pause, but when he spoke to me it was with greater respect, as though I'd invented something new.

"Well yes, I suppose it could be done, then we could give you the report afterwards," he agreed.

It took about four minutes to organise it all. The agent would meet me under the cover of darkness that Friday evening and then follow me home to identify Lukkas' car. He would wait for darkness; for me to close the curtains late in the evening and then fit the tracker beneath the car.

We met at the Park and Ride, in the shadow of the hotel. He was nothing like Elliot Gould, in The Long Goodbye. In fact, he was not much older than Hannah. A tall, lanky young man from Liverpool who assured me that it would all be fine. As I signed a contract I could hardly read in the dark and handed over the cash, I told myself that it was probably a lot less than Lukkas had spent on a woman.

I shook all evening and kept a fixed smile upon my face as Lukkas ate his dinner before the television, unaware of the young man loitering in the road. Then, just before bed time a message came to my phone which said, "Done."

I had expected to be on tenterhooks for the next few days, but it wasn't like that. For once, when Lukkas left the house, I felt peaceful, for it would defeat the object if he stayed at home and it was as though someone else was keeping an eye on him. Despite the disappearance of his underpants and the unnerving feeling that another woman was doing his washing, I relaxed for the first time in ages.

On the Monday morning, after the tracker had been fitted, I had a text from Adam. It took a few minutes to realise that it was in code.

"Can you call me? The pool has flooded," it said.

I rang him.

"Sorry," he said cheerfully, "but the tracker's come off."

"What do you mean, the tracker's come off?" I asked indignantly, falling into a chair in my disappointment.

"It's okay," Adam reassured me. "We found it on Sunday morning. It was on the kerb at the top of your road, no damage other than a few scratches. We think it must have brushed with a sleeping policeman. The problem is that the chassis of your husband's car is very low. Nowadays there's very little metal exposed at the bottom of cars like that, so the magnet in the tracker didn't work."

"Oh," I said. Why hadn't they told me that? "So, what do we do now?"

"The best thing is if I get the tracker back to you, show you how to use it and then you find a place where there's a significant bit of metal, I think the boot would do."

"Me?" It was a terrifying thought. Yet, I suppose I had successfully planted a Dictaphone in the car. I certainly wasn't going to spend all that money on nothing.

I had begun to feel like Mata Hari, a spy making dinner, making love, making Joe look for a job.

On the next Friday evening, I waited again until Lukkas was safely ensconced in his chair with a tray of Chinese food on his lap. Taking the car keys from his overcoat pocket, I stole outside to the garage on the pretence of putting away groceries in the outside freezer.

Fumbling with the heavy, camera shaped device, I opened the boot which had a thin lining of grey, felt material around it. Hurriedly, I pressed the starter button as Adam had instructed. I tried to control my shaking hand as I watched, terrified that Lukkas would catch me, or a neighbour come to talk to me, and finally decided that there was no more time to wait until the light on the tracker changed from blue to orange. I pushed the thing beneath the felt lining at the top of the car and the two magnets went home with a dull but satisfying thump.

After that, Adam's texts were enthusiastic.

"He's in Buckingham, at a place called Morton Avenue."

"He's parked close to a hotel in Milton Keynes."

And the next day, "He's been at the office all day except to make two short journeys."

I shared my thoughts with Adam.

"The thing is," he said, "when we don't draw a lot of conclusions, it's generally because the affair is being carried out inside the office, if you see what I mean…"

Inside the office? No, Lukkas would be very strict about that kind of thing. In the last ten years, he had fired a legal secretary when he discovered that he had been carrying on a relationship with someone inside the office. No. He might have fallen in love or sex with someone else, but he wouldn't humiliate me with a member of staff, not after all this time. I didn't believe it. I just couldn't face it.

No. I didn't believe it.

When the week ended, I removed the tracker myself and left it in a safe hiding place close to the garage for Adam to retrieve it. A few days after that he sent me the report. Nine sheets of locations, of latitudes and longitudes. Some of them were in London or

Buckingham, Milton Keynes and Banbury. Many of the locations puzzled me, one in particular-although he might have been calling on a client. It was a road in Abingdon, but firstly, in the middle of the afternoon, he had stopped outside a shopping centre in Milton for ten minutes, as though he were picking someone up. Perhaps the person who left little parcels in his car for me to find.

I had two and a half hours before collecting the girls from school.

I would have liked some company, my life often felt lonely now. But Charlotte and any other friends that might have come with me on this journey were doing sensible jobs, as I once had, besides-it probably wasn't appropriate to take other people on a journey to track down a straying husband.

The details Adam had given me lead me to a brewery on the edge of an estate, a rather smart estate, but beyond that a second estate crouched dispiritedly.

He could have parked here and walked to any of these houses. I wanted to give up in an instant, but I was also tired of not knowing the worst. I parked my car in the location he had parked his, finding a gap in the hedge which led to an alleyway to both estates.

The posher estate told me nothing, although I trundled around it for about half an hour. It was very new and mercifully small. I asked myself again, exactly what I expected to find. Love and jealousy were making a fool of me, I couldn't argue with that, I thought; as I wandered about like a female Colombo.

I came to the end of a second alleyway, flanked by iron poles. It led to the older, slightly tatty estate. As I talked to myself about the merits of returning to paid teaching instead of unpaid, private detective work, my heart gave a loud whoop. It could be closure, it could be closure, my internal voice said.

I was standing before a small, squat, concrete bungalow surrounded by broken, stone paths and in front of that was her car, just as I remembered it from her tenancy. A rusty blue Vauxhall with her half-remembered registration.

"Irina," I muttered to myself.

For the second time, I peered through the window facing the front garden, my heart beating an elated but discordant tune, like a badly played bongo drum.

"Hello, Laura."

The bongo drum stopped suddenly as I held my breath. Irina now stood in the doorway, her Chinese, silk dressing gown was almost the colour of the car and her eye shadow, I noticed.

I forced a smile, wondering whether her henchman, Gregory, was about. But the house seemed quiet.

She was beautiful, with her golden hair loose about her shoulders. My heart gave a little lurch for my lost looks.

"Do you want to come inside?" She asked, and she was serenely confident and in command, no tears this time.

I nodded and stepped through the door she held open for me. "Please, go inside," she said, indicating the living room with a nod of the head. I stepped through, feeling angry and foolish at the same time as scanning the well hoovered floor for traces of something. But her carpet was much cleaner than mine, free from the children's toys that Lukkas grumbled about.

"Please, sit down." There was no smirk of amusement on her lips as she offered the chair in her slightly husky, accented voice. I sat on the mock, leather settee with the colourful crocheted blanket thrown across the back. There was a faint smell of nicotine in the room, disguised by air freshener.

She sat beside me, crossing her slim legs, modestly pulling the dressing gown around her small, ballerina like body.

"To answer your question, Laura, no, it isn't me..." I opened my mouth to say something, but the saliva had dried up. She went on, "We became friends, quite good friends after I stopped being your tenant, but I've never had sex with Lukkas and I'm certainly not his mistress. I contacted him for some legal advice about immigration and after that we met incidentally, a few times," she added candidly.

She gazed at me, her brown eyes framed by plucked and painted eyebrows. "Lukkas is a very friendly person, very warm; he likes young people, men and women."

I found my voice, I couldn't resist the impulse to say, "Only if they are attractive, Irina. I like young people of all ages, I've spent most of my life trying to help them, one way and another."

She frowned. "Please don't take offence, Laura, Lukkas told me that he loves you very much and that when things are good with you, they are very good indeed."

"How kind of him," I mumbled angrily.

"But Laura, I am trying to help you and I have work soon, so listen." She leaned forward, fixing her eyes upon me. "Sometimes I have met Lukkas in a bar, in the city, The Porter's Lodge; you know it?"

I nodded, wondering where this was leading to.

"We don't meet by arrangement, he goes there quite often, I think. It's a meeting place for lawyers, so I go with my friend Helena, who works at the hotel. She wants to meet a wealthy lawyer. But Lukkas almost always comes there with a woman. Holly, she's called. They laugh a lot and I watch the way he looks at her. He likes her very much, I think. He pays a lot of attention to her and buys her drinks."

She must have noticed my face fall. She held my hand very briefly. "I don't know, maybe they are just friends, perhaps they just work closely together. But if you need to start looking somewhere. Look there…"

I thought of Adam's words, "When we don't reach many conclusions, it is often because the affair is carried out inside the office, if you see what I mean."

No. Please God, no. And yet it made more sense to me. I drew in a long, sad breath, only just remembering the bonfire night recording.

"The recording that was sent to my phone. Did it have anything to do with you, Irina?"

She shrugged. "No. Lukkas has used the pool at the hotel on several occasions. He has had a massage there, also. But no, absolutely not, I have no idea what that is about."

I didn't know whether to believe her. "Has Lukkas ever given you a lift, Irina?" I asked, thinking of the blonde hairs.

"Oh yes. I think he does give lifts. He gives lifts to the lawyer, Holly."

Does he? I bridled at the thought.

"Have you ever… left things in his car?"

"What kind of things?" she frowned. "I don't think I've lost anything."

Perhaps she genuinely misunderstood me. I chewed my lower lip, fixing my eyes upon her as though to trip her up.

She laughed then, shaking her head. "You are worrying too much. He said he loves you. In Russia, it is normal to behave like this in marriage."

I made no comment.

"Well, thank you for talking to me, I'd better be going, and you have to get to work."

I wasn't sure that I trusted her any more than before, though I liked her a little more. I wasn't sure that she was as principled as she made out and maybe she was a little jealous of Holly. I certainly was.

"So, we are friends now?" Irina smiled.

I nodded. Friends, at least far more so than we were before, I thought.

I drove home with a renewed sense of panic. No, Lukkas, please don't let it be Holly.

Two lawyers, I would be working against two lawyers to keep him, or two lawyers in a divorce. I didn't want to believe it, yet a voice inside me told me I had been wrong so far.

Yet, why should I trust Irina?

Because I had read the look on her face when she told me about Holly, it was a look laced with jealousy and if I knew nothing else, I was an expert now, upon the subject of jealousy.

CHAPTER THIRTY-THREE

Holly at Christmas

Later that evening, I printed out the rest of the material that Adam had sent me. I went into the garage to mull over the rest of the postcodes, crossing off any that were business related. I found a reading that was miles from anywhere, somewhere between Brackley and Bicester, close to the main highway. He appeared to have stopped there and waited for almost an hour. Why there?

I went back into the house and googled the place on a map finder. It was a motorway rest stop, with a garage and shops and... a Travelodge. The place meant nothing to me.

Holly. I knew nothing about her, but the urge to know was overwhelming, like a horrible itch that wouldn't go until I had scratched at it. How could you, Lukkas? But I couldn't accuse her, I had no evidence. He worked with Holly on a daily basis, relied upon her, confided in her. It didn't mean that he was having sex with her. All that I had was burgundy lipstick and bits of pink shawl. I would have to see them together, once more.

On the following evening I sent a message to Lukkas. "In Oxford, buying Christmas presents," it said, "Do you mind if I walk down, perhaps we could go for a mulled wine like we used to?"

I wasn't in Oxford buying Christmas presents, which meant that I'd have to go there now. I pulled on a clean dress and my best old coat and boots and drove into the city, now decorated with Christmas lights. I parked near the office and walked briskly to Marks and Spencer, where I bought three gifts. Then I walked back towards Lukkas' office, checking my phone for a reply. There was nothing.

When I arrived at his office there was a light on in the reception area, but it was empty. Above, at the very top of the building there was one light burning from Lukkas' floor. I pressed the buzzer and waited. No one answered.

Tom's portly figure turned the corner. He smiled broadly at me, seeming unable to conceal a sudden burst of laughter. It embarrassed me a little, but I smiled to hide my lack of confidence.

"Hullo," he said. "They're in the pub next door, but I have to get back, baby and all that…"

"Oh, okay, thanks," I smiled, hiding my humiliation. I tried to walk slowly, carrying my purchases, with the ridiculous feeling I'd never experienced in all the years I had been married to Lukkas, of being excluded in some way.

Three smokers sat at trestle tables outside the pub, overlooking the cold, grey river. I hesitated briefly then pushed the door open to a packed pub with a cheerful interior and log fire.

Lukkas and some of his staff were seated at a trestle table in a window overlooking the river. Their backs were facing me. Lukkas was sitting next to the girl, Holly. There were three other staff there, a young, blonde, fresh faced secretary, Josh and another young girl I had never seen before.

It was Josh who saw me first, "Hey, Mum!" he called over the noise.

At the mention of my name, Lukkas turned. His reaction was explicit, he glowered at me.

"Fancy a drink?" Josh offered, tactfully covering up for my hurt feelings.

I smiled uncertainly at Lukkas, hesitating. I didn't want Holly or the other staff to read my feelings. I had chosen to walk into the lion's den.

For the first time, I really looked at Holly, just as at the same time, she appraised me.

She wasn't beautiful, rather plain in some ways, and certainly older than I had thought her when I saw her with Lukkas. But she had an attractive curve of the lips and a mischievous light in her eyes. I could see immediately that Lukkas might be attracted to her. There was something else; dark, chestnut brown hair cut carefully in a bob; just like Betty, just like the girl in the restaurant, and it made me feel uneasy.

"Actually, we were just going," Lukkas said. The cold rudeness in his voice was unforgivable. He had never spoken to me like that before his staff. The fair-haired secretary regarded me uncertainly, almost with sympathy, but I smiled back. Who exactly did Lukkas mean by 'we'. Josh hated crowded pubs and I knew he would ask me for a lift home, the two young girls were not lawyers, they wouldn't be returning to work in the office at this time, so presumably Lukkas was referring to himself and Holly.

Lukkas, who never had time to go for a drink with me, nowadays.

"I'll get a lift back with you, Mum, if that's okay," Josh said.

"Okay, Josh, but I think I'd like a glass of wine first," I challenged. I was angry with them both now, Lukkas and Holly. Was he trying to impress her with his manly authority over his wife? Because clearly, she was amused by the whole thing, there was a sardonic curve at the corner of the plump lips.

"Okay, I'll get one for you. Dry white?" Josh asked before going to the bar.

As Lukkas sat down once more, his face angry and stiff, I noticed too the gash of dark, burgundy lipstick on Holly's face, the identical colour to the mark on Lukkas shirt and the stains upon the tissues that Lukkas couldn't throw away.

He had never cared about who I knew at his office, who I met with, but this much I knew now. He had been trying to keep me away from Holly and the realisation was like a dull knife sticking into my belly. I suppose you wouldn't want your wife to meet with your mistress, I thought.

As Josh bought my wine, Holly said, "Lukkas told me that you used to be a teacher."

I nodded, "Yes, at a large school in Oxford," I replied, sitting down opposite her, unwanted.

"My partner, John, is a Deputy Headteacher, actually. He works in Banbury, but he's close to retirement now."

Was she trying to throw me off the trail, had Lukkas tried to stop me from coming to the office over the past months because of her?

Banbury. I thought about the last entry on the tracker record, the service station where Lukkas appeared to have spent almost an hour.

"Nowadays," Holly smiled, "He's away a lot on teaching courses, that kind of thing."

I nodded. "That must be quite lonely for you," I said, adding, "Although Banbury is quite a busy little town, I guess."

"Oh, it is. I shop there, but we don't live in the town, we live in a little hamlet called Tadbury."

I stared at her long and hard, aware of Lukkas' nervousness as he watched me, a vibration disturbing the air between us all. In my mind's eye, I scanned Adam's list. There it was, Between Banbury and Bicester, Tadbury.

You are the one, Holly, who has been encouraging Lukkas to behave like this. You are the one who has tried to break me, break our family. My thoughts ran this way and that. I took a rather large swig of the wine Josh had brought to me.

In one swift movement, Lukkas drained his glass and stood up. He said nothing, not goodbye, not "I'm off then." He put his glass down heavily upon the wooden table and just strode out of the pub. I got up to follow him, Josh too. "Can I have that lift, then?" Josh asked optimistically, as though interrupting a scene from some heart-breaking film.

"If you wait. But I'm not going yet, Josh. I'm going to the office."

He frowned, but I couldn't read his face, whether he understood that Lukkas was in a temper or not was hard to tell. "Okay, I'll just get the bus," he shrugged.

Outside his office, Lukkas was moodily smoking a cigarette, one of those cigarettes he had accused me of encouraging. As I walked towards him, he snapped, "You're not doing it." "Not doing what?" I asked, genuinely confused.

"Coming into my office…" He snarled, dog like.

"You mean that I should cut back on family finances, so you can buy new computers for the office but that I can't come in now and make myself a cup of tea?"

He threw down the cigarette and stomped to the office and I followed him into the reception area. Then he threw an unpleasant smile in my direction like a spoilt child, locked himself into the corridor to the upper floors and disappeared.

I walked into the kitchen to make tea, then sat myself upon the settee, flicking through a magazine. But I wasn't reading it and as I looked up, staring morosely into the street, Holly returned, her black heels clip clopping on the pavement.

I left her to unlock the door herself, after all, she had a key to the kingdom.

"Oh," she said as she saw me there. There was a look of disappointment on her face. "I came back for my bag."

Did you? I wondered.

She retrieved the little black, wheelie suitcase from the corner of the room and glanced at me once more, before returning to the door.

"Holly," I said as she opened it, and she turned expectantly. "Why don't you get a car, you wouldn't have to rely on Lukkas for so many lifts, then. It's a long way to Tadbury."

Her face reddened, and she clamped her small, wolverine canine on her lip for an instant before staring at me. Then she offered the merest of smiles.

"Laura, why don't you compartmentalise your life," she said.

Leaving me with that, I watched her cross the road toward the train station.

Holly. I shuddered with fear and loathing.

I had been wrong perhaps, about all the women I had suspected. But of course, it made sense that it was Holly. When might it have begun? How long had she been there, at his firm? I had met her, years ago and had forgotten. She was one of many people I had met at one of many dinners.

Had Lukkas known her before he came to the firm? How easy it would be to carry on with someone who worked so closely with you.

But, I had no proof of anything.

After that, we drove home separately. As soon as I entered the kitchen, Lukkas threw his keys onto the kitchen table and faced me, one hand on his hip, looking every bit the Lawyer.

"Jealous cat!" He snarled. "So, you think I'm having an affair with Holly, do you?"

"I didn't say that, but I think she's a bit of a control freak, maybe that's what I've been sensing all this time. She's taken over the office and now she's trying to take over our life!"

"Really?" He yelled.

"Don't yell, the children are upstairs, watching television," I said.

But it was enough to bring Hannah and Joe down to the kitchen, which was what Lukkas wanted.

"What's the matter now?" Joe asked.

"Ha!" Lukkas spluttered. She thinks I'm having an affair with Holly Farrah now, my colleague!"

Joe shook his head slowly. "It's Christmas soon, Mum. You're not going to spoil Christmas with this stuff, are you?"

I sniffed, "I haven't spoiled the eighteen Christmases since you were born, in fact they've been spectacular if

I say so myself. I'm not going to spoil this one and anyway," I added, "I didn't say I thought that..."

Hannah sat at a kitchen chair, looking up at me. There was an angry bleakness about the short laugh and the shake of her head. "You really do need to get your brains checked, Marge, if you think that. She's been in the shop, she's a nice person, she would never do that."

I wanted to ask, "Is she?" But I said nothing. I looked slowly from one to the other of them. "Forget it, then," I said.

"Forget it?" Lukkas barked, "You've just been thoroughly rude to her in my office!"

I shook my head, "You were rude to me, you didn't even offer to buy me a drink, in fact you said that you were leaving."

Lukkas skipped over that. "Well, you've done it now," he warned. There's no way you are going to the Christmas Staff dinner. Not in a million years."

How, I wondered, had he known that I had been rude to her? He wasn't there at the time. She had spoken to him on the phone, she must have told him that.

Then Joe put his hand on my shoulder, his touch was light, this time, and I turned about. "Do what Dad suggested, please Mum, for all our sakes. Get a proper psychiatric referral this time. This has gone on long enough."

What was I supposed to say to that? "Oh, alright Joseph, anything for a peaceful Christmas?"

I turned my back on them all, putting the pre-prepared dinner in the oven, to heat. My head ached with tension.

"Now she's fixated with my colleague," Lukkas said as a parting shot, "If I'm not careful my business will suffer and it'll all go down the pan. I'm not having your grandparents here for Christmas if she doesn't stop."

I ignored him. I ignored all of them and went to read to the girls.

Much later that evening I thought about the word compartmentalise. "You should compartmentalise your life," Holly had said. I knew what it meant, and it was probably easier for childless Holly to do that than for me. Was it necessarily a good thing to do that? Didn't serial killers and criminals do it, shutting their feelings, their guilt, in a box?

When in doubt, google it. There were several references to affairs. It seemed that men were better at compartmentalising than women and that it was a tried and trusted method of keeping love interests separate. Had she meant to say it, was she taunting me?

Lukkas had been more defensive than ever before, but then again, he would be upset if he thought I had turned my attention to a trusted colleague. I didn't know what I believed any more.

CHAPTER THIRTY-FOUR

Gwen

I had Gwen's number in my tatty old phone book. I hadn't spoken with her since Lukkas told me she had agreed to leave the firm- for placing, he said, a spy camera on her desk.

I wanted to see her again, Lukkas had asked me not to contact her for the sake of the firm. I had always heeded what he wanted, especially when it came to our livelihood and the livelihood of other, good people who worked there, but not now.

When Gwen answered my call, that same evening, she sounded surprised but then defensive. Maybe she believed that I would be critical of her. I wasn't used to that caution where Gwen was concerned, she had always been open and honest with me.

"Oh, Laura, how nice to hear from you..." But it didn't sound like the bouncy, confident woman that had worked for him.

I paused before saying it. "Hey, Gwen. Could I come and see you sometime?"

"Yes, sure, it would be good to catch up."

"How are things?" I asked.

"Not too bad. I'm working for another Law firm, here in Thame. I'm working less hours, but what with Tony's illness and Dad to look after, I can't really manage full time now. When would you like to meet up?"

I swallowed. "Are you busy right now? Please say if you are, I shan't mind at all as I've rather taken you by surprise. I'll just come for a little while."

There was a slight hesitation whilst she mulled over my great cheek in asking it, but then she said, "Yes, sure. I'm not doing anything but watching the television. Tony has gone to bed and I'm not babysitting, for a change," she added. "Do you remember where I live?"

I left the house after serving the dinner.

"Where are you going to?" Lukkas asked me.

"Just to see Charlotte," I lied. He grunted as if he didn't believe me, but I turned away from him, grabbing my coat from the hallway.

I did remember where Gwen lived, although I had only been to her house once and many years ago, with Lukkas. It lay in a small cul-de-sac off the main High Street, right at the end of the town. I sat within the car for two minutes before getting out. She had sounded cautious, wary. I wasn't going to ask her about the incident with the spy camera, but I wondered whether she had caught rather more than the theft of paperclips on the spy camera.

I stared thoughtfully at her front door, the dark reminding me of the vision I had long ago. A vision of a lonely woman who lived in the countryside, someone clever, cunning, waiting for her lonely life to change.

When I knocked upon her door, she appeared in the hallway at once. We hugged. I followed her past the paraphernalia of wheelchairs and pushchairs and the tools of family life, into her living room, then ducking beneath the Christmas cards that hung across the door.

Gwen turned off the television, then offered a chair. "How have you been? I saw Hannah the other day, she looks well."

"She is," I agreed, "Now that man has gone."

In an instant, I admired Hannah for her will power, wishing I had the same resolve.

"I miss Josh," Gwen said, with a little smile, "and Heather, quite a few of them, really."

I nodded. "They miss you, too. What's the new office like?"

"Not too bad now that I've started to get into a routine. The staff are quite nice and of course, being in Thame, it's easier to get back to Tony and Dad, when I need to."

I nodded, relieved when she spoke sincerely about her situation.

"Tea?" she offered, "or something stronger? I've got some wine."

I accepted tea and waited in the living room for a couple of minutes whilst she went to the kitchen, looking at the many photographs of her family. She returned with a tray, laden with two mugs of tea and a plate of biscuits.

"How is Lukkas?" she asked.

"Fine at work," I said, "difficult at home."

Gwen laughed. "He could be very difficult at work, too, you know!"

I shook my head as she offered a biscuit. My lip had started to tremble once more as I said, "I think he's having quite a lot of fun there at present..."

She looked concerned then, as I clamped down upon my lip to keep it still.

"Laura, are you okay, what's the matter?"

"I'm fine," I said, shaking my head. I took a deep breath. "Don't fuss about it, or I'll feel worse.

I let my head fall back onto the chair and closed my eyes for a moment. "It's Lukkas, Gwen. Please don't tell anyone, I don't know what to do. I love him, but I wonder whether he's having an affair."

"Oh, I see. I don't know what to say…"

"The thing is, I wondered whether it's Holly in the office that he's having an affair with."

I looked at her. To my surprise, her cheeks had turned pink. "Oh," she said again. "What makes you think that, has something happened?"

"Not exactly, it's more of a feeling that I have, but I suppose I wondered whether you could shed any light on it."

She sat back, her hands held together in her lap and sighed. "I'm sure that Lukkas loves you," she said, as others had before her. "I admit that I never liked Holly, not from the start. She isn't popular, I know that much." She gave a small, mirthless laugh.

"I haven't had many enemies in my life, but I can't help feeling that she is one, that she resents me," I said.

"Holly is highly competitive. She resents anyone who disagrees with her, she wants to be the best at the expense of loyalty to her colleagues."

Gwen leaned forward again, placing a hand upon my shoulder and giving it a slight squeeze.

"The truth is that I don't know. There's only one thing I can tell you, but," she frowned then, her face creasing with worry, "I don't want you to repeat it, Laura. Seriously. I'm sorry for you but I don't want to fall out with Lukkas. I need my job now, we wouldn't survive without my money. If I tell you something, please keep it to yourself."

I nodded. "I'm not going to tell Lukkas anything. He doesn't even know that I'm here, Gwen. What is it?"

"Okay. About four months ago or more, shortly before I left the office, I was about to get the bus home. There was only Lukkas and Holly there. I said goodbye, then realised I'd left my bag upstairs so, I went back to their office. When I reached the top floor, I could hear giggling, Holly's voice, and noises. I pushed open the door very slightly and they were, they were…"

I wanted to shake the poor woman by the shoulders in my impatience. "They were what?" I asked.

She swallowed and pursed her lips at first. "I know it sounds very silly, but it was as though they were playing a game of chase. There were papers all over the floor and Lukkas was behind a desk, sort of panting, breathless; whilst Holly was on the other side of it. She was trying not to laugh when she saw me. I mean, I've known lawyers for a long time and certainly they act the fool, but it was all a little odd," she finished.

"Odd?" I repeated, furiously. "I'll say it was odd. For months and months, he's been telling me that he's so busy, he can't come home, can't be with our family and friends!"

She nodded. "But it doesn't mean that they are having an affair," she said.

Perhaps she was trying to comfort me, but she was right. I said nothing about the spy camera but wondered, yet again, whether she had filmed something other than the theft of paper clips.

CHAPTER THIRTY-FIVE

The Snow Queen

There were times during that Christmas, when the usual ordinary or delightful things escaped me and then, perhaps, I could have been accused of being absent minded.

Times when I read Christmas stories to the girls, all the usual favourites, but this year, the Snow Queen and Gerda's long journey to find Kay seemed particularly poignant. It helped to throw myself into the festival, decorating the house with ivy and mistletoe from the woods nearby (I had rather gone off the idea of holly in any form) making pretty but inedible biscuits with the girls but, on occasion, fear and uncertainty gnawed at my insides like a rat.

There was a strange kind of silence in the house when Lukkas was there. It unnerved me. It was as if he was a ghost, present, but in his mind-somewhere else. Once I would have put any preoccupation down to his work, but I no longer believed this.

Once when he was late home, I called his office, before he said anything I heard a female shriek, followed by a giggle. The thoughts that came to me after that were a torture. The only thing that stopped me from confronting him with Gwen's story was my promise to her.

At the last minute, like an ugly sister taunting me with an invitation to the ball, he told me I could go to the Christmas dinner with him. I thought it my reward for saying nothing about Holly, only afterwards did I find out that Hannah, feeling sorry for me, had persuaded him that I should go.

It was nice to be reunited with old faces and to meet new ones, but in between eating and conversation and the pulling of crackers, I looked guardedly at Holly.

She was clearly enamoured of Lukkas, hanging on his every word and gesture. It was as though she had to force herself to show interest in anyone else. She was small, softly spoken, reminding me a little of a librarian, but there was a depth to that. It was clear that she took a great deal of care about her appearance. Her hair was cut in a sleek, dark, chestnut bob, her eyebrows carefully plucked and painted black, rising in an almost medieval arch. She had bright, lively eyes, the eyes of a bird and her lips were painted in that same burgundy colour. Above her mouth, she had painted a beauty spot. She wore a plain, black velvet dress.

It was as if our confrontation in the office had never happened. Convention dictated that we both be adults. I didn't want to be an adult, I wanted to pull her hair.

Lukkas tried, oh how hard he tried, not to pay all his attention to her. I could see that, and it made me want to cry. But it was the last thing I could do. I stuck on my most cheerful and fearless smile, stifling the urge to compete with her all evening and mostly, I succeeded.

Heather stuck closely to me, a generous gesture but I wondered whether she, a perceptive woman, had noticed that their relationship seemed far more than a close, working relationship.

We spoke little to one another, Holly and I, unless we were part of a conversation begun by Tom or one of the others. Being with her, I gleaned much about her and noticed the small, clear nails, false nails like Irina's.

Towards the end of the evening, whilst we waited for a taxi, I went to the cloakroom and when I returned, it was to witness one of the older secretaries with her hand upon Holly's shoulder. "It's all right Lukkas, I'll take good care of her, I'll see she gets home safely," Mary was saying.

There were many younger, more vulnerable women working for him, now drinking what was left of the wine. Surely Lukkas might be concerned for their welfare too?

As we left in the taxi, Lukkas put his hand upon my knee. But I felt wretched and inadequate, barely succeeding in not pulling away. It was almost Christmas, I had promised Joe that it wouldn't be spoilt.

On the day before Christmas Eve; Ruby, Lilly and I set up the slightly wonky Christmas tree bought years ago at Woolworths. I much preferred real trees, but no one ever wanted to help me remove it after Christmas and the hoover always blocked with old pine needles.

In church on Christmas Eve, at the Christingle service, the vicar asked the children why Mary rode on a donkey and Ruby put up her hand to say, "Because she gets car sick?" I kissed the top of her head and hugged Lilly, glad of them both.

After church, Lukkas arrived with his elderly parents, having collected them from their home in Gloucester. We sat down for a Christmas Eve meal as we had every year since Lukkas and I married, so long ago. Lukkas sat beside his father at the dining room table whilst Josh and Hannah gave me a hand in the kitchen, although the way Josh kept picking at the food, I was afraid there wouldn't be any left.

Then Lukkas' mother, Marjorie, came into the kitchen; stately as a galleon in a new, buff coloured dress. She asked Hannah about her shop and joked with Josh before turning her attention to me. "And how have you been, Laura?"

I bridled at the tone of her voice, there was so much gushing sympathy in it and Marjorie didn't, as a rule, sympathise with me. It was as though I had some terrible tropical disease.

"I'm fine; good, thanks," I replied cheerfully and with a smile, as I stirred the sauce.

I looked sideways at Hannah who was studiedly avoiding my eyes.

"Good... can I give you a hand?" Marjorie asked then, understanding from my reply that she should drop the subject. But I knew in an instant that Lukkas had spoken to her. Lukkas had told her that I was mentally ill.

"Lukkas looks very tired, doesn't he? He works so hard..."

I agreed that he did and thought, he plays hard too by all accounts.

The day after Boxing Day, Lukkas had to go into the office, or so he said. I think his parents were disappointed, although they would never say that. I was left to amuse them on my own and decided to take them to the Henley Rowing Museum with the girls, so we could have fun in the Toad of Toad Hall exhibition next door.

There was a thin layer of powdery snow lacing the pavements which made it hard to push Derek's wheelchair, but I managed. Afterwards we ate lunch in the café there. I hoped they had fun, I thought so. Marjorie didn't ask about my health again, but once or twice I caught her eyes upon me, as though she was examining me in the manner of a doctor.

At home once more, we waited for Lukkas. My parents-in-law were safely ensconced in the warm living room before the television with a tray of sandwiches and cake. He had been gone quite some time. The sky beyond the kitchen window had turned the colour of a purple bruise.

I never used to fret like this, but I wondered why he took so long. At last I heard his key turn in the lock. I peered along the hallway, clutching a tea towel. Lukkas was stamping the snow from his black shoes on the doormat. His black, woollen coat was dusted with frost. When he looked up at me, his face was flushed a ruddy pink. He saw me but didn't attempt a smile.

Something was wrong, I had no idea what it could be. Tentatively I went forward to him and reached up to kiss his cheek. There was whisky on his breath, but I said nothing, I wanted normality, I wanted his love.

There were crystal stars that night, in a sea of black beyond the window. In bed, I watched Lukkas undress, pulling his shirt over his head. I loved every part of his soft body, knew every crease and fold, for he was older now and though his body was muscular it was a little plumper.

I smelled his scent beneath the aftershave and followed the line of his spine with my eyes as he lay down. In an instant, it was as though ice-cold water had fallen on my own, warm skin. On his left hip, to the left of his spine was a clear scratch, the exact shape of a sharp fingernail.

"You've got a scratch," I said, unable to keep it to myself.

"Where?" He asked gruffly.

I touched it and he twisted his head to look. "It's nothing," he said, "A nail or something."

But he knew that it wasn't that kind of nail. We both knew. I didn't want to row with his parents in the house.

He fell to sleep beside me, but I dreamed that night. I dreamt that my family were together in a boat, except that Lukkas was on a second boat. His back was turned away from us and he wore an old brown jacket he had long since thrown away, his hands thrust into the pockets as he used to.

He was sailing away from us, further and further away on a charcoal black sea.

CHAPTER THIRTY-SIX

The Kick

After that Christmas period, Lukkas suggested that we go to Nice for the New Year with two very old friends we had not seen in a long time. Simon had been our best man. He is a well-known journalist and his wife, Valerie, the writer for a popular magazine. I was truly happy at the thought. They live in London but for all we had seen them, they might have lived on another continent. They have two children who get on well with Ruby and Lilly but on this occasion, Valerie had left them with her sister.

It felt wonderful to get away from her, from Holly. It was good to relax after the effort put into the Christmas holiday, too. To escape the dull, colourless landscape for the blue of the sea in the Bay des Agnes and the yellow and ochre buildings of Nice, the Christmas trees coated with sparkling, white paint, festooned with tinsel and ribbons that caught the intense, late, afternoon light.

Looking back, it was another part of the false world where Lukkas loved me and only me. Once more, strolling beside our old friends, Lukkas held my hand tightly. Sometimes he kissed me, but when we were alone, he would slip into silence again.

We ate a sumptuous meal in a local restaurant on New Year's Eve, gorging on oysters. In fact, there were eight courses in all, and we ate on into the night, until finally, although Lukkas and Simon excused themselves from the dancing by saying they had drunk too much, Valerie and I joined the disco in a packed restaurant.

Every now and then I would retreat for a few minutes into a world of my own, as though some part of me was aware that these were the dying days of one life. I couldn't imagine the next.

Finally, towards midnight, we made our way home to our apartment and to the bottles of champagne. The French are good at doing New year and they are good at fireworks, especially in Nice where they drag floating rafts out to sea to set the fireworks off. There they explode into neon dandelions of red, white, orange and gold. After the fireworks, a great roar lifts from the crowds on the Promenade des Anglais and people sing and hug one another, just as we did on the balcony, wishing one another a Happy New year.

Lukkas kisses me on the cheek, it seems a sincere kiss, his eyes are shining, his face happy and for one, minuscule moment, I believe that he loves me. But then, straight afterwards he reaches for his mobile phone and as Valerie wishes me a Happy New Year, dancing up and down with excitement, I watch Lukkas retreat from the balcony, into the living room to text someone. It might have been one of the children, or his mother, but I know it isn't.

I watch him put the phone down on the kitchen table and reach into the fridge for a bottle of champagne. He is a little drunk. No, he is very drunk.

I pick up the phone whilst his back is turned to me, refusing to be intimidated and find the sent message. It is to Holly. It says, "Let's hope this is a great year for us both."

This is the thing he has wanted to do all day, I know it. I know it in my head and heart.

I sniff the air as if it is cocaine and put the phone down just as he turns away from the fridge.

"Heather, Tom? Are you going to send such a heartfelt message to them?" I ask quietly, but sarcastically, bitterly.

His eyes blaze in an instant; tiny pinpricks of glowing lava. "Oh, fuck off…" he says quietly, unheard by the innocent friends on the balcony.

I fuck off, without the heart or energy to tell our family, our friends, that I am thinking of them in this New Year.

I went into our bedroom, then, and slumped on the end of the bed, crying out my distress, my jealousy and hurt. I didn't move for a long time and thought, stupidly, of our names carved into a heart in a cactus leaf a few years ago, somewhere above us, in the hills beyond Nice.

After some while I reached for a lipstick, bought at the airport to make Lukkas want me a little more. I knelt on the tiled floor and drew a tiny heart with our names on either side of it, then looked up at the sound of his feet in the hallway.

When he entered the room, swinging through the door, he looked down at me with contempt. His anger swept over me, rendering me immobile.

In one, swift movement, but with the force of a footballer, he lifted his right foot from the ground, kicking the lipstick from my hand, stinging the tips of my fingers into numbness.

He looked momentarily guilty as I clutched the fingers of my right hand with my left and gave a small cry of pain and grief.

I rocked back and forth, holding my stinging fingers, as he left me there in a heap on the floor and walked out of the room to join Simon, just as though nothing had happened. Moments later I heard him laugh.

I wondered briefly what he would do if I walked back into the room and accused him in front of our old friends. But I didn't do this. After a while, I got up and fell onto the bed fully clothed, then I cried myself to sleep.

I awoke to Lukkas' face, staring at me. There was a softness in his expression which tore at my guts. I wanted to be held but flinched away. I couldn't speak, not a word. A stupid, dumb thing. It was all my fault, I told myself then.

My next thought wasn't of the text to Holly, or the blow to my fingers, but that I must look very old and ugly, with my puffy eyes and the lines in my face clear to see in the bright light pouring through the window. My hair lay messily upon the pillow and across my eyes. I felt stupid and vulnerable and unattractive. What was Lukkas thinking about me whilst I slept, and he watched me?

"Oh," I said, in a kind of sob. I sat up, stupidly trying to brush my hair into place with my fingers.

Perhaps I was going mad. Only the slight throb in my index finger told me that he had kicked me, that I hadn't imagined it. He had kicked my soul; all the energy had left me. I felt lifeless.

I didn't think of clever things. Not that he wouldn't want Simon and Valerie to know. There was no real mark on my hand. Who would believe it? All I felt was that I wanted to be forgiven for crimes unknown, to be loved again, for it not to be like this anymore.

"What shall we do today?" he asked, and he reached out and stroked my cheek with his finger.

"Would you like to go to the Museum of Modern Art? I think Simon and Valerie would like it and it's open today, apparently. We could have some lunch afterwards, I'll book a table. But first..." He moved closer to me, kissing my bare shoulder, then kissing my breast.

For the first time in my life, I shrank from his touch. I didn't want to upset him again, didn't want to reject him, but I couldn't bring myself to move. I felt ugly, undesirable, beaten in some way, defeated. I couldn't believe that he wanted to make love to me when I was so repugnant.

"What's the matter?" he asked in an encouraging whisper.

I didn't answer at first. Both my mind and my body felt leaden. "I have a bad headache," I told him. Not the truth, not "You kicked me, Lukkas." It hardly seemed real, any of it.

I felt disgusted, not only with him, but with me.

He told me that it didn't matter, then sat up in bed with his laptop in front of him, talking to me lightly about various restaurants that we might try, while I smiled and listened as though my world wasn't collapsing about me.

We said goodbye to our friends after the Museum, promising to meet up with them soon. Then we walked to the other side of the harbour, Lukkas told me a story he had read about in Nice Matins concerning a party on a yacht, a celebrity had put her heel through the wooden decking, apparently. I always listened to his stories, but my mind felt numb today, fuzzy. I ignored all the pretty younger women passing us who Lukkas stared after, and eventually he asked, "Are you alright?"

"Yes," I assured him, and smiled at him, feeling empty all the time, my movements mechanical, my thoughts in turmoil.

When we reached the glorious Monument Aux Mortes which is the windiest spot in all Nice and towers over the harbour, I sat for a moment at the foot of the pale rock. I was emotionally exhausted and the new pair of boots, Lukkas' Christmas present to me, were pinching my feet.

He sat down beside me, his eyes wandering to the pathway that stretches to Villefranche.

I watched him in profile for what seemed to be an eternity. He was staring at a place where people sunbathed in the summer months, there was a slight frown on his long face which had nothing to do with the sun, but after a while he took his sunglasses from his top pocket and put them on.

"I love you, Lukkas. I love you so much…" I said, because I did, despite the kick to my hand, despite everything.

"Do you?"

I drew back, shocked that he had said it.

"Yes, yes of course I do, what do you mean?" I felt desperate, suddenly, to prove it to him.

"What?" His smile was suddenly light hearted, his expression baffled.

"You said, 'do you' when I told you I loved you."

"No, I didn't. You must be hearing things. Sometimes I really worry about you, Laura."

He got up then, walking towards the main road, whilst I stared after him in bewilderment. I had lost the ability to argue with him. I was a nodding dog, afraid of losing him. Slowly, like a zombie, I followed him towards the pastel blue sea.

CHAPTER THIRTY-SEVEN

Big Kiss

In the end, I told Charlotte.

"Are you serious, Lukkas kicked you, he actually kicked you?"

Her reaction was intensely protective at first, then she stared at me from across the kitchen table with her fingers covering her mouth and for one bleak moment, I wondered whether she was questioning its truth. I could not bear it for a moment if Charlotte believed that I was lying, or mad.

"I shouldn't have said anything about the text to Holly, I probably caused it to happen," I said.

She shook her head, "Caused it to happen? What are you talking about, there is no excuse, you can't allow him to kick you and get away with it! He'll do it again. Let me talk to him…" she said angrily.

"No. No Charlotte, really. Thank you, but no," I said firmly.

"Do you know he's been sending me texts whilst you were away?" Charlotte asked.

I frowned, "Texts, saying what?"

"That you have something wrong with you, that you're vague and you invent things and tell lies, that you have a personality disorder and he wants me to help him do something about it."

"What?" I stared at her incredulously for a moment, then faltered; "You don't believe him, do you?" I asked, my voice betraying insecurity.

"Stupid man, of course I don't and if he's resorted to kicking you and lying about you, no wonder you're vague!" She wrapped her arms tightly about me and we stood together for a moment. When we were younger, I had been the bossy, confident sister, how things had changed.

At last she stood back, holding my arms firmly. "But go carefully, now, Laura. This Holly thing sounds feasible, but you already suspected several other women. I know what Lukkas is like, I'll never forget what that tarty prison warden who came to dinner said about him, that was a real eye opener, but tread carefully with your accusations about this Holly woman." She sighed. "Really, I think there's only one answer now. I saw the bruising on your arms in Italy, remember? Now, he's kicking you. Divorce him…"

I opened my mouth to speak and she cut across me. "Oh, I know you've been married a long time and you say you love him. But I've told you, you will get over it with time. You shouldn't be with him. He's behaving like a bully now; your love and adulation makes him worse."

It was after that incident in Nice that I started to write things down, recording what he did, what he said to me, when he lied to me or when I felt he was making things up. It was Charlotte's idea and a good one, because sometimes I had begun to question my own sanity.

At first, that's what it was, just a record of events which I would burn when Lukkas came to his senses.

But something else happened. I had the seed of a novel which grew inside of me, accelerating speed and gravitas as a freight train, running ahead of events.

The emotional truth, if not the whole truth. Like a demanding child, it refused to be ignored but it also gave me strength. The notes, written in long hand became a new kind of new love, replacing the love I had lost.

Day after day, I was in the grip of something new, my own affair, my own secret relationship and the passion I felt for it would not be supressed. I was intoxicated by this new excitement and laughed again with the girls. My confidence grew once more.

I wrote in the evenings, in secret, taking my note pad and sheets of paper to the spare room. For the first time in a long time, I ignored Lukkas whilst he watched the television, until the evening came when he pushed the bedroom door open so softly that I didn't hear him enter.

"What are you doing?" His voice was soft, unconcerned, but I heard the edge of suspicion and malice beneath.

"Just writing," I said, fighting with the impulse to draw the sheets of paper towards me.

"What are you writing?" His question demanded an answer. Once I might have said, lightly, "Mind your own business," but not now. Lukkas was a different person, a frightening person.

"Do you remember the children's book? I got a reader's report which said I should work on it…"

He lost interest then, asking me whether I had seen the TV remote, and when he left the room, my shoulders collapsed with relief and I gathered up my writing and determined to hide it from now on.

Towards the end of January, other, frightening things took place.

Mum became very ill. It happened slowly as illness often does, with pains in her stomach. Charlotte and I both attended the doctor with her and he prescribed various medicines, but a day came when she called us. Her stomach cramps were unbearable, she had to go into hospital. That was my concern then, for my mother, not for Lukkas.

On the evening that they admitted her, we decided that Charlotte would stay with her and be with her after an exploratory examination and that I would stay with Dad. He had scarcely spent a moment without her in his life, surviving to old age because of Mum's care. He had never learned to use a cooker or a microwave. Now, in the early stages of dementia, he was agitated and anxious about her illness.

Lukkas and the family were supportive, the children worried for their Nan. Lukkas gave me a hug for the first time in ages and told me that everything would be fine.

But I didn't trust him anymore.

Seconds before leaving the house with an overnight bag and a meal for my father, I hunted for the hidden Dictaphone, placed once in Lukkas' car. I left it beneath the travel cot in the corner of our bedroom, because at short notice, it was the only place I could think of where Lukkas wouldn't discover it. I suppose I had telephone calls in mind.

Then I left, to go to my father. I forgot about the Dictaphone for two or three days.

What they discovered was that my mother's stomach was riddled with tiny cancer cells, or 'tiny spots of cancer' as the doctor put it. They removed quite a lot of the cells during her operation, but by no means all of them, she would have to have chemotherapy.

I stayed at my parent's house for more than a week, returning to make dinner for everyone, to look after the children and walk the dogs and generally to clean up, which included wiping felt tipped flowers from the walls, grown tall on long green stems in my absence.

On the third day of Mum's hospitalisation, I took the Dictaphone from its dusty hiding place and once again left the house to walk the dogs. There was no wind that day, just a trace of frost and the sun breaking through at last to enhance the few colours of the landscape, the red berries on the bushes and the brown of the fields.

Yet again, I ran the device back and forth to the sounds I could identify. Ruby and Lilly quarrelling, Hannah chiding them before bed time, the television as Lukkas watched a sports programme on a French channel. Then nothing for a long time as Hannah made herself a cup of tea and drifted to her bedroom to watch television. The ordinary sounds of the house.

Later, Joe came down to the kitchen, followed by Lukkas' footsteps in his slippers. Lukkas asked him to wash up, Joe said he was going to pick his girlfriend up and he would do it when he got back. When he left the house, I heard Lukkas mutter, "Lazy bugger," but he returned to the living room then and turned the TV to a programme about the comedian, Tommy Cooper. All these things I heard.

Now the children were asleep, Hannah was in her room and Joseph had gone out. Another half hour passed, and I began to feel guilty and foolish about my suspicions.

Then Josh thudded down the staircase on his way to the gym. Lukkas followed him on his way downstairs, just as he had followed Joe.

They spoke briefly about a work-related issue and Josh asked Lukkas whether he had any cloths for the wind screen that Josh might use.

When Josh left, his old car complaining at full voice as he reversed, there was silence for a few minutes except for the kettle which Lukkas switched on, making himself coffee. In the distance, the television remained on. Lukkas was downstairs now. I heard his feet in their slippers shuffle into the dining room. I heard him set his cup onto the table.

Then I heard his voice, low, controlled, heartfelt. I caught several words. He cleared his throat like Colonel Hearty in the Disney Jungle book.

"Yes... I love you... bye-bye..." It was muffled, indistinct and I knew there were other adjoining words that I couldn't make out, but he had waited until the family had gone out for his opportunity, except for Hannah, safe in her bedroom.

In a panic, as though I could stop love, I whistled for the dogs and ran back to the house with them at my heels as though I could see that my roof was on fire.

Inside once more, I shut myself into the toilet and locked the door. My fingers shook as I ran the recording back and listened.

There was a sound after he cleared his throat, a name, but I couldn't be sure whose name. Then, more. "Yes... of course that's what it means... Big kiss, I love you, thanks for everything, bye-bye."

I slumped against the wall, filled with grief until after a little while, anger took over. On the night my mother was diagnosed with cancer, when I had been terrified about that? Really? How could you, Lukkas!

"I love you, yes of course that's what it means," the man who told me not to send him text kisses?

I forced myself to be controlled. We couldn't talk about this at home, there were too many people who would be upset. So, I sent him a text. I tried to be me, the me that Lukkas expected me to be.

"Could we go for a drink after your work? The last few days have been a bit heavy, what with Mum and everything," I said.

"Okay," came his returning text. "I've got an advocates meeting, but I should be able to get to the Vicky by seven."

I waited outside, sitting at a table overlooking the river and the sweeping willow trees, thinking about what I would say and how I would accuse him, still carrying the burning resentment inside me, the Dictaphone deep in my pocket. When it got to twenty minutes past the hour, shivering in the February cold, I went inside and bought a small glass of white wine and waited.

He came at half past seven and joined me at the small corner table I had chosen, to be away from other people.

"Well, this is nice," Lukkas said.

"Lukkas, I need to talk to you about something…" I began.

"Nothing serious, I hope. What's happening about your Mum?" He smiled sympathetically. Good Cop, bad Cop, I thought.

"It's not about Mum. I recorded a conversation between you and… someone else, on the night she went into hospital."

"Recorded me? You spied on me?" he glowered, folding his arms across his chest. If only he knew about the tracker, I mused. But I didn't make any comment. Didn't say, "You're cheating on me and telling my family that I'm mad?"

"I recorded you thanking someone on your phone, saying that you loved them. You say, "I love you, yes of course that's what it means," so my guess is that you'd sent them a text kiss."

It wasn't the reaction I had expected. He laughed, only briefly. "Let me have it then," he said softly. "Where is it?"

"In my pocket."

"Give it to me…"

I hadn't thought about that bit. "If you come outside then I'll play it to you," I said.

He nodded and picked up his drink, following me to the spot where I had waited, outside. He pulled the tail of his long, black overcoat over the damp seat and looked at me, holding out his hand. But I didn't hand it to him, I ran the Dictaphone to the time of the recording, raised the volume and held it to his ear.

"Play it again," he said at the end, his face betraying nothing. I ran it back again.

"It's not me," he said.

I felt at the end of my tether, furious at his denials. "Of-course it's you, you think I wouldn't know your voice after all these years?" I said in an angry hiss.

He shrugged. "You can hardly hear it, but it isn't me, anyway."

"There's a ghost in our house then, because before that it has recorded the family talking to you and leaving the house, apart from Hannah and the girls, who are upstairs. Oh yes, and it recorded Tommy Cooper on the telly," I choked over my wine. "You are such a liar, Lukkas. No wonder you're so good in court," I finished.

For the first time in my life with him, I could feel respect diminishing. The feeling made me sad. Lukkas had become a wilful child in my eyes. Perhaps he was more dangerous than that.

He faced me calmly. "Give the Dictaphone to me then, I'll get it enhanced for you. I know the best people for it, they'll do a good job," he said calmly.

I wanted to slap his face. He was so sure of himself, he had convinced our children in an act of group illusion, as well as people in authority. He was a liar.

"Who is she Lukkas, who are you talking to... Holly?" I asked, a choking sound emitting from my throat.

His expression changed in an instant, his features twisting into ugly malice.

"I suggest you leave her out of this!" he said sharply. So sharply that I didn't want to be there anymore. I swallowed my wine back and left him.

In my car, I sat for a moment, trying to calm down, half contemplating whether to go back to him.

I looked back over my shoulder at his figure in the black coat, hunched against the cold, then drove away.

Chapter Thirty-Eight
Variables

I drove to Jennie's instead.

I had to see her for two reasons, to thank her for the glowing reference which would enable me to do supply teaching when Lilly went to school full time and because she is a wise woman with a practical, rational brain and a good friend. I had needed a good friend all day.

I didn't cry, this time, but I had cried on the journey. Tears of anger, of frustration, half supressed sorrow. She knew that something was wrong when she opened the glass door to the house, the reddened, blotchy eyes said it all.

"Hello, stranger," she smiled, then checked herself and said, "Come in, what's happened?" And she had the house to herself, so before I had even sat down, wrapped my hands around the cup of coffee she made for me, words tumbled from my lips.

"So, what are you going to do?" She asked, when I finished, as several people have.

"I don't know," I sniffed. "I keep waiting for him to come back to me, I can't envisage what things would be like without him. But I can't stand it anymore. First, I found blonde hairs on his jackets. Now, for so long, I've been finding dark, chestnut coloured hairs belonging to this woman, Holly, the lawyer. On the white tiles in the bathroom after he comes home, too. Taunting me. It's horrible." I took a well needed breath.

"Lukkas said he needed her on court cases and that she was his close, working partner, that there isn't anything going on between them. But now he says that he must go to Milton Keynes on Thursday for a big child care case and that there is only Holly to go with him. Only he'll be staying overnight. He says that Holly will not stay, that she'll return home each day..." I stopped, conscious that I was ranting.

"You believe that?" Jennie asked.

"No. He will use office funds for them both to stay."

She nodded. "If Lukkas is having an affair, and it does sound probable, he won't be messing up his life and reputation with an unknown factor like this Irina. It will be someone attractive and intelligent and certainly it's more likely that she'll be another lawyer."

Jennie gazed at me over the top of her glasses whilst I resented her description of Holly as attractive and intelligent. Then she smiled suddenly. "But there's good news," she said.

I waited.

"Guess where I'm going tomorrow? I'm going on a two-day Education and Management course in Milton Keynes, one day before he gets there. I was just about to book a hotel there. Where's he staying?"

"Jennie, you can't... I mean, he knows you, what if he sees you there!" I cried. There was a long pause whilst she looked at me over the top of her glasses.

"Juror's Inn," I said. "He'll never tell me, but there's a half filled in car parking card on his passenger's seat."

Before I could say anything else, she picked up her phone and booked the room, a room that was street facing, so that she might see them arriving.

"You know, Laura. I thought you were cleverer than that, to allow him to stay at a hotel overnight with a woman like that. I mean, even if they were in separate rooms, it's hardly appropriate, is it?"

But Jennie didn't really know Lukkas as I did, she didn't know the way he used to sulk in the face of any objection. She didn't know, nowadays, how angry he would become.

It was late when I arrived home. Lukkas was standing in the garden, hidden behind the house, smoking a cigarette.

I went to him. He didn't ask me where I had been.

"Give me the recording," he said. "Where is it?"

"If it isn't what I think it is, why do you care. Just forget it," I said.

"But you won't forget it."

I didn't answer him.

I looked at him, I was thinking about this garden, about the parties we had here, for children, for friends, for our family and his staff. I stepped toward him to touch his arm in some, pointless gesture of love and hope, then stepped back instantly, as his eyes narrowed into tiny pinpricks of loathing.

Lukkas slept on the settee that night, whilst I lay alone in our bedroom.

He left the next day, a day earlier than his case in Milton Keynes. He didn't return that evening.

When Josh came home from work, I asked him if Holly had been in the office. He looked sideways at me, hesitated before answering and then said,

"She left at four, but she won't be in until Monday, apparently."

Then, I thought, she's gone to Milton Keynes with him.

Hannah asked me whether she might go out whilst I looked after the children that Thursday. I was pleased for her, she had hardly left the house except to go to work, since parting with Ben.

The girls and I played board games, we watched a wild life programme and I gave them a supper snack, after which I bribed them with the promise of a hamster, if they slept.

I lay upon our bed, trying to concentrate upon my notes, whilst I waited for Jennie's texts. In between, I thought wistfully about the time that Lukkas might have spent with me whilst in the company of Holly. I found it impossible to imagine them having sex, was then wracked with torture at the idea when I did imagine it. Perhaps it was all nonsense, in which case, no wonder Lukkas was angry. But did lawyers share rooms, surely you would have to be very well acquainted with someone to share a room? Would it be like a pyjama party, with innocent giggles, was Lukkas alluding to the idea of sharing a room when he said that the Legal Aid people would only pay for one lawyer to stay in a hotel?

At seven thirty I had my first text message from Jennie. "I have a room overlooking the reception, that way I can see who's coming and going. The course is good, but I'm knackered, now. I'm going to have dinner in the restaurant here."

"Don't lie down, don't fall asleep..." I said aloud.

In the kitchen, Joe and his girlfriend were embroiled in the start of a row. I pulled on my dressing gown and went downstairs to remonstrate with them because of the sleeping girls, and they heeded me by disappearing into the street to upset the neighbours with their argument.

When I returned to my room, there was a second text from Jennie. "Lukkas came into the reception area followed by a brunette in a pink shawl with a trundle case. Shoulder length hair?"

Oh no, no, no! I screamed inside.

Holly. She had worn the pink shawl to the Christmas dinner and I recognised bits of it from Lukkas' jacket. Still, that didn't mean they were sharing a room, and maybe it was on his jacket because she hung the shawl over it in the office.

"I'm hiding in the dining room, he hasn't seen me. He's gone to the reception desk and she's gone to the lift."

I thanked her. Despondently, I flopped back against the pillows.

I didn't want to humiliate Lukkas. I simply could not bear for him to lie to me anymore and tell our children, and the people in a community where I had lived and worked for so long, that I was mad. I was the one suffering humiliation. I knew one thing, even though I had pretended to myself it wasn't so, that Lukkas had to have what he wanted, regardless of any other consideration. That is how he had always been.

I didn't want to get it wrong any more. Lukkas' flirting got me down over the years, but this particular relationship, whoever it was with, was significantly different. It felt as though the other person hated me, was encouraging Lukkas to hate me and now had control over me. That, I wanted to remove. I didn't want this person to be able to control me through my husband. I blamed her, not him.

Choices didn't appear to exist.

Those were the variables that made the decision for me.

But I had to wait some time.

CHAPTER THIRTY-NINE

Goading

Three things happened. Practical jokes made against me, in the case of one of them, it was certainly a practical joke.

The time drew near for Lukkas to go away for his weekend with the boys. Last year they went to Lille in France, this time they were headed for Berlin. It didn't worry me when he went away with his friends, Holly wouldn't be there, so I felt at peace.

In the days before he went, Lukkas asked me to do something for him. I was pleased. He asked me reasonably and as he seemed to need me so infrequently, and as it related to his office; I agreed.

"We're going paperless," he said. "Everything is to go on computer files. We've been working at it for some time. If I brought the old files home, could you burn them in the incinerator for me?"

So, he returned one spring evening with a boot of pink files, each one bursting with paperwork and we carried them with Josh's help into the flowerless garden and dumped them on the ground next to the incinerator.

I looked around the garden and winced, my preoccupation with Lukkas and a lack of motivation caused by sadness meant that, this year, I had done nothing to improve or tidy the space. The ground was strewn with colourful, plastic toys, half chewed by the dogs. I was so worried nowadays about being depressed, that there was always the possibility that I was depressed. Each day, I awoke with a fear that I couldn't articulate to myself, let alone anyone else.

That evening, in the dark, I started the job of burning the paperwork. There is something cathartic and primeval about a bonfire. It attracted both Josh and Joe, who came out into the garden to talk to me and watch the flames licking around people's past lives as they drank coffee.

It took several days, there was an awful lot of paperwork. On the third day, I started the job a little earlier than before, risking the wrath of my Neighbours as it was still light. These were the more recent documents. I took out sheaths of paper in larger bundles, prodding them with my fingers to make them catch the flames. My fingers were becoming as my grandmothers had been, hardened to flame.

I stopped as I saw her name at the top of a new bundle, Holly Farrah, it said. It was impossible to ignore them. The bundle was a sequence of emails between an Oxford City estate agency and Holly herself. It was pertaining to a house just two roads away from Lukkas' office.

My shoulders collapsed in disbelief. The buyer was Lukkas, but Holly had negotiated the purchase. The buyer was Lukkas, Holly knew about the money he had spent, our money...but I hadn't.

Lukkas had bought a house without telling me. I dropped the loose papers onto the muddy lawn. Suddenly, I did not want to do this job anymore. "How could you, Lukkas!" I raged aloud.

I picked up the sheathes of paper. Underneath them, as though it had been stuck on one of the emails and had come loose, there was a yellow post it.

It was a drawing of two cartoon swans on the squiggled lines of a river, a doodle. Beside that drawing, an elaborate heart. Camouflaged within the heart's lacey pattern were the initials L and H and beneath this a message, in her writing:

"Chase?"

And the reply, in Lukkas' hand, on the same post it, "Yes, please!" I thought about the things Gwen had told me. Was the message intentionally ambiguous? I scratched at my anger until I could stand it no more.

I left my incinerating and pulled off my boots. Lukkas was in his study, I went to him and closed the door, without permission.

"You bought a house, a whole house without telling me?" I accused him. "Isn't that something you should talk to your wife about?"

He didn't look at me, carried on staring at the paperwork before him. "Not really, in the circumstances," he replied smoothly. "I bought it to boost the firm's income, as security," he said.

"But Lukkas," I reminded him, "You are the firm, it's your Business, your money, our money…"

He shrugged. I watched him, hating what he had done. "You bought it with her, Holly, who knows all about it when you failed to tell me; just a ten-minute walk from your office."

"So, what are you suggesting, that I'm carrying on with her there?" His voice had risen now. He did that, he was perfectly in control and knew if he raised his voice, it would bring the whole family running to see what the matter was.

"You-git," I said. "You utter, heartless, git. Burn your own guilty secrets."

After that, the things I found were either remarkably careless on his part, like the sheath we had no cause to use; or he left them deliberately, for me to find.

The hairs were not deliberate, but they were there each-and-every day. Holly's fine, dark hairs.

After I felt tortured by them for a long time, I remarked that it was "An odd phenomenon," saying perhaps we had another ghost in the house. Sarcasm may be another form of bullying, but I defy anyone to live the way I had without resorting to it, in the end.

Some weeks before Lukkas went to Berlin with his male friends, I came home from a parent's meeting with Hannah. He was in the bathroom, washing. He had taken off a crisp, white shirt and thrown it to the top of the wash basket, almost as though he wanted me to examine it.

I picked it up, as I did so, hundreds of small, short, dark hairs fell from the sleeves onto the wash basket. I leapt back in disgust, he must have heard my cry. But they weren't human hairs, or animal either, although they resembled horse hair in their tough, brittle texture. Someone had cut up a paint brush and stuffed the ends, each about four centimetres long, into the sleeves.

I shook the hairs out of the window, keeping several to show Charlotte and to prove to myself, more than anyone else; that I wasn't mad.

Lukkas doesn't do practical jokes for his own amusement. He had done it to make someone laugh. He had done it to make Holy laugh, I thought, laughing at me behind my back.

I lay awake for a long time that night, still unable to act, still believing that if I divorced him, I wouldn't survive. Anyway, he had control of all the money we had. It had been alright, I supposed, when he loved me, but now...

All our files; my Will, the mortgage documents, the details of our bank accounts; they had all been removed to his office. Holly had more access to them than I.

When he rose from the bed, I said, "That was a nasty thing to do."

"What was?" He asked with a sneer.

"The paint brush bristles..."

"God, you really are mad, Laura. What the hell are you talking about? I'm going to work," he said.

But he appeared not to have told Hannah and Joe at least, and I thought I had escaped.

I was pleased when Hannah asked me to go to the park with her and her girls on the Saturday, I said I would buy us all a hot chocolate in the newly opened coffee shop. So, we went in her car, visiting the Polish store on the way. Hannah seemed very bright and cheerful, joking with the girls and playing pop songs at volume in the car, to their delight. She was recovering from Ben at last, or so I thought.

The girls were happy too, whacking each other with catkins from the hedgerow. We were in the park for about an hour, until I had run them up and down on the zip wire so frequently that I felt the urge to pee, then we left the car in the car park and walked to the shop for our hot chocolate.

We hadn't been sitting for very long before Hannah's fingers touched mine. I looked up with a smile. "Mum..." I suspected trouble as she said it. It was the way she said it, the same way she used to ask for something when she was a teenager. "Just listen to me for a minute, without interrupting, cos I'm worried about you."

In an instant, the holiday feeling had dissipated. The innocent jaunt to the park had a darker purpose. I sighed, looking away towards the girls with colouring pens and paper, their faces smeared with chocolate.

"Please, Hannah," I started. But with her face set, determined like that, the resemblance to Lukkas was overpowering.

"You can't deny that you're behaving weirdly any more. All this rubbish about hairs in the bathroom, marks on Dad's shirts, hidden necklaces. You are being delusional. Dad is right, Mum."

I shook my head at her. They were his words, his propaganda. I wanted to shout in my frustration, but it wasn't going to help my case. I wanted to say, "Your father has been hitting me," but I didn't.

"You are driving Dad mad. It's not right, he's doing nothing wrong."

I looked about me, hoping that no one there would know us. "Hannah. I love Dad and I want us to be together as we always have, but you don't understand the way he behaves toward me or what's happening. You have his story, half of a story. Firstly, there isn't anything wrong with me and secondly, say he influences a psychiatrist as he influenced Dr Lamb…" She snorted in disbelief, but I carried on. "Say that, he knows so many people. If he succeeds in this and divorces me, I will have no access to our money, none at all, I will be dependent upon others, him…"

She shook her head and groaned. "But Dad loves you, he's told me that. He will look after you!"

I smiled. "He will look after me? Whilst he does as he likes, and I have no rights at all?"

She peeled off her jacket. Her cheeks were flushed in frustration. "That's it then, he's going to leave you if you don't get help. He spoke to me yesterday. You're putting yourself before your family, Mum. He's not bluffing. He says that he is going to move into Croft Street away from you."

I placed my fingers before my mouth, unconscious prayer. "I am not unwell," I pleaded in a whisper.

She ignored this. "There's something else. We have both decided that if you don't see a psychiatrist, you shouldn't have the care of the children. So, I'm going to find another childminder. Dad will pay."

"What, are you serious, Hannah?" I whispered miserably. They were arguing with each other now, about the crayons, but I couldn't bear for them to hear it. "You and Dad were the ones who asked me to give up my job and care for them in the first place. I love them, and they love me. Other than you, I know their needs better than anyone could. I've cared for them since they were babies, fed them, taught them, played with them. You couldn't be so cruel!"

But her expression was cold now, as though I were nothing to do with her.

"Then you had better take it seriously. I don't want you to treat him in this way. All this nonsense about Holly, now. You don't have long, as I said, I've started looking for childminders."

My heart sucked and pounded in panic as I fought to think clearly. It was time to talk to a lawyer, not Lukkas' lawyers, but someone else. I didn't speak to Hannah on the way home; but chattered distractedly with the girls; whilst all the time, my mind was in turmoil.

I left Hannah to bring the groceries inside and went upstairs to my hiding place in the sewing machine. I took out the card I had taken from Lukkas' pocket and locked myself in the bathroom with my phone. So many secrets, where there had never been secrets before.

An answer came almost instantly. The woman's voice was friendly and warm, I thought she must be my age or thereabouts. I told her my name and my relationship to Lukkas, I was anxious, I suppose. "It's a confidential call," I stated.

"I know Lukkas well," she said, the tone of her voice veering towards caution, now.

I started to explain, trying to speak slowly, to control my feelings. I told her that we hadn't been getting along, what Lukkas had said about my mental health, but crucially now, I told her about the threat of having my grandchildren taken from my care.

"I can't represent you," she explained, "I have too much to do with him. But there is no reason that you can't speak to one of my family team."

So, I waited, chewing my nails, for a young family lawyer called Alex to come to the phone.

CHAPTER FORTY
Extenuating Circumstances

During February, the chemotherapy our mother had begun started to take its toll. It is an odd thing, that you must be made very sick before you can get better. Charlotte and I took it in turns to take our parents to the hospital and there she sat, wired to the tubes via the pick line in her arm. She was so patient, she so wanted to live. Having always been a small woman with thin arms, she bore the pain and indignity of having a nurse stab and stab again at her forearm to find a good, strong vein. At one point, the nurse couldn't succeed in it and the hospital registrar had to be called to help. But our mother's courage and resolve to overcome it all was incredible.

The car parks around the hospital, filled to bursting by ten o'clock, told their own story of how common this disease is now. And in the wards, row after row of patients, mostly seated in arm chairs, like Mum. All shapes and sizes and backgrounds, Cancer doesn't care, and many of them awake and still smiling, especially the patient elderly, who bore everything with fortitude. The younger people were the more depressed, very often. Those whose lives had not been long enough. The young, tired to the point of exhaustion.

But there was an air of camaraderie, in a way. It was easier there to speak to strangers and listen to their stories. My father seemed more lost than ever. Every day his dementia deteriorated, forgetting why we were there, forgetting the 'C' word in a world that had been overcome with it. He simply understood that his wife was sick, and to that end, did everything he could to make her comfortable and happier.

But he couldn't cook beyond a cup of tea, didn't know how to use the microwave because Mum always did the cooking. She had been fiercely independent to the last, she liked to cook and enjoyed her own cooking and she prepared meals for them every night until the day came when her third course of chemotherapy made her so sick and ill that she couldn't stand without dizziness. Reluctantly, Mum took to her bed and we made their meals, but she hardly ate a morsel.

We tried everything, including the protein drinks which she said were "Slimy and nasty." They might have saved her life, but like Lukkas, she was most particular about food. Her weight went down very quickly until she moved towards six stone and we were reduced to feeding her in bed with one spoonful of jelly at a time.

On one of these occasions, I had been with her all morning and left the house at about eleven to go to my own. I had been at home for about an hour when I received a text from her. "Will you come back for a minute?" The text said.

She rarely sent texts, it must be something serious, I thought, fearing the worst. My father opened the door to me.

"Laura, how are you?" he asked cheerfully, forgetting that I had been with them all morning. He'd also forgotten to put in his false teeth and to shave, something our mother would have been cross about, so I reminded him and mounted the stairs to her room.

She had always had a lighter figure, but now, propped up against the pillows in the large bed, she appeared so small that it frightened me. If she didn't put on weight soon, we would have to take her to the hospital and ask them to put her on a drip, I resolved, she was now as fragile as porcelain.

I eased myself beside her upon the bed and took her small, weightless hand in mine. "What's the matter?" I asked, patiently, so that she knew that nothing was too much trouble.

"Lukkas has sent me a text," she said, and her smile wore a little thin.

My heart plunged, a heavy stone hitting the deep, black waters of a well. I knew what the text had to say even before she told me. How could he do this, just now, when we both needed to be so strong, was he doing this because we needed strength, to undermine us?

"And what does it say?" I asked quietly, silently hoping that it might say, "Get well, we both want you to be well."

In answer, she gripped my hand tightly. I felt the pressure of her thumb nail on my skin, the tension running through that touch.

"He wants me to encourage you to see a psychiatrist, Laura…"

Anger brought tears to my eyes, I was less than patient, then.

"Do you believe there is something wrong with me, Mum. Do you think that I'm mad?" I asked in frustration.

She released my hand then; a shadow of sheer weariness crossed her face. "I can't believe you do the things you do for people, for Dad, for me, for your Grandchildren and have a mental health problem, no. But I worry because your Grandmother was ill at one point, as you know, and because the truth is, well, I'm not there to see the things Lukkas is talking about and now, Hannah is frightened for you."

It was my fault. I had taught them to trust Lukkas over the years, all our family. How could I blame them? They had believed him a wonderful son in law, clever, generous with time and money, an important person. But they were in awe of him too, perhaps a little afraid.

"Has he said what he accuses me of?" I asked, trying to steady my voice.

She reached for my hand once more, breathing in the air slowly through the opened window, I knew that she was trying to reassure me that she loved me in any case.

"He says you are hiding things, that you plant things in the house, in his car, that you accuse him of having relationships with other women."

I wiped my eyes with the heel of my hand. All my life, my mother had faith in me, had always been proud of me, and now, this?

"Do you believe it, Mum? Because I'll tell you what I believe. Lukkas is having an affair, and the way he acts now, the things I find, are all part of that. One of my friends suggested that I try to be the better woman, but how can I be the better woman if he wants another woman so badly that he will lie about me, that's defamation of character, surely? How can I be the better woman if she, this woman, is pushing me away to her own advantage?" I blew my nose on a tissue from her box. "I haven't wanted to discuss any of this with you because it's humiliating and because you are so ill, and

I'm so ashamed of him for trying to draw you into it like this."

She breathed a small sigh. "Then divorce him, Laura; or do as he is suggesting, and get it over with."

I stared at her for a moment, startled by her suggestion, it felt like a betrayal.

"Mum, Lukkas has influenced Doctors in this before, he's lied to them."

"Then go to a Doctor he's never met, do your research, find someone who wouldn't know him from Adam. If there's nothing wrong, and Laura, I don't believe there is...you will be cleared, and he might just shut up."

"But it's inhuman to force me to do something against my will and based upon lies, Mum. Don't you see, that's my greatest objection? I thought you, of all people, would agree! What about my right? I know I'm absolutely sane, that I've been this me all of my life; this me who has used all she has to help him, to jolly children along, to solve problems. Lukkas never objected to flaws in my character then, so why now?"

She lifted her thin, claw like fingers, taking my chin in her hand. Her eyes were sallow smudges without colour.

"Do what you think, then. I know you've been having difficulties for some while. I know that you love him. But all of this has gone on for long enough. I know you've avoided seeing me at times because you are upset. That's not what I want." The sentences were shorter now, with her breaths. She looked so tired. All she wanted was sleep. "If you know there is nothing wrong with you, prove it properly and he can't argue, then leave him; or leave him now and be done with it."

I nodded, but there was a hard knot in my stomach, an ache of resentment.

"I'll promise you, not him, to talk to my doctor again," I said. "I don't want you to worry about this anymore, Mum. I just want you to be well. I'm going to tell him not to text you again. It will be alright, I promise. Just rest now and go to sleep."

I kissed her forehead and left the room, knowing that nagging my mother when she was so ill, was something I would never forgive him for.

Her name was Doctor Catriona Shaw. Doctor Evans helped me to find her from a long list on the computer. She said that she would ask whether Dr Shaw had ever worked with my husband and if the answer was 'yes', then she would find someone else.

I felt as though I was betraying Josh, I knew his view upon the matter. Furthermore, I felt as if I were betraying myself.

Charlotte promised that she would accompany me and was equally furious with Lukkas for bothering Mum with it all.

I told Lukkas what I had done. He was delighted, of course; although his delight wasn't mine. It gave way to disappointment when I refused to tell him the name of the psychiatrist I had chosen, and he sulked afresh, but I ignored him.

I resented what Lukkas had done, my smiles and responses were as feigned as his kindness and joviality over the next few weeks.

He promised me the earth, in fact. Suddenly attentive and loving in his manner. It was a tortuous game. He said that we would go to London to see a play, that he would take me to a dinner on the retirement of the kindly Judge and he kissed me.

"Who are you taking with you to your appointment?" he asked. "You may need someone to speak on your behalf. I shall take time off work to come with you."

"No, Lukkas, but thank you," I replied tactfully. "I am quite nervous, in fact, so I thought I would take Charlotte."

His voice was dismissive. "Charlotte doesn't live with you, she doesn't know the changes in you. If you won't allow me to come, then take Hannah."

I said nothing to this, sensing the order beneath the suggestion.

"Charlotte has known me all her life, she will do," I said, crisply.

To my surprise and relief, he didn't argue about it any further, but pursed his lips, thrusting them forward like an army officer dismissing an untidy uniform.

CHAPTER FORTY-ONE

A Hag in London

It was raining hard on the Saturday that Lukkas returned from the office to drive us to London. I said nothing about the mornings chance meeting in the supermarket with Heather, who told me they all had the weekend off because of electrical rewiring being undertaken there. I didn't ask Lukkas about it, or where he had been either, I simply wanted to have a nice weekend.

I was so looking forward to it. I'd been filled with trepidation at the thought of the interview with the psychiatrist and welcomed anything that would take my mind away from it.

If Lukkas wasn't exactly jovial, neither was he miserable. As he drove, he chatted to me about work as he would have in the old days. We arrived at the 'Chambers' hotel at about half past three. A hotel, Lukkas told me, he had stayed at frequently. We checked in at the reception desk and trundled our small cases to our room. I thought the plan had been to go straight to the Courts of Justice, but Lukkas had another idea.

He started to remove his clothes the moment that I closed the door behind us. At first, I thought he was changing out of one thing into another. I hadn't known him to want this with me, not during the day, for some years. I suppose I should have been thankful, believing that he still wanted me. But I mistrusted it so much, now. I had experienced a lack of love, lack of compassion and abuse which made me feel truly ugly. I was ugly, there was no point in arguing it, so why did he want this now?

So, I stood beside the bed, feeling very foolish as he stripped down to his underpants as though he did this every day, which he may well have done, elsewhere... and I could never compete with that. But if I rejected him, he would have reason to go to someone else, and so I stood there, feeling stupid. The fight within me, the complexity of it all, had become too much. It had never been like this when I was younger, even after I was young. Then I had faith that he loved only me.

I had reached the point of being scared about having sex with my own husband.

"Come on then," he said, impatiently. So, I sat on the edge of the bed like a young virgin and waited whilst he undid my blouse. After that, everything was mechanical; cold, strange, and unwanted by me whilst I did my best to pretend. I could no longer feel anything but old, ugly; that he could have any pretty girl and was forced to have me. But I acted as best I could. That the room was cold would never have defused our passion, once upon a time, but now it added to the pressure building inside of me. It was a new feeling to me, not to want sex with my husband, not to want to have to do this with anyone, ever again. I was relieved when it ended and Lukkas reached an orgasm and I could feel free of it all.

It was late when we reached the Courts of Justice, too late to go inside. Lukkas took my hand in his and lead me around the outside of the courts, all the while talking to me about his various cases whilst I listened attentively, pretending I had not heard these stories before. I was not fooled, there was a flatness in his voice, as though he were showing an old aunt about the place, as if he were having to try too hard and wanted to be somewhere else, or with someone else, and it was as though I was simply trying to understand this new Lukkas.

After this, we went to the Templar's Church, and there was a wedding taking place, so we viewed it from the outside.

When Lukkas smiled at me, I thought, even your smiles aren't the same, they are tinged with sadness. It isn't me that you want here, I'm second best. She has damaged us, and all is spoilt before we begin, and I hated her for that. The will to fight her was subsiding. But I kissed him, telling him how proud I was of his work although I was dying inside.

Lukkas returned what he could, that day. He held my hand so tightly, I believed he was afraid of losing me, too. Perhaps she wasn't always kind to him, at least I had that.

In the late afternoon we went to watch a parody of the Thirty-Nine Steps at the Criterion Theatre. We held hands and laughed as though laughter was a tonic itself. Then after it, we went to a near-bye restaurant to be served by a blonde, Russian waitress who reminded me a little of Irina and was thoroughly attentive to Lukkas, if not to me; but I didn't mind, didn't care, then. I had been married to him for a long time and whatever happened, that could not be taken from me.

Afterwards, we walked through Covent garden, watching a quartet of performers leaping into the air with their instruments as they played Rimsky Korsakov without faltering in the music, deserving the excited applause at the end of it all. I caught Lukkas smiling at me as I clapped and laughed and then, I believe the smile was genuine. He bought me the CD of their performances and we walked on, resembling the old, married couple we were.

As we wandered along Chancery Lane afterwards, we arrived at the glass frontage of a pub, the noise from within spilled over into the street and I saw Lukkas hesitate and felt sure that he had been there before. But when I suggested, "Shall we go inside?" he shook his head.

"No, it's too busy, let's go to the City of York," he said.

I gazed at the coop of cockerels and young hens, pressing close to each other in the packed room and suspected they were Lawyers and barristers, for the most part; maybe business people too. Just as he took my elbow to lead me away, a face, large and round as the moon, rose up at the window. His mouth gaped open in a huge grin as he saw Lukkas. Then he tugged open the pub door to greet us with a booming cry.

"Lukkas, Good God, it's you! Come in and let me buy you a drink!"

I sensed Lukkas' reluctance, studying his face with interest and sympathy, but there was no escape.

We followed the white shirt and loosened tie through the busy bar, with Lukkas holding onto my hand as though he thought I might get lost. I felt the protective squeeze of his fingers and wondered, momentarily, whether he needed reassurance himself.

"What'll you have?" the man asked, shoving his elbows between two younger men to reach the attention of the barmaid. He turned his large, brown eyes upon me with another, clear question. He had no idea who I was.

There was something that reminded me of the great British cad, Leslie Phillips or Terry Thomas, perhaps. I half expected him to eye up one of the many young women around us and remark, "I say!" or "Ding Dong!"

"Martin, this is Laura, my wife," Lukkas said at last.

A look came upon his face, a look of surprise, of amusement, perhaps?

"Laura, this is Martin, a fellow Lawyer," Lukkas said, without faltering.

"Fantastic!" Martin roared above the din, as though we had only just announced our engagement.

"D'you know, Lukkas, I'm getting married too!" Martin announced.

"Really?" Lukkas eyed him over his beer. "Who's the unlucky woman?"

"D'you remember the actress, Penny? At least, she's only had a few parts so far, but things are looking up at last, she has a small part in a new TV drama on channel five as a matter of fact. I popped the question recently and she agreed!" Martin beamed at me.

"Yes, of course I remember her, when's the wedding?" Lukkas asked.

"We haven't fixed a date yet, my cases keep getting in the way, but we hope for a date next Spring. Of course, you two will receive an invitation." It was generous of him, I thought, considering the fact he had only just become aware that Lukkas was married.

He handed me a glass of white wine just as a young, pretty, pony tailed girl lurched into Lukkas, spilling some of the wine onto his shoes. He put out a hand to steady her elbow and she fluttered rich, thickly dark, false eyelashes at him before stumbling away on her high heels to flirt elsewhere.

Then Martin asked a question that made me frown. I think the question was merely tactless, rather than asked with malicious intent, but it was as though meeting me had made him think of her. "How is... what's-her-name, dark haired girlie who came to work with you, fun sort?" he bumbled, and Lukkas' cheeks turned flaming red.

"Holly?" I ventured quickly, "She's well, isn't she Lukkas?" And I felt my own face burn like a woman having a hot flush in an airing cupboard.

I noted Lukkas' shoulders fall in despair, but I felt no sympathy for him at that moment, Martin had met Holly but seemed not to know about me. It just felt insulting. After that I hardly heard a word of their conversation and I drank my wine rather rapidly whilst I seethed inside. Little wonder that Lukkas hadn't wanted to come into the pub.

I imagined Holly, pressing against Lukkas' arm as I did. I heard her low, mocking laugh and saw the mischievous twinkle in her eye. The idea simply popped into my head, I had given no thought to it.

"You know, Martin, Lukkas and I are having a small party in July. You really must come with your fiancée."

Lukkas frowned at me, opened his mouth to speak and then closed it in a firm, sour, line.

"Holly will be there," I assured Martin.

Suspecting nothing, Martin boomed, "Splendid, love too!"

But it was not long after that that Lukkas gave his excuses. It had been a long day, he said.

In the street, he strode ahead of me, an imposing figure in his black, woollen jacket. I thought of Dr Jekyll and Mr Hyde. In the dark, the air heavy with mist, it was an obvious comparison; but real fear grew inside of me. His anger could render me senseless now.

I caught up with him and he stopped, heedless of anyone who might be listening, and turned to me, snarling. "What the fuck was all that about?" he spat angrily, "a party, invite Holly? We're not having a party, okay! What the hell are you playing at?"

He tore along the street again, hurtling ahead of me so that I stopped trying to keep pace with him, then bounded up the stone steps to our hotel, going in without me. I fumbled in my bag for my key, weary now, my own anger subsiding into regret once more as I followed him inside.

He had taken the lift, and so I mounted the stairs. When I reached our room, he was already stripping off his clothes to get into bed. I went to the bathroom, drawing off my coat. Lukkas hurled his shoes across the floor. "Count me out, have your bloody party but I won't be there, and leave Holly out of it!" he yelled.

I turned on the bathroom light and stared at myself in the mirror. "Hag," I whispered to myself, "Vile, wizened hag..." The make-up I had applied so carefully did nothing to hide my age.

When I climbed into the bed I rolled away from him, to the edge, but he turned suddenly, and in the light from the window I saw his face and shrank away too late to stop his nails from digging into my forearm.

"No more," he growled, "Leave her out of it."

Chapter Forty-Two

Florence Nightingale

As often now, the silence was safer. Lukkas said not a word over breakfast and drove from the underground car park past the elegant London buildings, too fast; so that I had to hold onto the car door as we turned the corners. He didn't appear to care about anything, the look upon his face was hard, filled with a resolve that frightened me. I didn't dare speak to him and stared from the window at the early morning mist, lying low across the fields between Oxford and London. Depressed.

When we arrived at home, he said he had to go to the office. Go then, I thought defiantly as the car climbed the hill.

There was no sign of Hannah and the girls, or Joseph. I took the dogs for a walk, attempting to lift my flagging spirits. When I reached the edge of the little copse with its low-lying stream, I had recovered. I marched back, my boots sucking at the soft mud. I pulled them off at the back door and went to our bedroom, then groped beneath the heavy mattress for my roughly written manuscript. I took it to Lukkas' study and started to write, the emotional truth. Gradually, the pain inside me stopped.

A couple of days later, my appointment to see the psychiatrist came through in the post. I shoved it to the bottom of my handbag, but in the end, it was Lukkas who needed the more urgent appointment with a specialist.

He returned, mid-afternoon, his angular body stooped as he clutched at his back. It had happened during the day, he said. It had been ten years since the operation on his spine and now he would have to be referred for another.

The back specialist, Mr Curtis Hodgson, was very stern on the matter when I drove Lukkas to the hospital. Lukkas must rearrange all appointments for the next six weeks. If he didn't do this, the damage to his spine would affect his kidneys and other major organs.

Having waited with Lukkas for this news, we then spent a further, hectic, forty minutes at the hospital as Lukkas rearranged his court appointments, searching for staff to stand in for him, whilst I completed the medical forms on his behalf and called his parents with the news, telling them not to worry.

But on the Tuesday morning, as he packed his bag for the hospital and I went in search of his keys, he looked up at me and said, "You're not coming."

I gave a short, uncertain laugh. "I'm taking you, aren't I? You can't drive or carry a heavy bag. You won't want to leave your car in the underground car park for all of that time."

"I'll call a taxi," he grunted.

"Please don't be stu...silly," I corrected myself, hastily. I had been called many things now, stupid, an idiot, a bitch, a hag; but I must not call him stupid. "Besides," I finished, to persuade him, "Your mother would never forgive me if I didn't take you."

He capitulated, eventually, but in the end, I was to wish that I had never gone at all.

The moment that I parked the car, he started to raise his voice. Taken that his pain was great, his anger was exaggerated in the extreme. Lukkas has always been a show man, an actor, but this performance made me shake.

"Go away now, leave me. I don't want you here. Go away or I'll call the police and say you are harassing me." He had opened the car door and his voice resonated in the underground building.

I gaped at him in horror. What would poor Mum think if he called the police, my father, my children, what would they feel? Yet he appeared to be serious. I wasn't sure, could a husband call the police on a wife for taking him to a hospital? What would he tell them? Lukkas knew everything about the law, I knew little.

I stared at him as he hobbled from the car. What on earth did Lukkas imagine that I would do, other than help him? I watched his progress, his limping, loping gait. I began to cry silently, at first, then smudged the tears away; angrily wiping them from my cheek bones.

Swearing silently, I jumped from the car and walked briskly after him as he reached the door to the lift. I followed him inside and he turned angrily towards me. "You do that, Lukkas. You call the police," I said.

He ignored me. He behaved as though I were invisible, even when we reached the reception desk. Being there was a defiance inside me. It is so easy to say, "Stuff you then," I suppose, and part of me wanted to say that. The opposite of having my pride trashed. Walk away. I didn't understand any of it. It was what I had always done.

"Do you have someone to carry your bags for you?" The grey-haired receptionist asked Lukkas, not connecting us at all.

"Yes," I said quickly, too aware of my reddened eyes, my dishevelled appearance. "I'm his wife, I'll carry them."

To my relief, Lukkas didn't argue. I lifted his heavy bag, following him silently to the comfortable bedroom at the foot of the corridor. He began to unpack whilst I stood at the large window overlooking tall, grey apartments to house the nursing staff.

"Go, now," he said quietly.

"Lukkas, please," I begged.

Just then, the nurse entered the room; short, plump, round face; from Nepal, perhaps. She smiled from one to the other of us but said nothing as she opened a file to read it and filled in a chart. Her smile faded to a look of uncertainty, as Lukkas asked coldly, "Would you ask my wife to leave, please?"

The nurse, poor woman, smiled apologetically at me.

"I would like her to leave," he repeated in a monotone.

She nodded, turning to me. "The difficulty is that we have to put the patient's needs first," she said.

I sighed, nodded, picked up my bag. "Yes, of course."

I looked briefly at him. "Goodbye Lukkas. Good luck, it will all be fine... I'll see you in the morning," I said.

As I wandered back to the car, I thought of it for the first time. Why did he want me gone today, why so badly? Was it because she, Holly, would visit him?

I did everything, so many tasks in one day, just so that I didn't have to think about him. I marched angrily across the fields with the dogs, weeded the garden; with hammer and nails I bashed at the fence which had blown down in the wind. I prepared two casseroles for the week, fetched the girls from school and then took them to the library. I did all that I could to take my mind off Lukkas' operation and his unfathomable, unkind behaviour and the possible reason for it.

Later, the family return from various visits to the hospital to tell me that the operation appears to be a success. Hannah regards me with a critical eye, believing that I had chosen to stay away, or that I had perpetrated yet another heinous crime.

At seven in the evening, I make my way back to the hospital with a bowl of fruit. I am afraid that Lukkas will spot me from his window, that his angry face will turn me away.

As I alight from my car and cross the car park, I see it. Holly's car. A small, grey, Fiat. I have seen it parked at the office, close to Lukkas' car. At first, I think, no. No. Because I shan't visit him if she is there. Again, she is more than welcome, where I am not.

I cross the car park to peer through the car window. On the front seat, there are legal files. On the rear seat, little golden sandals, made for tiny feet and a text book of Family Law. As though I have been chased away, I hurry back to my own car with the bowl of fruit.

That night, against my will, a rape of the mind, I imagine them making love in the office. I don't want to imagine this, imagining makes me feel ill. It isn't the truth, I tell myself. They are close, working colleagues.

I thought I would be Florence Nightingale to his wounded soldier. I experimented with the bedroom on the day he was due to come home, checking that Lukkas would have everything at hand, his desk, nibbles, pain killers.

I explained to the girls that their Grandfather was very poorly and that they would have to be quiet, making them a star chart so that they would cooperate.

When he came home, allowing me to collect him from the hospital without a fuss, this time, I prepared the kind of nutritious meals I thought he would like to eat and revelled in the fact that I would be the nurse, not Holly.

I gently changed his dressings, whilst he was aloof, moody, demanding; often silent; but I told myself the pain in his back would be great whilst Lukkas snapped and sulked. I told myself, like a mantra, you always reserve the worst behaviour for the people you love.

Lukkas asked me to collect two gargantuan files from the office, in order to prepare for a child abuse case. I went, early in the morning to collect them from his secretary. As I pulled into his car space, Holly's car followed mine. She smiled through the driver's window and I nodded back. As she got out, I said, "So, you do have a car then?"

Her expression was pinched, resentful. "You are jealous of me," I thought for the first time.

"Yes. I don't always bring it to work. It's expensive to park in Oxford. Sometimes I park at the Park and Ride's."

"Where Lukkas picks you up," I thought.

"Actually, Laura," she shut the car door, "would it be okay if I came to your house to visit Lukkas, a bit later in the afternoon?"

I raised my eyebrows. Now I understood why Lukkas, who had worn his sloppy pyjama trousers for the duration of his illness, who had only shaved every five or so days, in my company, had risen bright and early, shaved the silver bristles from his chin, put on his jeans and clean tee shirt and sprayed himself liberally with his best after shave.

I thought he was making the effort for me. What an idiot I was.

"I'm sorry, Holly. Perhaps another day, Lukkas was in a bad way when I left the house, it isn't really a good idea."

Her plump lips parted. How much she wanted to argue with me. Her bright eyes glistened with resentment, cold and bright, the eyes of a thwarted Snow Queen.

"Okay," she said.

No doubt they would text one another, no doubt that Holly would complain to him.

CHAPTER FORTY-THREE

Perhaps it was a combination of unseen family catastrophes which persuaded Lukkas to turn to me once again. I suppose it's what happens in life.

Lukkas returned to work, far too early. A combination of things, perhaps; he had always been diligent about the firm and whether I liked it or not, Holly was there. If nothing else, he was certainly smitten by her, preferring her company too mine.

Shortly after this, Derek, his father, now in his late eighties, fell in the living room, breaking his leg. It was all becoming a little too much for Marjorie to cope with.

For the next few weeks, we drove to visit them, at the hospital and at Lukkas' mother's home. This was our base as we explored the surrounding county for suitable care homes for Derek. He hated the idea, an elderly man with a lively mind, free from dementia... it was hard for Derek to accept the plan. We suggested that they move closer to us, as we had done before, but Marjorie said that she didn't wish to leave those friends whose funerals she had not yet attended and that was understandable too.

For me, it meant more weekend trips to visit them. I didn't mind at all. We would be at a distance from Holly.

Both Lukkas and I were relieved when, at last, having visited eight care homes in total, having asked question after question to ensure that we had found the right place, we settled on a beautiful home, the outside of which might have been the country residence of the Wooster's.

In the evening, after we had driven home and Lukkas had made a visit to collect something from the office, I had curled up in the corner of the settee to watch the news.

When Lukkas nuzzled my neck with his lips, I jumped in surprise.

"Thank you," he said, happily, "We couldn't have done without your help, you asked some very useful questions." He came to sit next to me then, kissing my lips, then wrapping his arms about me, even massaging my neck as I watched TV. I was suddenly elated, perhaps he had stopped all of it, whatever 'it' was. Perhaps we could start again.

When Lukkas let go of me at last, I floated into our bedroom, the sudden rush of happiness making me almost light headed, until at the bathroom floor, I hesitated. On the top of the pile of washing drooped a pair of his black underpants. This morning I had watched him pull on striped underpants. He had only one pair of black and they hadn't been there in the morning. Why would he change his pants, half way through the day?

My life was being reduced to pants.

I picked them up between finger and thumb. They were warm, damp, with the salty smell of frenzied sex. I dropped them onto the carpet, just as Lukkas came into the room. But for the first time ever, he didn't shout, didn't make a scene. He walked across the room to the place where the soft, black material lay, picked them up and dropped them back onto the pile. Then he sighed and turned to me, wrapping his arms about me. I felt the guilt inside him as it emptied itself upon me.

I said nothing. We stood like that for a while, but I knew I had to take control, to do something before the canker grew and damaged me for ever. I couldn't go through another year like this, I couldn't let this hell affect me for the rest of my life.

Unwittingly, Josh gave me the chance to end it.

CHAPTER FORTY-FOUR

Doctor Shaw

I was dreading the appointment with the psychiatrist, no matter how calm I appeared to be.

On the morning of the interview, the calm left me. I hardly slept the night before, my dreams were pictorial voices of my fears, my 'What if's?'

What if they found me mad after all, what if Dr Evans betrayed my trust and had told Lukkas the name of the psychiatrist, what if I was incarcerated in a mental hospital, all my freedoms removed, forcibly taken from my family? All these questions haunted me, whether reasonable or sensible. I was simply, very scared.

I had not told Lukkas or our children which date I would go, only that I would go. Before going to collect Charlotte, I went to the petrol station. I was shaking so much, my concentration on what lay ahead, I reversed into a car and had to apologise to an elderly lady and give her my insurance details. It wasn't a great start to the day.

Yet again, I sat in the Doctor's waiting room, although this time in the rather plush setting of the private hospital that Lukkas had paid for. He was keen for me to have 'treatment' as soon as possible, he said, although his idea of what treatment I would need varied from treatment for bi-polar illness, to personality disorder, to obsessive-compulsive disorder. I wondered why, in thirty years, these things had never been spoken of. I wondered about the ways in which various aunts, sisters-in-law, female cousins had been spoken of by Lukkas' parents as being 'mad'. Could so many unrelated women be mad, or was it just a term for dissent? Surely doctors didn't take such wide spread labelling seriously, not in this day-and-age?

Charlotte turned her attention away from the glossy magazine she had been flicking through and smiled an easy, relaxed smile. I smiled back.

Like Josh, she hadn't wanted me to do this at all.

I hadn't eaten anything. I had a cup of tea a while ago and my stomach was churning resentfully. I thought, this is what it's like to give up your freedom, to go to prison, perhaps.

When, at last, the receptionist called us to the desk, Charlotte hastily squeezed my hand as I used to hers when she was my little sister, so many years ago. No, Lukkas would not have done that, not have provided comfort. I was too riddled with fear and anxiety to think any more. I twiddled my fingers in my lap and stared at the other patients.

The receptionist led us along the long, brightly lit corridor to Sally Shaw's room and the woman came to the door to greet us. She was tall, well dressed but not imposing. Her brown hair was cut to her shoulders. I think she must have been in her mid-forties. She smiled at us both and for the first time that morning I faltered, felt as though I would run away and stepped back from the room. Dr Shaw gave a small frown but managed to retain her smile. I turned to Charlotte whose eyes widened in an expression of alarm, "Come on," she said quietly, gently touching my elbow.

I bit into my lip and gazed from one to the other of them. "Could we talk in the waiting room first? There's something I want to say about Lukkas, my husband…" My voice trailed away. In my mind, I had thought we should separate that, our 'relationship,' from the interview, but I didn't explain it as I should.

"Everything you have to say is confidential. The waiting room won't be the right place for that," Dr Shaw explained. So, I nodded, and we went inside.

The room was arranged to put a 'patient' at their ease. There was a low settee, which I sat on beside Charlotte, a small desk with winter flowers arranged in a vase. The room was painted like a living room, with pale, yellow walls. Dr Shaw sat opposite us, her long legs crossed, a pad and pen resting upon her knee.

There was never a time when she appeared to be studying me, I noticed, not throughout the entire duration of the interview, or assessment, which I suppose, is what it was.

She started by asking me about my background and during this time I began to relax. The questions were easy to answer, when I became relaxed, I no longer had to think about the answers. It was rather more like a comfortable interview for a job. I answered spontaneously and honestly, without pre-thought.

She asked about my interests and hobbies, she asked about my siblings. When she asked about my maternal Grandmother, who had a mental breakdown, I told her my family had always believed she had been exhausted and anxious after my Grandfather died. She had nursed him for several years leading up to his death and had few breaks from that care. But prior to this she had lived a very normal life and a happy one.

I told her that I felt Lukkas behaviour had changed a lot, but that he had insisted that I come. When she asked me why I thought he was insisting, I found it hard to explain. I didn't want to tell her that I thought he was cheating on me, that in the back of my mind I wondered whether this pressure was meant as a weapon to use against me in the case of divorce.

All the while, Charlotte said nothing, but listened. Only once did she nod, and this in agreement with me, when I stated that he had never, before the last year, accused me of having a mental health problem.

Before I realised it, I had been speaking for an hour and twenty minutes. Dr Shaw then asked me to wait in the waiting room as she would like to speak with Charlotte, alone. So, I shook her hand and left them.

I admit to hovering outside the room, then decided I might be accused of paranoia, so I took a deep breath and went to the water machine in the waiting area. I suppose that Charlotte was away for about ten minutes. When she joined me, she linked her arm with mine. "Do you think, she thinks I'm m...m...mad?" I asked, twisting my face into something grotesque.

Charlotte laughed. "We all know you're mad," she said, "But not in that way."

I took her home. Once she had gone I felt very lonely and weary. I suppose it was emotional exhaustion, not sleeping the previous night, concern about the assessment.

I stood in front of the garage. I looked at the rear of my damaged car. Lukkas would be angry about that, but his anger seemed to run with one thing or another without dimension or proportion. I remembered he had said he wanted the garage cleared, which would mean endless trips to charity shops and the dump to remove the accumulation of years. It might mollify him if I started now.

I lifted the garage door, ducking beneath it and faced the task that lay ahead. The corners were the worst areas, filled with boxes of books and toys, old lawn mowers and tools. I started removing things, lifting them and carrying them outside, until I came to a very old friend. Alison, a life-sized doll whose blonde curly hair was now scant, bought for me by my Grandparents in the sixties, played with by generations of children.

Her naked little body was still perfect, but her cheek had lain under the pressure of a box filled with books and was distorted and ugly. I picked her up and cradled her to me as once I might have done as a child, like an old woman with dementia, mollified by her care staff with a pretend baby.

"Please don't let me be mad," I said out loud, and started to cry silently, then.

In the week, Lukkas brought up the subject of the retirement dinner for the Judge. It would be better, he said, that he should take one of his colleagues, one of the other lawyers representing the firm. I didn't argue with him but nodded slowly.

"Who will you take?" I asked, aware of the sudden knotted pain in my belly.

His relief that I wasn't about to argue was palpable. "Thought I'd ask Lauren," he said. I almost sighed with relief. Lauren had a husband and two small children. She had been mentored by Lukkas and now had her own formidable reputation. It wasn't going to be Holly accompanying him, at least.

On the morning of the Judge's retirement, at the start of March, I stood between the tall fir trees in the park to watch Ruby and Lilly playing. The bare branches of the trees are suddenly flecked with small, green buds. Everything resembles a pointillist painting. The colours are points of light and dark, only the sky is a smooth blue, lit by a cold, crisp sunshine.

I shade my eyes as I watch Ruby and Lilly play with a little girl they met in the park, someone from their school. They are sitting astride a long wooden unicorn on rockers, laughing as the little girl's mother rocks them back and forth.

Later, after I have taken the girls back to Hannah, I stand in the kitchen, stirring the sauce. It is the day of the Dinner at the college. I would have liked to go, but I can accept that another lawyer might be better. I would have liked to listen to Lukkas' speech on the kindly Judges retirement.

Why would Lukkas want me on his arm, anyway? When he can have a young, attractive lawyer beside him? I try to force such negative thoughts from my head. Then, to my surprise, Lukkas comes into the house. This is a far earlier time than I have been used to on a Saturday morning.

He smiles at me. He is carrying a work bag and a small supermarket bag. He looks so, very happy... I can't bring myself to trust his cheeriness.

"You're early," I say.

"Yep, that's enough work for one day, especially if I'm going out later-on."

He leaves his bags inside the hallway, returning to the car boot to take out a dry-cleaning bag. Of course, he will have taken his best suit to be cleaned for this evening.

Suspicion overtakes me. Whilst Lukkas is busy, I go to the computer and send an email to Lauren.

"Lauren, I can't get hold of Lukkas. Are you still going to the dinner with him this evening?"

To my surprise, she answers quite quickly, within the half hour.

"It isn't me who's supposed to be going, Laura. Holly is going with him. I couldn't go, even if I wanted to. I've been off work for two days with the flu."

I feel so upset that I can barely contain my feelings. I tread the stairs to the living room, where Lukkas is eating lunch and watching sport on the television.

"Did you say that Lauren is going with you this evening?" I ask him.

"Yes," he says, without looking up. "Would you give me a lift to the High street?"

I hesitate, I don't answer him. He frowns at me, unused to this slow response.

"She isn't, is she Lukkas? It was never going to be Lauren. Holly is going with you, Lauren explained in an email."

"You emailed her?" He yells, loudly enough to disturb the magpies, roosting in the chimney.

After that, he didn't speak to me, not all the afternoon. Tired with it, tired with the silence, I walked the dogs and went to visit Mum.

When I returned, he was getting ready. He booked a taxi and left early. I had no evidence that he was having a relationship with Holly, I didn't want him to be involved with anyone, but Holly was my worse fear. He worked with her for hours on end, spent more time with her than ever with me, he would never extract himself, not now.

Again, I couldn't sleep. I tried on several occasions, tossing and turning in the bed until at last I decided to lay on the settee and watch the television. I could no more concentrate upon that, wondering, way past midnight, what they would be doing. Would they go to the Randolph Hotel bar, perhaps? Might they even go to the little house he had bought, which Lukkas told me he had rented to students.

At last, in the early hours of the morning, I went to lay on the top of our bed in my clothes and fell asleep. Lukkas must have arrived home shortly after that. I awoke to the sound of his taxi, his key in the lock, his footsteps on the stairs. I feigned sleep, smelling the whisky and after shave and he ignored me, his snoring telling me that he was asleep almost as soon as his head hit the pillow.

In the moonlight, through the open curtains, something gold and fine glistened upon his naked shoulders and upon the sheet beneath the duvet. Fascination and revulsion made me turn on the light, but he didn't stir. It was a powdery, gold dust, like glitter, yet so fine.

CHAPTER FORTY-FIVE

The Report

I called the surgery two weeks later. The report was ready for me to read, inside an envelope marked 'Confidential'. I felt sick with anxiety as I drove to collect it, then reluctant to ask for it, in case my cousin or any of the receptionists that I knew, had seen it. Some of the receptionists had children I had taught. It was all dreadful.

I sat in the car in the surgery car park to read it.

I assessed Laura at the Greengage Hospital in Oxford in February 2012. She attended with her sister Charlotte. Initially, Laura was reluctant to come into the consulting room, wanted to see me in the waiting area as she explained that she was here due to pressure from her husband and assumed if we spoke in the waiting room, it would not be a part of the consultation. I explained the issues around confidentiality and that the assessment begins when I first meet her anyway. She told me that she did not want me to share information with her husband and I explained that I could only release information to other parties with her consent, unless there was a concern about a risk to her health and safety, in which case I might need to share information.

She agreed for me to speak to or gain further information from her sister and her eldest son and her GP but did not want me to speak to her husband.

Presenting Complaint

Laura says her husband has told her he loves her, but that she no longer feels that he does. She says that she feels increasingly degraded and controlled by him. She says she does not feel unsafe or at risk from anyone but that she and her husband have argued far more, recently. She was adamant that she was not paranoid or mentally ill in any way. She feels her difficulties are all related to his increasingly controlling behaviour of her.

She says that her energy levels are generally good but that her appetite is less and that she has lost weight. She enjoys looking after her grandchildren, taking them to the park, reading to them and playing games with them and is still actively involved and enjoys them as usual. She says that there is some less pleasure in life now because she is distressed that her husband doesn't love her, but she denied any feelings of depression.

Previous Medical History

She denied any feelings of physical ill health, in particular denied any dizziness, weakness, pain, pins and needles, fits, headaches, unsteadiness or falls. She says she sleeps reasonably well but wakes often and feels anxious about her husband. She has never had any fits, epilepsy, cardiovascular problems or diabetes.

Drug History

She smokes normally less than five cigarettes a day but recently, because of her anxiety, she has smoked more. She drinks water and tea but, on some days, will have at least two glasses of wine. She denies ever having had a drink problem, says she is not on medication and denies any allergies or illicit drugs.

Premorbid Personality
She feels she is a normally sociable woman who is interested in others. She is buoyant, creative, generally happy and optimistic but she usually paints landscapes and has found it hard to do this during the time of her anxiety. I spoke to her GP who felt there have been changes in her over the past year but cannot define what those changes might be.

Opinion
Laura denied feeling paranoid or mentally ill in any way. However, the information I have gained from her GP and other doctors at the surgery may reflect a temporarily abnormal mental state. It is impossible to confirm a mental illness currently as it is possible that her distress could be caused by a change in her relationship with her husband. I could see no signs of psychosis.

Laura is adamant she is not ill and does not need any further medical input. She maintains that she is here because her husband threatened her if she refused to come. We are in a difficult position given this situation. Should she be referred to the NHS service they can visit her at home and see if the Community Mental team can build a relationship with her and over time, further assess her mental state, but we need her cooperation for this.

If she did come to you wanting some medication for sleep or stress, then a small dose of risperidone e.g. 1 mg initially increasing to 2mg if needed at night would be a good place to start pharmacological treatment.

It was signed by Sally Shaw.

I read it through twice, then collapsed against the seat with the crumpled report in my lap. So, my GP's had been afraid for my health. But then, Lukkas had spoken to them before I had and Lukkas was an eminent lawyer who used GP's in the giving of evidence, psychiatrists too.

Josh had said it was a dangerous game to play, to visit them myself, just because his father threatened to leave me. But in fact, she had found nothing. Did I want nurses to visit me? No, I did not. There were so many people in the world in need of help for genuine mental distress.

My first thought was that I would be happy to let Lukkas read this. But the next thought, leaping on top of the first was depressing, because I knew that when he read it he would not be pleased, not at all. It wasn't damning as he hoped it would be.

Lukkas wanted me to be mad. I shuddered, pushing the thought away. Of course, he didn't.

CHAPTER FORTY-SIX

Scribblings

Within two hours of his reading the report, I watched Lukkas' face pucker dramatically in disbelief and stifled rage. He had already phoned Hannah and Joe. He had stopped bothering with Josh, who remained silent on every point he raised. Lukkas felt more than a little disgusted with him for not taking his side.

They sat in the kitchen whilst I made tea, though felt as if I could do with a slightly stiffer drink. Once upon a time we would have met like this to plan a holiday, I thought, now Lukkas planned my incarceration in a mental institution.

"The report says you could be visited by a mental health nurse," Lukkas reminded me. This, after he had initially dismissed it as misguided nonsense and criticised the psychiatrist behind it.

But the report gave me courage. It was hardly damning, in fact it said I showed no signs of psychosis, that it was possible that a changed state of being was related to relationship difficulties with my husband.

"I don't want or need visits from a mental health nurse when there are people genuinely suffering with mental health problems," I said flatly.

I looked at them in turn, whilst they all stared back at me.

"Mum. Dad isn't having an affair, he wouldn't do that, and you claim to have found odd things in the car. The truth is, you put them there, didn't you?"

I shook my head. I wanted to shout but wouldn't. I kept my voice steady.

"No. I can't believe you think that. I've been depressed about the idea of us parting. I found the things," I insisted. I felt my anger rising at the lie, or was it possible that Lukkas didn't know someone was deliberately leaving things? I had always been more observant than him.

"Hannah, if you truly believed I had some dreadful problem, would you really ask me to babysit so often, allow me to care for the girls as you do?"

She screwed up her lips but had no answer for me.

"What you are is...afraid," I said, "and so is Joe, I get that. You're afraid Dad will leave, you're afraid that I am ill. I'm not ill and the report says, effectively, that the doctor couldn't find anything wrong with me. I don't think you should be party to these conversations between your father and me. These issues are between us."

Joe took his tea from me. His expression was gentle, and I believed he was about to speak up for me. But my heart sank when he said, "If Dad leaves, I blame you. He loves you and you could do something about all of this, but you won't." He looked toward Lukkas, who shook his head. At twenty, Joe's blustering confidence concealed a deep-rooted fear that the family would disintegrate.

"They are afraid with good reason," Lukkas grunted. "Who knows what you will do next? I'm your target, but now you're targeting Holly, too."

"Holly, in Dad's office?" Hannah scoffed. "Do you know how ridiculous that sounds? I've met her, she's alright actually, but you really think Dad would do that to you? And anyway, what would it do to his reputation if anyone found out? It's all nonsense Mum!"

She hung her head in her hands, her long hair swinging across her face, and I felt so sorry for her that I went to put my arm about her shoulder, but she pulled away immediately.

Lukkas' long body leaned against the kitchen sink. His face was impassive. "Then I refuse to go anywhere with you until you do, or to have any family here, or friends. I'm not going to the wedding in Nice, either. Even your mother agrees..."

"She does not!" I cut in, silencing him for a moment, losing my self-control. "It isn't what she believes at all. You've harassed her at a time when she's very ill. She doesn't know the truth, does she? She doesn't know about the way in which you've behaved..."

I had not meant to say that. It was hopeless, all going the wrong way. The only way to regain their approval would be to carry on with this mental health thing. Give in or divorce him, either way, I couldn't win.

I left them then, and this time no one tried to stop me. I went into the garden and through the gate, out into the darkened field, no longer able to think about what they were saying. I had no proof that he was carrying on with Holly, I knew only that he could do with his own psychiatric assessment.

Lyra had followed me. She pressed her pointed nose against my leg and I stooped down to place my arms about her neck, balancing in the mud.

I had the idea, then; the possibility of finding out. I just had to think how I would do it and when. I had to have the courage, too. I had to prove to our children that their father was lying. They would never stop loving either of us, whatever the case. After all, through everything, I loved him.

True to his word, Lukkas stayed away until late into the evening and hardly spoke to me when he returned.

The atmosphere over the next few weeks was such that I couldn't invite either family or friends. When I was not with Ruby and Lilly or Mum, the only comfort to be gained was through the occasional chat with Josh. Hannah and Joe rarely spoke to me. Again, my writing was my only source of release and of comfort.

The day came when Lukkas walked in upon my scribblings. I had been so intent on it that I didn't hear the door to the spare room opening. The sheets of paper, filled with my long hand, lay upon the coverlet. My thoughts, my experiences written down; my therapy, now.

"What are you doing?" His voice made me jump. His long face was etched with suspicion.

"Just writing," I said, trying to steady the surprise and guilt in my voice.

"Writing what?"

"Remember the children's novel I began? I'm trying to finish that," I replied, though I could feel my cheeks burning, pink as a child's.

"Let me read some of it…"

"No, really, I'd prefer you didn't, not until I really know where I'm going with it," I insisted, my fingers crawling across the pages like a large spider protecting her web. But he seemed to lose interest then, asking me if I had seen the TV remote control.

I stifled a sigh of relief when he left the room, but waited, like a frozen thing. When he went outside for a cigarette, I quickly took the sheets of paper to our bedroom and hid them once again beneath my side of the mattress. After that, writing when and where I could, I scribbled on loose sheets which I hid in the bookcase. Writing had become a way of recording reality, of knowing that these things were really happening, just in case; just in case something happened.

She had begun to haunt me. I could not escape. Somewhere, perhaps bored with her own life, perhaps ambitious, another woman dictated everything we did. Another woman dictated Lukkas' moods, the way I should dress, the way I looked each day, how I must feel. Another woman left things in Lukkas' car to distress me. She cared nothing for the life we had, not for our children or our grandchildren. This woman cared about herself alone.

Lukkas arrived home earlier, one Friday. I had collected the girls from school and made cakes with them for a cake sale. Hannah was now renting a house close by, which made it easier for me to help her. We made the cakes in her small kitchen and waited for her return from work. After this, I strolled along the lane which lead to her house and followed the road to mine.

It was late afternoon, but I could smell the bonfire half way down the road and thought, Lukkas will be annoyed. He told me off if I started a fire just five minutes before the local councils allotted time.

Then I realised that plumes of smoke were drifting across our garden fence. Baffled, I started to walk a little faster. Only Josh and I enjoyed the cathartic ritual of a bonfire, often with a beer in hand. Joe detested the idea, Lukkas would only tolerate bonfires on November 5th and loathed camping and camp fires.

So, who was holding a bonfire?

In the garden, flames burned steadily in the incinerator as Lukkas dragged sheaths of paper from the black bin liners that had held them. He wore an old woollen jumper and jeans I had not seen him wear in years, he appeared to be burning office notes, but he had asked me to do that job. It was so unlike Lukkas to do anything that involved mess or dirt, that I smiled, at first.

Lukkas smiled back, too broadly, too pleased with himself. Opening my mouth to speak, no words came out. I turned away from him, heedless of the muddy shoes I was dragging through the house, racing in a panic through the hallway, leaping two at a time to ascend the staircase to our bedroom.

The coverlet had been pulled aside where I usually lay. I lifted the heavy mattress, groping beneath it for the handwritten notes and carefully woven words that had been ready to go onto my lap top, desperately searching with cold fingers for the feel of the paper sheets.

There was nothing there and it wouldn't have mattered half so much had it been fifty-pound notes that my hands sought.

I flopped onto the edge of the bed, my hands in my lap, chewing the soft, inner flesh of my cheek in my stress, squeezing the tears from my eyes. All that work. It wasn't work to anyone else, it didn't matter to anyone else but me. I could never remember it all, never in the same way, with the same words. Gone, but for the more recent parts in the bookcase that presumably, for I had not yet looked there, Lukkas didn't know about.

It had taken ages to write and I hadn't the heart, then, to think about writing it all over again. To write anything worth writing means distancing yourself from others and in my family, with my responsibilities, that was no mean feat. But it mattered, it mattered so much to me. I didn't challenge Lukkas. It would lead to a row, his denial, and further pressure from Hannah and Joe.

As my sorrow subsided over the next days, so my anger grew.

CHAPTER FORTY-SEVEN

"People will be suspicious..."

I had no keys to Lukkas' office. I didn't know the security codes, even if I could obtain the keys.

Lukkas went away for his boy's weekend as planned. Then, on the Sunday of his trip, Josh's car finally ground to a halt. He asked me whether I could give him a lift because he was behind with paperwork.

I said yes, spending the rest of the afternoon in a panic. I didn't want to do it, it frightened me like the idea of the Private Detective, but it might mean that I would know for certain, instead of being goaded and teased and lied to.

It was one of the longest days of my life, I knew that I would falter if I didn't fill the day with activity, so I suggested to Hannah that I take the girls to the cinema.

We went to see a Tim Burton cartoon. I will never forget the film, because of that day. It was in black and white, but they didn't seem to notice that, they loved it, never moving except to eat popcorn and fizzy drinks. Sometimes, during the sad or scary bits, Lilly sat on my lap.

All the while I kept the plan of his office in my head, thinking and thinking. I could not implicate Josh, who must never know what I intended to do.

I had promised Lukkas that I would never use the Dictaphone again, but then, he had broken so many promises to me. I erased the songs that Ruby and Lilly had sung and put in new, long life batteries. These should last through the night and some way into the following morning, I thought.

I had no idea how I would retrieve it after it had lain there. It was enough to deal with today's espionage.

In the late afternoon, I cut a printing ink box in half, which would blend in with the environment of Lukkas' messy office, I thought.

I carried it all in my handbag as I followed Josh up the staircase to Lukkas' office, on the pretence of making a coffee, whilst I waited for him to collect the things he wanted. While Josh photocopied paperwork, I looked casually about the room; at Lukkas' desk, at Holly's too.

While Josh was busy, I looked at the desks and their drawers, at the waste paper baskets, the loose boxes and paraphernalia of files and then at last, noticed the loose paperwork jammed between Lukkas' desk and the wall and as Josh finished using the photocopier, I shoved the box, with the Dictaphone inside, beneath this.

All evening I felt sick with nervous anxiety, praying that it wouldn't be found by anyone. Lukkas would know immediately that I was the culprit and he would chastise Josh, too. I felt so jittery, thought that I would be sick, then lay awake until the midnight hour, when Lukkas returned from Berlin.

The problem of how to retrieve the thing shook me awake the following morning. Lukkas said he had a great time in Berlin, that was all, then he dressed and hastened to his office.

Cakes, I thought. When Lukkas took over the office, I would take cakes in on a Friday. I would buy Iced cupcakes and take them today.

The girls at reception seemed pleased. I went up to the top office. As luck would have it, only Josh was there, seated at his desk with a pen between his teeth. Both Lukkas and Holly were on a case together, he told me. Briefly, I wondered whether that case might be taking place at Lukkas' new house but retrieving the gadget from under Josh's nose was the predominant thought now. I sat on a chair as I talked to him and when he turned to the window, slid my hand to the door and shoved the box into my bag.

In the car, just a few streets away, I ran the machine back and forth, to nothing, it seemed, but the silence of the night in Lukkas' office.

I almost gave up, my heart not wanting to believe my head in any instance, I almost erased the whole recording in desperation, believing that it must have petered out by morning. The timing said that it was a fourteen-hour recording, not the seventeen hours I had thought it would last. It should have recorded Lukkas' arrival in the office at least.

Then, out of the silence, came a squeak, the squeak of the office door needing oil on the hinges.

It was about forty minutes after he had risen from our bed, so he must have driven straight to the office.

I listened as Lukkas stirred his coffee and opened the zip of his work bag. Ten or so minutes afterwards, Holly came into the room. She had arrived before him, I thought, my heart skipping a beat.

At the very first, the conversation might have been between any two colleagues, but there was something false about it, just as though, beneath the banter, they were desperate to say something else to each other.

"Hello," Holly's voice, the small, librarian's voice. The greeting was one, melodious, long note.

"Hi, just going over the case notes for today," and Lukkas cleared his throat again, like Colonel Hearty. There was something false about that sound too. It was as though they were acting something out.

She walked across to his computer, looking at it from beside him, I imagined her elbows resting upon the desk.

But it was nothing, I told myself, beginning to feel relief, elation even.

"So, how did your weekend in Berlin go?"

"Great, got a bit of a hangover, though. What about your weekend?"

"Oh, so-so..." It is a sad little sound, artificial, as though she seeks his sympathy. "I went shopping," Holly adds, a little more brightly.

"What kind of shopping?" Lukkas asks swiftly, briskly.

"Clothes shopping." Her voice changes, there is something cute, something sexy about it.

"What kind of clothes...?" His voice is flirtatious now, I can almost hear him panting. Lukkas hasn't shown interest in my clothes since I was in my thirties, perhaps that was why I stopped trying.

"Oh, just these..." I can hear a bag rustling.

Then he drools, "Never seen a contraption like that before, quick release clothing?"

I imagine what she might be showing him and am filled with loathing and disgust. Quick release clothing? I'm not there, but I am embarrassed, as though I am watching a pornographic film with my children.

"Oh, sorry..." she appears to have bumped into him, a strange collision considering there is no one else present in a large office. Holly coughs nervously. Then she squeaks, "Oh!" and gives a small sigh.

"What?" asks Lukkas, as though he doesn't know what.

"You grabbed my arm."

Grabbing my arm was a technique used by Lukkas when I was young, when he wanted sex. How dare he? They sound like two overheated teenagers.

There is a pause then, who knows what they are doing? Then Lukkas makes a pretence of opening the office door. Perhaps it isn't a pretence, but he says, "Just checking the corridor to make sure nobody is there..." and Holly giggles, "You're dreadful," she says, "Terrible..." But she loves it.

"I know," Lukkas agrees, equally attention seeking, "and I'm getting worse, but we've only got twenty minutes before anyone comes."

For a second, they say nothing, until I hear the dreaded, unmistakable sound of the slow kiss.

"So, this is your master plan? The one you were talking about last week?" Holly asks in a sexy whisper.

"What, spontaneous sex..."

"Sh! Keep it down," she says.

"It won't take very long," Lukkas coaxes.

Holly emits a whispered sigh, "Let's face facts, Lukkas. Spontaneous sex, uncomplicated? Ears will prick up. We need to be more careful than that."

"Quick release," Lukkas reminds her, kissing her again, his voice muffled. "One means of access."

"Nobody can ever find out about us."

"Never, ever," Lukkas promises. "I'm not going to divulge it to anyone."

"I'm serious, Lukkas. We'll have to be careful, but we can't change the way we've been working, or people will be suspicious."

How very clever, Holly. What an admirable way to discourage this. I hate her, there is little point in lying to myself, I hate the woman for good reason, and she is cleverer and even more manipulative than Lukkas.

"So, you've been thinking about me over the weekend, then?"

"Of course, I've been thinking about you…"

Then there is the sound of a slap, the way Lukkas used to slap me on the bottom.

"God knows how I'm going to concentrate on the trial now. What time are you free today?" he asks.

"I'll meet you at three, if you've time…" Holly purrs.

The office door squeaks open then. Josh, our son Josh, calls, "Morning."

I turn the device off. Bastard, Lukkas. You utter bastard. I knew, but I didn't want to believe in it. Holly Farrah, family lawyer, the nice girl?

My forehead lolls against the car window and I close my eyes. All I can see is Lukkas and Holly in the office and their foreplay.

CHAPTER FORTY-EIGHT

The Truth

It's past one thirty, when I reach home. The house is quiet, everyone is at work or school or just out. The dogs wag their tails and I turn them into the garden. I can't speak, can't breathe, can't think. I go to the fridge and pour wine into a mug. I feel dead inside.

Dully, a zombie, I go to the computer. When I set the recording, I hadn't accounted for such a conversation, for the lust in their voices, for the shock it would give me.

At least, I knew I wasn't mad, for there were times when I almost believed it.

I wanted them both to know, and my feelings made it imperative, so I transcribed some of the message, to him and to her, in two emails.

For a long while, there was no reply. Then Hannah sent me a text, and I could sense Lukkas' panic in her message.

From the transcription I had sent, there was an element of doubt in him or, worse still, he believed he could have me committed to some mental institution today, now; without further ado, in case I messed things up for him. He couldn't recall what they had said to one another, that was clear.

"Dad says you are going mad again, that you sent Holly an email. I am coming there now, you can't embarrass him like this."

Embarrass him? I, embarrass him after everything he had done? Perhaps he had forgotten the whole conversation, the kissing, the promises to her.

So, when Hannah and Joe arrived at the same time, moments later, in Joe's car; to whisk me off to the Doctor for my injection, I stood defensively against the wall at the front of the house.

"Please listen," I told them. "I've made nothing up. Your father is lying to all of us, as is Holly."

"Listen? To what?" Hannah screeched, "You've gone too far this time."

"I can prove it, but I don't want to," I told them. "I love you."

I was trembling a little, now, at the back of my mind, I wondered whether they would drag me off in the car. "I recorded them, Dad and Holly. He's been lying to you; to us. I can't go on any more like this, with her there, dictating everything that we do through your father."

"Where is this recording?" Joe asked, scepticism written all over his face.

I nodded slowly, so-be-it, before leading them into the house, into the study.

Hannah sat at Lukkas' desk, Joe behind her. I ran the recording back once more whilst they waited impatiently, then started it at the squeaking door.

At first, they looked blankly at one another and contemptuously at me whilst they heard the innocent pleasantries. Then Hannah's pretty face twisted to incredulity, whilst Joe hung his head. But I felt no triumph, no, it wasn't like that. What I felt was sadness for them both. What I felt was fear for their relationship with Lukkas, who had felt no guilt for the way he had affected my relationship with them.

"You don't need to hear any more," I said. "Turn it off."

"No," Hannah said, "Leave it." But she slumped further down at the desk, her head resting on the heels of her hands, as distraught as I had been.

And Joe thrust his lips in an expression like his fathers. "He sounds like a seedy old man and she sounds like a whore," he said.

I turned it off before the end. Neither of them tried to persuade me after that.

"How could he?" Hannah groaned. Then Joe put his arms about me, holding me against his chest. "You aren't mad then, you were right about Holly," he said.

Hannah got up too. She kissed me on the cheek. "I'm so sorry..." she said. "Do what is right for you, now." But there was a youthfulness, a lack of realism in her voice and I knew this would be harder than Hannah believed.

What was right for me? Yet, I had expected Hannah to get rid of Ben, to be free of an abusive relationship. My own relationship with Lukkas was wrong. He had no respect for me if he thought he could behave as he had.

"I feel as though I'm in shock, Hannah. I don't know what to do now, but nothing will be easy for a long time," I said, "Nothing will be easy."

They left after that, I will never know what their messages to him said.

Lukkas came home much earlier than usual, but I wasn't there, because I went to the pub. Not our usual pub, I didn't want to see anyone, or yet talk to anyone, not anyone who knew Lukkas and I. I went to the Red

Lion, a pub that Lukkas didn't like, and drank two glasses of very green Chardonnay in less time than was good for me and smoked several cigarettes until the point where I might have vomited. It was pure self-destruction, I no longer knew what I wanted, and it seemed the only answer.

"How could you, Lukkas?" I said it in my head, said it aloud and under my breath, said it again and again. I hated her, I knew in my heart that their relationship, this relationship, fuelled by sex, had been going on for a long time. I called her every name under the sun, mostly under my breath. I hated her, for she had destroyed my family, or had deliberately attempted to.

Then I left my wine glass in the garden, driving home in the rain, a mercifully short journey.

I admit to being truly drunk and ugly of thought and appearance, both, as I muttered vindictively under my breath. I wanted to slap Holly; I wanted to hurt her.

The house was quiet when I returned. Lukkas car was there, but there was no sign of him. Hannah had gone somewhere with the girls, perhaps, upset, she had gone to cry on the shoulder of a friend. I had no idea where Joseph was.

I felt sick, now. I had eaten nothing all day. The idea of them together filled me with revulsion.

I went to the computer to read my emails. There was one, only and that from Holly.

"I am sorry, Laura," it said. "Nothing actually happened between us."

I laughed, a bitter, drunken laugh. Not on that occasion, I thought.

I sent an email back to her. "You are as bad a liar as he is, and you are a false-hearted bitch."

I slumped across the desk and started to think more rationally about her involvement. She wanted Lukkas, she wanted his money too, family money that I had worked as hard to secure. It was she who had been in that office on the morning Lukkas accused me of hitting him with a frying pan, she who had created the joke with paintbrush hairs in his white shirt. Had she also been suggesting to him that he should accuse me of some form of madness? Had she put the idea of gaslighting me into Lukkas' head? How much all of this, how often?

I felt a rush of panic now. Lukkas had moved all our files, our documents, our mirror wills into the office. He had bought her a house, hadn't he? I was powerless. If he left me for her now, how would I track anything down, any of the information that I needed?

It was growing dark. Where was Lukkas?

Then I heard Josh's footsteps on the doorstep. His appearance was even more dishevelled and world weary than usual. His first words to me were sudden and his expression had an air of confusion about it.

"What the heck has Holly done?" he asked.

"Why? Why do you ask that?" But I didn't wait for his answer. "She's having an affair with your father," I finished tonelessly.

I would no longer refer to him as 'Dad', it was too friendly, too familiar.

"I recorded them in the office," I said, "carrying on, so to speak."

"Oh. I'm sorry, Mum." He didn't pause to ask me how I had done that, and I didn't want to explain.

"Why do you ask?" For a moment, optimistically, I wondered whether she had committed suicide, or at the very least, resigned her post.

THE DEVIL YOU DON'T

"Joe barged into the office an hour or so ago. He was in a bit of a state. He called Holly some pretty-dreadful names and told her that if she'd been a man, her would have punched her. Dad wasn't there, and the staff were a bit worried, so I had to persuade Joe to leave. It was all a bit tricky."

"Ah. Poor Joe," I said. I should have said more, should have said, "Gosh, that's dreadful..." But there was little point in lying to myself. I scarcely cared.

He gave me a hug, but food was the greater priority. I had failed to produce any, so I gave him some change and sent him to the fish and chip shop.

I wanted to feel calmer, but it wasn't happening, the anger inside me was like a bonfire out of control and wouldn't let me relax. Where was Lukkas? I wanted to shout at him, to hit him, to explode out of all proportion. All my efforts to be 'the better woman' had come to nothing.

I felt disgust with myself too and I felt no love for him at that moment, or if I did, it was manifesting itself in hatred. He had smashed all my beliefs, or so it seemed.

As I lurched against the washing machine, the kitchen door opened and Lukkas appeared at last with the dogs at his heels. He had been walking in the fields, as though there was nothing wrong, as though nothing had happened, or perhaps because of what had happened. He shut the dogs outside and smiled at me, calmly, as though he hadn't been carrying on with anyone, as though he hadn't asked another woman for unconditional, spontaneous sex.

"How could you, how could you?" I spat, "To lie to us all, to tell your children I am mad, and doctors and

God knows who else? How could you do that, how could you have sex with Holly?"

He took one step toward me. "No, no sex," he said.

"Really, Lukkas? My God, what a liar you are!" And I flew at his chest then, pummelling his chest with my fists in hurt and frustration whilst he said nothing.

"You've been setting me up, planning to leave me, stashing money away!" I accused him, "How could you treat me like that?"

I started crying then, still hitting his chest with the sides of my fists until he held my arms still and suddenly put his arms tightly about me and held me against him, whilst my tears soaked his sweater.

When at last I had stopped crying, I asked in a whisper, "How long, how many... conversations... like that?"

"A few," he said quietly, and he sounded drained.

"But for how long, weeks, months, years?" I implored him.

"About five or six weeks. Look, it was all about the chase, all about the romance," he said. "I love you, there wasn't any sex." He kissed my forehead. "Go to sleep," he said, "Sleep it off. I'll get my own dinner."

I went to our bedroom, exhausted, and climbed, fully clothed beneath the duvet. But as drunks do, I awoke a few hours later needing to drink water. It was after midnight and Lukkas was sleeping soundly beside me. I thought about the note from Holly I had incinerated.

"Chase?" And on the same post-it, in his writing, "Yes please!"

I imagined him chasing her around the office after dark, an office empty, but for them. Thought of the glossy, chestnut red hairs I kept finding on the bathroom floor. "Oh my God!" I wailed, an animalistic cry of pain. I could no longer sleep with him.

I left him then, not caring that the door was banged shut by me for a change, I left the bedroom we had shared all these years and went to the spare room to sleep.

The Mistress

When I awoke, Lukkas had already gone to work.

"Fire her, please get rid of her," I pleaded in a text. It was some time later that he replied.

"I can't. She's a good Family Lawyer. It won't happen again. I won't work with her."

How are you going to do that? I asked myself miserably, knowing now, as Josh had said, that she was his 'close working partner.' How were they going to avoid one another, even if they had the will power to do it?

Hannah was very kind to me that day, she didn't go to work, taking the children to school herself. She never took time off. I was very glad of the space, I really couldn't smile today.

I sent another text to him. "Please pay her off, whatever it takes, I don't care. I feel as though she is ruling my life and I hate it. It's humiliating too, how can I ever go into the office again?"

He didn't reply to that at all. I suppose it wasn't a case of sexual harassment, I suppose that he couldn't fire her.

I went from one extreme to another, one emotion to another. One moment I cried quietly to myself, picking up the pictures of Lukkas, of our family, our wedding, playing silently with my wedding ring. The next I was possessed by fury and found myself slamming pots and pans around or throwing things out of the garage, so the dogs hid from me. It was during one of the latter fits of rage that I sent Holly a text.

"You are a liar and a whore," it said. I was ashamed afterwards and I knew that Lukkas would be furious with me.

I had to wait for Charlotte to return from her school, to tell her.

At first, she frowned, and I knew that Lukkas had half convinced her. She looked at me with her head on one side, a lazy left eye closed, and I knew, as she admitted later to me, she was trying to assess my mental state. Wondering whether I was imagining this liaison. Lukkas was respected by everyone we knew, used as a lawyer by everyone, no less so, my family. She loved me, but she would doubt something like that happening in his office.

But then she sat at the kitchen table, listening to the recording and her features gradually changed, just as the children's faces had changed. She winced, gaped; shook her head and fell silent, staring at the hands in her lap. When it was over, she stood up and put her arms tightly about me.

"You can't tell anyone, Charlotte, for one thing, Hannah and Joe are so... shocked. For another, it's humiliating," I faltered.

She nodded. "Of course, it's humiliating, all of it, and of course I shan't tell anyone."

There was silence between us for a moment.

"So, what are you going to do now?" Charlotte sighed, at last.

"He denies an affair..."

"Does he? Of course, he does. He probably says it's your fault too..."

I smiled. She took my hand in hers.

"Enough is enough, Laura. Tell him to go. His behaviour is disgraceful, he thinks he can do what he likes, thinks he's God," she exclaimed.

I nodded, dully watching the rain beating noisily on the kitchen window.

"You're surely not going to that wedding in Nice, now?"

"We told Thomas's parents we were. I don't want to make excuses, we've known them for a long time."

"Look, Laura, I'm so sorry, but I honestly don't believe that Lukkas can love you at all now, to put you through this. He has other motives, doesn't he? You are a sort of, convenience, really. You sort out his home life whilst this bloody woman sorts out his office. Hasn't it occurred to you that he might want to divorce you now, but all this stuff about madness is so that he can stop you from getting money? I've been divorced, remember? Lukkas was my divorce lawyer. Most of the things I've learned about the devious tactics that people sometimes use, came from him. Lukkas knows every trick in the book and he's playing you."

I left Charlotte when her own family returned, arriving home at almost the same time as Lukkas.

It was clear to me that he had been crying, also clear that he was extremely angry with me. His eyes were hard and red and as he walked towards me from his car, his lips stretched back in a grimace. He held his face inches from mine.

"That's enough," he said. "No more abusive texts to Holly, just one more and she will report you to the police for harassment!"

I flinched at first, but when he said this, all fear subsided.

"Really, was that your advice to her? Let her do that and I'll show the police how she harassed me!" I shrieked at him, heedless of the neighbours.

"Vile, wizened hag!" he snarled over his shoulder, as he had done before, striding away from me.

We didn't talk for days after that. Every morning when I awoke, I would stare at myself in the bathroom mirror in a way I had never done before and lift my cheekbones with my fingertips, imagining my skin as it had once been. Once, I considered using pins, pinning my ears. I wondered how much blood there would be, as his insult rang in my ears.

After this, he persuaded Hannah and Joseph that nothing would happen again, that he was sorry. Again, they believed him. They spoke gently to me, but it was clear they expected me to forgive him. "You can move on!" Joe told me, as though it was that easy.

Lukkas had promised me that he wouldn't take Holly to Milton Keynes on cases any longer. I didn't trust it, not after everything they had done.

When he said that his new case was due to start in a week, that he would have to stay there overnight, I told him that I would go with him. For the first time, I didn't ask it, but insisted.

"What about the children?" he asked incredulously.

"I'll drive there in the evening and come back to Oxford in the early morning," I told him, knowing how hard that would be. But I would do it, oh yes.

I made it more, delightfully complicated by refusing to tell him which nights I would arrive. If Lukkas liked spontaneous, he would now get spontaneous surprises.

Every chosen evening, then, I would leave the supper on plates and race along the country roads to Milton Keynes, a place with many confusing roundabouts. I listened to radio four whilst cleaning my teeth and brushing my hair in transit. Not my best driving. As I approached the town, the American sky line, with its tower blocks reaching upward to luminate the sky, my heart would palpitate with a panic that I can't explain and would never forget.

When I arrived, I would dive into the downstairs toilets, hastily apply some make up, comb my hair into place and spray myself with perfume. I would then have to wait whilst the receptionist rang through to his room. How incongruous it seemed to me, wives wait here, girlfriends go up in the lift, unnoticed.

When I reached his room, he would answer the door without looking at me, an unwanted visitor who sat, sewing upon his bed whilst he read through paper after paper and I wondered what else he would be doing if I hadn't come.

Eventually, having bored himself silly, Lukkas would say, "Shall we have some dinner, then?"

I got to know several of the restaurants there. The food was nice, but the company did nothing for my ego. Lukkas was always quiet, or sometimes critical. I watched him on occasion, trying to fathom what he was thinking. Often, I thought about all the times I had been criticised for necessary expenditure whilst wondering who paid for the restaurants and hotel rooms. Sometimes he would say, "Stop staring at me," and I remembered an elderly uncle with dogs who would order them, "Look away!" when he was eating.

I asked him, he had promised me, that Holly wouldn't stay overnight in Milton Keynes. He had evidently changed his mind. She would be assisting him with his case, but she would return to Oxfordshire each evening, or so Lukkas said, rather grumpily. Presumably to ask it was an infringement of his human rights.

The towels were replaced each day, as were the soaps and the bed linen. My mind became alert to all of this.

When I arrived on the Wednesday evening, Lukkas was hunched over paperwork at the desk in his room. A sentimental feeling smothered me as I remembered a scene from years ago, a younger Lukkas, glasses perched upon his nose, studying for his finals, so long ago. Tears sprang to my eyes and I quickly went into the bathroom to staunch them.

As I reached to pick up a fallen hand towel, I saw the marks there. Several smears, again, the ripples of blotted foundation, sandy brown. The rose pink of lipstick marks too.

I looked at the other towels, unused, neatly folded, fluffy and white on a bathroom rack.

There was no anxiety inside of me, only anger and loathing. I carried the towel through to him.

"What are these?" I asked.

He gave them a cursory glance. "You are being ridiculous, you made them, with your own make up…"

I laughed briefly. It wasn't funny. "I never wear pink, it's a young person's colour," I said. "Besides, I put on make-up in the downstairs loo before I see you. All the towels have been changed since this morning. Are you wearing make-up during the day, Lukkas?"

Tension remained between us for the rest of the evening as we fought with our feelings against a row.

In the morning, having arrived at the plan whilst he slept, I accepted that these marks, these findings were not left by accident. She wanted me to know, wanted to hurt me and rock my stability or the make-up would be wiped with a tissue that could be thrown away.

When he rose from the bed to shower, I stood briefly at the hotel window, gazing at the tall, modern buildings, now shrouded in fog, then made my decision.

Hurriedly, I took my sewing scissors and cut a small gash in the wide hem of the heavy curtain. I took the Dictaphone from the bottom of my bag and placed the batteries inside, switching the thing onto record, then dropping the thing into the hem, I stitched it loosely, letting the curtain fall back into place. I dressed and said goodbye to him and looked back at the window once before driving to Oxford.

Again, that evening, I returned. As we chatted, quite amicably about Hannah's shop and his case, and Lukkas rubbed his tired eyes with finger and thumb, I looked up at the window sill. Two empty wine glasses stood there, their bottoms smudged with red wine, but quite clearly, even from the other side of the room, I saw the pink trace of lipstick turned to me. I noticed, too that the pillows had been rearranged, but thought it possible he had taken a nap.

I said nothing, but on the following morning when he was in the shower, once more I took the Dictaphone out and deftly repaired the damage to the curtain. As I drove home, once more, I listened.

It was an odd feeling to hear myself, yesterday, in history, kissing him on the cheek and wishing him a good day, the door to his room closing. There was silence for a few seconds as he paced the room. Then I heard his voice, loud and clear. "Yeah, go on, fuck off out of my life..."

Lukkas, who loves me so, very much.

I sigh and shake my head, then listen as he wanders into the bathroom, saying, "She's taken my fucking toothbrush..." His is identical to mine.

I listen as Lukkas starts up his lap top and then hear his fingers hammering away at the lap top. There is a buzz from his mobile phone, which he must have read because in a voice of the sleaziest enthusiasm, he replies to himself, aloud, "Just going for a little drive? Ooh yeah, ooh yeah!" And I am reminded of the Led Zeppelin song.

She is out there, somewhere, waiting for him. Perhaps in the parking lot I have just vacated. Waiting for me to go.

A few seconds afterwards, I hear him take his coat from the hanger and leave the room.

After this, there is silence for a long time, other than a dripping tap and the noises from the street outside. The room is ghostly until the chattering Polish cleaners arrive, talking animatedly to each other. They too, leave. Silence once more. Lukkas returns in the late afternoon and sits at his desk, working, until once more my knock is heard at the door.

Perhaps I should be relieved that he had no visitors, unless of course, they met elsewhere.

Ooh yeah...

CHAPTER FIFTY

She Wouldn't Like that

We went to Thomas's wedding two weeks later, but in all that time, we hardly spoke to one another. I had lost a lot of weight, was sleeping badly again. I was afraid of saying or doing the wrong thing, afraid that I was old and ugly now. I could not make up my mind what to do and to make things worse, Lukkas had convinced Hannah and Joe that his relationship with Holly was over and that nothing was happening, or would happen, between them again. They believed him sincere.

I felt as though I was caught on barbed wire. I did love Lukkas, despite everything, little point in telling myself that it wasn't so, but I couldn't live with her in our lives, any more. I loved our family, we had both worked to make it strong and now Lukkas had let this other person in, allowed her to smash it to pieces.

On the way to the airport Lukkas said, "I've booked myself onto a Captaincy course, in Antibes, for the day after the wedding. It's for three days, with a test at the end."

So, that was why he had arranged for our stay to be longer. He wanted to play power boats at sea.

I didn't mind the thought of being left to my own devices for that time, I never minded anything so long that we were away from Holly. Besides, for the first time in a long time, I had my own plans.

Lukkas and I had been invited to the wedding feast by Marianne and Serge, the groom's parents. We had known them since buying the apartment, they lived directly above us, and then, Thomas had been a boy of twelve.

When we alighted from the bus, we walked to the supermarket to buy wine, bread and cheese, intending to go out for a meal later. Once we arrived, we sat on the balcony and watched a golden sun settling on the wintry horizon. Lukkas read his texts twice. I said nothing to it. He had put his phone on silent, so that I wouldn't be disturbed by messages any more. Once I went to the dining room to wrap the wedding present for the following day. I stared at the back of his head, at his dark hair, now turning grey, at his broad shoulders and the pain inside my chest was a hard pebble.

Stupid, really, to imagine that such a small thing would change anything, but I walked out to him and put my hand upon his shoulder.

He had a dreamy expression on his face as he watched the setting sun, it was one thing that frightened and upset me about his silences. Was he thinking of her, Holly? Was he imagining what it would be like to be here with her, instead of me?

"Lukkas," I started, "If I bought you a wedding ring, would you wear it?"

He didn't look at me, instead he said, "I don't think she would like that very much, do you?"

My lips parted in shock. Did he really mean to hurt me that much or was he simply lacking in any emotional intelligence?

"She? Presumably you mean Holly? Would she also mind if we slept together after all this time? Should I text her and ask for her permission?"

It was sarcasm, but presumably he took it seriously. He rose from the chair, flexing his back and pushed past me. "Don't start on me, Laura. I'm going out, you do what you like," he said, picking up the apartment keys.

At first, I felt like crying again, but something else took its place. I watched his tall figure for a moment, leaving the apartment, then over the balcony, striding through the ornate garden gates towards the centre of Nice. I turned to the small case I had left in the hallway and took out an old exercise book that Ruby had cast away.

With the smells of dinner cooking in the other apartments, and the sound of the passing cars and motorbikes in the main road and the voices on the promenade, I started to write once more, perhaps, ironically, it was the only way to be with him and to remember what he once was to me.

As it grew dark and the street lamps illuminated the bejewelled palm trees in front of the beach, I began to forget that Lukkas wasn't there in reality. My heart started to feel whole again, and my self-esteem grew, little by little, as I worked at my writing and put everything else aside. The story I had once woven, destroyed by Lukkas, returned to me.

When he came back almost three hours later, I saw him from the balcony first, then heard the noise of the lift outside our apartment as he approached. In panic I ran to the bathroom and locked myself inside, pulling the chain, running taps, making as much commotion as I could whilst I stood upon a stool to stuff the little exercise book on top of the cupboard where only the spiders would find it.

"What have you been doing?" He demanded suspiciously as I left the bathroom. Perhaps my cheeks were red, perhaps he felt disappointed by the fact that I had not been crying.

I shrugged. "Sleeping, watching the television. Oh, and I called Charlotte..."

I didn't ask where he had been but fetched my coat and gloves and meekly followed him back into the street to find a restaurant. But there was a warm glow of optimism inside me, of happiness and excitement, even, the feeling of a childhood Christmas; which had everything to do with my writing and nothing to do with Lukkas and it took me by surprise, for it hung within me like the warmth of love.

The blue bikes, the Velo Bleu, are a very common sight in Nice, a symbol of environmental friendliness. They have gradually taken the place of cars. You pay for a card, a similar system to the bus card, which enables you to retrieve a bike from one of the well-placed bicycle racks. The Spring and Summer months can be frustrating, often the bicycles are all gone when you arrive. Which was why, I suppose, Lukkas didn't have his customary lie in the next morning but leapt out of bed, saying, "I don't have to start this Captaincy course till after lunch. Shall we go on a bike ride?"

I smiled but was unable to keep the bemused frown from my eyes. Hot and cold, hot and cold ran his moods. But then, anything to keep him in a good mood, I supposed. I know how much he used to love a bicycle ride. We kept our own, second hand bikes, bought at a junk shop, but they were stolen when we left them at the rear of the building. We have ridden far afield, to Villefranche and Liberation, generally he loves to ride beside the sea.

So, we descended to the sunny street in the lift before all the bicycles disappeared and examined two to make sure they were in good working order.

Lukkas unlocked one for me then pulled a larger one from the rack for himself, stooping over it as he examined it, looking every bit the part in a white, short sleeved shirt and shorts. Handsome, assured.

"Where do you want to go?" I asked.

"Nowhere in particular. Shall we head up Gambetta, towards the railway station?"

"Okay," I agreed. It wasn't the usual route, of fresh, sea air and market places, but perhaps he had some reason to go to the railway station.

Lukkas took off and I followed him. I hadn't anticipated the amount of traffic, I hadn't ridden in heavy traffic before in France. Once, I had almost ridden into a car when I momentarily forgot which side of the road I should be on. But Lukkas thought me a fool enough and I was determined to keep up with him.

He pedalled fast from the start, his strong leg muscles lifting the wheels from the road to the pavement if anything got in his way for a moment. Our rides were leisurely as a rule, it was as though he was in a great hurry to get somewhere, and I remember feeling the sinking hurt inside as he sped away from me without once turning to see whether I was alright, as he would once have done.

Determinedly, I raced behind him along the Boulevard Gambetta, past the shops that were just opening, traversing the narrow spaces between the shops and the impatient, constant traffic.

My bike wobbled on several occasions and I almost lost him, but I kept a tight hold on the handlebars until I saw him far ahead. He had almost reached the station. But he didn't turn right as I had expected, or slow down or stop and wave. He just kept going.

The memory of his recorded words came back to me. "Go on, fuck off out of my life…" Sudden, indescribable sadness, where there should have been anger.

It was almost as though he wanted me to… but I couldn't face my own thoughts, just then.

He didn't turn towards the sunny, suffocating, trapped heat of the platforms beneath the ornate roof, but turned left, still peddling so fast, towards Liberation. Perhaps the very name meant something more to him. He sped hurriedly across the shining river of moving cars towards a road on the right, whilst blindly, obstinately, I followed him; swerving away from a taxi and almost into the path of an oncoming bus. The driver blasted his horn and glared at me. I held up my hand in apology and stopped.

I stopped, breathless from my exercise. No, Lukkas, you won't kill me, I thought. I shook my head. The very idea was paranoia… that's what Lukkas would say.

I turned my bicycle around and walked it back along the pavement.

CHAPTER FIFTY-ONE

The Captain of another Heart

Thomas, the Groom, was a rather delicate and sweet natured young man, only a few years older than Josh, a violinist employed by the Nice opera house. The bride was a beautiful young woman from Madagascar who had lived in Nice since she was a toddler and whose family took over the wedding party, a robust, chattering, joyful crowd who revelled in being both French and from Madagascar. Thomas' family and friends seemed a little startled by their exuberance at times, but they took it all in good part.

It was a very happy occasion and I felt proud to be invited to it, for Lukkas and I were the only British people present. I love company, love parties as Lukkas used to, but he was hardly the life and soul of this one.

Lukkas' French is perfect enough that he reads complex novels. I get by with mine, often by understanding a little and nodding and smiling a lot, but I'm not shy. At this reception, in the early evening sunshine at one of the beach restaurants, the food and wine and the generosity of our hosts and the other guests was touching. Yet I couldn't help but be embarrassed about Lukkas, who sat alone for such a long time at a bare trestle table, away from the wedding party.

I went to him twice, to talk to him, to encourage him to come with me and he did. He smiled then and made a little conversation, but as soon as he could, he would wander away again to sit on a wooden table, staring towards the sea.

In the end, I gave up. I almost forgot that he was there. It was mesmerising to watch the young and old dancing to the modern African music. Sometimes I tried to chat with people around me, but most of the time I found myself swaying and dancing on the spot and even that was liberating. Still, I looked over my shoulder a few times to see where Lukkas was. Once he would have been at the very centre of the party, but not now.

We left long before the other revellers, giving our excuses to the bride and groom and to Thomas' parents, saying that Lukkas felt unwell. From the balcony, I watched the wedding party going on long into the night. As for Lukkas, he carried on drinking wine the moment we arrived home.

For the next three days, Lukkas caught the bus to Antibes at eight thirty each morning. When he left, I walked for a while and chatted on the phone with my mother. Angrily, I threw grey pebbles into the sea after speaking with her. I was afraid of losing her to cancer. Much as I hated Lukkas' treachery, the feeling ebbed and flowed now, as though he was less important, at least. I owed so much more to Mum. Once, her voice weak and croaky after the recent bout of chemotherapy, she asked tentatively, "You are alright, Laura, aren't you?"

"Just ignore the stupid texts from Lukkas," I said, "He has his reasons, Mum, but they're not honest reasons."

Love for her made me want to write all-the-more. I didn't have time to eat, didn't have time to smoke. It was as though the world was coming to an end and I had to write it all down. In a poignant way, my world was coming to an end and I could feel it. It filled me with fear and panic but with a sense of purpose too. This person I once saw as a knight in shining armour had turned into the most abominable villain, it seemed, and recounting my feelings in a story cleansed me of it.

Each day after his Captaincy course, Lukkas would return with a schoolboy smile on his face as though I was his mother and should pat him on the head. Then, finally on the third day, he returned to tell me that he was now 'Captain' Lukkas and we celebrated over dinner.

"Let's go out in a motorboat," he said, on the day before we were due to go home. "Okay," I agreed, hesitating a little. The weather had changed, no more sunshine, there had been a fierce wind on the previous evening and the clouds beyond the balcony doors were various shades of purple-grey, as though a child had mixed all their colours on a palette. I was a little perplexed. I rarely got sea sick and I'd been on various boats off the coast of France and Cornwall in rough seas, but Lukkas detested rough weather at sea. Maybe he simply wanted to put his new skills to the test, I thought.

He called the boatyard in Villefranche and after breakfast, we took our kagoules and caught the bus there. It wasn't raining then, but the clouds were spreading like a purple bruise overhead.

Almost as soon as we arrived there, as I helped Lukkas unwind the mooring ropes from the wall, the first heavy drops of rain started to fall, hitting the shining, green harbour waters with heavy plops. I saw the young boat boy produce his own phone, warning Lukkas of the weather report, but Lukkas pouted and shrugged like a Frenchman and the boy smiled and held his palms open, grinning at me as though to say, "Bonne chance."

Lukkas filled the boat with petrol, and with Captain Lukkas in charge at the helm, we wove in and out of the other small vessels, which were mostly heading in the opposite direction, I noticed pensively. But if the weather was bad, at least I was determined not to rain on his parade. I might be a vile, wizened hag, might be a stupid woman; but I wasn't a scaredy-cat, so I tried to keep a fixed smile upon my face as the rain fell in a constant drizzle, blurring the vision.

By the time Lukkas had taken us far enough into the ocean for the harbour to be a small speck in the distance, the rain was fell like small, hard stones and the waves were gradually building higher and higher so that the boat smacked against them each time they met with the hull, almost as though they were made from solid material.

Lukkas' determined smile became a grimace of concentration. But this was what he wanted, I supposed, to test his management in rough weather.

I sat beside him, stifling my anxiety as the larger, rolling waves pushed us this way and that. There were no other boats in sight, there was none to help us if we got into any trouble. On several occasions, he looked at me as though I might challenge what he was doing, but although I repressed a couple of shrieks, I didn't object, because I wouldn't be cowed, and because of Holly, because I would be stronger and braver than her.

By the time the cliffs below Monaco came into sight, Lukkas was hammering the speedboat at full throttle into the path of the largest waves he could find. I looked nervously at him from the corner of my rain filled eye, wedging myself into the seat beside him with my foot pressed hard against the fibre glass panel to the hold, where the life jackets were stored. As I thought about putting one on, conversation now made impossible, I caught the expression upon his face.

The skin across his cheekbones was pale and taut and, in the rain, like whetted stone. His profile harsh in its expression and angry. In an instant, he whipped his face toward me as though his cheek had been slapped. The look in his eyes made me freeze in panic. He smiled demonically just as the little boat lifted on its stern, pushed up by a giant wave so that the nose pointed skyward, almost tipping me out and over the side, but my foot, wedged so hard against the fibre glass panel, held me fast and cracked it. I shrieked, then stared at him. For an instant he stared back, not asking me whether I was alright, not even commenting upon the broken panel which would have to be paid for. His eyes locked with mine and my fear gave way to sudden depression, in that moment when our eyes met he told me what he had wanted.

I shivered as I had not done with my clothes soaked to the skin and the rain creeping beneath the cagoule.

"Are you trying to kill me?" I asked dully. I didn't mean it as a joke, nothing about it was funny.

"Don't be stupid," Lukkas said. That was all he said, dismissing the idea with a grin. "We'll go back now, shall we?"

I don't know how other people react if they believe that someone they love wants them dead. But there was no shouting, no remonstrating, no anger then. My hurt was subdued, but I knew. I chewed my lips constantly as he steered back towards the port. There was something he could not deny, no matter how he tried to. I had seen the look in his eyes as I bounced from the seat towards the water.

Lukkas had wanted me to go overboard. Lukkas had wanted that, whether the idea had been pre-planned, or not.

Lukkas hated me, he wanted me dead. I ought to have been frightened, I supposed, but there was something more dreadful to me than that. It was the realisation that the person I had loved so passionately would be prepared to do that to be rid of me.

CHAPTER FIFTY-TWO
Revelation

"You go, you go to her," I said, on the plane coming home. "It's not worth murder. Go." Again, we had scarcely spoken since the incident. We had been waiting a while for the plane to take off, all the while, I kept my eyes firmly fixed upon the window and the runway beside us. I had hardly eaten, slept badly. It was as though my heart had stopped beating.

"Murder? You really are off your trolley. There is no, 'her.' If you are speaking about Holly, I told you, I hardly had anything to do with her and won't again," he hissed angrily, "But you know that, it's you who wanted to get rid of me."

I didn't reply. There was no reply to give and no point in arguing with a liar who no longer loved me. This was the end, at last, and still I hoped it wouldn't be, just as I knew it had to be.

This was the last time that I saw our apartment in Nice and it was the last time that Lukkas and I were in each other's company, alone. The last time, after thirty-four years.

I remember sitting with my forehead against the plane window, peering down through the clouds at the mountains of Nice, tears running from my eyes before falling into a dull and desperate sleep.

Sleep would be my only escape for a long time to come. Living without ever seeing him was harder by far than anything that had gone before. I knew he would never come home now, we were finished at my choice as well as his, but his absence hurt as much as if he had died. He saw our children, and they were kind and loving to me, but they wanted him in our home and they missed that. They missed their family for a long time.

I could not listen to music, then, or watch television, or go to any of the places we would once have gone to. My tears would start unbidden, in public; humiliating me. I thought about him every second of every day for a long, long time. The ghost of Lukkas as a young man, a middle-aged man, an older man. The things we spoke of, the times we had laughed, these things would not let me alone.

Our children believed, even then, that their father might return. They had stopped calling me mad, but a month after he had gone to live in the house close to his office, Hannah sent a text to me saying that Lukkas would join us on holiday if I went, even now, to see a psychiatrist called Grace Sharrow. He father had never heard of her, so she said. But I looked the woman up on google, only to find that she was on two committees with Lukkas.

I didn't go to see her.

We went on holiday to Italy, to Lake Como and Hannah and Joe and Josh made it their business to love me and look after me. Often, Joe would ask me anxiously, whether I was happy, and I found it impossible to lie to him, so I told him that I was contented. But at night I dreamt of Lukkas frequently and by day, would think of him too and wonder about him.

He carried on providing money, but it was never enough, and when we returned from that holiday, I experienced a panic about finances such as I hadn't felt since I was a student. I took students in, as many as I could manage in the house. They slept in the room Lukkas and I had shared, and I slept on the sofa in the living room. I hadn't wanted to return to teaching because of the children's needs after school and because our mother needed help in the day time now. Her cancer had made her very weak, but it was her love and the love of my family that kept me strong enough to get through it.

I resolved three things, though, but I didn't know how to achieve them. I would not fail, I would not fail my family and I would not spend the rest of my life missing Lukkas and worrying about money. The latter things would help me achieve the former.

The way to fight my feelings about Lukkas came to me after some while. I could no longer think of the good times we had, wallow in them beneath a duvet. I forced myself to focus on how dreadfully he had behaved. Lukkas made this easier for me by telling our friends that I required psychiatric help. I know that this happened, either they told me, or they would watch me for odd movements, so that sometimes I had the urge to break into a silly dance or imitate the movements of a chicken. He made it easier for me to think badly of him by sending me texts to say that he would stop my finances, or stop paying bills, or sell our house. He made it easier by appearing to hate me, now.

Charlotte, Monica, Valeria and Jennie made me go out with them, eventually, after I had refused so often through dull spirits. Valeria introduced me to a man of my own age, but I am not interested in men or in a relationship like that, and I will never be again. I worked too hard on our relationship, mine with Lukkas, ever to care about such things.

Lukkas seemed not to want to divorce me, although, 'not prepared to divorce me,' is probably the best way of putting it. Mutual friends told me the term he used was 'estranged'. I hated the term, it reminded me of women without purpose, who visit tea rooms on a Saturday afternoon.

Then, one day, almost a year after he had gone, Josh said, "I think it's time to get a divorce." I had taken my wedding ring off, then put it back on, then offered it to Joe to sell when he was short of money, but he refused. So strange, that the gold band which had felt so much to me had become a useless symbol now.

I didn't know any divorce lawyer who would not know Lukkas. Neither did I trust lawyers any more, I suppose it might not be understood by some people, but I had two lawyers plotting against me, that was how it felt. It was improbable, untrue, that Lukkas had not talked with Holly about me.

His vindictiveness now affected me badly. He would say things to the children, so that I came to dread their visits to him, although he was their father, and they needed those visits.

"Dad said you won't get a penny if you divorce…"

"Dad said you would be best to take the house and forget everything else."

"Dad said he's going to stop your allowance next month, so you'd better get a job now."

"Dad says he's taking the car."

So, it went on. They didn't tell me to upset me, but because they were afraid for me and didn't understand how the father who had always told them he loved me could now behave as though I was public enemy number one. I had started to feel more at threat than I had before, although I told them not to worry.

But Josh was right, as he was right about many things. I needed a lawyer. I finally made the decision after Lukkas suggested to Joe, once more, that I was mad and that I should not have the care of our grandchildren. I had been trusted to care for them for seven years by then. I was appalled he should say such a thing.

I contacted several lawyers, using names other than my own. Lukkas has a good reputation and a keen, if dubious, sense of humour. He is well liked by all those people who don't really know him, but he's an excellent representative for abused children and God knows there are still plenty of abused children in the world.

Eventually I chose a firm with a reputation for lawyers who could be as intimidating as Lukkas himself; eventually, I chose Alex.

When I was first introduced to the woman who would become my lawyer, I faltered perhaps, when shaking her hand. She introduced herself as Alex and she was small and slight, one of the most attractive women I had ever met and softly spoken, with a slight Welsh accent. I didn't think she would ever stand up to him in a divorce court or, I thought, he will flirt with you and win you over.

But none of these things happened, and I grew to have faith in her, in fact, I grew to see her as a friend, certainly as someone that I could trust, and she has never let me down.

I knew from the start that her firm's fees would be high but knew too that to get any kind of reasonable settlement, this was the firm that I would have to use. How I would pay them was another matter. I approached four, different banks. None would lend me the money. I was estranged, had no salary now and no potential to earn or guarantee of a divorce settlement.

I had not borrowed money from my parents since before our marriage but from her bed, my mother held my hand, told me not to worry and lent me a few thousand to pay my first bill. She was not wealthy and had cancer. I was ashamed to ask for it and she knew that.

Then Charlotte came to my assistance, lending me the money for my second bill and I knew at every interview with Alex, even though she reduced my bill, and I know that she did; I would need more.

In the end, I returned to teaching. I combined visiting and caring for Mum with supply work in a secondary school on a large estate in Oxford to which the police were called nightly. It wasn't a bad job, but every night I fell into a coma on the settee, at least exhaustion resolved my sleepless nights.

The girls had to go to the After-School Club, which they didn't much like at first. But they grew used to it in the end.

One Saturday afternoon, Hannah came without the children. She told me that she had come for a cup of tea, which wasn't very like Hannah. There was a look of dejection on her face as she sat at the kitchen table and knowing her well, I let her talk about all kinds of unimportant matters before she said, "Dad is living with Holly."

The knife that I was using to slice an onion slid from the skin into the chopping board. I took a deep breath.

"What, the Holly who he is not carrying on with?" I asked with an air of resignation. "How do you know that?"

"I'm sorry Mum," she said, and I knew she was upset about it too. "I don't know for sure, but I went to visit him there last week and there were some bits and pieces in the house that didn't add up."

"Did you ask him?"

She shook her head.

"Then you don't know for sure."

I didn't want to know. I was trying to rebuild my life, trying to pretend that Lukkas meant nothing to me. Anyway, I was trying to move on, trying to forgive him, though there were things I will never forgive. I had poured my life into my children and Lukkas deliberately tried to set them against me. He had been planning to leave me for a long time, whilst pretending to love me, the removal of our files from the house to the office and the purchase of his house without telling me, told me that. Nothing I had ever done indicated a mental illness, but he had gone as far as to text Mum and lie to her.

We hugged before Hannah left and perhaps, then, her restored faith was enough for me. But I couldn't stop thinking about what she had said over the next few days.

Alex had told me not to go near his home under any circumstances.

But on a misty Monday morning in November, the indignance I felt at Lukkas' telling my lawyers that he was not carrying on in a relationship with someone else, got the better of me, and I drove to find his new home.

Lukkas' small, terraced house lay at the end of a narrow lane. I parked my car in a nearby Cull de sac and walked to it with the Dictaphone in my coat pocket. I would never be able to place it inside the house, but where there's a will, there's a way, as they say.

Yet again, my heart beat like a Tom-tom drum, but it was very early still and curtains, including his, were still drawn against the chilly November sky.

I walked stealthily towards Lukkas' door, checking over my shoulder that I wasn't being observed by a neighbour and on the pretence of putting the letter in my hand through his door, I quickly stooped and shoved the Dictaphone beneath the leaves under his living room window. It didn't look as though it would rain. I had nothing to lose.

It was two days later before I had an opportunity to retrieve the thing, and as I had a whole week's supply teaching, I didn't have the opportunity to listen to it until the following weekend.

This time, I did not have to wait very long to hear the events of the day, both in the little lane and in the small house. I admire the machine, it is made of sturdy stuff and its range is incredible. Through the brick wall, the Dictaphone recorded a great deal of the conversation and activity inside, and I had been parted from Lukkas for so long that I didn't expect what I recorded to hurt me, but I suppose that it did. Yes, it hurt.

If Holly wasn't living there, she must have stayed over the previous night and in the early morning. They had a small argument, a lover's tiff. I don't know what it was about and really, I don't care; but it was Holly's husky voice and she yelled at him once, telling him to "Back off." Then she cried, I could hear the break in her voice.

She crashed about in the little kitchen as though she were washing up, dropping a plate, I heard it smash.

She turned on a liquidiser as though she was pureeing my guts and finally came to the front door in her clicking heels and crashed about outside in the front porch.

Lukkas would never have tolerated that behaviour from me, I thought, in cold amazement. That she had cried didn't touch me, how often had I cried?

She appeared to grab a broom and swept the front step in angry fervour and once she even bashed the Dictaphone, which resounded with a metallic clunk. And surprise, surprise, she clicked a lighter and puffed on a cigarette, so, perhaps I hadn't been the one to encourage him to smoke after all!

As I listened to this other world in this other place, whilst I sat in a lay bye on the motorway from Oxford, I heard Lukkas calling her from inside the house in a wheedling, dramatic tone which reminded me of Sir John Gielgud. He had never used that tone with me either, never wheedled; but I had, and pleaded and begged, to no avail.

"Hollie..." A deep, pleading tone to his voice as he called her back inside.

I heard her footsteps once more as she put out the cigarette but with her foot and kicked it aside, a heavier tread than if she had been wearing shoes, so I think she must have worn boots.

After that, a few noises in the street and bird song, but quite a pause before the most terrible sound I had ever heard in my life. It would not hurt me now, but it hurt me then.

I had seen that the bathroom window stood open. This was an old preference of Lukkas' and mine. Two smokers who liked fresh air.

Now, I heard, without detachment, as though I were present in the room, the sound of her high-pitched orgasm, floating through the window into the foggy morning. "Oh, oh, oh...!"

The most dreadful thing about it was that it sounded like me. I was so upset by the sound, that if Lukkas had come crawling to me on his knees at that moment, or at any time, I knew it would be easy to say no to him. Easy.

The remainder of the day was an even greater revelation.

Later, I think, Holly went into the office, or perhaps to the court. For I heard her drag her little black case through the door and on the doorstep, the sound of their slow kiss and she said, "Lukkas, Lukkas, get off!" in a shocked whisper, as though people might see them.

There was nothing then, for almost two hours, except a mouse or maybe a rat, cracking nuts within range of the Dictaphone, snuffling in the leaves. Until Lukkas opened the front door to someone. That someone didn't speak. Lukkas said, with a small laugh, "Well, go inside then..."

They were male footsteps, a heavier tread, a flat heel. Maybe, I thought, he is seeing a client at his home. But there was something about his laugh...

A whole hour passed whilst I waited, hearing nothing. It came to early evening. I hadn't heard the guest leave but heard another man's voice approaching the house and the heels of a woman walking beside him. The woman didn't speak, but her companion said, "Don't forget your coat, this time."

Then the man knocked upon Lukkas' door and I heard Lukkas greeting them, the man said, "I've been telling Rose that you are a lawyer, she's interested in becoming one herself…" The voices withdrew into the house.

As the door opened, I heard music from within and thought, "He's having a party." And after that there were several knocks upon his door, but the only voice I recognised was Irina's. She appeared to come alone, and she was the last guest to arrive.

The music and the distant voices of his party must have gone on until about nine thirty in the evening, but what puzzled me was that Holly appeared to have disappeared from the scene entirely, as though she didn't even know about it.

After nine, the first people to leave were whoever Rosie was, and the man accompanying her. They said goodbye at the door and I puzzled a little over what her escort said to Rosie. "Well, that was a bit of a surprise, wasn't it?" he asked, as they walked along the pathway.

Then people began to leave in one small group, chattering as they walked in the direction of the City centre, I wondered whether they were going to one of the local pubs.

Irina was with them, I heard her heels and pleasant, accented laugh. I assumed Lukkas had gone as the door banged shut.

I was about to run the machine forward, as the street fell silent once more, except for the sound of a train and distant cars passing. But I heard a distant snippet of conversation from within his house and minutes later, two sets of male footsteps heading in the opposite direction to the party goers, retreating, without any conversation, into the distance.

After this, the sound of the night set in. A few November fireworks exploded in the sky above, the mouse chewed at berries and sweet wrappers in the bushes. The noise of the trains passing nearby, the sound of cars screeching, as they turned sharply in the Oxford car park.

My lips parted at the sound of Lukkas' voice about two hours later into the recording. His voice was distant, he was returning, and in conversation with another, perhaps the person he'd left the house with, the person who he had told to go into the house in the afternoon.

As they approached the house; a young, cultured, male voice which somehow belonged to the University said, "So, we'll go to the shop to buy fags, yeah? Then pop back in."

"No." And it was Lukkas.

"Why?" But his question was contrived, as though he already knew what Lukkas' would reply.

"Because it's dangerous."

They walked on, passing his house, their footsteps going towards the town centre. Their conversation was low, barely audible then.

I had almost stopped listening, needing to return home to various tasks, but wondering who the other voice belonged to. I ran forward, stopped, ran forward, stopped again. I did this for almost an hour of the recording time and then I heard them coming back.

There was no conversation, just male, drunken giggling. But it was Lukkas, it was him with the young man. I heard the key, very close to the Dictaphone as he tried to get it into the lock, then muted laughter and a "Sh!" from Lukkas, followed by hushed laughter from them both.

Giggling, drunken male voices. Seconds passed, and the young man cried out in surprise. "Oh!" They went into the house and closed the door.

Years ago, at the death of my sister, I had been in denial. It manifested itself in several ways, I repeatedly returned to the place of her death, I picked up the phone to call her weeks after she had gone, people said that I talked of her as though she were still alive. I think it is a condition that I suffer from, denial.

Even after hearing that recording, I kept telling myself that there must be another explanation. Perhaps Lukkas was a saint, after all. Perhaps he was harbouring an illegal immigrant and that's why it would be 'dangerous' to return to his house with another man.

But, at last, I had done with denial. Really, there was only one answer.

CHAPTER FIFTY-THREE

The Mask

Almost seven months after Lukkas had gone, I looked at my reflection in the same mirror before the fireplace where I had examined myself after persuading Dr Griffiths to give me pills. Then, I had been bitter about everything, bitterness caused by hurt and the growing acceptance that Lukkas no longer loved me, that he wanted a 'Trophy wife.' Then, I had thought, nothing has changed, a man can no longer put his wife away in a nunnery, can no longer force her to take tablets, but he can have a good try.

I still held a little of that bitterness inside me, but I put my feelings to good use. As, gradually, I made life work for me, I could accept what Lukkas was and what he wasn't. I was able to accept what I was, too. Lukkas and Holly would be old, one day. The only disloyalty was that I would have cared for Lukkas no matter what he looked like, but he hadn't been able to do that for me. Far from it, he had stopped loving me and then attacked me in every way.

The newspapers are filled with photographs of old men with women half their age. It's impossible not to be cynical about it. I was confused about Lukkas' sexuality and if he was gay, sad; because, had he told me, I would have understood. Perhaps, if that was the case, Holly was simply a respectable cover for something he couldn't admit to, just as I may have been. What I see is that Lukkas is fickle.

My looks didn't matter now, beyond being clean and tidy. But I made every effort for our mother to look 'nice', because she cared about appearance and she was now very gravely ill. Because of this, and our father's dementia, I stopped the supply teaching for some, long while. At least, where I had once wanted to cry before her about Lukkas, I could now be resolved not to do so, to care for her, to be more of an emotional support for her and even to make her laugh and make every day that she had left, a little brighter.

The business of divorce had begun. I had been awaiting a text from my lawyer, Alex, when another text popped up on my phone.

It was from Irina, of all people.

"Hello, Laura. I want to tell you something, could you meet me at Macdonald's in an hour, at six?"

She meant my local Macdonald's, of course. I frowned, totally baffled by the suggestion. She knew where I lived, why not come here? What on earth did she want to tell me? But I was curious. I told her that I was waiting for the girls to be collected by Hannah, that I could meet her at half past. Ruby and Lilly were happily covering the kitchen with glitter and paint, and now it mattered not if they made a mess, their grandfather no longer lived with me.

I turned my attention back to the mirror. I might not care what I looked like, nowadays, but I wasn't inclined to look a mess before the ultra-glamorous Irina, as I had done when I arrived at her house a year before.

Lukkas had sent me a proposal, earlier in the week. I wasn't inclined to take it, it was very mean. Alex said I should not reply, that we would go through the court.

I had felt lonely and frightened at times, but I hadn't resorted to the bottle; I had so far managed to sort things out and I hadn't gone to pieces without Lukkas, as he had told me I would.

Our children and grandchildren all rallied around me at birthdays and other celebrations. Lukkas came to a restaurant for Joe's birthday, but he only paid for himself, before disappearing into the night and back to his new life to leave me with a considerable bill.

Irina. It was important to me that she should see me differently; composed, clear headed. I changed out of the sweater with a smudge of chocolate spread on the shoulder and pulled off my jeans and boots. I pulled on a woollen dress, bought once to make Lukkas love me more. I brushed my hair and pulled it behind my ears. I hooked my oldest and nicest pair of earrings, the only ones to have survived the grasp of toddlers, through my ears.

Irina was there before I arrived, sitting at a table close to the window, entirely incongruous in a light blue, silk dress, a white, faux fur jacket and with a necklace of dainty pearls around her small neck. Her appearance was elegant, I was glad that I had made some effort.

She rose from the table to greet me, there was an unmistakable impish curve at the corner of her red painted lips.

"How are you?" She asked, and I was grateful for one thing, that the question lacked the patronising expectation that I was suffering, that I would indeed be falling to pieces.

"I'm okay, thanks Irina," I said honestly.

She dipped her head towards the coffee cup on the table. "Cappuccino, I hope that it's not cold, I can get another…"

"It's fine, thanks," I smiled.

We sat down at the small, round table, whilst the restaurant thronged with the ordinary people from all walks of life, all seeking instant, cheap satisfaction for the belly. Those on long journeys, those from the estate, opposite. All heedless of the reports about the possible risk of dementia in old age from burger build up. I am one of those people, in a rush, I have used the place to feed my grand-children. Seated opposite Irina in her elegant shadow, the place feels very different and the experience provokes an inward chuckle as several people gawp at her.

I sipped the coffee and waited, until she looked down at the brown, manila envelope in her lap and I realised that she had been holding onto it all this time.

"I have come to show you something, it concerns Lukkas," she said. "Something that might help you."

"Lukkas and I are getting a divorce, Irina. I don't think there is anything you can do to help me as far as that is concerned. It's over, we're finished."

"Perhaps so, but, you know, Lukkas is living with this woman, Holly? She has a flat in Oxford, but they are spending more and more time together, I think."

I nodded. I didn't want to give her anything, I wanted to move forward, I couldn't think of anything more to say about it.

I nodded slowly. "I realise that," I said, after a slight breath. "My children have cottoned on to it, they are not very happy about it. It's hard," I explained, "But in the end, it will be alright, they love their father."

Her long nails tapped upon the envelope. I noticed the expensive, gold watch on her slim wrist and wondered how she had come to afford such a thing. I watched the small, Korean girl, clearing the floor of sticky, spilled juice. A few seconds passed. Then at last, Irina drew some photographs from the envelope.

"Lukkas' relationships are complicated," she said with a smile. She shrugged her small, ballerina like shoulders.

My mouth twisted into a wry smile, "Yes, Irina, I think I understand this too."

I took the photographs from her, three of them. They were coloured photos, blown up to A4 size, with small time differences, each one mirrored the other except in one instance.

Two men stood before a small but sleek sports car, very like Lukkas' own car. One of them was Lukkas, the other a younger, slimmer man with hair as black as Lukkas' had once been.

I thought that I recognised the distant landscape. It could have been anywhere in Oxfordshire or the surrounding counties. Closer to the car was the edge of an ornate and beautifully tended garden. Large, stone urns were heavy with plants more suited to the Mediterranean. The car was parked on a weed-less drive. Perhaps I had visited the place with Lukkas, once upon a time.

"A friend took them. Lukkas was at a wedding where I was also a guest. Look at them Laura," Irina said.

I turned my attention back to the photographs. Lukkas wore his most elegant grey suit and most glorious, enigmatic silk tie. He looked every bit the gentleman. In the first two photographs, Lukkas was laughing with the other man, who was almost as tall as he. He was leaning a little towards him. I brought the third photograph to the top of the pile and stared at it in wonder, but I think I had known, as though some small voice had been telling me to wake up and understand the obvious.

In the third photo, I could read the number plate on the front of the sports car. The two men were standing close by it. 'Nero5ZX' I read aloud. Nero, the Roman Emperor who burned Christians alive to light his palace gardens at night time. I couldn't say that I was a fan.

And in this photograph, they were kissing. Not kissing on the cheek, as French men do, but mouth upon mouth, as lovers do.

"She doesn't know. Holly doesn't know," Irina said.

I felt compassion for Lukkas then. He could have told me, could have confided in me. It would have been alright. Was I a front for him, to hide his sexuality? Was he fond of me all along, but scared? I would never know now, but if this was the case, it is what she would be now, Holly would be that. That's how he would conceal it if he hadn't the courage to admit to it.

"I'm glad you brought them to me, Irina." I looked up at her. I didn't know why she had done so, or what her expectation was, but perhaps now, I could find peace. If she had believed that I would use them, she was wrong.

"I had a sister once, she died from cancer aged thirty. She had so much potential. Before she developed cancer, she opened-up to me. She told me that she was a lesbian. As a young woman, she had never been happy as a girl. Know what, Irina? I was impatient with her. It didn't fit in with my middle class, 'I'm married to a lawyer with three lovely children, life style.' I sighed and shook my head. "Just at the point where she needed a friend, I let her down. My mother, my sister and brother were the tolerant ones, not me. So, I understand much more now, than I did then. You can't help your sexuality, to a large extent. I love Lukkas as I loved my sister, there is little difference in it."

In front of her, I held the photographs between my thumbs and forefingers and tore them through, once and then twice. Irina gave a little jump as I started to do it, but her shoulders quickly relaxed, and she was composed once more, looking neither pleased nor displeased. I don't know what I believed about her, whether she was truly friend or foe. No doubt there were copies of these and there was little that I could do about it, except to do nothing of my own accord.

CHAPTER FIFTY-FOUR

A New Life

I live alone, now, in reality; I am seldom alone.

I sold the house to rehouse us. I like my new home, I'm happy where I am and above all, it's mine.

I live with the dogs and Hannah's cats. Josh lives in a rented flat and Joe lives with me, although he and his pregnant girlfriend are now on the Housing list.

I'm never truly alone and it is okay. Often, it's very much better than 'okay'. When I was a young teacher, I was befriended by a little old Jewish lady, a neighbour. I will never forget her. She came to Britain as a child, having lost all the people who loved her in the holocaust. She was thought of as a little eccentric, for company she had four mongrel dogs and dozens of cats, she also had a goat in her garden. She had few friends, so I was quite proud of the fact that she appeared to like me. Then, I felt sorry for her loneliness, now it makes perfect sense to me.

I love my family and friends, they are all that I want. I never, ever want to be in a relationship with another man. I know women who yearn for it after divorce, women to whom a second relationship is a real ambition. I believe it is a mistake. I would far rather be alone, truly.

Joe, who would ask anxiously, once, whether I was happy, but understood at his heart that it wasn't so, now knows that a miracle has occurred. I am happy, frequently. Our children, especially Hannah who had wanted us to stay together so much, not only accept my single status but do all that they can to make me happy. They are my strength, they are my friends.

I no longer cry in bed at night, no longer feel that I don't want to get up in the morning. I can listen to every kind of music without getting upset, I can appreciate art and can concentrate on novels. I see and appreciate the colours of the seasons again. Gradually, what happened moves further and further away from me in time. I act the fool and giggle a lot.

In my new garden, I look up at the stars. I hear snatches of conversation between Lukkas and I, conversations from the past that are still fresh in my mind. The stars remind me of a time when we walked the dogs late at night on the beach in Polzeath, walking hand in hand, leaping across the tide pools in a path constructed by moonlight.

Now, Lukkas spends all his holidays in Nice at 'our' apartment, with Holly, that same Holly he wanted to have me put away in a mental institution for. I believed his love for her would be the end of me, but it wasn't so. Truly, I don't care. I have people to love and who love me. Besides, I don't believe that she is his only love, or ever will be.

Lukkas told me more than once, towards the end, that I would be a lonely old woman if he left, that I would have nothing. Thanks to my lawyers, it isn't so. Thanks to my family and some good friends, it isn't so. Each day brings new worries and new problems to solve but I can solve them, and I do so.

There is a photograph of Lukkas and I, sitting on my crowded mantlepiece. We are younger, the photograph was taken before we had children, we are locked in a passionate kiss. The photograph amuses me now. Lukkas once loved such photo's, he must have taken hundreds of photographs over the years, too many, and for what? Photographs can be sincere, but they also tell lies.

Joy, happiness, is found in unexpected places now. Joy is not a man and a woman after all. Joy is having Hannah as a friend, once more. The closeness to her revived. Hannah takes me in hand at first and I don't mind. Between us, Charlotte, Hannah and I plan for the fun we will have, cook the Sunday roast and hold things together. Josh and Joseph are wonderful too, but it is Hannah that I lost, the Prodigal daughter.

"I've had enough of men, I'm going to be a Lesbian," Hannah says, to make me laugh. Or perhaps she is serious.

Standing beneath a shop awning one Sunday morning, Ruby; who is eight years old, now; and I, wait for a shop to open. We were caught in the rain which has dampened our clothes. As we wait, Ruby munches on a croissant and I drink coffee. We attempt a conversation in French, laughing at our mistakes.

In the background, a street guitarist sings as he plays 'After the Gold Rush.' He has a good voice and the lyrics seem so important, although I don't understand why; but I do know that I'm so much older and wiser. I like who I am.

A good eighteen months after Lukkas and I divorced, I met with Charlotte and Steve in 'The Bat and Ball,' a pub of our youth. It wasn't a very jolly meeting, for Mum had died almost two weeks before, with us all at her bedside. We were meeting to discuss the minutia of her funeral, the hymns and tributes, prior to a meeting with the vicar. Our love for her was great, she had so much courage at the end. We were resolved that her funeral would be perfect.

We were embroiled in an impassioned argument about whether we would ask for flowers or donations when the conversation came to an abrupt halt. Steve looked up at a place above my head, grinning broadly and I twisted my neck to see what he was staring at.

It was my gamekeeper friend of the Barbie doll incident. "Hello, Steve!" he greeted him. The two men shook hands whilst Charlotte and I waited for an explanation.

"School friends," Steve said, "But I've not seen Rob for years. These are my sisters, Laura and Charlotte..."

So, his name was Rob, or Robert, presumably. He was still wearing the heavy, green coat, opened to reveal a brown sweater, with a small hole, I noticed, towards the neck. And jeans, over a pair of lace up walking boots. He smiled down at me. "I know one of your sisters, I had to warn her of the dangers of being shot in the pheasant season!" he smiled.

Charlotte looked at me then, with her own, knowing smile, labelling me a sly-boots for keeping the man a secret. I would have it out with her later, in the meanwhile, I contented myself by narrowing my eyes at her.

Steve asked him to sit down with us, buying him a pint of beer. I felt a little prickly about it, because I was recently divorced, because Mum had died, but my brother is the friendliest person I know. Charlotte explained why we were there on this particular occasion and I listened and smiled but said very little.

"I'm so sorry, I wouldn't have intruded if I'd known. I remember your mother, she was such a nice person. She let me stay at your house on two occasions when my bike broke down," he smiled. He glanced quickly from Charlotte to me, as though we might remember it, but presumably he was a good five years younger than I. I would have been at college, or possibly just not interested in my brother's younger mates.

"When is the funeral? I would like to come..."

And I kind of like him a little more for that, he didn't have to say it. I have a sudden crazy impulse to call Mum on the phone and tell her about him, about our gathering in the pub, about all the things that have happened since she died.

I meet Rob a couple of times after that. The first of them is whilst walking Jack across the fields. He waves at me and I wave back, some distance from him. I don't want to talk, not to him, not to anyone, that morning. I feel like this after Lukkas has gone, sometimes. The things that happened keep repeating themselves because I am still incredulous at them, still questioning them, telling myself that I might have done this, or I should have done that.

At Christmas, I meet him again. Monica and Steve invite him to a drinks party. We chat a little. He is divorced, too, he tells me. He has two, teenage children. They stay with him at the weekend, sometimes. His son is about to go to University. He's easy to talk to, I talk rather too much with the mulled wine as encouragement, then stop, suddenly, remembering Lukkas. A sort of self-consciousness and sadness overwhelm me, and I withdraw from him when it's polite.

The following Spring, as I walk the dog past the tumble of moss painted stones from a long-broken wall, staring through the woods that are suddenly rich with colour after a dull winter. I am deep in thought about Lukkas and Mum and my prodigal daughter. How different life is now. An ancient motorbike drones in the distance where once a Roman Villa stood. Where once, as a child, my father, and later my sons, played army. And here, before D-Day, the American soldiers made their camp.

The motorbike comes toward me and I hasten to grab Jack, who Lyra taught to chase motorbikes. It's him, it's Rob. He slows down, then stops, wheeling the bike in my direction. I don't feel anything about it, but I don't mind, either. We walk together along the winding path and talk about inconsequential things and if I am not yet fully happy, I am content for a while. That, for the moment, is good enough. For now, contentment will do nicely and I will show our children the way to trust themselves above anyone else.

Lightning Source UK Ltd.
Milton Keynes UK
UKHW011009150919
349822UK00001B/38/P